Tc

THE DRAGON CHARMER'S APPRENTICE

A LEGENDS OF TIVARA MYTH

JC KANG

Cover Art by ชาณัตถพล แสงกระจุย

Maps and Cover Layout by Laura Kang

First Edition: September 2021

To Elena Huyhn-Vy, for your Patreonage

Prologue:
Initiation

The sparkling gemstone atop the pyramid pulsed in Mai's ears, its rhythm drowning out the Tivari High Priest's blessing. *Sing*, her heart cried, not caring if it would ruin the solemn initiation.

None of the other children on their first pilgrimage seemed to even notice the sound. Beside her, palms pressed together, her best friend Ying wore a radiant smile. So calm!

Mai's eyes darted back and forth. Where was Fei, her other best friend? She'd disappeared when the Tivari acolytes had bathed her. Maybe they'd put her at the back, so that her limp wouldn't slow down the lines to the initiation.

As they drew closer to the base of pyramid, Mai's heart whirred like a cicada. The robes they'd dressed her in were so pretty and smooth, but now her sweat was ruining them!

The boy in front of her knelt, lowered his hood, and bowed his head before the Tivari bishop.

Up close, the grey ceremonial robes brought out the bishop's turquoise skin. He was so tall and handsome compared to Cleric Pyuz back home. Revealing his fangs with a smile, he set the amulet representing the Red Sun of Tivar on the back of the boy's neck, and spoke in the guttural language of the Tivari.

With a shriek, the boy's body went limp. He crumpled to the ground.

All eyes turned to him. Mai covered her gawk. Was he okay?

"Nan harbored wicked thoughts," the bishop said. "His soul will pull Tivar's chariot for all eternity."

Blood rushed from Mai's head. Her legs wobbled. She didn't know Nan; he must've come from another village. Nobody else had died today.

The bishop gestured toward some acolytes, who dragged the body away. Now all eyes were on her, the next in line.

Had she recited her vows correctly? What if Tivar rejected her? She'd never have a chance to say goodbye to Mother, Father, or Baby Ling. Not to mention the eternal torture in the afterlife.

She knelt. Hands trembling, she lowered the hood and bowed her head.

The bishop loomed above her. The amulet felt hot against her skin. His harsh gibberish sounded the same as the words he'd spoken to poor Nan.

The amulet pinched.

Still alive. Mai blew out a breath. The burning subsided. Like her parents before her, she wore the initiation scar on the back of her neck.

"Welcome to Tivar's flock," the bishop said. "You will serve the Tivari until you receive Tivar's Rest."

Mai's heart swelled. She'd proven herself worthy of the gods.

Chapter 1:
Unseen Voices

Had Mai known a Tivari god would pass overhead today, she wouldn't have worn her oldest, most threadbare dress. Then again, the chafing skirts she had on now weren't much worse than her nicest clothes.

Humming, she looked up from where she'd finally pulled a particularly stubborn weed near the base of the rice stalks. In the distance, a line of flames flickered across the sky, engulfing the gold-gilded chariot of a Tivari god. They usually only descended at harvest time, to accept sacrifices of rice, wheat, and chickens. If they were coming now, maybe a nearby village had sinned and now faced divine punishment.

Around her, the workers continued their shoveling and hoeing, the chariot's roar too far away for the others to hear. Their hums joined with hers, harmonizing with the cicada buzzes, bird chirps, and wind in the rice heads.

Not even Cleric Pyuz on his armored horse noticed the sound. Slapping his coiled whip in his palm, he was probably too busy barking orders.

Then, he turned his horse and glared at her. The whip cracked.

Pain seared across her cheek. Her hum, and the symphony of summer with it, fell into silence as the snap echoed across the valley. The villagers all stopped their work and gawked.

It'd landed so close to her eye. She lifted a hand to the wound. Warmth oozed between her fingers. The Turtle's Egg!

The priest's snarl exposed the full length of his tusks, the sharpest part of the Tivari's otherwise blunt features. His turquoise skin glistened with sweat. He raised the whip again. "Back to work, Six-two-one-three!"

Mai recoiled and shielded her face. The last thing she needed was a scar next to all the pimples. Several lashes had already left permanent marks across her back.

Dropping his hoe, Li scrambled over and interposed himself between them. He turned his back to the priest, wrapping firm arms around her. The air cracked again.

A wince contorted his handsome features. Her fault. He looked over his shoulder. "Please, Cleric, Mai had a good reason for resting. Tell him, Mai."

"Insolent." With a grunt, the priest drew the holy rod from his side and pointed it at Li.

Mai shuddered. What fell magic would it unleash this time? Last week, Cleric Pyuz had reduced hobbled Old Shu to ashes for working too slow; and a month ago, Shu and Meng for doing things men shouldn't do together. She wiggled free of Li's arms and staggered around him, putting herself in the rod's line of fire. She pointed to the sky. "Please, Cleric, I heard a chariot, and had to admire the gods' glory."

He followed her finger.

The roaring grew louder, and the flaming chariot loomed closer and closer. The ground shook. Now, everyone was looking up at it.

The priest's jaw wiggled, sending his tusks rocking back and forth. He looked at them. "On your knees!"

Along with the other villagers, Mai knelt and pressed her forehead into the dirt. Her cheek stung.

The chariot was right overhead now, so huge it blotted out the sun. Its crackling flames tortured the souls who bore it through the skies.

It was so loud that even when Mai covered her ears, they still hurt. Her chest squeezed around her racing heart, choking out her breath.

Then it passed. The sun shined again.

She peeked up.

Cleric Pyuz harrumphed and sheathed the rod. "Back to work. Laziness in life means—"

"Eternal labor in the afterlife," they all finished in unison.

He bobbed his head. "Yes. If you don't make your quota, the gods will curse you." He turned his horse, off to whip other sinful workers.

Out from under his watchful stare, she gazed at Li.

His smile, forced or not, shined like a second sun. "You came to my rescue."

No longer at risk of whipping or disintegration, the memory of his sculpted chest and strong arms wrapped around her sent her stomach fluttering like a swarm of butterflies. She smoothed out her dress. "We won't make our quota without you." By Tivar, did she just say that?

At the edge of the rice field, the three village beauties all eyed her, grinning and tittering at her misfortune. The priest might oversee Sweetfield village, and the headman might report to him, but The Gang ruled over the boys.

"She'll be even uglier with that scar," said one.

Just a few steps away, Ying rose. She brushed off her husband's restraining hand. Like a rabbit, her eyes never leaving Cleric Pyuz's back, she worked her way to Mai's side. Her husband just glared.

Ying looked over her shoulder at The Gang. "Don't listen to them. They're so lazy, they'll be pulling Tivar's chariot in the afterlife."

Mai shot a glance at them. They used their beauty to trick stupid boys into doing work for them. Surely Ying was right. They'd be punished for all eternity.

Ying dabbed the cut on Mai's cheek with her kerchief, the one Mai had woven for her. "Are you all right?" she asked.

The coarse fibers stung, but Mai nodded all the same. "I think so."

"I'm sorry I didn't warn you that the cleric was so close," Ying said.

Li chuckled. "I think you were thinking of places you'd rather be than here."

"The places we could sing together!" Ying's smile was radiant, even more so with the glow of her recent marriage. "Where is it this time? The gorge? The Wall?"

"The dragon bones, I bet." Li's grin widened. "I'd sure love to see them, too."

A tingle ran up Mai's spine. Myths and fables talked about a world that had once existed beyond the dozen villages and rice and wheat fields. Since children, they'd sung songs about the enormous wall from the lost Empire of Cathay, when the sun shined larger and brighter. Not that she'd see anything more amazing than the nearby pyramid. She squinted in its direction, barely able to pick out the monument to the gods from the surrounding mountains.

She sighed. Even if those legendary places existed, escaping would just get Mother and Father tortured. Chances were, she wouldn't even make it very far before a vicious madaeri tracked her down, or a wandering ghost claimed her while she slept.

Ying pressed the cloth into Mai's palm and returned to work with the others.

A smile formed on Mai's lips, unbidden. As hard as life was, the gods favored her with good friends like Ying and Li. Again, the scrapes of shovels and hoes set a rhythm for her heart. The bird chirps resumed, sending her spirit soaring. She fought the urge to raise her voice in song.

Li met her gaze, then flicked his eyes to Cleric Pyuz's back. With a grin, he pantomimed choking his shovel haft.

If only she could bring herself to giggle like the beauties in The Gang. Twirling a strand of hair, she attempted a futile smile. Pain lanced through the cut in her cheek. She knelt to resume weeding—

—and froze.

Cleric Pyuz was staring at her as he rode back. He adjusted the neckline of his grey mesh armor, with fine and supple links that hugged his stout form and moved without a sound. He wiped sweat from his prominent brow. "Of all the villages in this godsforsaken world, I get stuck in the hottest, most humid cesspool of them all."

At least in this, Mai agreed. Still, her heart pattered at his approach.

"I'm saddled with the most useless workers." Cleric Pyuz pointed to nearby buckets. "Six-two-one-three, go refill the water buckets. Be back before the mid-waxing crescent, or I will mark your other ugly cheek."

Eyes never leaving his, Mai hurried over and picked up a pole. If only she could whack the Tivari off his high horse. But that would get her tortured and killed, though not before having to watch the same fate inflicted on her family. Instead, she looked toward the Iridescent Moon to the south, never moving from its reliable seat in the heavens. It was now well past its second waxing crescent; there wasn't much time. She bowed low. "Yes, Your Holiness."

He turned his mount and headed toward The Gang, the joints of the beast's metal armor making no sound, even to her keen ears. She slid the wooden buckets' handles to either end of her pole, and hefted it up to her shoulders.

She followed the irrigation ditches, their muddy waters sealed off to keep them from flooding the rice fields close to harvest. Each footstep followed the cadenced scrapes of workers. The birds and cicadas resumed their song. Nobody else ever seemed to notice the primal harmony. Despite her fatigue from the day's work, the surrounding music invigorated her. Away from Cleric Pyuz, she hummed, synchronizing all the disparate sounds.

Pain in her cheek forgotten, her heart floated on the notes. Even if she was plain compared to most of the other village girls, none could sing like her. When she sang, even flirty Li ignored The Gang to listen. A smile flitted across her lips. Mother and Father wanted her to marry Skinny Fang, but maybe, just maybe, Li would ask. Maybe Cleric Pyuz would approve it.

The White Moon was rising in the east, while the Iridescent Moon waxed halfway between the second and mid-crescents to the south by the time she reached the river. Its waters rustled over stones, adding to the summer's song. She clambered over the large, smooth rocks toward her favorite pool.

As always, it glowed a bluish hue, beautiful like the Blue Moon, Lydath's Eye. Her hum echoed off its placid surface, filling her with strength and confidence. She crouched over and studied her reflection.

The whip's cut ran down the middle of her right cheek, right between a ridge of pimples. Her hum came to a stop. Her heart, drifting on her melody up till now, sank. If the wound healed like the ones on her back, it would leave a scar that would make her triangular face look even more like a fox's. Her eyes were much too large for her head, and if her jaw was any shorter, she'd look like a praying mantis.

She dipped the hem of her dress in the water. Pausing for a few seconds to watch the ripples, she dabbed the wound. The roughspun cloth, even when wet, chafed. She let out a long sigh. Her voice might be beautiful, but Li would surely pick a beautiful face. And even if he chose her, they'd be stuck in the village for the rest of their lives.

Pulling her finger loose from her hair, she found a flat, round stone and skipped it across the pool. One, two, three bounces. She watched as the ripples spread out from wherever the rock had hit, blending together in countless patterns. After a harrowing morning, it was comforting to get lost in them. It—

A quiet breath hid among all the other sounds of nature. Her heart leaped into her throat, and she raked her gaze over the surroundings.

Nothing.

Just her imagination, perhaps. With a last scan of the area, she reached over and closed her fingers around one of the buckets. She dipped it into the pool and the water gushed in.

There it was again, the same breathing—closer now, out of harmony with the crickets, birds, and wind. She looked in its direction.

It was just a summer's haze above the water.

Still, it sounded as if something was there. Never breaking her focus from the waves of air, she reached for the other pail.

The haze shifted. Not in some random pattern, but with the same intent as nature's music.

A ghost? Her fingers slackened, and the bucket's handle slipped from her grasp. She bolted to her feet and turned to run.

"Wait." A voice, clear like a nightingale's song, called from the vapors.

The hairs on the back of her neck stood on end.

"I won't hurt you," the voice said. Male or female, it was impossible to tell.

Still, it was so melodious, her heart threatened to burst. "What are you?"

Silence.

Eyes still locked on the haze, she retrieved the bucket and filled it. Maybe it was just her imagination. Yes, from the heat and the stressful morning.

"Can you see me?"

The way her nerves jolted, it felt like Tivar had ripped her soul from her body. She squinted. Still there was nothing more than the shifting air. She shook her head.

"How did you know I was here?"

She cocked her head. How… "I heard your breathing."

More silence.

Then, "Why did you watch the ripples in the pool?"

Maybe she was losing her mind, talking to nothingness. "They are calming. It's pretty, how they spread out and split when they hit each other."

Again, silence.

"Will you sing for me again?"

It had to be a ghost; maybe some poor man lured to the river by a water spirit's song, and drowned. Even in death, it wanted to hear music. Still, she'd visited this spot more than ninety-nine times over, and never heard water spirits or ghosts before.

"Please."

At least the ghost was polite. Mai looked around. How embarrassing it would be for any of the water girls to stumble onto her talking at thin air. The gossip would spread like bamboo shoots after a spring rain. Li would never look at her the same way again. "Why do you want to hear me sing?"

"Your voice. It is unique. Special."

Not that it got her anything more than a lashing from Cleric Pyuz. Perhaps this was some kind of Tivari trap.

"Trust me."

Its accent didn't sound like the guttural Tivari. It was melodic, like poetry. It couldn't hurt to sing for it. She lifted her voice into song, starting a hymn to celebrate the gods visiting on their flaming chariots.

"No, not one of their songs. I want to hear one of yours."

Her forehead scrunched up. What could possibly entertain a ghost? Perhaps an ancient song, one of those her people never sang in front of the Tivari. The lyrics, which recounted cautionary tales from the mythical land of Cathay, might be considered sacrilegious. She hummed the tune about the building of the legendary Great Wall, a monument to Cathay's first emperor, at the cost of far more than ninety-nine lives. Note after note captured the workers' toil, rising to a crescendo as they reached completion.

"Yes, that is it. Your music. Your legacy. Their gods are not yours."

She rubbed the scar on the back of her neck, the mark of obedience to the gods, which she'd received as a child. The voice's words were nothing short of blasphemy. She shook her head. "Tivar and Lydath created the Tivari in their own image. It was by their grace that they created us as lesser beings, meant to serve and be rewarded in the afterlife. Why else would the Tivari have the power of magic, while we don't?" How bizarre it felt to lecture the air! But still, facts had to be set straight.

"Oh, but you do have magic. Or at least, some of you do."

Such nonsense. She frowned, sending pain searing across the cut on her cheek.

"You do. With your music."

She shook her head.

The haze came closer. "It's true. Surely, you have held your friends spellbound with the beauty of your voice. That connection is magic."

It was true, the villagers would listen to her whenever she sang. Still— "That is just the quality of music."

"No, there is more to music. A Dragon Song can bend others to your will."

Mai twirled a strand of hair. If that was true, it might be possible to charm Li away from the other girls.

The voice continued, "It can summon typhoons and rout armies. It can free you from the yoke of slavery."

Slavery? The word tasted strange. "What is—"

"It's how you work for the Tivari your entire lives, until you die, with no freedom to choose."

Even if it were possible, what would mankind do without the Tivari to guide them from sin? She couldn't hold back her laugh, even for all the pain in her cheek. She covered the cut with a hand.

The shimmering air was right beside her. The voice sang.

Wondrous, like a shower of shooting stars. Her eyes widened.

Resonant, like thunder rumbling across the valley. Her shoulders shook.

Soothing, like spring rain on the thatching of her parents' hut. Her limbs relaxed, all tension fleeing.

The haze pressed right up to her face. Warmth flooded over her cheek, and the pain disappeared.

"Look at your reflection," the voice said, now from a few paces away.

Mai knelt by the pool and looked down. Beneath the flakes of dried blood, her cheek was smooth, as if it had never been cut. The pimples were gone, and even the blemishes had healed over. She gasped.

"This is the true healing of the gods, channeled through sound. Have you ever seen your Tivari priest do as much?"

Cleric Pyuz only brought pain and suffering with his magic. She stared into the haze. "Who are you?"

"I am an Elestrae."

"What is that?"

"Your people would call us fairies. The fairies call themselves elves, and they call us angels."

They were cute words, belonging to bedtime stories and cautionary tales. "Show yourself to me. Please."

"Come back here tonight, when the moon waxes to its third crescent. I will reveal myself, and also teach you how to invoke a Dragon Song."

Teach her? To heal with only the sound of her voice? Li would surely appreciate such a talent over the silly giggles of pretty girls. Still, leaving the village and the protection of the gods past dark was dangerous. Ghosts roamed the land, ready to drag others into an afterlife even worse than hell.

Chapter 2:
Blasphemous Rumors

Cicadas whirred and frogs trilled in summer's symphony. Sitting in the village square with her friends and family, Mai stared at the heavens as she absently nibbled at her rice. In the west, Lydath's Eye opened three-quarters, while the White Moon to the east waned towards new. Yet it was the Iridescent Moon in the south, now waxing to its second gibbous, which preoccupied her. In order to meet with the angel, she only had a phase to slip away and make her way through the darkness and ghosts to the river.

"Eat." Mother prodded her with a finger to the shoulder. "Your hips are too skinny to make babies."

A familiar set of footsteps approached the village square, accompanied by an equally familiar chuckle.

Mai peeked up through her lashes and turned her head just enough to see Li.

He was just coming for dinner with several other villagers. With his shirt off in the summer heat, his sculpted chest and arms glistened with sweat. He slapped the skinnier, homelier Fang on the back. "Lydath's Eye will fully open in three months. It's the perfect time to make babies."

If her face could flush any brighter, they wouldn't need the firelight to see. Other unmarried women, Little Sister Ling included, giggled and cast adoring eyes at him. The three members of The Gang batted their eyelashes.

Ying, still glowing from her own recent marriage to dour Qiu, sidled over and chopsticked some carrots and potatoes into Mai's bowl. She gave a nudge. "Here, have some more, and offer it to Li."

It wasn't like Ying to give up food. Mai searched her eyes. "What about you?"

"I'm not hungry."

Not hungry? Mai shook her head. "You must be jo—"

Father stood and beckoned Skinny Fang. "Come, sit with us. Beside Mai."

"Yes," one of The Gang said. "Go sit beside Mai."

The other two giggled.

Mai's eyes strayed from Li to Fang. Though best friends, they might have been opposites in every regard. Li, outgoing and handsome; Skinny Fang reserved and plain. He was also lanky, just like her. Maybe that's why everyone except Ying thought she and the latter would make a good pair.

Perhaps fate had different ideas. She glanced up at the Iridescent Moon again.

There wasn't much time for her to make it to the river, but Li was approaching with Fang. As the new arrivals found seats on the logs, Mother rose and went to the central cauldrons and filled two bowls with rice and vegetables. She returned and offered the meals to Li and Fang.

Ying nudged Mai, her whisper tickling her ear: "Offer Li some of your stew."

How would that even be possible? Mai would have to reach over Skinny Fang—

Bowl in hand, Li wiggled his way between her and Fang. He leaned in, his face close.

It did little to cool Mai's cheeks. Thank Tivar the flickering firelight hid her blush. Her pulse quickened.

Ying nudged her, while across the fire, The Gang members muttered.

Li ran a finger across her cheek, sending sparks up and down her spine. "The cut..." he looked up at the others. "It's gone. Was it my imagination? Didn't the priest drag a whip across her face?"

Ying nodded. "I saw it, too." She twisted over and studied Mai's cheek.

"What?" Father stood and crouched in front of her. His eyes roved over her face. Apparently, her non-existent wound was on display for everyone. "What did you do?"

"Something stupid," one of The Gang whispered to the other two, too quiet for anyone but Mai to hear.

"I looked up at the god's chariot." She would've turned her head, but that would have given others reason to crowd in and look at her cheek.

Li snarled. "Cleric Pyuz is such a Turtle's Egg. So moody! That's the seventh time he's whipped you."

With their hips touching, it was hard to tell if the vibration was from Li's growl or her own pattering heart. And apparently, he'd been keeping track of her.

Fighting the urge to fan herself, Mai glanced back at the Iridescent Moon. "He's whipped me for being late. For being early. For not harvesting fast enough." She envisioned each of the scars across her back.

By contrast, Li had never been whipped at all, until today. She leaned back and examined the cut across his back, which was smooth from waist to nape—save for the blotch they all had at the base of their necks from their childhood dedication ceremony to the gods. Maybe like the invisible elf angel, she could learn to heal his wound with a song.

Mother sighed. "Without the Tivari's guidance, we would stray from the grace of the gods."

Around them, the villagers murmured in agreement.

"Sin in life can only be redeemed with pain," Skinny Fang said.

For whatever else he lacked, Skinny Fang had a pleasant voice. If only he spoke more. Or sang more. After all, if Father and Fang's parents had their way, they'd be married before Lydath's Eye fully opened. Of course, Cleric Pyuz would have to approve.

"In any case," Li said, his breath tickling her ear, "I could've sworn I saw blood on your cheek."

He looked up toward a group of workers who'd witnessed the scene. They all nodded.

How could she explain about the haze and the voice? They'd think she was crazy, or worse, dabbling in witchcraft. Li, and maybe even Fang, would avoid her. Of course, if Hazy Voice could really teach her how to charm someone, or heal injuries, they would all admire her. Maybe even The Gang.

Then again, Hazy Voice might not wait around for her. She looked up at the Iridescent Moon, now waxing closer to the third gibbous. Not much time now. Setting her rice bowl down, she stood. "I'll tell you what happened when I get back."

Li stood. "Where are you going? I'll walk with you."

Mai chewed on the inside of her lip. As tempting as the offer was, it would be irresponsible to risk someone else's soul. And perhaps Hazy Voice might not appear if she came with a stranger. She waved her hand back and forth. "I just need to stretch my legs. I won't be long."

25

"I need to stretch my legs, too." Li passed his empty bowl to Mother.

"I...I..."

Fang threw up his hands. "Mai has to go relieve herself."

It was hard to tell if Li's eyes or mouth were rounder or wider.

So much heat flared in her head, it might rival the Tivari gods' flaming chariots. Her eyes darted from Skinny Fang to Li. His gaze dropped to the ground, then back up, sending hers down. Picking up her skirts, she escaped the village square and made her way among the huts. She glanced over her shoulder. Tivar forbid Li should follow her in order to sneak a peek.

Of course he wouldn't.

She passed the chicken coops, then the woven trays of sourberries. Foods left to dry there would sometimes disappear, taken by hungry ghosts. She shuddered and hurried on.

At the edge of Sweetfield village, out of the firelight, it was quite dark. She blinked several times, letting her eyes adjust. With the White Moon near new, and the Iridescent Moon never providing much light, even as it neared full, she had to rely on blue sheen from Lydath's Eye.

She took a few deep breaths and listened. Leaving the village at night was forbidden, for their own sakes, but Cleric Pyuz was never around after dark to enforce the rule. At least, not that the villagers knew of. Even now, there was no sound of his coarse breathing, or the stomping of his armored horse. Then again, the beast never made a sound.

She rubbed the scar on her neck. No one ever broke the rules. Even if a sinner managed to survive marauding ghosts, disobedience in life meant punishment in the afterlife. Tortak had many ways of inflicting pain on a soul. Yes, this was a bad idea. Why risk eternal torture?

Then again, Hazy Voice had claimed the Tivari gods were not truly the deities of mankind. Mai ran a hand across her smooth cheek, healed by the grace of the true gods. She took a step toward the fields.

An eerie howl pealed through the darkness.

Blood running cold, Mai froze. Hazy Voice had said there were no ghosts, but nothing living could've possibly made that sound. She chewed on her inner lip. A life of back-breaking work in this tiny village, with only a rare pilgrimage to the pyramid, wasn't worth living. If there was no risk of damnation, then let whatever howled come for her. With one last look back at the village, she headed toward the river.

Thank Tivar the hard-packed dirt along the irrigation ditches was flat and more or less clear of rocks. A careless step might trip her, cut a sole, or sprain an ankle. Eyes straining in the dim blue light, she followed the path through the fields toward the river. Frogs croaked, setting a rhythm for her march. If there were ghosts out tonight, surely the birds and beasts would quiet, for all animals possessed a certain understanding of the dark things that moved at night. Wind rustled through the rice stalks, the breeze raising her skin in chicken bumps. Fireflies flashed, seeming in beat with the sounds. Far in the distance, blue light sparkled at the pyramid's summit.

Up ahead, the river's rustling grew louder. Not only that, a soft blue light glowed above her favorite pool, illuminating a trail between the wispy trees to the river bank.

When she reached the pool, she gasped. The light gleamed up from the riverbed, which snaked its way south toward the pyramid. The glow was especially bright from the floor of the pool.

"You are late."

Mai swung around to the source of the voice. Again, no one was there. "Where are you? Show yourself."

The air glittered just a few steps away, revealing a lithe figure about the same height as her, lowering the hood of a cloak. The cloth shimmered like the underside of a storm cloud when lightning flashed. The blue light, filtered by the water, sent rippled shadows across the figure's face.

And what a face! Mai sucked in a breath.

Male or female, it was hard to tell in the shifting shadows. Still, such beauty didn't seem possible. Perhaps it was that light, but Their large eyes appeared to be the most peculiar shade, perhaps that band of color near the bottom of a rainbow. An oval face framed Their thin, high-bridged nose and full lips. Their ears tapered into points.

When They spoke, it sounded as if all the angels in heaven were singing. Mai's heart fluttered. Had They been beautiful before, Their voice made them divine.

"I am Aralas, messenger of Solaris, God of the Sun." They dipped heir head in greeting.

"Are you...a man or a woman?" Face hot, Mai chewed on her lower lip. It would've been polite to ask in a more roundabout way, but how was she supposed to address an angel?

They laughed like a concert of ceremonial bells heralding the arrival of the Tivari gods' flaming chariots. "Man." They...no, *his* eyes studied her.

The piercing gaze made it feel as if she were naked, her gaunt frame on display despite the dress. She crossed her chest and down *there* with her arms. "Aren't angels supposed to look like the Tivari?"

His lips pursed like he'd sucked on a sourberry. "The servants of the orc gods are demons."

The word *orc* sounded so foreign. Her forehead scrunched up.

"Tivari...that is glorified name the orcs gave themselves."

Mai's head spun. This Aralas had to be lying. "Aren't angels supposed to have wings?"

He looked over his back and shrugged. "A slanderous rumor."

JC Kang

Slanderous might be too big of a word for her, but *rumor* made his meaning clear. Li was the subject of many rumors among the village girls, after all. "Then how do angels fly?"

With a grin, he hummed several melodious notes. He rose off the ground with nothing but air beneath his feet.

"Tivar's Scythe," she muttered, though it would've been more impressive had his hair not flopped into his face.

His smile melted. "Do not invoke the Corrupter by name."

"I'm sorry." She bowed her head.

"You are forgiven, Miss Mai."

"How do you know my name?" she asked, cocking her head.

"I am an angel, after all." In a most undivine way, he blew hair out of his face with a puff of air.

Still, she bowed lower this time.

He laughed again. "You need not show such deference, Miss Mai. The gods created you to be free."

She looked up. "Free?"

Nodding, he knelt by the pool.. His arm extended from beneath the cloak. Fitting tight around his slender arm, his sleeve was the same lustrous grey material as the cloak. His hand brushed through the water. "Do you know why the water here is so blue?"

She shook her head.

"In the beginning, the God of the Sun—Solaris in my language, Yang-Di in yours—presented the world as a gift to his consort: Ayara in our language, Guanyin in yours." He gestured toward Lydath's Eye, looming large in the sky.

"No, that is Lydath, Tivar's Queen, watching over us."

"Lydath is an orc god. The Corrupter's Whore, who does not deserve a seat in the heavens. The Blue Moon is the Eye of Guanyin."

Whore was a term to describe the immoral behavior that had led to the fall of Cathay. What did that have to do with the gods? "I'm so confused."

"They have deceived you for generations. Guanyin is your creator. So moved was she by Yang-Di's gift, that she shed a single tear. It fell to the earth, landing not too far in that direction, forming Tear Drop Lake." He pointed south.

"Do you mean the lake near the pyramid? The one which we are forbidden to approach?"

He nodded. "Forbidden, because its healing waters would expose all the orc lies. Your ancestors sprung forth from where her fertile tears fell, and thrived under the protection of the elves, and established the Empire of Cathay."

Mai's head spun. Myths of the decadent Cathayi empire spoke of elves, but never as protectors. Everything Aralas said contradicted history.

31

Tivari history. It dismissed tales of the Cathayi empire as children's cautionary tales at best, sacrilege at worst.

"Then why do we serve the Tivari?" she asked. "They tell us Lydath created us for that purpose."

His mane of lustrous hair rippled as he shook his head. "The elves and orcs fought for supremacy of the world. In the end, Tivar appeared in the sky as a red sun, outshining your yellow sun. In the Year of the Second Sun, Guanyin's Eye faded to grey. Elf magic lost its power, and the orcs nearly wiped us out. The survivors went into hiding. Without the protection of the elves, the kingdoms of men, dwarves, and madaerae fell, and all your people were enslaved."

Dwarves...the short pixies were supposed to be fairy tales. Yet so were elves, and here stood a living, breathing elf angel. As for madaeri... She'd never seen one, but rumor had it they were vicious and wolf-like, and that the Tivari used them to track down wayward humans. It was hard to believe the beasts could ever have kingdoms. "Why are you revealing yourself now, after so many centuries?"

Aralas searched her eyes. "The Sun God has decreed that we overthrow the orcs. I am searching the world for people like you, who will help."

"Help?" Mai's jaw must've gaped wide enough to fit her entire rice bowl. When she regained her wits, she said, "I don't understand. We have food to eat and a roof over our heads."

"What happens to the lion's share of food you grow?"

"We sacrifice it to the gods. They will reward us in the afterlife."

He chuckled. "Serving the orc gods will not bring you salvation. What if you could keep the food for yourself?"

Her forehead scrunched up. What were they supposed to do with extra food? It would just go to waste.

"What if you did not have to suffer punishment?" He extended a delicate finger and ran it over her cheek, right where the cut had been.

Whether the tingling came from the memory of the cut, or just the gentle caress of his finger, she couldn't tell. Though, even if he'd healed that wound, she still had six long scars across her back from Cleric Pyuz's whip. "It's impossible to defeat them."

"You outnumber them, two hundred to one."

However many a *hundred* was, "The Tivari have holy rods, horses, and armor."

"You have the spark of magic."

Maybe he meant humans in general, or her specifically. Still, all she really wanted magic for was to heal the sick and wounded, and maybe impress Li into liking her. Getting involved in a rebellion that at best would leave humans without guidance, or at worst condemn her immortal soul, ranked about as high on her list as having Skinny Fang's babies.

He lifted her chin. "All you have to do is awaken it."

"How?"

His hand brushed along her jawbone to her ears. "You must hear the heartbeat of the world itself. Let me take you to a place where it is loudest."

Was it worth it? If he taught her, no doubt he'd want her to take part in this crazy rebellion. She found the Iridescent Moon, now waning well past the third crescent. "Where is it?"

"The dragon's grave."

Mai shuddered. Only one dragon remained, the rest hunted down by the Tivari ages ago. Of course, rumors travelled about the grave near Frawdok's Purse Lake, which was supposedly haunted by a dragon spirit. Thankfully, it was too far away. "Even if we could get past Tivari patrols, it's days away. I need to get back home soon, or else Cleric Pyuz will punish my family."

A charming grin flitted across his face. "How about if I could take you there in a blink of an eye?"

She suppressed a snort. "Sure. What do you plan on doing, riding in the seat of one of the gods' flaming chariots?"

He raised his voice in song. She'd never heard anything so beautiful, and her heart soared. Then, he placed his hand on the back of her neck.

The world spun around her in flashes of colors. Darkness crowded around the edge of her vision, and filled in until all went black.

The Dragon Charmer's Apprentice

Chapter 3:
Dragon Bones

The whir of insects buzzed in Mai's ears. Her eyes fluttered open to the night sky. She blinked, bringing Aralas' face into focus. By Tivar's Grace! Her head was resting on his lap. How humiliating. She bolted upright.

Pain flared on the top of her head as she crashed into his chin. "Ow!"

Rubbing his jaw, he grinned. "All that hair didn't cushion the blow."

Her cheeks burned hot. Li always made fun of her unruly locks.

The elf angel's smile only broadened. He jumped up and helped her to her feet. Then he pointed. "Look."

They stood in a flat, treeless basin surrounded by mountains. Just a few dozen paces away, several columns jutted long and straight out of the ground, rising to nearly twice the height of a man. They appeared to form a ring, encircling nothing but empty space. The light from Lydath's—no, *Guanyin's*—Eye gave them a bluish sheen.

"Is this...?"

"The bones of Pyarax." It would've sounded ominous had his hair not flopped into his face.

Mai shuddered nonetheless.

Aralas, however, didn't seem frightened by the prospect of a dragon spirit haunting the place, and his voice was so calm and reassuring. She looked to the Iridescent Moon, which had waxed no further than it had been by the river, though it did seem just a little lower than usual. "How did we get here so fast?"

"Magic," he said. Then he uttered a foul syllable, reminiscent of Cleric Pyuz's curses. A white light shone in his cupped palm.

She gasped. Not so much because of the magic, but because in new light, he was even more stunning. His eyes were the color of newly opened violets in spring, and his hair might've been the molten gold of the Tivari gods' flaming chariots.

He raised an eyebrow, affording her a curious glance.

Heat rushed to her head. She must've been staring.

JC Kang

He puffed hair out of his face, and grinned. "This was once Cathay's center of culture, where magic thrived. That's why the orcs forbid you from coming here."

Nodding, she looked around. It was just flat, open land, with none of Cathay's fabled golden cities. Nothing about the desolate basin spoke of Cathay's mythical greed, sloth, and wickedness, which had led to its collapse.

He scrutinized her. "We will see if we can awaken the spark of magic inside of you, as people did in millennia past. Close your eyes. What do you hear?"

She did as she was told and listened. "Cicadas buzzing, the wind, cricket chirps—"

"What is special about them?"

"All the sounds of summer sing in concert with one another, they—"

"Yes, you are very perceptive, but deeper. Listen."

What else was there? She opened her eyes. "Frog trills—"

"No."

His answer was so terse, her neck and shoulders tightened. "The croak of toads—"

"Nothing so obvious." He shook his head. "Perhaps this is too much for a human."

Maybe if she had ears as big as his, it would be easier. "A stream nearby, a—"

He sighed. "I thought since you heard me, you would be able to hear the pulse of the world itself."

Mai's shoulders slumped. She was such a failure. If the supposed spark of magic didn't awaken in her, she would never be able to win over Li. Never be able to heal her family and friends.

"I should get you home before you get in trouble." His voice, so beautiful before, now droned in defeat.

She blew out a long sigh. The breath sounded smooth at first, yet beneath it was a nearly imperceptible stutter, coming out at regular intervals. She closed her eyes again.

There it was, a pulse coursing beneath her feet. Slow, resolute.

She hummed, using the beat as a guide. Her muscles had been wound up and knotted from his terse rebukes, but now they relaxed.

"Yes, you hear it!" His alluring smile, though not visible through her closed eyes, floated in his words. "Follow it. Trust your ears."

Continuing her hum, one foot in front of the other, she followed the thrum. It grew louder with each step. Her heart fell into rhythm with it. It was almost as if—

A rock dug into her foot. Eyes fluttering open, she shifted her weight, only to stumble. Her arms flailed. Wind rushed in her ears. A column rushed toward her face.

Aralas' arm swept under her chest, preventing her forehead from a meeting with the column. He was stronger than his slight frame suggested. With a gentle lift, he eased her back into a standing position. Their faces were so close, his gaze so intense. "Are you all right?"

Was she? She searched his eyes, their violet now shrouded by shade, yet still mesmerizing. His arm remained around her, lingering just beneath her breasts. Such closeness should've shared their body heat, yet he felt no warmer than the air around them. Could he be…a ghost?

Brushing off his embrace, she took a step back. "I'm fine."

His smile made up for any warmth his body lacked. "I am sorry, I should have been paying more attention. I was so hypnotized by your connection to the energy of the world."

"Energy?"

"Yes! It wells up here, stronger than most places in the world." He waved his hand in an arc. "Everything in nature responds to it. It becomes an underlying beat which lays the foundation for all the songs in nature. You can borrow that pulse to bend others to your will."

That would be how she could win Li over.

He chuckled. "You haven't learned to hide your emotions, have you?"

By Tivar, she must be wearing the most ridiculous grin. She tried to arrange her face into an expression of disinterest.

He burst out laughing. "Now you just look constipated."

A pout formed on her lips, unbidden.

With a last chuckle, he took her hand in his and placed it on the column. "A dragon bone. What does it feel like?"

Mai shuddered. The Tivari allowed them to keep a few of the chickens they raised, and on special occasions, the villagers might slaughter one. The very thought of handling the carcass of a creature that once lived made her stomach roil. Now, her hand was pressed against a bone.

And not just any bone, but that of a *dragon*.

"Well?"

It felt almost like the smooth, cool surface of the armor that Cleric Pyuz's horse wore. Like the vibrant pulse of the world. "It resonates, like the string of a pipa."

"Yes. Everything has a resonance. Come." His hand took hers, intertwining his long, thin fingers with her stubbier ones. Unlike his body, his palm was warm.

A pleasant tingle ran up her arm.

"Lead the way," he said. "Come, let us continue. Close your eyes. I will make sure you don't trip this time."

She closed her eyes and listened. Again, the thrum of the world filled her ears. As he had said, all the other sounds

41

seemed to join with it. Perhaps that was the reason why natural sounds always seemed to harmonize with one another, and even why the villagers worked in beat with it.

As she ambled toward the source, he would give her tugs or pushes, until at last his grip tightened around her.

She opened her eyes. They had entered the circle of columns. The ground here was flat and felt smooth beneath her feet. He sang several incomprehensible words, yet the feeling was like the hymns they sang to the Tivari. A wind picked up from the east, making his hair billow like sheets of liquid gold. The columns all vibrated, some at a low pitch, others high, interacting in a chorus. This must be what the rumors mistook for the dragon spirit.

Her heart buzzed like dragonfly wings.

"Use your ears," he shouted over the bones' chimes. "Find where the sound is most intense."

Closing her eyes again, she wandered around. No matter where she went, the music's intensity remained the same. "I can't. There's no difference."

"Can you tell where I am?" he called. He started to hum.

With closed eyes, how was that even possible? Still, she listened. His melody mingled with the chorus of dragon bones. He was moving, circling somewhere far to her right. Tilting her head, she turned her ear toward him. She took too many steps to count, trying to follow his hum.

Then his song came loud and resonant, carrying over the song of the wind in the dragon bones, as if he were humming right in her ear. She opened her eyes.

He stood nearly a hundred paces away, and wasn't even facing in her direction. How was it even possible for his voice to sound so close? Not only that, but from where she stood, it was clear the dragon bones formed not a perfect circle, but rather an elongated one.

"An ellipse," he said, twirling his finger in a wide....elongated circle. It was as if he'd been reading her mind.

He chanted again. The wind subsided, along with the echo of the dragon bones. He turned to face her. "Well?"

"How come you sound so close?"

"Such is the nature of dragons." He patted his stomach. "They have a stone in their belly, the source of their power. Pyarax's dragonstone must've been right about where I stand now, before the orcs slew him and took it."

She cocked her head. "Why would they?"

"Dragons are selfish and powerful. As immortals, their goals are hard to predict. After the orcs conquered the world, they worried the dragons would turn on them. The slaughter was known as the Dragonpurge. Only the two mightiest still remain."

Either the Tivari or Aralas were lying. "Two? We only know of Avarax."

Aralas ran a hand through his hair, brushing loose strands from his face. "There is another, who watches over your people."

"The Guardian Dragon? He's just a legend."

"*She* is real. She lives not far from you."

Mai snorted. *Not far* was relative for someone who could travel weeks away with a word of magic. "The Guardian Dragon from our stories is supposed to protect us. Why would he—*she*—allow the Tivari to enslave us?"

"Unlike Avarax, whose sheer power necessitates an uneasy coexistence with the orcs, she survived through cunning and guile. She will reappear, when your people are ready to rise up against your masters." His gaze locked on her, intense even at a distance. "The spark of magic is alive in you. You will lead, and the Empire of Cathay will rise again."

She shook her head. With all its sins, Cathay had deserved to fall. "All I want to do…" is marry Li and have his babies. "…I can't lead. My own parents don't even entrust me with any responsibilities."

He took long strides toward her, his legs swishing out from beneath the cloak. Like his arms, they were covered in a grey fabric. "You have a rare gift. One you will squander if you stay content in your little village."

"Can't you do it?"

"Success will depend on a coordinated, worldwide effort." He arrived at her side and placed a finger between

The Dragon Charmer's Apprentice

her eyebrows, soothing the tension there. "I am training others in the various magic arts, and it will require all of you, rising up at once."

Just how big was the world? Cleric Pyuz had suggested there were many more people than the inhabitants of the surrounding villages. Mai had travelled no further than the pyramid, to witness the arrival of the orc gods in their glorious flaming chariots. "Let me think about it."

"Don't think too long. The training isn't easy, and will take time." With a finger, he drew a triangle across the sky, from Lydath's Eye to the White Moon and finally to the Iridescent Moon. "A conjunction of the moons is upon us. Magic will wax to its strongest. It will give us the greatest chance of success."

"What if we fail?" No doubt, the punishment would be severe. Torture and execution.

"You will have to wait another three hundred years for the next conjunction." He traced a finger from the moons and down her cheek, where Cleric Pyuz had whipped her.

She shuddered. Three hundred years meant dozens of generations living under the Tivari's whips.

His ears twitched. He closed his hand, snuffing out the light. When he spoke, it was in a whisper. "An orc patrol is coming this way."

Her heart leaped into her throat. Cleric Pyuz must've realized she was missing, and used his magic mirror to report

45

it. Now the Tivari had come looking for her. She took his hand. "Hurry, take me home."

Aralas chewed on his lower lip. A tremor wavered in his voice. "I…I can't. I must rest before I can channel enough energy to teleport."

Chapter 4:
Hide and Seek

Mai's heart thrummed loud and fast in her ears, almost drowning out the clopping of approaching Tivari boots. Her limbs felt as if she'd carried buckets back and forth from the pool for hours. Her eyes darted about, searching for some place to hide, but there was only open space. Even if they ran, they'd never reach the columns in time.

"Take a deep breath," Aralas whispered, tickling her ear. "Feel the air sink deep into your belly."

What good would a deep breath do? The footsteps sounded so close. The Tivari would appear between the columns any second now.

Frowning, he set a finger between her eyebrows again. "Do it."

She sucked in a draught of the hot summer air, and expanded her chest and stomach as if to sing as loudly as she could.

Puffing hair out of his face, he cast a reassuring smile. He pulled the hood over his head...

And disappeared.

Leaving her alone, in the forbidden ruins of Cathay.

Her breath stuttered. A chill crawled up her spine, her heart raced. How could he do that?

"Keep breathing," he said from right beside her.

Something draped over her head and pushed her to her knees. In the stuffy darkness, his slender arms pulled her close, her head pressed into his solar plexus. The cloth was smooth and supple, but as before, there was no warmth. Her shoulder pushed up against where his man parts should be, but there, too, seemed flat. His heart didn't even seem to have a beat. Perhaps angels did not have hearts, or reproduce.

As before, his voice was soothing. "Take a deep breath with your belly. Harmonize it with their bootsteps."

With a brusque sigh, she closed her eyes and listened.

The marching boots had cleared the columns. They came closer. They were almost upon them.

Surely they were as good as caught. Sweat trickled down her forehead. Every fiber of her being screamed to flee.

Breathe, his voice spoke in her mind.

Her heart jolted. She started to jerk back.

His hand held her firmly to him. *They can't see us through my cloak, unless you panic. If they see us, we are both dead.*

Her hands quavered of their own accord. If he hadn't wanted her to panic, he shouldn't have spoken in her mind, or told her the consequences of panicking. Through her terror, he kept a firm hold. She took a deep breath, expanding her stomach to pull the air deeper. Despite the stifling confines of the cloak, the air seemed cool.

Good. Now listen. Listen for the very beating of their hearts.

How was that even possible, unless she put an ear to one's chest?

Just do it, he said, a stab of impatience in his tone. *Keep breathing.*

The deep breath stilled the trembling in her hands. Her mind cleared. She turned an ear toward the approaching Tivari, but all she could hear were the boots and their hoarse exhalations.

The footsteps paused, right next to them.

Here's your chance. Listen!

They grunted in their foul language, drowning out all other sounds. Still, in the breaks in their dialog, there were nearly imperceptible thumps.

Yes, that is it!

How could he know what she heard?

I do. Just coordinate your breathing. One breath for every five of their beats.

The Tivari conversation continued, but now she could hear their hearts above it. Strong. Single-minded. Just counting their beats was oddly calming.

They resumed their march. The sound of Tivari heartbeats faded, and eventually so did their boots.

The cloak lifted. The humid summer air poured in.

She opened her eyes and blinked. Faint light from Lydath's Eye cast the dragon bones in an eerie blue. Aralas was nowhere to be seen.

"Where are you?" She squinted, looking for the haze.

"Find me." Like when they first entered the circle, his voice seemed all around her.

She peered through the dim illumination, yet there was no sign of him.

"You won't find me with your eyes." His mirthful tone danced around.

He was toying with her. She snorted.

"Imagine what happens when you cast a stone into your favorite pond, how the ripples spread out from the source. Imagine what happens when it hits a reed, or if you threw two stones not far from each other. Think of sounds rippling out and interacting like that."

What a strange notion. Still, he'd been right about hearing the Tivari heartbeats... She blew out a sigh. The sound of her exhalation echoed evenly through the dragon bones, but from one direction, it was somewhat muted, like the ripples in the pool splitting around a waterbug. Pulse picking up a beat, she turned to look.

The haze of his magic cloak flashed for a split second before disappearing.

She clambered to her feet and started to hum.

The sound reverberated back. Again, one spot seemed muffled for a brief moment before shifting. Maintaining her hum, she used her ears to guide her, chasing after the quiet spot as it headed toward the columns.

Then, that muted space disappeared. He must've gone past the edge.

Emerging from the ring, she stopped humming to catch her breath. She hunched over, hands on her knees.

Just to the right came the gentle pulsation from earlier in the day.

She turned and looked.

Aralas, no longer hooded, poked his head out from the other side of a column. The dim light cast his features in a ghostly glow.

Perhaps he was a wraith, one who played games with her in order to drag her down to hell. Her fists clenched.

Then he stepped out, beaming so bright he seemed to light up the night sky. It brought out the beauty of his fine features.

If he was a wraith, he was a very good-looking one. Her stomach fluttered like a swarm of butterflies.

He took her hands in his. "You have just taken the first few steps in learning a Dragon Song: evoking magic through music."

Whatever evoking meant. They'd hidden from the orcs, which seemed to have more to do with his cloak than anything she'd done. "I didn't do much."

He ran a finger up her arm to her heart. "You breathed. You listened."

"I do that every day. There's nothing special about that." She looked to the Iridescent Moon, now waning close to the fourth gibbous. Only a phase before midnight, and a phase had already passed. Everyone must think she was really constipated. Or...if the Tivari had been sent by Cleric Pyuz...

"I will take you home now," he said.

She favored him through narrow eyes. "I thought you said you needed to regain energy."

He chewed on his lower lip. "That wasn't exactly true. I wanted to test you."

"You risked my life?" Heat blazed in her head. She pounded repeatedly on his shoulders with both hands. "We could've been killed."

He caught her wrists. Her arms strained through his grip.

"Without great risk," he said, "you cannot achieve great things. Today, with orcs about to find us, your breath calmed your spirit and allowed you to connect to the pulsations of the world. It empowered your already acute ears to hear beyond what is normally possible."

Her arms relaxed. She'd always been able to hear not only sounds which escaped her friends and family, but also patterns within those sounds. She offered him a tentative nod.

"You are progressing faster than I thought. You even figured out what comes naturally to bats and dolphins."

Mai shuddered. Whatever these dolphins were, if they were as nasty as bats, then being compared to one seemed insulting. "Had I panicked, and the Tivari saw us, would you have been able to save us?"

If he chewed on his lip any more, he'd look like a goat munching on weeds. "I had full confidence that you would succeed."

She harrumphed. "I want to go home."

He nodded. Chanting several beautiful words, he drew her close.

Colors swirled around them. Darkness encroached on the edges of her vision, but this time, didn't fade to black. Wind gusted around them. Air rushed past her ears in a roar.

Then, all was quiet. She blinked several times.

They now stood in the rice fields, cast in the light blue of Lydath's Eye. The edge of the village was several dozen paces away. Shadowed forms, silhouetted by the central bonfire, moved among the huts, calling her name in hushed whispers.

Oh, that couldn't be good. Pulling free of his embrace, she took a step toward home.

His hand captured her wrist. "Will you continue your training?"

Was it worth risking her life? Her family's lives? Her soul? Just to learn to get people to like her? Because there was no way she was going to take part in, let alone lead, a rebellion against the Tivari. She was bound to be in enough trouble as it was.

"Think about it," he said. "In the meantime, keep practicing what you learned tonight. Deep breathing, listening. While you are working, close your eyes and listen to how your friends move about. That is the foundation of the magic of sound."

"I will consider it."

"Mai!" Li's voice called from the village.

She turned. At the edge of the hovels, Li stretched a torch out as far as his arm would reach. The flames flickered shadows across his face.

A face which didn't seem all that handsome compared to the elf angel. She turned back.

Aralas was pulling the hood over his head. He blinked out. "Come back to the pool in three days," his voice floated in the summer breeze.

Mai stared at the space where he'd just stood. Three days. Well, he'd be waiting longer than that. She turned and trotted back toward the village.

Li wrung his hands. "Who was that?"

How could she answer without sounding crazy? She shrugged.

He squinted out into the space. "A ghost?"

"I was by myself." Hopefully, the lie would end the questions.

"No, I'm sure I saw and heard someone. What were you doing out there?"

"I, uh…personal matters." Not exactly a lie, but certainly not the truth, and to tell a man about personal matters would normally make her face flush a peculiar shade of red. Now, nothing.

His eyes narrowed. "For an hour? You never take that long."

Now, heat flared in her cheeks. Was he keeping track of when she relieved herself? She covered her mouth.

"I mean... I, uh... Nobody takes that long." His heartbeat, clear in her ears, picked up a few beats, similar to the tremor that wavered in Aralas' voice when he'd lied about not being able to whisk her away to safety.

She glared at him. "Have you been spying on me?"

"Of course not!" His heart fluttered again.

His heart!

Now that she knew how to hear the heartbeat, it was hard to ignore. One thing was for sure, he was paying attention to her. It was part disconcerting, part flattering.

"Do you keep track of everyone?" she asked.

He shuffled on his feet. "Oh, of course. Women, men, everyone."

Another lie. She scowled.

He returned the look. "You couldn't have possibly taken so long, and I know I saw someone. It's dangerous out there."

"Mai! She's over here!" Little Sister Ling rushed over and wrapped her in a tight embrace. "Everyone is looking for you!"

In seconds, Mother and Father rushed over, along with a few of the other villagers. Even quiet Skinny Fang came.

Ying, glowing in the joy of her recent marriage, clasped her hands and pulled her into a hug. "We were all so worried!"

Mai's shoulders relaxed in the embrace of her best friend. Cleric Pyuz must not have found out about her absence, or else he would've detained her parents.

Father's relieved expression melted into anger. "Where were you?"

"Yes," Li said, hands on his hips. "Where were you?"

She looked past the growing crowd. "Where is Cleric Pyuz?"

"Probably sleeping," Ling said.

She craned her head and looked toward the far end of the village. The domed top of his house, striped like the paper of a wasp's nest, peeked out above the villagers' stick-and-straw hovels. The lights were out.

Perhaps she could tell a little of the truth. "I met a spirit. He's the one who healed my wound." She looked at Li and pointed to her cheek.

Ling gasped. "Witchcraft!"

"It's too dangerous," Father said. "You can't trust the spirits. They will lure you first to sin, than to death."

57

Mother nodded so fast her head might fall off.

"Shhh," Ying said, pulling Mai close and looking over her shoulder back at the village. "We can't let anyone else know. Especially not The Gang."

If those tittering gossips found out, they'd threaten to tell Cleric Pyuz in order to make Mai take on some of their chores. Or worse, really tell the Tivari.

Mai shuddered.

Aralas might not really be a spirit, but he'd nearly gotten her killed. And even if she'd wanted to help him overthrow the Tivari, no one else would join in. It was settled.

Chapter 5:
Indecision

Mai knelt by the stalks of rice, plucking weeds from near their bases. Whereas she'd always been able to hear the synchronized sounds of tools cutting into the earth, in the three days since her meeting with Aralas, she'd started detecting breaths and heartbeats on a regular basis. It would've scrambled her poor brain if all these noises, and those of nature, hadn't harmonized with each other. Unlike at the dragon bones, where the pulse of the world had been so clear, here she could only guess its underlying beat from the other sounds.

The tone shifted in her ears. Covering her head with her arms, Mai stood and took two steps back.

A whip cracked through the air where she'd just knelt.

Her heart leaped into her throat. She looked up.

Astride his horse, Cleric Pyuz stared at his whip as if he'd just found at toad in his meal. He then turned and glared at her. "I... I, uh.... I swear by Tivar, you are the most useless worker ever. Lucky for you, I am feeling magnanimous today. That was a warning. Next time I catch you daydreaming, I will have you tied to a post and whip you until you can't sit or lie down. Now back to work." He stared at his whip again.

"Yes, master." Mai bowed low. Whatever *magnanimous* meant, it wasn't worth trying to find out if it was good or bad. She kneeled down and resumed her weeding.

Her heartbeat stuttered. The more she listened to the chorus of sounds, the more shifts in their regularity became evident. By Tivar, she'd just sensed Cleric Pyuz's approach, and even his intention to whip her. As amazing as it was, Aralas' skills risked infuriating the cleric.

Aralas! He was supposed to return tonight.

She looked around at her friends and family, working so hard. Mother, wiping sweat from her brow as she paused from plucking weeds. Ling, smiling as always, pulled carrots from their furrows. Li's toned arms flexed as he dug a trench. Fang's wiry frame strained as he shoveled dirt. Ying waved at her with a broad smile.

It wasn't just Mai's life and soul she was risking.

They'd all warned her against meeting the spirit, for her sake, without even considering the danger to themselves.

Danger she was inviting by learning magic.

It wasn't worth the risk. A rebellion was certain to fail; and perhaps, if Li was paying attention to her personal habits, she could win him over without using magic.

She let out a long sigh. Now that she'd learned how to listen for their heartbeats and breaths, she couldn't unhear them. A power lay just within her reach, one she couldn't ignore.

"Let's sing!" Ying said. "What was that song—"

"Line up!" Cleric Pyuz barked.

A pit formed in Mai's stomach. Nothing good ever came from an inspection. She looked up at him.

He was alternating between speaking to his magic mirror and taking stock of the villagers. He pointed to Fang. "You, get the others from the village."

Everyone hurried to comply as they abandoned their weeding and harvesting. Shovels and hoes clanked as they hit the earth. They formed three lines: men in back, women kneeling in the middle, and children at the very front.

Ying knelt next to her and leaned in. "What do you think this is about?"

Mai tried to keep her hands from trembling. Had Cleric Pyuz found out about her little adventure the other night? Perhaps he would publicly punish her.

The Tivari guided his horse back and forth, counting with his finger.

Mai counted, too, as the last stragglers—predictably, The Gang— filed in. Ninety-nine and twenty-two members of Sweetfield village in total, with two of the women plump with babies in their wombs. All there. All hearts beating rapidly, stuttering in and out of harmony with one another. Was that yet another heartbeat, twice as fast as everyone else's, coming from Ying's flat belly? Another baby?

Turning, Mai looked at her friend. Of course! That would explain Ying's lack of appetite, that radiant glow, and the constant smile.

Mai's spirit soared. Making babies was a special kind of magic. She'd be married soon, and carrying a baby of her own. Hopefully Li's and not Skinny Fang's.

The armored horse came to a stop in the middle of the lines, silent as always. Cleric Pyuz glared at them. "I have received unprecedented news from the gods."

Whatever pleasant feelings she had over Ying's pregnancy melted as Mai's stomach clenched. Whatever unprecedented meant, news was not usually good, and certainly not during a line-up.

Cleric Pyuz guided the horse over and stopped right in front of her. By Tivar, something awful was about to happen. Her palms clammed up. She snuck a glance at his wand, but avoided eye contact.

"There is talk of discontent. Are any of you unhappy with your service to the gods?"

All the villagers bowed and shook their heads in unison.

Headmaster Wang, Ying's father, raised his head first. "Of course not, Your Holiness."

"I should hope not. In one village, a priest caught a foolish girl dabbling in the dark arts from your fables of the Empire of Cathay. They were forced to torture and execute her. After all—"

The villagers spoke as one, the Gang most enthusiastic of them all. "All the pain of life will be redeemed in the immortal soul."

The words tasted bitter as they tumbled out of her mouth. Her pulse pattered. By Tivar, Cleric Pyuz was looming right above. His gaze seemed to bore into her. Now, whispers erupted all around. At her side, Ying broke into tears.

Mai's breath came out ragged, out of harmony with the staccato of her heart. She clenched and unclenched her sweaty hands. Cleric Pyuz must have found out about her meeting with Aralas. Was this her day to die? She took a deep breath, letting her stomach expand. Her heart settled into its normal, steadfast beat.

"I certainly hope none of you would be so foolish." He wheeled the horse around.

Mai blew out a long sigh. Everything was all right. Of course, there was no way he could know that she—

Cleric Pyuz spun, yanking the holy rod from its sheath. He levelled it. Blue light crackled out.

It enveloped Ying.

Her mouth gaped in a silent scream. Then her body disintegrated into ashes.

Mai's own heart stopped. She tried to draw in a breath, but her chest tightened. She could only stare at the mound of dust that had just been a living, breathing human. Not just any human, but her best friend. And her unborn child.

Tears welled in her eyes. All the times they'd spent together, sharing secrets. Protecting each other from The Gang. By Tivar, no.

Ling's husband Qiu moaned, his cry breaking the silence. He pushed toward what remained of his wife, freezing as Cleric Pyuz leveled his wand.

He grinned ear to ear, making him look even uglier than usual. "Luckily for Six-two-one-eight, her sins did not warrant torture. She will enjoy everlasting paradise, basking in the grace of Tivar."

Mai's sob caught in her throat. If what Aralas said was true, the orc gods provided no salvation. Ying was gone.

He pointed the wand at Qiu. "Six-two-one-four, you will marry Six-two-one-three under the Open Eye of Lydath."

Mai stifled a gasp. She was Six-two-one-three.

Still looking at Qiu, Cleric Pyuz shifted the wand to her. "You will ensure she behaves, or else the gods may demand both of your souls."

Choking through his tears, Qiu sank to both knees and pressed his forehead to the ground.

Mai's head spun as she prostrated herself before the priest. It was just three months until Lydath's Eye fully opened. Three months until she had to marry a man who was jealous of her friendship with his wife. Marrying Father's choice, Fang, was out of the question; and it wasn't like she'd really ever had a chance with Li.

"Back to work." Cleric Pyuz turned his mount and headed back toward his house.

Qiu glared at his back, his hate palpable from the torrential song his heart sang.

The wail lodged in Mai's throat broke free, and she collapsed near Ying's ashes.

After a few moments, more cries and murmurs joined her. Villagers crowded in, many comforting Qiu.

He collected Ying's remains in cupped hands. "She was with child, too."

Midwife Yu put a hand on his shoulder and nodded. "Her pulse said it was a boy."

He stared at the ashes in his hand. "We don't even have a funerary pot to honor what is left of her and my son."

Oh, Ying. Tears blurred Mai's vision. Cleric Pyuz usually only disintegrated the elderly, when they got too old to work. What had she done to deserve death, not just for her, but a potentially hearty boy? Stifling her own sobs, Mai set a tentative hand on her future husband's shoulder.

He recoiled and glowered at her. "You. You ugly Turtle's Egg. You irritate Cleric Pyuz with your incessant singing, and disappear into the night. Ying never did anything wrong, and she gets punished!"

Mai flinched, each of his accusations biting worse than a whip. Tears stung her eyes. The disjointed sounds roared into her ears. She clambered to her feet and stumbled blindly away.

Somewhere behind her, Father's voice rose. The words sounded muffled through the roaring in her ears, but the tone of his exchange with Qiu sounded like a heated argument.

The cacophony was too much. She broke into a run, toward the more harmonious sounds of nature.

A whip cracked in the air somewhere in the distance, clearing her ears. "Back to work. You will miss your quota and I will have to punish more of you."

Tears blurred her vision and skewed her already poor sense of direction. Still, somewhere in front of her, the sounds fell into order, giving her a sense of comfort. She pushed through stalks of rice, their blades chaffing her arms. The wind rustled through their unharvested grains, setting a more regular rhythm.

Then, she stepped into a clearing. Crickets chirped, cicadas buzzed. The rice stalks swayed, singing their own song. Everything sang in harmony. She blinked away the tears and looked.

She had run far, to the where the rice fields met the wispy trees. Each slogging step took her toward a large boulder. Setting her back against it, she sunk to the ground and pulled her knees to her chest. Then she lowered her head and cried.

This was all her fault, for listening to the elf angel and his silly ideas of rebellion. With the gods on the Tivari's side, there was no chance of success, only misery and death. It was better to labor and make babies and grow old than to be smote by the holy rod.

Even if it meant giving up on Li. Even if it meant marrying Qiu, who hated her.

"I am sorry for your loss." Aralas' voice floated on the air.

Mai lifted her head and looked around.

He was nowhere to be seen.

"The sorrow you feel, you can harness that. The intensity of your emotion will impel your voice."

That sorrow now mixed with anger. A curse rolled off her lips. "Show yourself, you Turtle's Egg."

Her voice filled the area, wrapping around the boulder, but also a spot atop it. She squinted.

The haze from three days before wavered there. She scrambled to her feet.

"Good. You have been practicing."

"And what good did that do me? It got my best friend killed." She jabbed a finger at him. "You *knew*. You could've stopped it."

"I can't be in two places at once," Aralas said. "By the time I arrived, it was already too late. Even still, what would have happened if I had intervened?"

Anger burned in her face. "My friend would still be alive. The village might've believed a higher power than the Tivari gods looked after us."

"Maybe. But then what?"

What was he talking about? She glared at him.

"What then?" he repeated.

Her shoulders slumped. "More Tivari would've come."

"Yes. They might've wiped out the entire village. Not only that, they would know that the True Gods have sent emissaries. There might only be one overseer in each village now—easy to overcome when the time is right. Imagine dozens of them, watching your every move."

She shuddered. Tivari all around, eating their food and imposing on the villagers, would make life horrible.

"Now that you have started to learn magic, you must consider the repercussions of evoking it. That is why I implored you to listen. There is a time and place to use it."

That didn't make Ying's loss any easier to accept. No, it was harder. It was Mai's fault Ying had died. Tears pooled in her eyes and rolled down her cheeks.

The haze shifted; whether that was because of her tears or because he moved, it was hard to tell. "You can blame yourself. You can wallow in self-pity. It changes nothing."

Leave it to a man not to understand the benefit of a good cry. Her head drooped.

"Or, you can let Ying's wanton murder fuel your righteous anger. Fight, so that no human ever has to die on a Tivari's fickle whim."

So many of his words were big, but at least humans not dying on a whim made sense. She sighed.

"Take a deep breath. Feel it fill your belly, and visualize it sinking to your feet."

Snuffling the gunk in her nose, Mai did as she was told. With a deep inhale, she let her stomach expand. In her mind, she pictured the air sinking to her feet.

The pulse of the earth was there, barely perceptible through her soles.

"Good! Now grip the ground with your toes."

She scrunched her toes up. The heart of the world beat clearly through her heel and the ball of her foot, and thrummed in her ears.

"Now—"

"Mai!" Li pushed through the rice stalks. He looked left and right. "Who were you talking to?"

She squeezed her eyes tight to clear the tears. He wouldn't believe it, and even if he did, he wouldn't condone it, especially after what had happened to Ying. "I... I, uh, was talking to myself."

He brushed her tears away with his thumb. "Your eyes are so red. Are you all right?"

Yes. No. She could only give him a vacant stare.

His arms wrapped around her. The warmth was so comforting.

Her shoulders trembled, and her tears flowed freely now.

He ran his hand over her mess of hair, smoothing it. "There, there. Qiu is wrong. It's not your fault."

Wasn't it? Had she never listened to Aralas, she would've never tempted punishment. She buried her face into Li's firm chest.

His chin rested on the top of her head. "It's okay."

This. This was all she ever wanted, though not with the heartache of losing Ying, nor the guilt that it was her fault. She melted into him.

The pressure of his chin shifted, replaced by the warmth of his lips on the crown of her head. Heart buzzing like a swarm of cicadas, she arched her neck. His lips trailed down to her ear and then to the side of her neck.

As he lavished kisses there, she pulled back. "Why me? You could have any girl in the village. One of The Gang."

"Your voice," he murmured through his kisses, "I have always loved hearing it." He pinned her back to the boulder.

Heat flared inside of her. He liked her. Liked her voice. She wrapped her arms around him, digging fingers into his back. Still, as much as her body screamed this was right, her heart knew it was wrong. Ying was dead because of her, and now she belonged to her widower. Panting, she shook her head. "This isn't right. Ying is…is..."

"I know. But you must live a life full enough for the both of you. Experience what she is no longer able to." Li's hand ventured up her dress, tracing a line up the inside of her thigh.

Her ragged breaths reverberated against the pulsations of the earth. Another sound hid among it.

Aralas' breathing. He was still there. Watching.

Chapter 6:

Painting Magic

Mai's heart thrummed in her ears, setting a beat to her ragged panting. Li's lips claimed her neck as his fingers crawled up her thigh, coming closer and closer. Every nerve tingled with need. Back pressed against the boulder, she lifted the leg to his hip. His bulge pressed against her. A moan escaped her attempts to stifle it.

The sound reverberated into the boulder, and lightened at the top. Right where Aralas still sat. His heartbeat might've been a drum pounding.

Why was he still there? Surely an elf angel would have the sense to give them some privacy.

Yet there he lingered, like the voice of her guilty conscience.

This was so wrong. She pushed Li's hand down and out of her dress. "I can't. I can't do this. I'm to be married to Qiu soon." Ying's husband. It was all wrong.

He pulled back, eyes wide like the village dogs when they were denied a treat. "It's so unfair. Qiu hates you. Let's exchange vows, here and now."

"And go against Cleric Pyuz's decree?" She shook her head, though not because marriage to Qiu was the least bit enticing.

He claimed the space between them. "I am the hardest worker. He likes me. I will beg him to change his mind."

"When has he ever changed his mind? He will sooner whip you." She backed away as much as the boulder would allow. Its coolness doused all sense of need, its resonance with the steadfast pulse of the earth slowing her heart.

"Then we will run away." Desperation clung in his voice.

Her chest knotted up. "To where?"

"There's a rumor of a hidden valley," he said, urgency rising in his voice as he pointed east.

She shook her head. "The priests will send their madaeri to track us down. Our fate will be worse than Ying's. Our families will suffer, too."

His shoulders drooped. "You are right. Still, there has to be a way. Give me three days' time to come up with a plan."

Three days wouldn't make any difference. She nodded all the same. "Three days."

His face brightened and he clasped her hands. "I will find a way, I promise."

If only it were possible. Ying's death made the truth so clear. Aralas was right—they lived and died at the Tivari's whims. Even if Cleric Pyuz allowed them to marry, he could execute either one of them, or their yet-to-be born children, for nothing more than his hate for hot, humid days. Their entire village lived at the mercy of his impulses.

Reluctantly, she freed her hands from Li's grip. "We shouldn't be seen coming back together. You go first."

His puppy-dog expression exposed his naiveté. Waving, he turned and skipped back toward the village.

She let out a long sigh. Everything she'd ever wanted, she'd let go.

Aralas blew out a sigh. "I thought he'd never leave."

"I thought the same about you." Mai stepped away from the boulder and looked up.

Aralas sat there, his legs kicking back and forth. The grey fabric shimmered in the sun.

Even given all that had happened today, his irrepressible grin somehow felt comforting. The tightness in her chest eased.

He blew hair out of his face. "Giving yourself to him now would bring nothing but pain."

She nodded. It would've only been a temporary reprieve from harsh realities. The reality that every man, woman, and child lived at the whims of the Tivari. Was such a life even worth living?

He hopped down from the boulder, landing without a sound. He locked his gaze on her. "If you overthrow the Tivari, you can make your own choices."

Yes. Maybe then, she could marry Li without fear or regrets. Maybe her friends and family—no, *every* human—could live without fear or regrets. "If we survive."

His grin melted. "Indeed. Just know, if you play the role that I foresee, you will change. What you want now may be very different from what you want in the future."

She squinted. Li appeared as a dark splotch, bobbing atop the golden sea of rice stalks as he headed back toward the village. No matter what happened, he would always be the one she wanted.

"Are you ready to learn? To take the next step?"

Mai turned to the elf angel. What had started as a desire to learn to enchant someone had awoken her to the reality of enslavement. The constant threat of punishment for her, her family, and her friends. Ying's brutal murder today.

Pointing to where the edge of Lydath's Eye had just started to peek above the horizon, barely visible in the noon sun, she asked, "The Tivari say that Lydath created humans to serve them in life, and their gods in death. That isn't true, is it?"

"The Blue Planet is Guanyin's physical manifestation in this world. It is true she created humans, but the Tivari have appropriated it into their own mythology, corrupting the image of Guanyin into Tivar's foul whore, Lydath."

Hope sparked in Mai's chest. "What happens after we die? Where is Ying now?"

"Was she a good person?"

"The best."

"She will bask in the grace of Yang-Di for a time, until she is reborn into a better life in a better world. A world that you will help create."

Mai nodded. Learning to use the power of music had goals that reached beyond the desires of one woman.

"Are you ready?"

With a heavy sigh, she nodded.

"Good." His glowing smile returned. It brightened the storm cloud that had gathered over her mood.

"Mai!" Her family's voices called out in the distance.

Aralas placed a hand on her nape and uttered a single syllable whose harshness was worthy of a Tivari curse.

The colors of the world swirled, and the edges of her vision darkened for a split second. Then everything brightened.

The rice fields were gone. They now stood before a wall of white rock, rising a dozen feet above them. To the right, it sloped over into an overhang, while the path beside it narrowed and dropped down a mountainside to tumbling river rapids. It looked like nothing she'd ever seen.

"Did we just shift through the ethers again?" She looked at Aralas.

Hunched over, he seemed a shade paler than usual. He nodded.

"You weren't so tired the last time," she said.

"You are perceptive. I had to use a quicker invocation of magic. It drains me more than the other type."

She shook her head. "I just didn't get dizzy this time."

He straightened. "Yes. Once you get used to teleportation, it is far less disorienting."

That was good, if this *tele-whatever* was going to become a regular occurrence.

"Come." He beckoned. "Stay close to the cliff."

"Cliff?"

He pointed to the wall of rock.

They worked their way along the so-called cliff, the rustle of water over rocks carrying up from below. Swishing and scraping sounds grew louder and louder as the sheet of rock sloped above them. They came to several waves on the rock face, painted in broad strokes of reds, blues, and yellows.

The uncertainty in the pattern seemed to project off the wall, into the air. Mai's heart wavered, and her steps became less sure. Maybe this wasn't a good idea. Maybe—

Her bare foot twisted at the edge. Pain flared in her ankle. She started to tumble.

Aralas caught her wrist, jerking her shoulder.

With only one foot on solid ground, her weight dangled precariously off the ledge, providing a view of the rocks her body would smash on if he let go. Her heart, beating tentatively just a second ago, almost stopped.

"Steady, now." He tugged her back onto the path. Draping an arm over her shoulder, he pointed to the colorful lines. "Kang was a talented cave painter before we found him. These are the first strokes he made when learning how to evoke magic in his art. What do you feel when you look at them?"

Not like she wanted to relive that feeling, and risk splattering on the rocks below. Whatever a painting was, it wasn't worth experiencing it again. She turned her head and squeezed her eyes shut.

"It's okay. I have you. Take a deep breath."

Of course, breathing. She sucked in the air, filling her belly. Her pulse, as it had when surrounded by the Tivari under Aralas' cloak, settled into its normal rhythm. Reassured, she opened her eyes and studied the lines. Though the feeling wasn't as evident as before, her heart again wavered. "Uncertainty. There is indecision in the lines."

Aralas nodded. "Yes. His emotions at the time remain etched in the cliff face, and project on anyone who sees it."

"How is that even possible?"

He grinned. "The same way I will teach you to evoke emotion through your music."

The two arts seemed completely different, but... She studied the lines. Indeed, like music, they had a pattern, a discernable rhythm to them, only fused into the image instead of carried through sound.

"I had him start here for a reason: his art makes a perfect guardian for the start of your people's new empire."

She looked up at him, incredulously. "Empire? That sounds like the stuff of children's stories."

"It's more. It's part of your peoples' past, and now a beacon for your future." He moved her to the side of the path closer to the cliff face. "Come on and see."

It sounded so...hopeful. She accompanied the elf angel along the path, looking at the paintings.

They evolved into more complex and wondrous images. The intertwined hand prints in red and orange stirred a nostalgia for childhood, when Mother held her hand. A guard dog in blacks and greys seemed so lifelike, it made her palms sweat. A long silver dragon, like those from the tales of the lost empire, seemed to be in motion, dancing around a woman with silver hair. It sent a shiver up her spine.

And if what Aralas said was true, the same emotional effect could be evoked through music.

The rhythmic scrapes, set to the cadence of the water rustling below, grew louder, echoing against the overhang. Up ahead, a silhouetted figure worked on the cave wall. As they got closer, the man's form took shape.

He stood a head taller than her, or perhaps it was the effect of his wild hair that made him seem tall. His head turned toward them. His prominent nose might've stood out against his small eyes even more had his face not been so filthy. His smile revealed several missing teeth. "Aralas, welcome back. What do you think of my new painting?"

Mai looked at the work. And gasped.

The image of Aralas couldn't be more lifelike, even if it did make him look a little thinner, perhaps somewhat feminine. It was as if he emerged from the stone, golden hair rippling in the wind, and out of his face for once. Those violet eyes stared into her soul. A fist-sized gemstone seemed to sway from a chain around his neck. The thin elf blade raised above his head looked as if it were about to slash down, while his other hand pointed a holy rod forward.

"Tivar's Scythe!" She squeezed Aralas' hand, just to make sure the elf angel beside her was the real thing and not the image charging off the wall.

"Do not invoke the Betrayer here." Kang pointed a stick of bird feathers at her. His excited expression melted, replaced by a scowl.

His anger was so palpable, it was as if it pushed her back. Her foot nearly slipped on the ledge again.

Aralas' grip tightened around her. "It's all right, Kang. I have not told her everything. I want her to see it with her own eyes."

Her heart, which had nearly lurched to a stop from a second brush with death, picked up a notch. "I'm sorry. It is…habit."

Kang's lower lip jutted out. "One which you'll need to correct."

She would've sunk to her knees had there been enough space. Instead, she bowed low. "I'm sorry."

Aralas patted her on the back. "It's all right. Get in the habit of calling on the Heavens—instead of Tivar, Lydath, and the other false gods—when you are here. Come along."

Mai gave Kang a perfunctory nod, and he returned the salute. Then she hurried along with Aralas. Up ahead, the overhang arched over, forming a short tunnel through the rock. Blades of sunlight formed a hazy curtain on the other side.

The closer they got to the opposite mouth, the quieter it became, until right at the edge it was eerily silent. Mai's heart beat loud in her ears. Her fingers trembled.

Aralas tightened his grip on her hand. "Yes, it is unsettling, especially for someone used to hearing the pulse of the world. You'll be fine when you pass through the veil. Close your eyes." He pulled her through the curtain of light. Whatever a veil was, it flared orange on her eyelids.

Enthusiastic shouts rang out in unison. Birds chirped. A waterfall roared somewhere in the distance. Mai blinked several times.

When her vision cleared, she sucked in a breath. Tree-covered mountains encircled a basin below. At the center stood the largest structure she'd ever seen, besides the pyramid. Its white walls looked flat, and instead of thatch and straw, it boasted steeply pitched, red-tiled roofs. Surrounding it were dozens upon dozens of smaller buildings of a similar architecture.

Her ears tracked the waterfall to the far end of the basin, its rumbling waters setting the beat for all the other sounds. It poured out of a gap in a grey wall, which snaked up and around the mountains along the east side of the vale.

Her head spun. The children's stories were true. The Wall...

"Welcome to Cathay." Aralas' arm slid down her back and under her arm. "This is where you will learn more about your peoples' magic."

The Dragon Charmer's Apprentice

Chapter 7:

The Hidden Kingdom

The chorus of chants grew louder as Mai descended into the basin. Eyes closed, she clasped Aralas' hand and let him guide her down the mountain path. A light breeze blew through her hair.

He released her hand. "Keep your eyes closed."

Her chest constricted. The path wasn't that wide, and without his gentle tugs and pulls, she might very well take a nasty tumble down the mountainside.

"Keep breathing. Listen to each of your footfalls as they connect with the pulse of the world." His hands gave her a push.

She stumbled forward two steps before regaining her footing. Her hand shot out to the rocks on her left. Still, where her soles met the ground, the rhythm of the earth resonated through her and echoed in her ears.

Aralas swatted her hand off the wall.

The Turtle's Egg! Rubbing her arm, she took several more tentative steps, one step for two of the world's heartbeats. The sound radiated out from her feet, dying out just a half-pace to her right, but echoing off the cliff-face to the left.

Her slow pace sped up, now one stride for each pulse of the world. Whenever the sound of steps hitting the ground petered out too close to her right foot, she edged to the left. The more she listened, the easier it was to distinguish her location with the chorus of chants. They were getting closer and closer. How long they walked, it was hard to tell.

"Yes, that is it." Aralas' hand rested on her shoulder. "You may open your eyes."

When she did, she found they were at the bottom. She looked back up the way they'd come. It was quite a far distance up, and the path had been quite narrow. Impressive, but... "I don't see how listening to sounds will lead a rebellion."

He grinned. "It's just a start, a foundation. Not only that, but there are others, like Painter Kang, who have roles to play. And not just people who look like you, but those with pale skin and fair hair, and others with dark skin and coarse, curly hair. The orcs have enslaved you all. It will require all of you to use what special talents you have to win."

Her head spun to think there were other kinds of people besides her own, all toiling under the Tivari. "Teach me more."

"It starts now." He spoke a guttural word—and disappeared. The air filled in the place where he'd just stood with a pop.

Find me, he spoke in her mind. *You have an hour. If you can't locate me by then, you are not yet ready to begin.*

Her hands trembled. What if she failed?

Right now, there was only one direction, a gorge between two tall cliffs. She hurried deeper in, skidding to a halt just past a crevice she would've missed had her ears not picked up a faint clanging. She squeezed through and gasped.

Hundred of houses spread throughout a basin ringed by mountains. The entire area had to be a dozen, dozen times larger than Sweetfield village, and the buildings were closer together. It might take days to explore. An hour just wasn't enough.

Remember how I sounded when we first met. Use your ears as you navigate through town.

He'd been right beside her that day! Not only that, now there were so many different, clashing sounds in this so-called *town*. The waterfall drowned out most other noises, while the occasional toll of a bell seemed to magnify the clang of metal on metal. The chorus of chants still assaulted her ears.

Good, you are hearing how all the sounds interact with each other. Now find me. You've already wasted several minutes. Don't go into the trees. You'll get lost.

He was listening to her thoughts again.

Yes. Yes, we are. But you knew that.

His voice sounded a little different, perhaps higher pitched? And *we*, not *I*? Was there more than one elf angel, or was he harboring illusions of godliness like the Tivari High Priest, speaking with the divine *We*?

She clenched her jaw and set off. The Iridescent Moon sat in its usual spot, though here it was barely visible just above the ring of mountains. It now waned toward new. She had to find him before it waxed to its first crescent, or else... Hopefully, she'd come across his unique sound.

Not likely. It was so hard to concentrate, given all the new sights and smells. Her stomach rumbled at the scent of something roasting, the aroma mingling with a sweet, smoky fragrance as it wafted on a light breeze.

Up ahead, the clanging grew louder. She followed the sound to a squat, open building with smoke circling out of the roof. Inside, several men hammered at long knives and short, pointy triangles.

Two were not much more than half the height of the others, but they were brawnier. Bulbous noses poked out above coarse mustaches, which were red like their voluminous beards and bushy eyebrows.

Red! It didn't seem possible for hair to be that color. Beneath the smudges of soot, their skin looked pale. They hummed the most beautiful tune as they hammered at a flat stick that glowed blue like Lydath's Eye...no, Guanyin's Eye.

Her heart fluttered like a duck taking flight. Could these be dwarves? They were supposedly just fairy tales.

Then again, so were elves.

One barked out orders in a thick accent. "More heat in the bellows. Ye'll be stuck hammering bronze if ye can't melt iron, let alone istrium."

Whatever bellows, iron, and istrium were, they must be important by the way the bare-chested young men crowded around the dwarves bobbed their heads and rushed off to the fire.

The one who'd spoken resumed his humming, clear and resonant. It beckoned Mai to join in, and she hummed just loud enough for her alone to hear.

Or maybe not.

One of the dwarves looked up and met her eyes. "Like our song, do ye? Come, come into the smithy and accompany our tune."

She craned her neck to get a good view of the Iridescent Moon. It had already waned to new. Still, it was impolite to refuse a male. With a bow, she entered.

Grinning, the dwarf resumed his hum. Like the war chants in the distance, it followed the pulse of the world and the beats of their hammer.

Mai joined in his song, louder this time.

The dwarf looked up from his work. "Less uncertainty, more emotion. Hum with the resoluteness of your heart."

Resoluteness. It was everything she wasn't. Still…Mai held an image of Father in her head as she hummed. Her spirit soared.

The stick glowed an even brighter blue.

The dwarf nodded. "That's it, lass. You're almost as good as the Dragon Charmer. We forge a sword fit for a Nothori King. It shall be named *Tamskelti*, the Ice Reaver."

Swords, Nothori Kings: they might as well have been speaking gibberish. And who was this Dragon Charmer? With a bow, Mai backed out of the building. She looked up to find the Iridescent Moon's phase had moved a sliver. Given the small amount of time she had to begin with, she'd wasted too much singing with the dwarves. With a sigh, she followed the chorus of chants and continued deeper into the enormous village.

People looked up from making food, crafting interesting objects, and other work. Some nodded as she passed. A few afforded her curious glances.

The clanging from the dwarves' smithy grew softer as the chanting got louder. Up ahead, the path between the buildings opened up into a large open space. Dozens of bare-chested young men yelled as they danced with sticks, not unlike the so-called sword the dwarves were making, but smaller. At their head, a male elf—not nearly as handsome as Aralas— led them through the movements, making the humans look clumsy in comparison.

Several had the same image painted on their chests: a snakelike creature, but with legs, each ending in five claws. A mane of silver flared from behind its horns. Without a doubt, it was a painting of the legendary Guardian Dragon— who Aralas said was female.

Its fearsome expression sent a chill up Mai's spine. Her hands trembled. It took every last drop of discipline to keep from turning and fleeing. Instead, she took several steps back.

A hand pressed firmly between her shoulder blades.

Mai's heart just about stopped. She turned to find a pretty girl about her own age, with large dark eyes and a thin nose. Her clean, smooth skin brought out the color of her dress, which was like a cloudless sky on a crisp autumn day.

How was such a shade of blue even possible in cloth? Mai reached out and ran her hand over the long hanging sleeve. It was so soft and cool, unlike her own roughspun shift. And really, in retrospect, many of the other people she passed were similarly dressed. She pulled her hand back.

The girl laughed, refreshing like a bubbling brook. She extended her arm and let the sleeve flutter in the breeze.

"Yes, I felt the same way the first time I saw silk. Once you wear it, you will never want to let your old clothes touch your skin again."

Mai stared at her. Her mouth moved, but no words came out.

"I am Wenhui," the girl said with a giggle. "What's your name?"

"Mai."

"That's a pretty name." Wenhui pulled her arm back. "What skill do you have that the Elestrae brought you here?"

Elestrae. It's what Aralas called himself. Elf Angel. Mai's voice sounded husky in her own ears. "Music."

Wenhui's pretty lips rounded. "Oh, very rare. Very special. Very powerful. The Elestrae probably need you as a back-up, just in case Yanyan fails."

Mai's heart just about sank into her stomach. Her skill was rare, but not unique, and apparently there was someone even more talented. Perhaps this Yanyan was the Dragon Charmer that the dwarf had mentioned. She straightened. "Why is she called the Dragon Charmer?"

Wenhui's pretty lips formed an even prettier circle. "She woke the Guardian Dragon from a thousand years of slumber, and bent it to her will with only her voice."

"What about you? Do you have magic?"

Wenhui held up a needle and pointed it at the dancing men. "None of them has a talent like us, but they are learning to fight. I tattoo the Guardian Dragon into their chests so that they will have an advantage when we are ready to attack the Tivari outpost near the pyramid."

Tattoo. The word was new, but clearly related to the paintings on the young men's skin. Mai looked back at all of them, none of whom looked big enough to wrest a holy rod away from a Tivari. Still, the lifelike dragon on their chest sent chills through her. "You drew that?"

"Yes," Wenhui said with a smiling nod.

"That's amazing."

"Yanyan can do the same with her voice." Wenhui spoke the name with the same tone the villagers used to worship the Tivari gods. "With a starburst, she could probably rout an entire Tivari army."

Mai's stomach knotted. Aralas had made it sound like her gift was special. "What's a starburst?"

"It's a jewel from ancient times which magnifies magic." Wenhui made a fist near her neck. "Aralas has one."

Aralas. She looked up at the Iridescent Moon, barely visible in the bright sunlight, and inching inexorably toward new. If she didn't find him soon, he'd still have this Yanyan. She turned to Wenhui. "Can you take me to Yanyan?"

Wenhui's radiant smile was so reminiscent of poor Ying's. "I would love to, but I need to finish Ku's tattoo." She beckoned toward the training men.

A good-looking young man in the front, with only a snarling dragon head on his breast, lowered his sword. Placing his right fist in his left palm, he bowed toward his comrades. Then he hurried over. He bowed his head. "Hello, Wenhui."

"Hi, Ku." Wenhui clasped Mai's hand and pulled her forward. "Ku, meet Mai. She is new. You should show her around sometime."

Ku afforded her a cursory glance and dipped his chin before gazing at Wenhui.

Mai bowed her head, as she would salute an older peer, but studied Wenhui in the corner of her eye.

If the girl's chuckle was any more nervous, it might be mistaken for her wedding night. "All right then. Are you ready for the rest of your ink?"

Ku shuffled on his feet, but nodded.

Wenhui turned to her. "He's such a baby. He's scared of the needles."

"Do they hurt?" Mai looked at the sharp implements in Wenhui's free hand.

The tattooist shrugged. "All I know is that Ku screams louder than anyone else."

He could also flush redder than anyone Mai had ever seen.

"Come on, Ku." Snorting, Wenhui tilted her head in the direction of one of the buildings. Numerous whip scars crisscrossed his back. She then turned to Mai and pointed toward the middle of the basin. "Yanyan lives closer to the palace, but she might not be there. Listen for her voice, though. She is always singing, and you won't mistake it for anything else."

In this, Yanyan did not sound too bad. Perhaps she could be a friend. A mentor. Bowing, she started off toward whatever the palace was.

"Come by tonight," Wenhui called. "You can join Ku and me for dinner."

Mai looked back. Wenhui was waving. Beside her, if Ku looked any more disappointed, she'd think he was the one who'd lost his best friend today. Maybe it would be better not to join. Hopefully, Yanyan would be just as kind as Wenhui.

She wandered deeper among the buildings, watching people engaged in both strange and familiar activities. Her ears twitched at all the sounds. Hammering, scraping, whistling, plucking, swishing, chopping. All followed the same resolute pulse of the world.

One sound carried above the others: the resounding twang of a musical instrument. Some notes roared like pouring rain, while others whispered like the sweet secrets passed between lovers.

Then, a voice like no other joined in. Clear as a crisp winter morning, it sang the praises of snow. Resonant like the echo of thunder in a valley, it extolled the power of nature. Thick like honey, it pulled on Mai's soul, drawing her closer to a building with a red-latticed veranda wrapping around its side.

She followed the music around the corner, drawn like bees to honeysuckle.

Legs bent out to the side, a stunning woman sat on the stone-paved veranda. Her bare feet were so clean and smooth and small, in comparison to Mai's feet, whose callouses had callouses. Luxurious locks of shiny black hair framed an oval face with a pearl-smooth complexion. Her thin, high-bridged nose, large eyes, and full lips evoked images of fairy tale beauties.

In one arm, she cradled a pear-shaped wooden instrument with ridged frets along its neck and upper body. Her other arm curved at an elegant angle, long fingers swimming across four strings. If Wenhui's dress had been beautiful, the glossy red gown this woman wore was nothing sort of extravagant, hinting at the soft curves beneath. Its borders were embroidered in gold like the Tivari gods' flaming chariots.

Where those borders ended and Aralas' molten gold hair began was uncertain. At least it was out of his face for once. He'd changed out of the form-fitting grey suit, and now wore a sparkly purple robe. His head was nestled in her lap, one arm draped over her hip.

With her musical talent, so far beyond Mai's own, this could only be The Dragon Charmer.

Mai's stomach twisted. In comparison, she was dingy and mousy, and there was little chance Aralas, or any man for that matter, would look at her with those same adoring eyes. She smoothed her dress out.

Still strumming and singing, Yanyan looked up from her instrument. Her eyes met Mai's and narrowed. A smirk marred her delicate beauty.

Mai's chest squeezed. It was the same kind of smirk the prettiest village girls flashed at her and Ying.

Aralas' head turned, his gaze falling on Mai. So enraptured by the Dragon Charmer he must have been, that he looked at Mai in confusion for a moment.

A look of recognition bloomed on his face, and his eyes shifted to his wrist. He bolted to his feet, nearly bashing his forehead into Yanyan's instrument in the process. He shook his hair out, and it fell in perfect waves about his shoulders—though not into his face as usual. "Well, it looks like you just made it. I was worried you would get too distracted singing with dwarves, so I had Yanyan play a song for you." He extended his hand and helped the beauty to her feet.

Had his voice pitched higher? Gentler?

Yanyan bowed her head. "Anything I can do to help, my lord." The sincerity in her tone didn't match the cruel quirk of her lips.

He lifted her chin and smiled. When he spoke, his voice pitched high and his tone softened. "I am sure you will be of great help to Mai."

"As you command."

"Very good. I must visit my budding sorceress, Makeda, now, so she's ready to confront the Tivari. I will leave Mai in your capable hands." He nuzzled his head into her throat.

Arching her neck back, Yanyan giggled.

Mai pursed her lips. Why did her stomach knot the same way it did when Li flirted with other girls? Was it because Aralas was so unearthly handsome? That couldn't be it, and he really wasn't even a male, but rather some ethereal mix of genders. And, he was so…annoying. And scary.

Yanyan lowered her chin and their gazes met again.

Mai straightened her posture.

The same smirk flitted across Yanyan's face, even as Aralas lavished kisses on her neck. His hands…just what were they doing inside her dress?

Mai flushed hot.

"I must be off." He pulled away from Yanyan, admiring her as he fiddled with a lock of his hair. Without even looking at Mai, he spoke a guttural word. The air popped as he vanished.

Yanyan straightened a loose lock of hair and studied Mai. "Aralas thinks you have talent, but I fail to see what's so special. Come along now." Sweeping up the instrument, she turned on her heel and went into the building through an arched doorway. "I am going to prove him wrong."

Chapter 8:

Unwanted

Mai barely heard the music over the growling of her stomach. She hadn't eaten since the morning, well before Cleric Pyuz had murdered Ying. Still, Yanyan insisted on teaching her how to play the pear-shaped instrument—a *pipa*—immediately.

Besides a reed flute and the wooden bowls she'd tapped out patterns on, Mai had never touched an instrument before, let alone a real one. Hungry, fingers sore from plucking and pressing into strings for hours, she had to fight back tears as she tried to follow Yanyan's lead. Whereas the beauty could bring out the most delightful sounds from her ornate pipa, Mai failed to elicit more than flat twangs from the plain wooden instrument resting in her lap.

"Heavens, you really are pathetic." Settled on the edge of a delicate-looking chair, Yanyan let out a long sigh. "Maybe the Tivari will flee because their ears hurt. Seriously, if our liberation relies on you, we might as well give up now."

Mai glared back. What an arrogant Turtle's Egg. "Can't we just sing? Aralas said my voice was special. I made the dwarves' sword glow blue."

"Feisty girl." Yanyan harrumphed. "Feisty, but ignorant. Just because you could copy a dwarf's simple hum doesn't mean you can charm a dragon. An instrument makes the power of Dragon Songs easier to project."

"Maybe if I got to use the real instrument," Mai muttered under her breath.

Yanyan scowled. "What was that?"

Mai shook her head. "Nothing."

"Remember, girl, I have excellent hearing." The Dragon Charmer strummed out a short melody, and sang the words. "Repeat yourself."

Whether it was the rise and fall of the pipa's notes stirring her heart, or the persuasive tone in Yanyan's voice, Mai felt compelled to answer. "I said, maybe I could play if I used a nicer instrument." Tivar's Scythe, she had just said that out loud, forgetting all her manners.

Yanyan's laugh echoed in the room. With a smirk, she proffered the ornate pipa, while swiping Mai's from her hands. "Go ahead and try. It is a magical instrument. The soundboard is the scale of the Guardian Dragon. The strings are made with twisted elf hair."

Mai tentatively received the instrument.

And almost dropped it. Its subtle buzz made it seem alive.

Yanyan raised an eyebrow. "So you can feel it? Maybe you aren't so hopeless, after all. Follow me." She played a series of notes on the plain pipa, which came out jubilant and clear. Apparently, it wasn't just the quality of the instrument that accounted for her skill.

Gritting her teeth, Mai plucked out the same combination. If the sounds from the plain pipa came out flat when she played, these came out as a barely audible hiss. She strummed harder, but the instrument refused to make the same resonant sound that Yanyan had effortlessly elicited. How mortifying. Shoulders slumping, she snuck a glance up.

Yanyan stared, no doubt with a rebuke on her lips.

Silence.

Yanyan set the pipa down. "I can't."

Couldn't what? Mai fidgeted, waiting for the insult.

Blinking several times, Yanyan narrowed her eyes. "Get out."

That was sudden. Mai cocked her head.

"I said, get out!"

If that's what this woman wanted, so be it. With a sigh, Mai clambered to her feet. Spinning on her heel, she marched through the doors and out onto the veranda.

She breathed in the fresh summer air. Maybe Yanyan was right. Learning the magic of music really was hopeless. Maybe it would be better just to go home, wherever that was, and wait for this rebellion to free them. Clearly they didn't need her, since they already had the amazing Dragon Charmer.

She trudged down the steps and plodded along the hard-packed dirt road through the town. Savoring the symphony of sounds, she wandered back toward the training men.

Whereas before they had performed some kind of dance, now they engaged in some kind of pair work. Swords glinted as they clashed and clanged against each other, the movements following the pulse of the world. It was a thing of beauty, one which would have been more wondrous to watch if Mai's stomach didn't clench anytime a blade came too close to someone. It was amazing nobody lost an eye.

She sighed. Despite lacking a talent for magic, these men were training so hard. If mankind were to be free, they all had a role to play, and there was no way she'd be swinging a sword around. She looked back in the direction she'd come. Sucking up her pride and absorbing Yanyan's insults might be—

"Ow!" The voice had the same quality as Ku's, only a pitch higher, coming from her left.

"Heavens, stop being a baby," Wenhui said.

Mai turned her ear to the source of the conversation.

"I'm sorry." Ku's tone returned to normal.

Whereas most of the artists had been so rude, at least Wenhui had been friendly. It would be good to have someone to talk to in this strange place. Mai followed the sounds to another wooden house. She paused to admire the planks, so wide and long they couldn't have come from any kind of tree near her home. Not only that, the loops and whorls had rhythm of their own, like Kang's paintings and Wenhui's tattoos. She looked in through a square window.

Lying on a table, Ku flinched and wriggled as Wenhui ran a needle across his chest. Scowling, she dabbed the point into a dish of red dye and drew more lines. Her hand movement was so fluid, like the fighting men's sword dance. However, she stood in the most peculiar way, with her knees bent, both bare feet firmly planted, toes curled into the floor. Her spine was so erect, so straight...

Similar to the way Yanyan sat while playing the pipa. The same way Aralas had told her to feel the pulse of the earth at the dragon bones. Yanyan had never said anything about that.

"Owwww!" Ku screamed again, sounding not unlike Ying when she found a bug on her.

Mai's heart squeezed at the thought.

"You want to feel real pain?" Wenhui snarled. Her head jerked toward the window and her gaze met Mai's. Her scowl melted when their gazes met. "Come in, come in. Don't be shy. You can help me."

Bobbing her chin, Mai rounded the doorway and into the room. She paused at the dozens of paintings of the Guardian Dragon all stuck to the wall on reed-thin, white rectangles the size of her face. Her mind spun, not just from the dizzying array of different poses and swirls of color, but also from the range of emotions the sweeps of brushstrokes evoked. Some sent chills up her spine, while others drained the blood from her head, and yet more filled her heart with courage.

One stood out, both from its prominent position in the middle of the others, and its larger size and subject matter. It was Aralas, dancing with a pair of thin straight swords. The starburst jewel hung around his neck. Like in Kang's mural, the elf angel's golden hair didn't flop into his beautiful face. Mai's stomach fluttered like dragonfly wings, and all her worries washed away.

"Come on, don't dally. You can help me retrieve dyes." The tattoo artist beckoned her, and motioned to a shelf with dozens of fine ceramic jars, each with some kind of picture scribbled on them. Her tone turned belligerent. "Get me medium indigo."

Wen had pointed in the direction of jars. Along the edges, many of the dried violet and dark blue dyes looked exactly the same. Mai shuffled on her feet. "I'm not familiar with that word."

"Indigo," Wenhui snarled. "The color between blue and violet on a rainbow. I need a darker shade of it."

Mai stared at that general color, where at least five jars looked to be on the darker side, yet might've been the same for all she could tell. She held one up.

"No." Wenhui shook her head.

Mai reached for an—

"Heavens, no!" Wenhui jerked a finger toward the third.

"Ow!" Ku screeched again.

"Shut up!" Wenhui afforded him a livid glare before settling back on Mai with equal anger. "Can't you read?"

Whatever good feelings Mai had gotten from looking at the painting of Aralas, they'd since fled. Hands trembling, she retrieved the third jar.

Wen swiped it away. "You'll just slow me down, and this idiot," she jerked her head at Ku, "will faint from his low pain tolerance at this rate. Stay out of my way."

Bowing her head, Mai took a step back. She bumped into a table, sending several more jars rattling.

Wen threw her hands up and jerked a finger toward the door. "Out!"

Tears threatened to spill as Mai's heart clenched. So much for finding a friend here. Thrown out for the second time in a few minutes. Bobbing her head, she turned and fled out the door.

Just like back home, she was useless. She wasn't special, just a contingency in case the real Dragon Charmer failed. Outside, she leaned her back against the sturdy wood, choking back sobs.

No, just like back home, Mai wouldn't let anyone see her cry. Taking a deep breath and burying her negative thoughts, she looked around. She would have to rely on herself, assuming they still even found her useful. For now, though, Yanyan had given up on teaching her, and Wenhui didn't want her around. Until Aralas came back, there was nothing to do except practice and explore.

Closing her eyes and opening her ears, she set off, this time focusing on her posture. As before, all the sounds joined in a concert, with the underlying pulse of the world setting the rhythm. Each of her footfalls sent their own sounds out, interacting with all the others. She sidestepped one rock on the ground, but stubbed her toe on another. Undaunted, she hummed. The way her hum spread out revealed where the buildings were. She walked down the middle of the road, where conversations stuttered to a stop as she passed.

How long or far she walked, it was impossible to tell just from the sounds. Eventually, the surface beneath her feet changed, going from a dense hardpack that carried the crunch of her footfalls well, to a softer surface. From the sound of it, something large loomed ahead of her. She opened her eyes.

Trees towered high above her, each easily twice her girth. They looked nothing like the short, spindly smoothbarks back home, and might've been a wall given how close together they grew. Their lowest limbs were so high up, save for one, where a coiled length of red thread hung.

Never before had she seen so many trees in one place. Their gnarled bark and dark green needles, many strewn on the ground, contrasted to the smooth sheets of bark and wide leaves she was used to. The air felt cool and refreshing in her lungs, and the primal pulse of the world echoed in her ears.

It beckoned her deeper.

Aralas had said not to go into the trees.

Then again, he'd also forced her to question everything she knew to be true.

She turned and looked first at the Iridescent Moon, waxing to its mid-crescent, then back at the so-called town. Right now, it would be nice to get as far away from it as possible, if only for a short reprieve. Eventually she'd have to return, to learn the magic of Dragon Songs from a woman who didn't even like her.

For now, though, the trees called to her. She wouldn't go far.

Several steps into the mass of trees, the late afternoon sun barely filtered through the trunks and branches, casting the afternoon into twilight. Everything looked the same. If she got lost, would anyone even know she'd left? Would they come looking for her?

It smelled so cool, so fresh. She stretched out both arms so that her hands touched two trees. The pulse of the world carried through their trunks, magnifying its sound.

Bending her knees, she dug her toes into the ground. She straightened her spine, just the way Yanyan did when playing the pipa, just the way Wenhui stood when painting the tattoo on Ku. She closed her eyes and heard her own body harmonizing with the trees. Everything tingled, from fingertips to toes. Her pulse quickened, roaring loud and torrential in her ears. Her insides writhed like dozens upon dozens of fish squirming over each other in a shallow river pool. An immense source of energy lay just beyond her reach, like a vast field of power trickling through a pinprick in a wall. There, ready to tap into.

Every impulse screamed for her to sing. She hummed, letting the pulse of the world guide her. Her spirit soared to a place only music could take her. Even though she was plain-looking, music made her feel pretty, maybe as beautiful as Wenhui, maybe even as gorgeous as Yanyan in her extravagant gowns. Then, her limbs went slack. Blood rushed from her head. A dark tunnel in her field of vision narrowed. All went black.

Chapter 9:
Awakenings

"Mai! Wake up!" The voice sounded like Ying's, though the gentle shake felt like Mother's, beckoning Mai from sleep.

Impossible. Ying was dead, murdered by Cleric Pyuz. Mother was far away, probably worried sick wondering where she was.

Head buzzing, Mai tried to force her eyelids open.

"I think she's waking up." This voice sounded like Li, though like Mother, he couldn't possibly be…

Just where was she? With supreme effort, she opened her eyes. Vision blurred, she blinked several times.. Green and brown smudges came into focus.

She was lying on a bed of needle-like leaves. Brittle lines of sunlight peeked through the trees vaulting above her, and a cool, fresh scent filled her nose.

A silhouetted face encroached on her field of vision. "Mai, are you all right?"

Mai jerked up to a seated position. Her head spun all over again.

An arm hooked under her. "Easy," said the male voice.

She took a deep breath of the cool air. The fog in her head lightened, even if her empty stomach was still grumbling. She blinked several more times.

Wenhui, still in her blue dress, and Ku, now clothed in a high-collared shirt, blew out long sighs.

"Thank the Heavens. You shouldn't have wandered off," Wenhui said, tone sweet and eyes gentle.

It was such a change from earlier. Mai tried her best not to glare. "You told me to leave."

"I didn't mean for you to come to the forest."

So this place, with its countless tall trees, was called a *forest*. "I didn't know what else to do."

"Luckily you didn't go too deep, or we would've never found you." Wenhui smiled, again radiantly like Ying. "I'm sorry about earlier. In order for my tattoos to convey ferocity, I must channel my anger."

Mai's forehead scrunched. *Use your emotion to impel your voice*, Aralas had said. Perhaps emotion had been missing from her attempts to play the pipa. She studied Wenhui.

The tattooist tilted her eyes down. "I don't like to be that way. You saw my picture of Aralas?"

Mai nodded. In the corner of her eye, Ku frowned.

Wen fixed him with a vicious stare before turning back to her. "It made you feel happy, right?"

"Yes."

"I painted it when I was happy. I have it there for when I'm done working. Otherwise, I will be angry at everyone and everything for hours."

"That's not the only time you look at it," Ku muttered under his breath.

"Heavens, will you shut up?" Pink tinged Wenhui's cheeks. "In any case, I'm only mean when I'm drawing those tattoos on the warriors."

Ku harrumphed. "Not exactly."

Wenhui lifted her chin and snorted. "I don't like to do it. I don't like feeling that way. But we all have to make sacrifices."

Ku's lower lip protruded.

The two made for interesting friends. A giggle escaped Mai's best attempts to bury it.

"Come on, let's get back to town." Wenhui pointed to a red string which trailed through the forest.

Ku started winding the thread around his hand.

Mai followed them through twists and turns among the trees. "Is the string so you don't get lost?"

Ku nodded. "These are elf trees. Our elf teachers disappear into the forest every night. Their homeland supposedly lies in a valley deeper in, but no human has ever laid eyes on it. The magic here will make you get lost in the forest."

Mai closed her eyes and listened. The heartbeat of the world pulsed strongly here, rippling out from the ground itself. Yet above them, there seemed to be so many quieter sounds. She looked up.

The dappled sunlight cast blurred shapes in the treetops, in regular patterns. There seemed to be laughing or talking coming from there. There had to be someone there.

"Yes," Wenhui said. "You see it, too. That's part of the magic, meant to disorient you."

Looking up, Ku threw up his hands. "By the Heavens, I still don't know what you're talking about. It's just the tree tops."

Wen shrugged. "Only someone who can sense the magic of the world would be able to notice it. Now come on, poor

Mai's stomach has been rumbling this whole time, and she needs to be refreshed if she stands a chance of learning how to use her gift."

Flushing, Mai put a hand over her stomach. She hadn't eaten since the morning; no wonder her limbs felt so listless and her head so light.

Before long they cleared the forest. Above, the Iridescent Moon already waxed to half. It had been waxing to mid-crescent when she first entered the woods, meaning she'd spent two phases in there, and more importantly, it had been ten phases since she'd eaten anything. Something aromatic danced on the breeze.

As Wenhui took them deeper into the town, the scent grew stronger. At last, they came to a building where several men and women were working over fires, tossing chunks of red, green, and white vegetables in large metal pans. The sizzling foods and scraping of spatulas created their own concert. Wenhui motioned Mai to a bench where a dozen people were already eating, then she and Ku went to get food.

Mai watched the cooks. Unlike the villagers back home assigned to cooking duty, these people wore broad smiles and laughed as they worked. Wenhui set a ceramic bowl decorated with blue dragons in her hands. It was so delicate and pretty compared to the wooden ones back home. Vegetables topped rice, the steam rising off of the dish sending her stomach into rumbles worthy of a Tivari god's flaming chariot.

By the time Ku handed her chopsticks, all sense of manners disappeared. She shoveled the food into her mouth.

113

The sweet and salty flavors erupted over her tongue. "Tivar's Scythe," she mumbled through her mouthful, "I've never tasted anything so good."

All conversation went silent. Every eye glared at her. Several people tapped their index fingers together, a sign of warding evil.

Her chopsticks froze over the bowl. "I'm sorry, I was just so hungry."

"She's new." Wenhui stood and waved her hands, and the others resumed their eating. Then, she sat and leaned in. "You used that name. You mustn't, not here. Not the Corrupter's, nor his Whore."

Mai's face flushed. Of course—Aralas had told her to invoke the Heavens instead of the Tivari gods. He'd mentioned the Whore as Lydath. "What do you call the Blue Moon?"

"Guanyin's Eye."

Mai nodded. Aralas had named her, and claimed mankind had sprung forth from her tears.

"The Tivari took our gods and twisted them into foul perversions." Wenhui's pretty smile curled into a frown. "This is what the rebellion is about, winning not just our freedom, but reclaiming our very gods."

Reclaiming gods. Her head spun. "There's so much to learn."

Wenhui's head bobbed. "Learning the truth of our creation is even more important than whatever role you play in our liberation. Hurry up and finish."

After just a few swallows, her energy was already building, much faster than when she ate the food back home. Then again, no one else was eating as fast as her. She mumbled through her stuffed mouth. "How is the food so…filling?"

Ku patted his stomach. "Right? I could never go back to the bland millet porridge we used to eat every day."

Wenhui giggled. "I try not to think about it. As for the food here…the cooks put their heart into it, just like I put mine into my work. And you, into your music."

Ku's lash scars marked him as a former slave, but Wenhui moved through this world like a fish in water, as if she belonged here. Mai leaned back and looked at her neck. The telltale scar of obedience marred her otherwise smooth neck. "Where do you come from?"

Wen rubbed her scar and tilted her head toward Ku. "We're both from Hualian village, near the pyramid."

Mai nodded. The region supposedly boasted a scenic valley. "How did you escape? How long have you been here?"

"We escaped two years ago." Wenhui's radiant smile melted. "One evening, our village priest caught me painting on a rock. He executed my father and mother that day."

Why did the Tivari always reserve executions for offenders' friends and family? Mai shivered. Back home, perhaps Mother, Father, and Ling were all facing some kind of punishment for her disappearance.

"The priest decreed that my fingers were to be broken in front of the rest of the village, at dawn the next day." Wenhui's voice cracked. She hugged her shoulders and tilted her head toward Ku.

He nodded. "I helped her escape that night. We ran into the mountains. But the next morning, several of the priests tracked us with madaeri." Ku shuddered. "Their shrieks haunt my dreams."

Mai shuddered. Villagers whispered rumors of their sharp fangs, coarse hair, and vicious nature. Of course, none had actually seen or heard one.

Tears glistened in Wenhui's eyes. "They found us so fast. Their unholy rods were pointed at us. I thought for sure they would drag us back and torture us in front of them all."

"But then," Ku said, "Yanyan and Aralas rescued us. She sang…"

"It was the most glorious sound ever." Wenhui sighed. "And the Tivari priests fell into a daze."

"What about the madaeri? Did they attack?" Certainly, the vicious little beasts could snarl and bite.

Ku's forehead furrowed. "We never saw them, nor the one that accompanied Aralas and Yanyan. We saw their shadowed shapes among the distant underbrush, and it apparently convinced the others to run away with him. It was so strange. It was almost like they were intelligent."

"What happened when the Tivari recovered?" Mai asked.

Wenhui's shoulders shook.

Mai started to reach over to give her a comforting hug.

"I sang a Dragon Song of forgetfulness." Yanyan's unmistakable, mellifluous voice came from the entrance.

A pit formed in Mai's stomach. If only she could do the same.

Yanyan glided over, her wondrous red dress billowing like clouds. Red and gold slippers now graced her perfect feet. Mai's plain, roughspun dress chafed more than ever.

Hip-bumping Mai over, Yanyan sat down beside Wenhui and draped an arm over her. "I know, it still gives you nightmares."

Mai's stomach twisted. Yanyan was better. At everything.

Yanyan looked over her shoulder. When their eyes met, she smirked. She leaned her head on Wenhui's. "There, there." Her words hung in the air, heavy and soothing.

Wenhui's shoulders relaxed.

A sigh escaped before Mai could stifle it.

Yanyan turned to her. "You left before our lesson was over. If you want to give up, just say so. Only a select few can use any kind of magic. Fewer still can invoke the magic of a Dragon Song. Still, everyone has a role to play." She nodded at Ku, then lifted her chin to the young women who were washing the bowls and chopsticks in a trough.

What a Turtle's Egg! Heat flared hot in Mai's head. Was that all she was good for? Cleaning dirty dishes? No. She bolted to her feet and curled her toes into the ground. Knees bending slightly, she straightened her spine. The pulse of the earth carried through her and echoed in her ears. Again, her belly squirmed like dozens of fish in a small pool. Now what to do?

Eyes narrowing, Yanyan floated to her feet. "Good. You have some fight in you. Save it for tomorrow, when we try to start your lessons again. Now sit."

The last two words trilled.

Mai's heart responded, its beat shifting to match. Her toes relaxed and her spine turned to jelly. Against her efforts to resist, she plopped down onto the bench.

Throwing her hair over her shoulder, Yanyan harrumphed. She turned on her heel and glided toward the door. At the threshold, one of the dishwashers brought her a full bowl of rice and food.

Yanyan looked back. "Wenhui, would you join me for tea tonight? We can watch the moon."

If Wenhui's nod was any more enthusiastic, her head might fall off.

"Good." Yanyan flashed a smile. "Come at the first gibbous."

With a swirl of color, she glided out.

Mai blew out a long breath. What had she hoped to accomplish in confronting a master of music? She hadn't even tested the stance, or learned any Dragon Songs. No, Yanyan had provoked her, and made her look like a fool.

"Yanyan is nice." Wenhui patted her on the back. "She's like a big sister. You'll come to like her."

Mai bit her lip. If Yanyan was nice, then Cleric Pyuz was a saint. Still, it was clear she wouldn't make any friends if others thought they had to choose between her and Yanyan. "I don't know what came over me. My insides felt out of sorts."

Wenhui grinned. "I'd let you look at my painting of Aralas again, but I don't think that could help now. That feeling you are describing, I got that a lot when I first started learning to paint magic. I know just the person we can see about it."

Chapter 10:
A Different Kind of Magic

Cricket chirps and frog trills replaced the sound of work as dusk fell over the town. Mai followed Wenhui and Ku through the streets, while craftsmen closed up shop and headed toward the building where they'd just eaten. Many held glowing rocks, which cast a light that didn't flicker like a torch. As they passed, several looked at her, then exchanged whispers with their friends.

Curse her keen ears. The whispers might as well have been shouts.

"That's Mai."

"The one who confronted Yanyan."

"I've heard she can't do magic, though."

Each rumor felt like the sting of Cleric Pyuz's whip. This was worse than all the giggling village girls back home.

Wenhui skipped along, oblivious. At least the tattooist wasn't holding the friction between Mai and Yanyan against her.

Mai hurried to keep up.

They came to a rounded building, made with the material that looked like one continuous stone. A rectangular wooden board hung below the red-tiled roof, with squiggly black lines written on it. On either side of the board also hung dried lizards, snakes, and large insects.

Mai shuddered. "What is this place?"

"Doctor Wu's." Wenhui pointed at the wooden board.

When Mai studied the symbols, which flowed in a clear pattern, her tight shoulders and neck loosened. "What is a doctor?"

"Heavens!" Wenhui giggled. "Someone who can heal your wounds."

The village had a healer, who was good at setting broken bones, mixing poultices for bruises and cuts, and brewing herbs to chase away sickness. Mai had none of those ailments right now. She followed Wenhui to the open door, from which a soft white light shined.

Wenhui bowed her head. "Hello? Doctor?"

"Come in, come in." The voice sounded female.

Mai's nose scrunched as she entered. On the inside, the single room was oval-shaped. The walls were lined with several ceramic jars, all with wavy lines painted on them. A table stood not far from the middle of the room.

The most beautiful eyes met hers. Luminous blue, like Lydath's...*Guanyin's* Eye.

Mai couldn't help but stare.

A woman?! A woman couldn't possibly be a healer, could she? From her smooth skin, Doctor Wu might not have been much older than Mother, yet her hair was a lustrous silver. She nodded in greeting, the motion so dignified and regal it made her plain grey robes seem even more majestic than Yanyan's luxurious gown.

Whatever compelled her, Mai bowed low in response.

"I'm not a Tivari priest, Mai. You don't have to bow so low." Doctor Wu's laugh was like jingling of bells.

Reassured, Mai straightened. "How do you know my name?"

"Aralas told me about you. He's right. You have a voice that really can tame a dragon."

Mai searched the doctor's beautiful eyes. Aralas had said nothing to her about charming dragons. "Like Yanyan charming the Guardian Dragon?"

The doctor snorted. "That's what they say, thanks to Aralas. I wouldn't trust anything that comes out of that rascal's mouth."

Rascal, indeed. Mai opened her mouth to speak. "Then—"

"I'm not surprised you came to me on your first day here." The doctor patted the table, the rhythm of her taps following the pulse of the world. "Come, get out of those filthy clothes and jump on up. Ku, Wenhui, you may take your leave."

The doctor might not be a Tivari priest, but she sure spoke with similar authority and carried herself with an even more awe-inspiring presence. Mai stared at the table before looking to her new friends. Bent at the waist, they were already backing out. Wenhui closed the door behind her.

Hands clenching and unclenching, Mai shouldered out of her dress, leaving her only in a loincloth, and perched on the edge of the table.

"Show me your wrists," the doctor said.

Whatever for? Mai stretched out her arms.

Doctor Wu placed three fingers on each wrist. Her face scrunched up, making her look older. "Now your tongue."

Such a strange request. The healer back in the village never looked at her tongue when she was ill. Mai did as commanded.

"Keep your tongue still." Doctor Wu's beautiful blue eyes roved back and forth. "To connect to the vitality of Mother Earth, all your pathways must be open."

Mai cocked her head. "Pathways? What are they? And why are they closed?"

"Lie down."

Mai's dubious stare died quickly, and she did as she was told.

With a snort, Doctor Wu placed a finger on her belly, then traced a line to her chest. "Imagine the food you eat and air you breathe like the source of a river. You've lived a life eating food which does not nourish, so there is not enough water to course through all the irrigation ditches. Some riverbeds are dry, while water stagnates in others."

The doctor spoke of bodies like they were the trails between the fields. Mai's head spun.

"You tried to make a connection to the vitality of Mother Earth without proper instruction. Lucky for you, your base energy is strong. Very strong. No wonder a certain diva is worried about competition."

Mai clapped her hands together. At last, someone who could see what was happening. Then again, the doctor hadn't been around earlier, so how could she know?

The doctor's glare froze Mai's hands in place. "Don't let it go to your head. A small seed can grow into an elf tree, but if it never lands on fertile ground, its potential will remain unrealized."

124

"How can I progress?"

"With practice. But first, I will open your pathways." Several needles, gold like the Tivari gods' flaming chariots, flashed in the doctor's hands.

Mai shuddered. She started to protest.

The first needle, in the web between her thumb and pointer finger, sent a jolt all the way up her arm and into her face. Doctor Wu grinned. "*Hegu*, the peaceful valley, commands the head."

The throbbing in Mai's mind suggested the doctor wasn't lying about commanding the head, but there was nothing peaceful about it.

Before she could respond, the doctor stabbed her in between her big and second toe, sending a heavy, numb sensation up her leg. "*Taichong,* Extreme Rushing, balances *Hegu*." On the opposite leg, a needle went in right below her knee, while another went into the other arm, in the crook of her elbow. "*Zusanli* boosts energy, *Quze* balances it all."

The doctor inserted several more needles, with a final one ending in Mai's belly. "*Qihai*, The Sea of Energy."

Childhood tales told of vast expanses of torrid waters, infested by monsters which swallowed up anyone foolish enough to wade in. If there were such a sea of energy in her, it must've been hit by a legendary typhoon. Her body throbbed and buzzed. Jolts coursed up and down her spine. Though not exactly torture, it certainly wasn't the way she expected to learn the magic of Dragon Songs.

Doctor Wu patted her on the stomach, right over the writhing fish sensation. "Breathe deeply. Feel the fresh air in this valley fill your lungs and go all the way to your belly."

It was similar to what Aralas had said. As Mai did as she obeyed, her limbs relaxed. The writhing sensation in her belly subsided.

"Now rest," Doctor Wu said. "I will be back."

What? "You just want me to lie here, and—"

The lights blinked out, leaving only the moonslight streaming in through an unshuttered window. Tiv…Heaven forbid any man walk by and peek in to see her naked body.

Mai shuddered, but shook the idea out of her head. How bizarre this day had been, starting with the tragedy of Ying's death, progressing to a passionate moment with Li, to discovering a place where fairy tales came true. A failed lesson in magical music had led to a nap in an elf forest, and now being stuck and stabbed like cloth being stitched into a dress.

If it brought her any closer to learning to playing her part in the liberation of mankind, perhaps the unpredictable twists and turns of this day were worth it.

"You can get up now," Doctor Wu said.

Get up? With all the needles sticking in her? Mai lifted her head and found the doctor in her peripheral vision.

"Quickly now, the diva is already waiting for you."

"At this hour?" Mai blinked a few times. The needles were gone, and a smooth sheet covered her. Sunlight streamed in from the window and open door. It had only seemed like minutes since Doctor Wu had treated her. "Is it already morning?"

Doctor Wu nodded. "You had so much stagnation, the acupuncture wore you out. I daresay you were almost an equally tangled mess as the diva when she first came. After I took the needles out, we couldn't rouse you, and you slept here."

Which sounded like a good thing, since no one had told her where she'd be staying. Mai stretched her arms and legs, which felt lighter than usual. She kicked her legs over the side of the table and slid to the tile floor. The world pulsed into her soles, stronger than the day before. Tiv...no, *Heavens,* it sounded so...clear. It resonated through her as if her body was Yanyan's pipa string.

The way she felt now, she could take on the Tivari High Priest, his army of Templars, and a horde of snarling madaeri all by herself. Nothing the diva could do could possibly deter her from learning the magic Dragon Songs. She straightened and started for the door.

"Don't go out naked." Doctor Wu chuckled, then pointed her to a green swath of so-called silk draped over the back of a chair. A pair of matching slippers rested in the seat.

Mai's face flushed hot in embarrassment, but her heart leaped. She ran her hand over the smooth fabric, then held it up. While not nearly as wondrous as Yanyan's, or even

127

Wenhui's, the undecorated dress was probably just as fine as anything Cleric Pyuz wore.

"It is about your size," the doctor said. "I gave the tailors your measurements, and they will make alterations so the next one will fit better."

Whatever tailors were, Mai would be sure to thank them later. When she slid the dress on, the hem dropped only to mid-calf, and the sleeves hung a little past her palms. Still, it felt like wearing a cloud. Slippery and cool, it made her roughspun dress seem like a potato sack. Which it probably had been, before being repurposed. How satisfying it would be to burn it. Her eyes strayed to the ugly shift.

Doctor Wu laughed. "You'll need to keep it, for when you go back to save your parents."

Parents. Mai's stomach leaped into her throat. She'd been worrying about fitting in in this wondrous valley, and had forgotten all about her family and friends. "I need to get back to them."

"Not yet." Doctor Wu patted her on the head. "If you go back now, they'll just torture and kill you. The best way you can help your parents is to learn the power of Dragon Songs."

Was there enough time? Mai's jaw tightened. "It is near rice harvest, and the Tivari will need all hands." Though the Tivari's need for labor hadn't been enough to spare Ying.

"Well, go hurry back to the diva." The doctor wagged a finger at her. "Don't send your energy pathways into a tangle again! It will slow your progress. You don't have that much time before harvest is over to learn enough magic to defeat your village priest."

Mai started to—

"Or perhaps, something more insidious."

Chapter 11:

New Friends

From somewhere in the distance, the strums of Yanyan's pipa called out to Mai as she hurried down the street. She hadn't paid much attention to the roads the day before, and her sense of direction was fair at best. Still, the music might as well have been a beacon.

Even with the thick-soled slippers, the pulse of the world still coursed through her, louder than ever, and set the rhythm for all the other early morning sounds. Dwarves hammering metal, warriors shouting in their practice, cooks scraping and scooping, they all had an order to them. Up above, even the swirling colors of the Iridescent Moon, now waning to its half gibbous, seemed to follow the beat.

The steadfast regularity should've been reassuring, yet a pit had settled in her stomach. The rice harvest would begin within the next several weeks, and the last two phases of the White Moon. Cleric Pyuz must've reported her disappearance and sent word to the High Priest at the pyramid. While she might be safe from the Tivari's madaeri trackers here, no doubt Cleric Pyuz was working her family ragged. After harvest, he might very well torture and execute them.

She took a deep breath all the way into her belly, as Aralas had taught, and let it go. Her shoulders, which had already started scrunching up, relaxed again. Her family's plight needed to provide motivation, not drag her down. Using Yanyan's music as a guide, she lengthened her stride and redoubled her pace.

One of the dwarves waved at her as she passed the smithy. "Good morning, lass. Ye have an extra spring in yer step."

"Aye," the other said. "I bet her hum could enchant our blades even better today."

Whatever a lass was, it didn't seem like an insult. Not with their broad smiles. Mai bobbed her head in greeting and continued. Though most of the buildings looked the same, the area seemed more familiar. After a few minutes she passed the open space, where a different group of soldiers practiced with poles with metal tips. Ku was not among them.

Continuing her search, she paused to peek in Wenhui's window. The tattoo artist was busy berating an unfamiliar young man as she worked ink under his skin. Maybe it was better not to exchange greetings.

At last she came to the right house, obvious not so much from the red-tiled eaves and white plaster walls as from the music emanating from within. She shrugged her shoulders to loosen them again. Now that she'd had seen more of the town, it was clear that Yanyan's home was one of the nicest, even if its occupant wasn't particularly nice.

The music's tenor, which at first had sounded like gay birdsongs, shifted. Now it sounded like those same birds eyeing a determined predator. Every nerve fiber screamed at her to turn around.

No, she wouldn't give up. Not today. Mother, Father, and Little Sister Ling depended on her. She took a deep breath and filled her belly, just as Aralas had taught. Today, she'd show her.

She turned the corner of the veranda, and froze.

Yanyan sat there, her cheeks aglow with a vibrancy that hadn't been there yesterday. Her long fingers danced across the pipa strings like a spider pricking through its web. The sound, while melodious, had an eerie feel to it. She looked up and met Mai's eyes. "So you came."

As soon as the music stopped, the sense of dread eased. Mai took a deep breath to chase it away for good. "Yes, Senior."

A bittersweet smile flitted across her lips. "I played this song for you, and only you. Aralas has taught you to breathe correctly, which helped you redirect the magic into the ground. As much as I loathe to teach you, I lost a bet with him last night. You have earned your lesson." Her eyes narrowed. "For today."

Who knew what Mai had done to anger the diva? If the lessons of the Tivari were true, perhaps their souls had warred with one another before birth.

And as for Aralas, he was already back from teaching...what was her name again? Makeda? Apparently he'd spent the night here. No wonder Yanyan looked so radiant this morning. Then again, the elf angel wasn't equipped in *that* way. Mai shook the thought out of her head. She took another deep breath to banish the last of the foreboding and squelch the retort on her lips. "Thank you, Senior."

Yanyan peered at her. "Doctor Wu treated you last night, didn't she?"

"How did you know?"

"Her needles sing a song with your body, just like everything else. No doubt you notice the obvious sounds, and perhaps you already perceive more than most. There is even more. Do you hear my heartbeat?" Yanyan placed a hand on her chest.

Mai closed her eyes and listened. Her own heart thrummed loud in her ears, beating once for every two pulses of the world. A barely audible beat came from Yanyan. She opened her eyes.

Yanyan's eyes were closed. "Your heart and mine beat at different frequencies. If I can project my song at the right beat, our hearts will harmonize, and I can bend you to my will."

So that was what had happened yesterday, not once, but twice: first, when Yanyan commanded her to repeat herself; and then at mealtime, when she was commanded to sit. Mai nodded.

"You nod. Do you understand?"

Perhaps. Maybe. No. Mai sighed and shook her head.

Yanyan snorted. "Good. Admitting you don't know is the first step to learning. Let's see how well you listened. What did I just say?"

Why did she talk in riddles? "You nod. Do you understand?"

Yanyan's mocking laugh and genuine laugh sounded very different, and now it was definitely the former. "Before that, about our hearts."

"Our hearts beat differently. Harmonize our hearts, and you can bend me to your will."

"Close. Everything, both living and inanimate, has a beat, a resonance. Now *sit*."

The last word trilled, filling the space between them. Mai's heart fluttered for a split second. Compelled, she sunk cross-legged onto the veranda beside Yanyan.

Yanyan smirked. "There is a process: Calm. Listen. Project. Harmonize."

Mai gaped. Aralas had taught her to calm herself with deep breathing. He'd taught her how to listen. "Yesterday, you wanted me to project."

Yanyan laughed. "That, and learn how to play a pipa. Now, try again." She proffered the ornate instrument.

Mai stared at it for a few seconds before receiving it in both hands. Whereas the pipa's pulse had felt faint yesterday, today it coursed through her. She nearly dropped it. Again.

"Be careful!" Yanyan scowled. "Heavens, you are stupid. But you hear its vitality, don't you?"

Mai nodded.

"Good. Most people can't even hear it, let alone coax a sound out of it." Yanyan's lips curled. "Projecting its sound is impossible, save for me, and maybe you."

Mai studied the strings and resonator. "How do you do it?"

Yanyan laughed again. "You hear the pulse of the world, I assume?"

"Yes."

"Most people can't sense it, and those who can, perceive it differently. From what I've learned, Wenhui sees it. The dwarves feel it in their bones. Some of the cooks taste it. The trick is to link the pulse of the world with the life beat of the instrument, with your body as a pathway. Now—"

Mai stood. If her eyes were any wider, they might be as large as Aralas'. That explained Wenhui's posture when she worked her art. And Yanyan's, even if it was more subtle than Wenhui's. She kicked off her slippers and curled her toes into the wood, the wood whose very ridge patterns followed the pulse of the world. She bent her knees and straightened her spine. The world's song coursed through her.

Closing her eyes, Yanyan sighed. "I hate you."

Mai bent her elbows. The pipa's vitality resonated in her core. She ran a finger across the strings. Joyous, vibrant twangs echoed in its resonator. Her spirit soared, whether from the improvement over yesterday, or the melody. She looked up.

Yanyan's quivering smile was impossible to read, at once bitter and content. "I really hate you. You and I are the only humans to ever coax the sound out of the Dragonscale Pipa."

Mai's chest filled. Heavens, she'd never been special, beyond a voice which did little for farming. Now she had done something that only one other person had.

"Don't let it go to your head." Aralas said, stepping out of his house. The pitch of his voice was again slightly higher. He stretched his arms and yawned.

When he lowered his hands, the high collar of his long purple shirt dropped to reveal a discoloration on his neck that hadn't been there yesterday. The outfit looked nothing like anyone else's clothes around here, and would've made him look strikingly handsome—almost beautiful— if it hadn't been so rumpled. His half-lidded eyes gave him the appearance of having just awoken, and his golden hair looked almost as disheveled as Mai…though it didn't flop into his face as usual. He shook it out, and it fell into a perfect cascade about his shoulders.

Yanyan's smile, ambiguous before, beamed now. "You're awake."

He knelt down beside her and lifted her chin. "Yes, with more work to do. Today, I need to visit our bronze-skinned allies in the South. More lessons in teaching them to swordfight with magic. Unfortunately, they're not ready to take on the Tivari. Only Vanya is picking it up."

His tone, combined with Yanyan's pout, suggested Aralas was teaching this Vanya more than fighting with magic. A frown formed on Mai's lips of its own accord. Heavens, why did it matter who the annoying, genderless elf angel shared a bed with?

She cleared her throat. "I'm so worried about my family and friends. Cleric Pyuz will punish them because I left."

Aralas tore his adoring gaze from Yanyan and looked at Mai. "More likely than not, he sent madaeri to hunt you down. When they didn't find you—because there is no way they can track someone whose scent just disappears—he will probably just keep your parents as bait to lure you home."

The idea of snarling madaeri sent a shudder up Mai's spine. Hands on her hips, she stomped. "Bring them here."

"Let's see." The elf angel counted on his fingers. "Your father, mother, and Ling. And what was that strapping boy with the grabby hands' name? Li? And maybe add Skinny Fang for good measure."

How Aralas knew her family members down to Ling's name, not to mention Li and Fang—

Aralas closed his eyes. His lips moved, but no words came out for a few seconds. "But wait. Even if I had the ability to whisk them all away at once, what would the priest do to the rest of the village?"

He'd probably slaughter them all. It didn't seem right to sacrifice everyone else, just to save her family. In the corner of her vision, she caught Yanyan rolling her eyes.

"I can bring one a day." Aralas peered at her. "Who will you save, you will you risk? And if villagers start disappearing, the Tivari will suspect something, and you can bet the rebellion will fail."

Mai's shoulders slumped.

Aralas lifted her chin just as he had Yanyan's, his fingers soft on her skin. "The best way to save your family—no, mankind—is to learn Dragon Songs."

Mai gave a reluctant nod. "I just wish I knew they were all right."

"They are." He chanted several melodic words, and then swept his hand in a wide circle.

Where he'd marked, the air shimmered. A familiar image of rice fields appeared. People hoed and weeded.

There!

Mother and Little Sister Ling held baskets of carrots and sweet potatoes in the crook of their arms as they walked back toward their house. The picture swept to the right and centered on Father, his usually jovial smile twisted into a frown as he worked.

Mai could only gape.

"See? They are fine. Though from the look of it, they miss you."

Mai gave a tentative nod.

"Now," Aralas said, fiddling with some of his hair, "learn how to play a pipa. And other instruments. It's easier to evoke and project a Dragon Song with the Dragonscale Pipa, because it lends its own vitality to you. But regular ones are different. You have to give them life."

He spoke a word, and the plain pipa from yesterday materialized out of nowhere and into his hands. Oblivious to, or perhaps not caring about Mai's gawk, he swiped the magic pipa from her arms and replaced it with the new one. Compared to the first, it felt lifeless.

He turned to Yanyan. "Now, my sweet, you lost the bet and promised to teach Mai. If she has progressed to my satisfaction by the time I return, I will do that thing you like." Flashing a devilish grin, his eyes roved over her body as if he was undressing her.

It was so…wanton. Mai's heart juddered. It was all she could do to not imagine Aralas looking at her like that.

Yanyan's face flushed a color even redder than her dress. She tilted her chin and looked up at him through her lashes. When she spoke, her voice sounded uncharacteristically demure. "Okay."

Just what had the elf angel done to tame the diva?

Aralas took Yanyan's hands and drew her close. One hand slipped into the fold of her gown. He left a trail of kisses up her neck and finally claimed her mouth.

Face hot, Mai shuffled on her feet. It was as if he'd forgotten she was standing there, or perhaps he just didn't care. Try as she might, she couldn't look away. And it wasn't just her face that felt so hot.

Aralas pulled back, Yanyan's lower lip between his teeth. When he released it, he vanished.

Fanning herself with a hand, Yanyan blew out a sigh. Her eyes narrowed as a smile formed on her face. "You *will* learn to play the pipa by tonight."

Chapter 12:

The Dragon Charmer's Challenge

M ai pressed on frets and plucked at strings, the sound coming out clearer the more she practiced. The pipa proved to be quite logical in the way its notes progressed, and it only took a few hours before she no longer butchered the songs Yanyan taught.

Still, she had to do better. Not just to save her family, but also to avoid yet more rebukes from the diva.

As the Iridescent Moon waned to new and the sun shined bright overhead, Mai's stomach rumbled. Her butt hurt from sitting on the veranda for so long, and her back ached from trying to keep it straight. She adjusted her legs, shifted her weight, and let her spine relax.

Yanyan looked up from her instrument and smirked. "Keep your knees together. Do you want your audience to see *everything*? If that's your *magic*, you don't need to learn to evoke the magic of Dragon Songs."

Said the woman who let an elf angel grope her. Gritting her teeth, Mai adjusted her skirts.

Yanyan rolled her eyes. "Heavens, you can put a pig in a nice dress, but she'll still be swine. Just when I thought you were learning something. If you can't even sit still for a few phases, you will never be able to evoke the most powerful Dragon Songs."

Mai settled back to her original position. She straightened her spine again, imitating the posture both Yanyan and Wenhui used when projecting magic. If only she were allowed to stand and dig her toes into the veranda, it would be easier to connect to the pulse of the world.

The diva hadn't taught about stance. On purpose, perhaps.

Yanyan harrumphed. "Now, follow along. Don't look at my fingers. Listen, and repeat the Song of Spring." She plucked out dozens upon dozens of high and low notes, including shifting twangs and changes in intensity. The music floated like a spring breeze carrying a snow of cherry blossom petals.

Eyes closed, head bobbing, Mai held the melody in her head. With a deep breath to settle her spirit, she sent her fingers flitting across the strings. The Song of Spring wasn't that hard to copy. It was getting easier and eas—

"Wrong."

Fire flared in Mai's head. She glared. "I didn't make a mistake. It was correct."

Yanyan huffed. "Technically, yes. But it is so rote, so...dead. Remember what Aralas said? You must give the instrument life. You must infuse your emotion into it. Again."

Mai shifted on her sore butt. This was impossible. The only emotions she could conjure right now were confusion and anger. She sunk a breath into her belly, settling her mind, and plucked out the tune again. The song was coming out correctly, and—

"No. Too much uncertainty. What do you hear when I play?" Yanyan strummed out the first stanza again.

"It sounds whimsical."

Yanyan threw her hands up. "Finally. Again. Whimsically this time."

Whimsically.

Whipped by Cleric Pyuz. Ignored by Li. Now, scolded by Yanyan. Nothing in Mai's life could bring out a whimsical mood. Except maybe Aralas' fickle kisses on Yanyan's neck. Holding that memory in her mind, Mai tried again. The notes came out clearer.

Yet as she played, in her mind, Aralas was no longer kissing Yanyan. Somewhere in the middle of the song, he'd started kissing *her*. His mouth claiming hers. His hands on her body, sending shivers up her spine. His smoldering gaze and her primal moan rippled into her music.

"Is that whimsical?" Yanyan's mocking laugh doused whatever lustful images danced in Mai's head. "Your music screeched like a cat in heat. What were you thinking about?"

Just when the heat of arousal had subsided, Mai's cheeks flushed hotter than the Second Sun. Heavens, how could she even begin to think of a genderless elf angel kissing her? "Let me try again."

A conspiratorial smile formed on Yanyan's lips. "You were thinking about the clouds and rain, weren't you?"

"Clouds and rain?"

Lips turned up in a conspiratorial smile, Yanyan crawled over like a prowling tiger. Her whisper tickled her ear. "You know, the joining of man and woman. Or sometimes, of woman and woman." She trailed a finger from Mai's chest downward.

Heavens, it was so...wanton. One of the many perversions that had led to mythical Cathay's downfall. Swatting Yanyan's hand away, Mai scuttled back.

"Oh, you *were* thinking about that." Yanyan flashed a lurid grin. "You have someone back home, don't you? A strapping young farmer with dark skin and calloused hands?"

Li. Mai's cheeks somehow managed to burn hotter. Still, try as she might, she couldn't remember what he looked like, even though it had been only a little more than a day since she'd seen him. In this moment, he was just a faceless name.

Throwing her hair over her shoulder, she played the Song of Spring again.

"Oh, you won't get out of this that easily." With a snort, Yanyan swept up her pipa and played a new tune, one which harmonized with the Song of Spring. The notes rose and fell in harmony with the pulse of the world, drowning out Mai's own playing.

Mai shook her head. She wouldn't lose, not now. She improvised her own music, the pipa yielding to her fingers, evoking threads of her determination with its notes. The harmonics complemented the diva's.

Yanyan responded with changes of her own. Note battled with note, like the warriors' swordplay the day before. Louder and louder, yet still melodious.

The fury in the music battered Mai, but she wouldn't give in. She redoubled her efforts, infusing each pluck, each strum with her resolve. Their spontaneous duet climbed toward crescendo.

Sweat collected on Mai's brow. She couldn't falter. Not now. She stole a glance at Yanyan.

Her rival's skin glistened as well, her calm expression giving way to clashing eyebrows and tight lips. Her song wavered as their musical duel reached its climax.

Mai's heart soared. Victory was at hand.

Yanyan gritted her teeth. Two rapid sweeps of her hand across the strings launched a torrential soundwave.

It roared in Mai's ears and knocked her down. All four of her pipa strings snapped with a discordant twang. Thank the heavens the sonic blast had also ripped the instrument from her hands, or else the unravelling of the silken threads might have cut across her face.

Hand over her cheek, Mai glared at the diva.

Yanyan's chin lifted, her lips curled into a smirk.

Applause broke out from the periphery of the yard.

Mai's heart just about leaped into her throat. She turned.

Dozens of people were gathered, including Wenhui, Ku, and the dwarves, all eyes wide, all mouths gawking, all clapping. There were so many people, there to witness Yanyan again putting Mai in her place. Her spirit, soaring just a few seconds ago, sank.

Yanyan scurried over on all fours. Despite the furrows in her forehead and tilted eyes that expressed genuine concern, the tone of her voice sounded forced when she spoke. "Are you all right?"

Was she? Her eyes strayed to the pipa, its strings frayed and unraveled, then to Yanyan. Stifling a frown, she nodded.

Wenhui shuffled to the veranda. "Your duet was amazing." She offered a hand.

Taking it, Mai climbed to her feet. Blood rushed into her legs, and she stumbled.

Ku stepped up and caught her. He now wore a dark-blue silk robe with a fearsome dragon embroidered on the front in stitches of red and gold. Like the tattoos, the image sent a chill up Mai's spine.

He shook his head, his expression one of disbelief. "Both of you were amazing. I've never heard such a performance, except maybe when Yanyan summoned the Guardian Dragon."

Mai looked from one to the other, both of them nodding. Perhaps this wasn't a total loss. She'd dueled with a superior musician, who'd had to resort to an underhanded trick to win. In the corner of her eye, she found Yanyan.

The diva favored her with a raised eyebrow before her expression returned to its usual calm. She shrugged. "Mai has much to learn, but she's making progress."

"Progress?" Ku gestured back toward the center of town. "I heard both of you all the way at the palace."

Whatever the palace was, wherever it was, it must have been far away given the awe in his voice. Behind him, other young men in the same style of dark blue robes all nodded in unison.

Ku grinned. "If you play with that intensity when we launch our attack on the Tivari High Priest, we will surely win."

"Did you ever doubt me?" Yanyan flashed a broad smile and batted her eyelashes.

The warriors all shuffled on their feet and gawked, looking much like the silly village girls fawning over Li. It didn't seem possible that men could act more stupid.

Flashing a modest smile, Yanyan bowed. "I am honored by all your attention. Now, please, Mai must continue practicing." She flashed a smirk at Mai.

The diva was so...two-faced. She put on quite an act to win the adoration of everyone. A pit sunk into Mai's stomach. No one would believe her if she said Yanyan was so cruel. She looked again at the severed pipa strings. If Yanyan could do that to an instrument, there was no telling what effect it would have on a living being.

On Cleric Pyuz, maybe.

Mai took another deep breath. She would have to tolerate the abuse at Yanyan's hands if she was to have any hope of saving her parents. It also meant packing a lot of practice into the couple of months before harvest ended to get half as good as the diva.

Wen turned to Yanyan. "Would you break for the morning? The Census Ministry has commanded Mai to present herself before them."

Yanyan bowed her head. "If the ministry commands it, I am in no position to refuse."

A pit formed in Mai's stomach. As much as her poor butt probably needed a break, it meant losing practice time. And who knew what this ministry-thing wanted? She bowed to Yanyan. "Thank you for your lesson, Senior."

The diva forced a kind smile. "You are welcome."

Then, with an expression that was impossible to decipher for all the different emotions tangled in it, Yanyan dismissed Mai with a wave of her hand.

Chapter 13:

Bureaucrats and Bureaucracy

The rhythm of everyone working bombarded Mai as she followed Wenhui and Ku down a street toward the center of town. Even though she really couldn't spare a minute from practice, her legs and butt were thankful for this reprieve.

"Where is this ministry?" Mai asked. They still hadn't told her what a ministry was.

Wenhui pointed toward a long white wall, which started from a nearby tower. "Across from the palace. We're almost there."

Ku had mentioned something about having come from the palace after hearing the musical duel. As they walked, Mai studied the red-tiled roofs of buildings which peeked out from above the wall. "What is a palace for?"

Wen drew a rectangular shape with her hands. "It's like the priest's house in your village, only the emperor lives there."

"Emperor?" Mai's forehead scrunched. The individual sounds of the word implied a child of the heavens. "Is that Aralas?"

If Ku's face twisted any more, it would look like he'd sucked on bitter melon.

Wenhui, on the other hand, giggled. "No, silly. The emperor is a human. Aralas is an elf angel, the messenger from the gods who mandated that the emperor will rule over us all."

"The emperor must lead us in overthrowing the Tivari, first," Ku said.

"He will." Wenhui's quick nod and confident tone could've convinced the Tivari to surrender without a fight. "Heaven wills it."

Mai chewed on her lower lip. The Tivari said the same to justify mankind's enslavement, yet it was the priests with their unholy rods that enforced it. Here, in the Kingdom of Cathay, it was soldiers training with swords. Perhaps it mattered less what the Heavens or Gods willed, and more about which side believed it more, and had better weapons.

151

She let her hand brush over the wall, which towered at least three times her height. It was so smooth, it felt somewhere between wood and stone. She paused at red double doors, easily twice her height, with dozens of gold-colored nubs set in a rectangular pattern. This palace must be huge, bigger than even the pyramid, if the length of the walls were any indication.

Above the doors hung a wooden board, painted gold, with more wavy lines. The pattern was different from the ones above Doctor Wu's house, but still followed the pulse of the world. Whatever was in the lines made Mai's spine turn to jelly, and she felt compelled to bow. "Are we allowed to go inside?"

"Ku is," Wenhui said. "He works here, guarding the emperor. For the rest of us...well, the next time will be during the Harvest Moon. The emperor will address all of us. It's a rare chance for most of us to lay eyes on him." Her tone held nothing short of adoration, and she clapped her hands.

Ku harrumphed. "I see him almost every day. He may be a talented fighter and a brilliant strategist, but he's still just a man."

Scowling, Wenhui poked him in the ribs. "Don't speak ill of the Son of Heaven."

Mai looked from one to the other. Wenhui's fanaticism felt so much like the reverence that kept mankind enslaved to the orcs. They continued walking, until they arrived at a building across the street. Like the others, it had steep, red-tiled roofs, with yet another wooden board. It, too, had a different set of blocky lines.

"Here we are," Wenhui said. "The Census Ministry."

"What exactly is a ministry? And a census?" Mai peered at the board. If the dull lines, which guttered her energy, were any indication, it would probably be akin to watching mud dry. Her time would be better spent practicing.

"It is an organ of government. It conducts the official business of the emperor."

Mai's mind spun. Organs, government, official business. All words that didn't make sense. "What happens here?"

"You'll see." Ku opened the door and gestured Mai in.

"I have to go back to tattooing," Wenhui said. "You can find your way back to Yanyan's, I assume?"

Mai nodded. Despite the foreboding weight growing on her shoulders, she walked in.

Inside, the building was easily a dozen times larger than any place she'd ever been. Shelf after shelf had tube shapes stacked in the same tedious order as the lines on the signboard. Men in blue silk robes sat at several identical tables, all holding sticks with some kind of black dye at their fluffy ends. They drew blocky lines on rectangular sheets that looked like the peeling bark of the trees back home. If this was the official business of the emperor, it had to be boring.

A man approached and gave her a curt nod. "I am Secretary Chu. You must be Miss Mai. We have been expecting you. Where are you from?"

"Sweetfield village."

"Where is that?"

Before yesterday, the world consisted of only a handful of villages, and… "An hour's walk north of the pyramid."

"Ah, the Fenggu region." He pointed to another man sitting at one of the tables. "Meet with Scribe Ju."

As she approached, Scribe Ju looked up and motioned her to a wooden stool across the table from him.

Bowing her head, she plopped down. It felt sturdier than any chair she'd ever sat in.

The man dipped his stick into black dye and held it above the sheet. "What is your family name?"

"What's that?"

He rolled his eyes. "The common name passed down over the generations. Your father and grandfather and your siblings would all share it."

She shrugged. "Why would we have such a name?"

"Bumpkin," he muttered, just loud enough for her ears to make out. He sighed and pointed to the shelves. "It's how we keep track of families. Heavens forbid you marry a cousin. Which is to say, since the emperor's word is that of Heaven, it is forbidden to marry a cousin." He looked up from his work. "You didn't marry a cousin, did you?"

Li shared a distant relative—whether that was a great-grandmother or great-great grandmother, perhaps Father would know—but they didn't use family terms with each other. Still, cousin was such a broad word, and now subject to an emperor's order. Perhaps they were exchanging one type of tyranny for another. She shook her head. "I'm not married."

"Good, then I don't have to ask about your husband's name." His stick swept across the paper in quick swishes.

"What is this?" She pointed to the mark, but had to pull back as he swatted at her hand. She looked up.

He was glaring at her. "Your new family name, Wei." His eyes returned to their work.

"Why that one?"

He looked back up. "We have several hundred from the register of names to choose from. *Wei* just happened to be next in the queue. If you would prefer another family name, you can lodge a letter of complaint with a secretary in the Ministry of Oversight."

Not like a name mattered, but still, it seemed to be arbitrary, and buried under layers of rules. She sighed. "I don't understand, why is all this important?"

Scribe Ju stared at her the way she looked at Little Sister Ling when she had to explain something obvious. "The only way to ensure order, stability, and prosperity is to establish consistent rules and follow them."

"But who comes up with these rules?"

He set his stick down with an exasperated sigh. "The emperor, of course."

She shifted in her seat. "But how do we know it is good for us?"

"The emperor didn't just come up with random decrees. No, it's all based on the ancient knowledge of Cathay, which the Tivari tried to keep from us. We have recreated it all here, from the writing system," he held up the stick, "to architecture, from steel-smithing to the weaving of silk. It's all to practice a functioning government, which we will bring to our people once we defeat the Tivari."

If this was good or bad, they'd find out if and when they won their freedom. Still, the rules did seem to work in establishing this large, developed town. "How long has this kingdom been here?"

He shrugged. "I've been here for five harvests, and the town was already about this size. You would have to lodge an information request with the imperial archives if you wanted to know an exact date."

Mai wasn't even sure what a date was, nor did it matter enough to lodge requests and complaints. More concerning was that after five years, he, like Wenhui, followed this emperor's rules without question. "How come the Tivari gods in their flaming chariots haven't located this valley and rained unholy vengeance on us?"

He harrumphed. "I thought I was the one asking the questions."

In all likelihood, he didn't know. Mai bowed her head nonetheless. "I'm sorry."

With a smug grin, he dipped the bushy end of the stick into the dye again. "Now, I want you list all of your family members, starting with siblings, then moving up to parents, and their parents…"

***

The clanking and scraping of the cooking tools at the stoves helped rouse Mai from her boredom-induced stupor. After a couple of phases answering Scribe Ju's endless questions about her family, she would welcome a certain two-faced diva's barrage of insults, if only she could put her hands back on a musical instrument.

Right now, learning Dragon Songs was her most important task, if she was to prevent Cleric Pyuz from torturing her family…which was now surnamed Wei, without any input from her. Yes, at the very least, she'd save her family and village. It didn't matter if this new Kingdom of Cathay replaced the Tivari or not; it would no doubt collapse under the weight of its unwieldy rules. She chopsticked chunks of food into her mouth and swallowed with the least amount of chewing possible. There was no point in being late and giving Yanyan another reason to rebuke her.

Finishing her meal, she returned the bowl to the wash area and headed back out into the street. As she walked, she listened to the pulse of the world and moved her fingers as if playing the pipa. Hopefully, her muscles hadn't forgotten the morning's lessons.

A low rumble vibrated through the air.

It sounded familiar, like…oh, no. Mai looked up, tracking the source of the sound.

In the distance, a line of flames flickered across the sky, engulfing the unmistakable gold-gilded chariot of a Tivari god.

A pit formed in Mai's stomach. They usually only descended at harvest time, to accept sacrifices of rice, wheat, pigs, and chickens. If they were coming now, maybe some nearby village had sinned and now faced divine judgment.

Or perhaps the Tivari gods had finally discovered the new Cathayi realm.

Which one was it this time? Immolz, God of the Sun, preparing to scorch the earth? Or Deluk, God of Storms, coming to batter the crops with wind and ice? Heavens, let it not be Tivar himself, descending with his scythe to smite the unfaithful.

Every instinct screamed at her to find cover. Her eyes darted left and right, before settling on a house with an open door. A perfect hiding place. She took one last look.

Everybody else continued their work, never looking up, unaware of the danger. Of course, nobody could hear as well as her, with the exception of the diva. No doubt the weapon-hammering at the forge helped drown out the sound.

So many people would be caught out in the open. Mai took another look at the hiding place. It would be so easy to save herself. To live, and protect her family and friends from Cleric Pyuz.

She ran to the group of seamstresses embroidering dragons into blue silk robes. She pointed at the chariot, now growing larger. "A Tivari god is coming."

The women's eyes widened and looked in unison.

Not waiting, Mai raced to the next building, where two men worked at bending a long, curved stick with a string connecting both ends. "Hide! Tivari Gods!"

The roaring grew louder. Mai had to reach Wenhui, if not to warn her, then to die with a familiar face. She continued her mad dash, yelling the warning to everyone she passed. At the training square, she hunched over, panting for breath as she spoke. "Tivari...gods."

The fighting men all lowered their weapons. In unison, their heads turned up.

The flaming chariot loomed closer and closer. The ground shook. Buildings rattled. Wenhui came out of her house, freezing in her tracks as her eyes locked up.

Mai's heart sank.

Maybe the reborn Kingdom of Cathay would've never succeeded in the first place, but who knew the rebellion would be so short-lived? And if she died here, there was no hope for her family.

Chapter 14:

Unwelcome Visitors

The rumbling ground drowned out the pulse of the world in Mai's ears as the flaming chariot approached. It now loomed high overhead, ready to rain fire, pestilence, lightning, or Heavens-knew-what on the fledgling Kingdom of Cathay. Whatever luck had managed to keep the valley hidden from Tivar's all-seeing eyes for so long had run out.

Every nerve screamed at her to do something, anything. But her legs refused to move. Try as she might, the ground shook too much for her toes to grip. The pulse of the earth, which had coursed through her this morning, now seemed so far, so distant. Her voice died in her throat; not like she had trained in anything that could possibly affect a god. Perhaps not even Yanyan nor Aralas could do anything, either.

Not far to the side, the warriors, who had been staring at the flaming chariot with dread fascination, turned away in resignation.

It was right overhead now, so huge it blotted out the sun. Never before had she been so close to one. Its raging flames tortured the souls who pulled the chariot through the skies. It roared in Mai's ears, forcing her to cover them. Her knees buckled to the ground.

This was it. Her shoulders slumped. She closed her eyes and hung her head. Waiting. Hopefully, the Tivari's unholy vengeance would be fast and painless. And if what Aralas had said was true, the afterlife would be neither serving as handmaiden to Lydath, nor eternal torture at the hands of Tortak; but perhaps something better.

She waited for death to come.

And waited.

The moans and flames softened and faded.

Mai looked up.

The chariot had continued on its way, leaving a trail of smoke that cut across the sky, directly above.

Was that it? Perhaps it had been Tortak, sowing the seeds of some horrible plague that would ravage everyone here. She looked around.

People went about their business. The warriors seemed to have resumed their training.

Wenhui ambled over and helped her up. "Are you all right?"

Mai gave a tentative nod. "How are we still alive?

"Why wouldn't we be?" Wenhui cocked her head.

Mai pointed at the flaming chariot, now just a flicker in the distance. "I thought for sure the Tivari gods would punish us."

Wenhui patted her on the back. "It's quite a sight. One of the gods flies by every so often, but they can't see us."

"Why not?" And to think, she'd been running and screaming through the town, like a crazy girl.

Wenhui gestured toward the mountains, into the forest from yesterday. "Elf magic. We are at the edge of an ancient spell. It has cloaked this area from the Tivari for thousands of years." She lowered her voice. "There are rumors that the magic is waning, which is one of the reasons Aralas wants to defeat the Tivari soon."

Mai chewed on her lower lip. Perhaps the elves weren't helping mankind out of generosity, but rather for their own survival.

"Well, I have to get back to work." Wenhui tilted her head back toward her house. "For now, there's no need to worry about the chariots of the Tivari gods. They—"

Mai held up a hand. "Do you hear that?" Rhythmic puffs of air followed the pulse of the world.

Creases formed in Wenhui's brow. She looked up. "I don't hear anything different."

Mai tracked the source of the sound, her line of sight following the flaming chariot's dispersing trail of smoke. A red splotch marred the clear blue sky, following the contrail. She pointed. "What is that?"

"A bird maybe..." Wenhui squinted. "All I can say is that it has wings, flapping with the pulse of the world."

Mai nodded. "I hear the pattern, too."

"Oh, Heavens." Eyes widening, Wenhui froze in place.

Mai peered at the red spot, which grew larger which each puff of air. Now the wings stood out clearly against the blue backdrop.

The nearby dwarf hammering came to an abrupt halt. The warriors' martial shouts quieted. Even the bird chirps ceased. All around them, the world fell into silence, replaced by a palpable, collective fear. Heartbeats quickened in unison, all pounding loud in Mai's ears.

Deep-rooted, primal dread crawled up her spine as the gusts grew louder and the shape took clear form. Four legs protruded from an oval body. A long neck ended in a triangular horned head, while a tail drifted behind it. Jaws agape, it seemed to be sucking in the smoke left by the flaming chariot.

Heavens, a dragon. A real dragon.

The Dragon.

Wenhui clutched Mai's arm so tightly it hurt. The warriors threw themselves to the ground. Screams erupted from the far end of the town, joined by a chorus of shouts and cries. Even if elf magic hid the town from orc gods, surely a dragon would hear the commotion.

Like when the chariot passed, every nerve screamed at Mai to flee and hide. Live, and she'd have a chance to protect her village. Still, whatever else she thought about the new Cathay and its rules, the people were kind. They'd be ripped to shreds and eaten alive.

She took several deep breaths into her belly. The terror subsided, leaving behind an unease that roiled her stomach. She bent her knees and curled her toes into the ground. The echoes of people shouting coursed through her, threatening to send her into panic again.

If she could be influenced by their fear, perhaps she could settle them with her calm. She raised her voice in a hum, the beat slow and steadfast to counteract the torrential vibrations of terrified heartbeats and frenzied screams.

Like a ripple spreading across a pool, the people around her eased into nervousness. Still, there were too many townsfolk, too much collective fear to calm.

The dragon broke out of its straight path and veered into a circle. With its wings outstretched, it was so huge, easily three times larger than the flaming chariot. It cast a shadow that shrouded the basin in twilight.

It seemed to emit a sound, like a swarm of angry bees, hidden in the swooshes of its wings. It encroached on her own hum, like a river lapping up against its banks. Energy welled up from the ground, coursing through her. Mai's body felt light, like a feather pitching in the wind. Her spirit floated as euphoria took over.

"Stop humming!" a voice called.

Keep humming, her own bones seemed to whisper in her. Mai fixed her gaze on the dragon, who veered in tighter and tighter circles.

Turn! An instinct tugged at her, turning her head.

Doctor Wu was loping over, her arms waving. "Stop humming."

Her heart sunk. To obey the doctor meant an end to the bliss she felt.

Doctor Wu came up, beautiful blue eyes searching her own. "Stop humming."

The light feeling gushed out of her limbs like water spilling from a bucket. The steadfast pulse of the world seemed to rise up and engulf her. Her head felt like the anvil from the forge. Her hum faltered and came to a stuttered halt.

Mai looked up.

High above, the dragon's luminous blue eyes peered right at her.

Her heart lurched to a stop.

Doctor Wu's arms enveloped her, pressing her ear to her chest. The steadfast beating of the woman's heart was soothing. Her slow, deep breaths relaxed her knotted muscles. "Breathe."

Mai took deep breaths, but still couldn't tear her gaze away from the dragon's eyes.

The dragon's body straightened as its head turned away. Its last circle arced wider. With two flaps of its wings, it resumed a straight path, following the dispersing remains of the chariot's smoke trail.

Pulling away from the doctor, Mai let out a long exhale. The warriors picked themselves off the ground and brushed themselves off. Around them, trembling people were catching their breaths.

"That was Avarax," Doctor Wu said, voice cracking. "He's never come this close to Cathay."

Mai shuddered. The Last Dragon, the only one who'd survived the Tivari gods' Dragonpurge. "He found us."

Doctor Wu shook her head. "Impossible. He may be powerful, but elf magic keeps the town unseen and unheard, even from the Last Dragon."

"Why was everyone panicking, then?"

"That's your instinctual reaction to a dragon."

She shivered. "He looked right at me."

"Yes, he sensed you, and you alone. Your voice calls to him." The doctor patted her on the back. "Thank the heavens you have only learned the basics of projecting your voice. If you were any better, he would have surely found you, and the town, too."

Project. Yanyan had said that was part of learning Dragon Songs. Now, it looked like mastering the art carried the risk of attracting the Last Dragon's attention. "How did Yanyan get so good without Avarax finding her?"

"Aralas suspected your voice, and yours alone, calls to his dragonstone."

Mai nodded. Aralas had mentioned dragonstones when they'd visited the bones of Pyarax. "Where is it?"

Doctor Wu gestured toward one of the warriors. "See his tattoo? The Guardian Dragon is chasing a flaming pearl."

Maybe that's what the tattoo looked like, but... "I didn't see a flaming pearl.... Unless the flaming chariot is a pearl?"

Doctor Wu burst out laughing. "No. The tattoo is based on old paintings from the lost Empire of Cathay, which in turn is just a concept. They probably never saw a real dragon."

Mai's mind swam. "If the dragon doesn't chase its dragonstone, where is it?"

Doctor Wu placed a hand over her chest. "Where a heart would be. The dragonstone propels its lifeblood, not with a beat like your heart, but with its vibration. I imagine that someone with your keen hearing could detect it."

Mai's forehead scrunched up. There had been so many sounds when Avarax had circled overhead. The most distinct was the buzzing which had sent jolts of euphoria though her. "Would it sound like bees?"

"It's hard to say." Doctor Wu shrugged. "It probably depends on whatever he is doing, and his mood."

Mai put a hand on her forehead. "I heard a buzzing, like a swarm of angry bees. It made me feel...happy. Silly happy."

Doctor Wu nodded, her expression intense. "That was his dragonstone, then. It responded to your hum, and you, in turn, felt its tug. As powerful as she has become, not even Yanyan can do what you can: if you master the power of Dragon Songs, you, and only you, will be able to bend even the mighty Avarax to your will."

A shiver crawled up her spine. To think that she, a slave girl who no one paid heed to back home, could possibly control such a powerful being.

"Be wary, though. If you fail, he can control you, and all your power, too."

Chapter 15:
Pulse of the World

Mai sat in front of Yanyan's house, listening to the pipa strings vibrate as she restrung and tuned them. The diva had yet to emerge this morning, but had left the instrument and its strings lying on the veranda. The sheet with squiggly lines might as well have been gibberish, but no doubt explained what her first job of the day was.

The pipa's notes came out clear, but failed to soothe her worries. Not even the deep breathing exercises calmed her racing thoughts. She'd jumped at Aralas' offer to teach her Dragon Songs, in hopes of impressing the villagers, and especially Li. Now she risked drawing the attention of a real dragon. A shudder crawled up her spine. She needed to learn the magic to save her family, but she couldn't help them if a dragon ate her first.

"Good morning!" Wenhui's cheery voice called.

Mai looked up from her work. She was so distracted, she hadn't even heard Wenhui's approach. She bowed her head. "Good morning."

Wenhui studied her. "That was scary yesterday. I'd never seen a dragon before."

"Didn't you see the Guardian Dragon when Yanyan woke it?"

Wen shook her head. "That was before I came. Even so, I don't think it would've prepared me for Avarax. I thought for sure he saw us."

Mai nodded. "So did I."

"I wonder what made him stop his circling and fly away."

Perhaps it would be better not to say. Mai looked down at the pipa. "If you have never seen the Guardian Dragon, how do you tattoo it?"

Wenhui shrugged. "I just use the old paintings in the imperial archives as a basis."

If the Guardian Dragon was as fearsome as Avarax, maybe it wouldn't be worth laying eyes on it. Mai shuddered.

"In any case, Yanyan left a message for you." Wenhui pointed at the sheet of paper the strings had been lying on.

Mai nodded. "Yes, to replace the strings she broke."

"Not just that. You are to meet her at the waterfall at the waning mid-crescent."

No wonder the diva hadn't appeared yet. She'd already left. Up to the south, the Iridescent Moon waned well past its second crescent, leaving little time to reach the waterfall. Mai hung her head.

Wen chuckled. "It's all right. Out of all of us, only Master Scribe Xuan could read and write when he first got here. He had to teach us, and even now, less than a quarter of us can."

Which also meant that the diva had left the message here knowing Mai couldn't read it. She gritted her teeth. "Which is the easiest way to the waterfall?"

Wen pointed at the sheet again. "It says to follow your ears, and take the pipa with you."

Of course. With a bob of her head, Mai hurried toward the waterfall's roar. As with all the other sounds, its pattern followed the pulse of the world. By the time she scrambled over boulders to reach the base of the falls, the Iridescent Moon had already waned past mid-crescent.

Yanyan sat at the pool's edge, at the far end across from the waterfall, her back to Mai, a pipa at her side. Her feet kicked in the water, sending up splashes. She didn't even turn, yet her voice carried over the water's roar. "You're late."

Mai bowed, contrite. "I'm sorry. I can't read."

"Speak up. I can barely hear you over the water."

"I'm sorry," Mai shouted.

Yanyan turned and beckoned, and Mai worked her way over the rocks and came to her side. Yanyan gestured to the spot beside her.

Mai sat. Even so close, she had to shout to hear herself over the waters. "Thank you for teaching me."

"Of course, you know it was not my choice." Yanyan's voice came out effortlessly.

How could her voice be so clear, so close to the raging water?

"I heard your hum yesterday, when Avarax appeared." Yanyan shuddered.

The diva hadn't been anywhere nearby. Mai asked, "How did you hear it?"

"The echo of a Dragon Song, even from someone as inexperienced as you, goes out into the world." She tossed a stone into the pool, where a ring rippled out into the waterfall waves. "You tried to influence many people, didn't you?"

Mai hung her head.

"Don't be embarrassed. It is possible, but after you connect to others, you have to learn to project."

Project. Doctor Wu had said projecting any more would've revealed her location to the Last Dragon. Not a good idea. She shook her head and shouted, "The doctor said my voice draws Avarax."

Yanyan turned and favored her with a raised eyebrow. "As much as I would love for you to give up, you can still learn a Dragon Song."

"How?"

"Don't use your voice." Yanyan pointed at the pipa.

Hope welled up in Mai's chest. She could still learn the ability to save her family, without risking a trip down the dragon's gullet. "Please, teach me to project."

"It's not easy. In order to project sound farther, you must hear and borrow the energy around you. You must listen for the most opportune moment. That is why Aralas wants you to practice listening." She pointed at the waterfall. "Go stand behind it. Play your pipa loud enough for me to hear."

Mai stared at the rumbling waters. "That's impossible."

The diva shrugged. "Give up, then. You'll never know if you don't try."

It apparently didn't matter to Yanyan, and she was throwing out any excuse not to teach. Mai lifted her chin. The only harm in trying would be the wound to her self-esteem. Climbing to her feet, she hopped and skipped to the other end of the pool. The silk dress clung to her skin as thickening mist soaked through. It would probably damage the pipa as well. A long flat ridge passed on the other side of the cascade, the sheet of water forming a tunnel.

The Dragon Charmer's Apprentice

Mai peered through the translucent wall.

Yanyan's blurry form rose. "Go ahead, play."

Even at that distance, through the water, it sounded like the diva was right beside her. Keeping her eyes fixed forward, Mai played the Song of Spring.

"You'll have to do better than that."

Mai gritted her teeth and plucked a string as hard as she could. The pipa emitted a disjointed note.

Yanyan burst out laughing.

Humiliation and anger washed over Mai. No telling what shade of red her face was.

The diva covered her mouth. Then, she cradled her pipa and strummed.

The notes danced on the waves, tangible in their clarity. It was as if all the workers on the Great Wall rose up in angry rebellion against the First Emperor of legendary Cathay.

Mai's embarrassment and uncertainties melted. Her spirit wavered, uncertain.

Yanyan snorted. "It is not the strength of the pluck that matters, but the intensity of your emotion. Once you have seized the song's emotion and made it your own, root yourself to the ground, align your spine, and let your heart impel your sound."

Of course, so incredulous she'd been, Mai had totally forgotten all the lessons from the previous days. She dug her toes into the ground, bent her knees, and straightened her spine. Like she'd done yesterday, she imagined Aralas' whimsical smile. Pipa in hand, she plucked out the notes, sending her heart soaring.

"Better," Yanyan said, "but not good enough. Hear me from over here. Only the power of my intent can compel my voice beyond its physical limitations. Hear the waterfall's roar, and let it to lend you its strength. Now, one more time."

Mai closed her eyes and listened to the tumbling waters. The way they spilled off the cliff above, the way they splashed on the rocks beside her, echoed as a rhythm in her ears. Without conscious thought, her fingers danced over the pipa strings, melding with the song of nature. Perhaps her hands created the music, or maybe the music moved her hands. Clear and resonant, the melody filled space and rode out on the sound of the waterfall.

It sure sounded like her song projected. She looked up.

It was hard to tell through the water what the diva was doing across the pool, but it looked like a nod.

In that moment, Mai's heart raced. The light feeling of euphoria must've been how a fledgling bird felt when taking flight for the first time. She'd done it. Really done it.

"Don't congratulate yourself too soon," Yanyan said, the sneer carrying in her voice.

Mai stifled her snort. Leave it to the diva to diminish any accomplishment besides her own.

"Oh? You think you've accomplished anything more than a simple trick? This time, the waterfall helped carry your song." Yanyan's hands swept across her instrument's strings.

The song came out so clearly, even from the other side of the wall of water. Not only that, the strings of the pipa cradled in Mai's arms resonated, answering Yanyan's call with a harmonic refrain.

Mai's breath quickened. Was that doubt creeping into her heart? Maybe, but she'd already done the impossible.

"Now, switch places, and let's see if I can even hear you."

With a deep breath, Mai vanquished her uncertainties. Right now, the way she felt, she could do anything. She emerged from the waterfall.

The diva's lips quirked at an interesting angle. Her expression was no easier to read, even without the wall of water between them. She beckoned.

Mai climbed over the rocks as Yanyan approached. At the halfway mark, Yanyan lifted her chin and turned her head as they passed each other.

Such a diva! Doctor Wu was right. Well, two could play at that, and Yanyan couldn't very well refuse to teach her, since Aralas had commanded her to do so. Mai didn't deign to look back until she reached the opposite end of the pool.

She turned around.

Yanyan hadn't reached the waterfall yet. No, she was…

If Mai could gape any wider, her chin might drop to the ground.

The diva was now hanging her gown from a small tree, whose branches hung by the side of the pool. She now wore nothing more than what she was born with.

No words in Mai's vocabulary could describe the magnificence.

Back home, the women would bathe every several days in the river pools. Lanky with sun-leathered skin, none could begin to compare with Yanyan's smooth, white flesh and shapely figure. No wonder Aralas fancied her, since it certainly couldn't be her sparkling personality that won him over.

Mai tightened the drenched dress on her stick form. With physical perfection before her eyes, she'd never felt so plain.

Yanyan looked over her shoulder, exposing enough of her lip to reveal a crooked smirk. She crossed one leg in front of the other, embellishing her rounded hips. "If you weren't so self-conscious, you wouldn't be soaking wet."

Mai's lips pursed of their own accord. Maybe the diva had stripped to keep from drenching her gown, or maybe it was just to flaunt how much better she was in every way.

Not for long.

Her fingers itched to play, to prove herself. Aralas had said she had even more potential than Yanyan, after all. She bent her knees and dug her toes into the ground. Straightening her spine, she listened to the sound of the water tumbling onto the rocks. There it was, the pulse of the earth, waiting there for her to follow. She strummed across the strings.

The sound came out clear and strong.

From the other side of the falls, where Yanyan was little more than a shadow, she said, "I can hear your anger, but I cannot feel it. Again."

At least the diva had heard it. Mai listened for more sounds. The birds chirping, the wind in the tree branches. All followed their own beats, yet still mingled with the waterfall. She plucked out the Song of Spring again.

"Almost, but not quite," Yanyan said, her voice as loud as if she were standing right beside her. "You need to fill the space between the beats, like..."

A fish splashed.

"...a fish. When the carp swims against the current, it doesn't charge head-on. Now, whether it is your anger, or jealousy, or embarrassment, seize it. Listen for the right moment, and play."

Mai's stomach clenched. The diva was mocking her! So be it. Holding the stance, listening for the beat, she played the song again.

"You are progressing well," Aralas said.

Mai's heart just about leaped into her throat. She turned.

The elf angel was lowering the hood of his cloak. He shook out his lustrous hair, which fell into perfect lines over his shoulders.

Heart settling back in her chest, Mai gazed at him. It had only been a day, yet it seemed like forever since she'd last seen him. "Were you here the whole time?"

Lifting her chin with a finger, he shook his head. "I was waiting to hear your song from afar." When he spoke, it was again slightly higher in pitch than when she'd first met him. Maybe his voice in her head was a little deeper?

"How far is afar?"

"I have been teaching others." He pointed. "To the south, where bronze-skinned warriors can fight faster than your eye can see. In the deep south, where sorceresses can warp reality. And to the East, where real priests have embraced the True Gods to evoke their righteous anger and healing compassion."

Just the idea that there were different types of people and magic made Mai's head spin.

"You have made progress." His smile was so radiant.

Her stomach fluttered like a swarm of butterflies. She might never be as beautiful as Yanyan, but she would make herself worthy with Dragon Songs. So worthy that Aralas would look at her the same way he looked at the diva. "You came here just to tell me that?"

He laughed. "No. I promised Yanyan I would visit her when you reached a certain level."

Her heart sunk as she watched him saunter over the rocks toward the falls. Unlike Yanyan, he didn't bother to disrobe, and his form remained hidden by his cloak.

Before he turned into the space behind the waterfall, he looked back at her. If he was trying to suppress a giddy grin, it wasn't working. "Keep practicing. Put a candle behind the waterfall and try to put it out with your music."

His voice was so encouraging, so hypnotic. The way his eyes locked on hers turned her spine to jelly. Genderless or not, he was mesmerizingly handsome. She started to follow him.

He held up a hand. "Just not now."

He disappeared behind the wall of water to join Yanyan, his cloak slipping off behind him.

Chapter 16:
Strange Bedfellows

The waters tumbled down the falls, the roar setting the rhythm for the blue and white moonslight dancing in the pool. Mai sat at the opposite end, strumming pipa strings to harmonize with the sparkles in the ripples. A week had passed since Aralas had challenged her to snuff out a candle on the other side of the waterfall, and she'd come back every night to practice.

It was hard to tell whether it was her music or the occasional breezes which caused the flame to flicker. Or perhaps her plucking had caused the breezes. In any case, she'd yet to succeed.

Perhaps because it was so hard to concentrate. Now, as with every waking hour—and some sleeping hours as well— all she could think about was Aralas. The look he'd flashed when she'd made a breakthrough in projecting sound burned in her mind's eye. It had to have a deeper meaning, especially the way he smiled.

But no, he'd summarily dismissed her before disappearing behind the waterfall with a naked Yanyan.

Footsteps approached from behind. Too light to be a man, too heavy to be a child. Hesitant.

"Are...are you going to eat?" Wenhui called.

Mai turned around.

The tattooist stood at the tree line, a tentative foot pawing at the grass. She sheepishly held up a rice bowl.

"Oh, hi." Mai beckoned her over.

Wenhui approached like a timid rabbit, looking much like her murdered best friend had.

Mai's stomach twisted. Poor Ying. All the villagers might share her fate if Mai didn't make a breakthrough soon. Still, it didn't explain why the usually bold Wenhui was so nervous. "What's wrong?"

Wenhui straightened. "I think, I think your magic is growing stronger. Your music made me feel so...uncertain."

Mai looked down at the pipa. Her feelings for Aralas must've found their way into her song. Even if the candlelight remained unaffected, perhaps she could now influence another person. She set the instrument down, and gestured at the spot beside her.

In three quick steps, Wenhui joined her. She placed the warm rice bowl into her hands.

Even after these weeks in Cathay, the beauty and delicateness of the ceramics compared to the wood and crude pottery back home never ceased to amaze her. Staring at the flame behind the cascade, Mai picked at the food.

Wenhui leaned into her field of vision and met her gaze. "Why is there so much uncertainty in your music? Are you having second thoughts about learning?"

"It's not that." Mai shook her head. Of course not. Not with Mother and Father's lives at stake. It had to be Aralas getting into her head. How much should she say, especially if she wasn't sure how she felt herself? How could she be so attracted to a genderless elf angel?

Wenhui leaned back and kicked her feet in the water. "My first paintings evoked uncertainty, too."

"Because you were unsure of the power?"

"That, and, well..." Wenhui's lips twitched.

The smile was strange enough that Mai, still chewing rice, leaned over to see.

The tattooist's pretty features were contorted into something of a smirk.

Mai's brow scrunched up. "What is it?"

"Aralas was teaching me. He'd lean in over my shoulder, and his breath would tickle my ear. Sometimes, he'd press against me." Wenhui shivered.

Some of the young men back home would get too close to the other girls, but never Mai. Still, the idea of it sent a shudder down her spine. Who would've thought an elf angel, a messenger of supposedly good and moral gods, would be so rude? "It must have been so uncomfortable."

If Wenhui's head shook any faster, she might send her hairpins flying. "Heavens, no. He was so... handsome. I couldn't believe he would take such interest in me. Especially since he and Yanyan have been lovers for as long as I've been here."

Yanyan again. Mai's lips pursed.

Wen shrugged. "In any case, whenever he was with me, he gave me so much encouragement. I felt like I could do anything."

Mai nodded. It made sense. Years in the village, and nobody had paid much attention to her. Here, someone so handsome had taken interest in her.

"My art progressed in leaps and bounds. Then, one day, he was looking over my shoulder as I drew. The next thing I knew, he was kissing my neck." Wenhui blew out a long sigh. So much nostalgia hung in her breath. "Later, he was kissing elsewhere. And then..."

Waiting for Wenhui to finish her sentence, Mai held a bated breath. Her butt had slid to the edge of the stone, and she might've fallen into the pool if she hadn't caught herself. She looked over.

Wenhui's smile was so radiant, so much like Ying's. It was also clear she wouldn't finish her story without a little prodding.

"Did you...?" It would explain why she'd made such an amazing drawing of him.

Wenhui's face flushed red, even in the blue moonlight. "Not really."

"Not really?" How could that even be an answer? It either happened, or it didn't. Unless his lack of man parts made it impossible.

Wen giggled. "Let's just say, we did more than kiss."

That could mean anything. Mai snorted. "So what ever happened between you?"

Wen sighed. "I thought I could wrest him away from Yanyan."

"What is it about her?"

"Her voice. He loves her voice."

Just like his own voice made him so irresistible. "Then why does he stray?"

"It turns out, he gets easily infatuated with those of us who can use magic. The painters, the calligraphers, the embroiderers. Even Kang."

The homely painter with the wild hair she'd seen the first day! Mai shuddered. All the signals Aralas had been sending, even if she'd interpreted them correctly, were nothing special. To him, she must be just another conquest. It didn't even matter that she was a woman.

"Whoever he's with, it's just a passing fancy. In the end, he always goes back to her. Now, a couple of years later, my brief time with him is just a fond memory." Wenhui climbed to her feet and took the bowl from Mai's hands. "Don't think I regret it. Not all things are meant to last, but that doesn't mean they don't have value."

Mai nodded. Memories, good and bad, did have value.

Wenhui waved. "Don't stay out too late."

Waving with one hand, Mai retrieved the pipa. When the tattooist disappeared into the woods, she let out a long exhale. Aralas' feelings were nothing more than infatuation, if they were even that.

Her sigh mingled with all the other sounds…except in an empty spot on top of a boulder. She stared at it.

"I thought she'd never leave." Aralas materialized as he pulled down his hood.

Mai glared at the playboy, covered as always by his cloak. There was something different about him; a sadness in his eyes much like the first time they'd met, and then when he brought her to Cathay. "How long were you there?"

"Long enough." Aralas shrugged. His voice sounded just a little deeper, exactly the same pitch as when they'd first met, until the day he brought her to Cathay.

It was soothing, making it hard to be angry at him for eavesdropping. "Is it true?"

"I can neither confirm nor deny what I may or may not have heard." Whether he was counting on his fingers or studying his fingerprints, he was undeniably grinning.

"Really? Kang?" She raised an eyebrow. Even with his lack of man parts, Aralas said he was male. The Tivari expressly forbid men lying with men, or women with women. Perhaps the True Gods didn't care.

"Does it matter?" He jumped off the boulder, the cloak flaring out and revealing the elf angel's slim body for a split-second before he landed without a sound. As always, his hair flopped into his face.

"I just want to understand. Why would you ever be attracted to us?"

He blew his hair out of his eyes. In long strides, he approached. "Human lives are so short, like the blossoms on a cherry tree. The ephemeral nature of your beauty makes it all the more precious." Now close, he brushed her hair behind her ear.

The touch sent a shiver up her spine. Still, whatever ephema-something meant, it didn't explain the elf angel's tastes. Her lips quirked into a frown.

He held up a hand. "You know, elves were not always beautiful. We were once hideous and almost blind."

Mai shook her head. That couldn't be possible. The few elf teachers in town were stunning, though none could compare to Aralas.

"It's true. Listen to my story, and let it guide your music." He was right next to her now, and pointed to the pipa in her hands. "Have you extinguished the flame yet?"

She shook her head. "Almost. I can make it flicker."

"Play." He blew strands of golden hair out of his face with a puff of air.

"What do you want to hear?"

"Whatever you want." His eyes bored into her. "Whatever in my story stirs your heart's desires."

Even if her mind screamed warnings, her heart knew what it desired. Gazing at him, she strummed. Her fingers pressed on the frets, drawing out a song perfect for this night.

"In the beginning, the luminous, ageless Koralas dueled with Tivar. Koralas prevailed, but Tivar's poisoned knife cut him." Aralas slashed a finger across his forearm. "We sprang forth where his blood touched the earth, yet we were tainted by Tivar's venom."

As he spoke, the rhythm of his voice made Mai's hands seem to play of their own accord. Notes clashed with one another in quick strums.

Aralas grinned. "Koralas shined so bright, he never saw our repugnant forms down below. Yet every morning, he heard our voices, singing his praise."

Was it the tone of his voice which guided her? The music had turned jubilant, like the elf songs must have been, singing in awe of the gods.

"He allowed his bright white light to fade to soft yellow. Then he saw his creations, physically corrupted by his archenemy." He pointed to the Blue Moon. "He sang a song so sad, his consort, Araya, wept. We drank her tears, which cleansed the taint from our blood. We grew tall and beautiful, recreated in the image of Koralas and Ayara as we were intended."

Her music reached crescendo as he spoke. With him, she could do anything.

He was right up against her back now. Her body tingled.

Aralas whispered in her ear. "Not only that, we could now see in so many shades of colors, we could appreciate the beauty in everything. To us, humans are unique, exotic. Your short lives make your beauty all priceless."

His voice rolled over her. Heat blossomed in her. Heart racing, she turned her head toward his and leaned back into him.

He backed away.

She gasped. Her fingers swept across the pipa strings, emitting a melodious chord before she shot a hand out to catch herself. The Turtle's Egg! She turned and glared at him.

He flashed a mischievous grin.

All the fire inside her fizzled out. Her lips pinched. "What's so funny?"

He pointed to the waterfall. "You extinguished the flame."

Just like he'd snuffed out her rising passion. How mortifying. She looked back at the cascade. Behind it was only darkness.

"Calm. Listen. Project. Harmonize. You've been putting the power of Dragon Songs together, but needed to take this last step: to do, without trying."

Had his overtures all been part of a lesson? Mai's shoulders slumped. She was nothing special, just another human in a long line of humans. Unlike Wenhui, and even Kang, she didn't even warrant affection beyond what it took to teach.

He gestured toward the Iridescent Moon, now waxing to half-crescent. "I must be going."

"To see Yanyan?" The jealousy in Mai's tone surprised her.

With a word, he disappeared.

Chapter 17:
Echoes

An early autumn breeze sent ceremonial bells chiming from within the palace as Mai walked outside the walls. Borrowing their resonant ring, she hummed. Over a month had passed since she'd first started learning to project the power of Dragon Songs, and three weeks since the last time she'd seen Aralas, by the waterfall. Though she'd improved with constant practice, she had yet to master the fundamentals.

At least, that was the assessment of Yanyan, who reveled in minimizing Mai's every accomplishment. As demoralizing as it was, Mai worked all the harder to listen, connect, and project. Now, she approached the palace's main gates, to practice on instruments in the Hall of Harmony.

Standing guard, Ku nodded at her. Despite Mai's initial impressions, Wenhui didn't like her village-mate as much as he adored her, and the tattoo artist tried time and time again to match Mai with him.

Mai bobbed her head as she entered the palace grounds. Ku wasn't a bad-looking young man, but her own heart...well, she couldn't even remember what Li looked like. Every time she tried to imagine his face, Aralas' beautiful elf features appeared in her mind. The memory of his voice sent her heart aflutter. Even if their last encounter had ended with his rejection, all she could think about was him. It was like he and music were intertwined in her head.

Unlike the rest of the town, the palace's grounds were paved in white stone, which sparkled in the sunlight. Straight ahead, across the broad courtyard, the red-tiled roofs of the main hall rose taller than any structure Mai had ever seen, besides the pyramid. From what Wenhui had said, the emperor held audience with his ministers and generals there, but she had never seen him.

Soon.

The full Harvest Moon was just a few weeks away, and then the entire town would gather in the courtyard and hear the Son of Heaven speak from the deck of the main hall. Mai's eyes strayed to the right side of the deck.

That's where she'd be that night, playing a drum duet with Yanyan.

Her stomach twisted into a knot. The rice harvest would be done by then. Cleric Pyuz would undoubtedly punish her family for her disappearance once he didn't need their hands for working the fields.

Just a few weeks to save her family, and she had yet to learn any Dragon Song that could defeat him.

She let out a sigh and turned toward the Hall of Harmony. The rack of progressively larger bells outside the double doors caught the breeze again, their clear ringing settling her heart. A guard opened the doors for her.

Though she'd visited many times to practice, the size of the interior still never ceased to amaze her. The cavernous hall was larger even than the Census Ministry. Dozens of instruments lined the walls, including a two-stringed *erhu*, a magnificent twenty-one stringed *guzheng*, several flutes, and a pipa. She'd practiced all of them at one time or another, and lost herself in the different yet similar sounds they made. There was a logic to them, an order that seemed to be lacking in affairs of the heart.

Affairs of the heart... She shook out thoughts of Aralas again, specifically the memory of Aralas disappearing behind the waterfall with naked Yanyan. He was supposedly off teaching other races of humans now.

Mai came to the set of three drums in the middle of the room. The largest, which must've been four times as big around as her waist, rested on its side on a stand. Two other drums flanked it to either side. Rumor had it that all three had been carved from a single trunk of elf wood, and their silvery-white striking surface came from when the Guardian Dragon shed its skin in an elaborate dance, while Yanyan sang to it.

Mai snorted. On the night of the emperor's audience, she was to perform a drum duet with the Dragon Charmer, yet the diva had yet to practice with her. In fact, she hadn't appeared in days.

She picked up a pair of drumsticks hanging from the drum stand. Closing her eyes, she found the pulse of the world in her ears. She aligned her spine and pounded out the rhythm of the planned duet onto the center drum.

With a quick turn, she faced the lower drum and rapped out more beats. Faster and faster she drummed, sending her spirit soaring. There was an order to music, a beautiful logic, which propelled her twisting and turning, in and among the three drums. It was as if her body moved of its own volition, carried by the push and pull of the sound. Perhaps she looked plain and awkward compared to Yanyan, but now, music made her feel beautiful. The drumbeats spread through the hall, filling every corner.

Almost every corner.

Just like when she hummed among the dragon bones, there was something else in the room. Something which the sound wrapped around.

Human-shaped.

Maintaining her dance through the drums, she turned her head toward the interloper.

Nothing was there; at least, nothing her eyes could detect.

Her ears, however, sensed the empty space not far from the corner, which now moved. It was circling in stuttering steps, moving in between the beats, but breathing with them. It was trying to hide its position from her. If not for the lesson in projecting sound between the waves of sound from the waterfall, she might never have realized it was there.

It danced with her now, circling step-for-step on the opposite side of the center drum. When she rotated right, it spun left. When she rounded the center, it mirrored her on the other side. With its breathing pattern, let alone the invisibility, it could only be Aralas.

As they danced through the drums, they seemed to be made for one another, his Yang to her Yin, a perfect whole. While she oftentimes got lost in her music, it now seemed his energy was guiding her. Or perhaps, her energy was guiding him. It seemed impossible, but they moved with each other in perfect harmony. It felt so...right.

How long it went on, it was hard to tell. She should've been drained, but instead, her body moved effortlessly, with a vitality she'd never felt before.

Still, as much as she wanted it, as right as it felt, the bliss didn't belong to her. It should've been the diva dancing with her lover among the drums. She sighed. Instead of circling the center drum in the set pattern, she struck the center drum one last time and stopped the song halfway through a verse.

Aralas, still unseen, careened into her. They fell toward the hard wood floor.

He spoke a guttural syllable.

Their descent slowed like a floating bird feather. Though invisible, his lithe form landed on top of her. He was so light, more like a child than a man.

It was so wrong. She started to sit up.

Soft lips nuzzled into her neck, pushing her back down.

A shiver ran up her spine, even as heat flared inside her. If only she could see him! She closed her eyes and sucked in a sharp breath as her back arched of its own accord. She brought one hand to the back of his head, while her other hand pressed into his back. The fabric of his cloak felt smooth and cool.

One of his hands pillowed the back of her head, while the other brushed down from her waist to her thigh. He lavished kisses up her neck, to her ear. Fire raged inside, unlike anything she'd ever felt before, even when Li had kissed her. Not even at the waterfall, when he'd come so close. If only—

His mouth claimed hers. His tongue slid across her lower lip, probing, seeking entry. With a gasp, she parted her lips, inviting him in. The nudges and prods on her tongue, slipped inside her lip, across the roof of her mouth, all followed a rhythm, echoing the pulse of the world. Energy jolted up and down her body. Her fingers acted on their own, digging into his back.

The hand on her leg ventured back up. It loosened her lapels and slipped between the silk folds. Smooth and hot, it rested on her bare breast. A finger traced a lazy circle around her nipple, making her insides clench. A primal gasp escaped her lips.

She tried to bend her knee, to bring him closer, but his weight on the dress constrained her. She needed to have him up against her. Wiggling a little, she loosened her skirts. With the increased space, she bent her knees and tilted her hips into him. She brought her hands to his firm butt and pressed him closer.

Just as she'd felt when Li had pinned her to the boulder, a firm bulge pressed against her. Maybe she'd been mistaken about Aralas being genderless! Maybe divine beings were like ducks, who kept their parts tucked inside their bodies until ready to use.

What a silly thought in this moment! It didn't matter. Who cared how an elf angel was equipped, as long as he could make her feel this way. She moaned again.

The doors swung open.

The weight lifted off her.

Pulling the lapels of her robe together, Mai propped herself up on an elbow and turned to the entrance.

Ku rushed in, sword flashing in his hand. "Are you all right?"

"I…" what could she say?

"Your face. It's so red."

If the heat in her head was any indication, she must've been glowing bright enough to light up the hall. She brushed the sweat from her brow. "Yes, I'm all right."

Ku sheathed his sword. "The sound of your drumming filled the palace grounds. It sounded like there were two of you in here." He peered around.

She closed her eyes and listened. Nothing. If Aralas was around, he was holding his breath.

"But then, the music stopped so suddenly. Then, you cried out. I thought you'd hurt yourself...but it looks like...like." His eyes strayed to the drumsticks. Red tinged his cheeks.

Certainly no redder than hers must be. No telling what he must be thinking. She tightened the dress lapels tighter and stood up. "I just slipped, but I'm quite all right."

His gaze raked across the hall one more time before he bobbed his head and backed out. "All right then. I'll leave you to your...practice."

The last of her arousal drained away. She climbed to her feet.

When Ku closed the doors, she looked around. "Show yourself."

No answer.

She closed her eyes and listened.

Nothing.

Not even his breathing, not even the near-imperceptible sound of his music.

Still, it felt like he was still there. Borrowing the pulse of the world, she hummed different notes, even if it would attract Avarax. The sounds projected and resonated in the stringed instruments and bells, filling the room with sound.

She turned to the hole in the sound.

"Good," his disembodied voice said, deep and hoarse. "You have mastered the *Seeing Ears* technique, so much that you can hear through my own cloaking magic."

Heat rushed to her head. "Is that all you can say? What about what just happened?" She gestured to the spot where they just been lying entwined with each other.

He materialized, his hood coming off and revealing the beautiful golden hair she'd fingered into tangles. When he blew it out of his face, his cheeks were flushed. "I was lost in the moment."

"Turtle's Egg. You can't just keep taunting me like this." Her aching face muscles wouldn't allow her to frown any more.

His foot came out from the folds of the cloak and drew circles on the floor. "I can't help it. When I teach you magic, I give you a part of me. When you make that magic your own, you, in a sense, own a part of me."

Her forehead scrunched up. Whatever he was saying made sense, in a twisted kind of way.

Opening the fold of his cloak, he took her hand and placed it in the center of his chest. Through the cool fabric and his softened chest muscles, a light pulse beat against her palm. "Remember at the dragon bones when we were hiding from the orcs? You couldn't hear my heart. You almost can now. When you do…no, that's why I had Yanyan take responsibility for instructing you."

She yanked her hand away. "I don't want you."

Brushing her hair behind her ear, he sighed. "Yes, you do. The same way that, when we danced, I wanted you. It is always that way—a raging fire in the heart that demands union. When two souls intertwine so completely, it the only outcome. I can't control it. You must understand. This is the power of Dragon Magic. It takes my every last drop of control to keep from tearing your clothes from you."

She snorted. No one had said learning Dragon Songs would make her another one of the elf angel's playthings. "Go back to Yanyan. That's what you always do."

His head drooped. "It has nothing to do with her. And she is not here, anyway."

Her face slackened. "What? Where is she?"

"She is on a quest, vital to success of the rebellion."

"And you aren't with her?"

He shook his head. "Even if I was not needed elsewhere, I cannot help her. Just like you, and only you, can affect the mighty Avarax; Yanyan, and only Yanyan, can succeed at this task."

201

The dragon's name sent a shudder through her. "When will she be back?"

He shrugged. "When she has accomplished her goal."

So flippant. She searched his eyes.

"You, too, have a mission. It will test and hone your skills, and prepare you to save your family, and Li."

Mai's heart twisted. What had Aralas said that night they left? Maybe her desires would change? The Turtle's Egg! Why did her desire have to be him? And even if he couldn't be hers, Li would never seem the same. Not after she'd seen so much. Still, "Is Li still all right? And my family?"

Aralas nodded. "I have kept an eye on them, and for now, Cleric Pyuz only works them hard."

All because of her. It felt as if the anvil from the dwarf forge was sitting on her shoulders.

"Come, let me introduce you to some friends."

Chapter 18:

Newcomers

Following Aralas out of the palace, Mai heard the townsfolk's murmurs. The chatter grew louder and louder, mingling with shouts, suggesting he was leading her to the cause of the commotion. Crowds of people had gathered around the training grounds. Even with their backs to the elf angel, the people parted for him.

In the middle of the smooth gravel, a young woman dueled with three warriors, including Ku. Judging by the number of men sprawled across the field, moaning and clutching wounded body parts, there had been a few more when it started. She moved like a blur, dodging incoming stabs and chops like a dragonfly buzzing among rice stalks. With two hands, she held a strangely-shaped sword—made of silvery metal, the tip was wider than near the hilt, and it had no guard—yet she never used it to parry or strike.

Instead, she shoulder-butted her opponents to the ground as if they were the village children trying to tackle Li. The ripples in the pulse of the world scattered, though in a clear pattern. In a few short seconds, she stood alone, untouched, unbeaten.

Mai could only gawk. Not just because of the impossible speed and skill with which the woman fought, but also her appearance. While her shiny black hair would make her indistinguishable from anyone else, her skin was light brown, like the rice fields after harvest, or perhaps bronze. Though her eye color was the same as everyone else, their shape was rounder, and her features were less angular. With the high collar, her smooth blue dress matched the style Aralas had worn when he bade Yanyan to teach Mai.

While Mai held back at the front row of spectators, Aralas entered the ring. When he brushed the woman's hair over her ear, her serious expression melted. Her eyelids fluttered, and she gazed at him with adoring eyes.

Mai's stomach twisted.

He whispered something in the newcomer's ear and pointed at Mai. The woman's piercing regard met hers. She strode over, pressed her palms together and bowed her head. When she spoke, her words came out as gibberish.

Mai offered a tentative bob of her head and then, eyebrow raised, looked from her to Aralas.

With a laugh, he came over. He held up a small black pebble on his index finger. "This magic bauble will help you understand Vanya." Before she could protest, he placed it into the divot in her ear.

Vanya pressed her palms together again. She bowed her head, revealing the same black pebble affixed to her ear. "Greetings. You must be Yanyan. Our people have heard of you."

Of course everyone had heard of the Dragon Charmer. Mai shook her head. "No, I'm Mai."

"What the hell?" Vanya's respectful posture relaxed. She looked at Aralas, her head bobbling up and down, side to side, in an interesting rhythm.

Eyes shifting to Mai, he shuddered. "I need to protect your virgin ears from Vanya's foul mouth." He plucked the pebble from her ear and whispered into it. The name *Aralas* stood out from all the other gibberish. With a grin, he pressed it back onto her ear.

Vanya was scowling. "You said she sings Dragon Songs. If not her, then who the hill is going to teach me?"

Mai's gaze swept between the two. Teach the warrior? Apparently evoking magic through music wasn't so rare, after all.

Hair hanging in his face, Aralas laughed. "No, Yanyan isn't here right now. I have another teacher in mind for you, Mai, and Makeda." He lifted his chin to the right.

Mai followed his gesture. If Vanya looked different, the young woman standing in the crowd of people looked even more so. A boy touched her skin, as dark and rich as fertile loam, while an old woman on the other side ran a hand through black hair as coarse as rice chaff. Even in the early autumn heat, Makeda's clothes exposed so much of her, there was no way she could be hot. A blue crystal hung from her neck. She disengaged from her curious admirers and walked over.

The same black pebble shone in her ear. She clasped Mai's hands. "Greetings, I am Makeda. I trust your family is healthy?"

A pit formed in Mai's stomach. Her family. Surely Cleric Pyuz hadn't executed them yet, but he could make their lives unbearable. "I don't know. I haven't seen them in a month."

A look of understanding bloomed on Makeda's face. "Yes, I have not seen my parents for years."

"Did your village priest punish them?"

Releasing her hands, Makeda shook her head. "The Tivari thought I had died. Unfortunately, my parents thought so, too."

Mai chewed on her lower lip. What must her parents think? Li had been the last to see her, by the boulder. Maybe they thought she'd been taken by Ying's ghost. Maybe Cleric Pyuz believed the same.

Aralas cleared his throat. "Well, now that we have made introductions, follow me while I explain your quest."

Again, the bystanders all made way as he walked through them. Vanya and Makeda hung on his heels, chattering among themselves like old friends. Or perhaps rivals in love, the way they jostled to get closer to the elf angel.

Mai hurried after them, thinking. With the exception of Painter Kang, everyone who could use magic seemed to be female. The seamstresses who embroidered the palace guards' robes, Wenhui, Yanyan, now these two…all women. She cleared her throat. "What makes Kang so special that you decided to teach him?"

Aralas looked over his shoulder. "He had the talent."

"But why didn't you choose any other men?" she asked, as the hammering from the forge grew louder.

"Not many men have a knack for magic." He gestured to the craftsmen working in their shops. "Magic knits into the fiber of your very being. In this, women have something extra."

Makeda turned to her and clasped the crystal around her neck. "Almost every woman of my people could learn sorcery, but to hide it from the Tivari, we have only been able to sneak into villages at night and teach simple spells."

"Us, too," Vanya said. "Although some men have shown talent in Dragon Fighting, the women seem to be better."

Mai nodded. Apparently, it was not just about the elf angel's own taste in humans which determined who could and couldn't learn magic.

"Here we are." Aralas bowed to the dwarf, Master Blackhammer, at the forge.

The weaponsmith grinned at Vanya. "How's your *naga*? Does she feel like an extension of your arm?"

Mai suppressed a gasp. Whereas the dwarf had spoken with a thick accent before, now his words sounded perfect in her ears. She ran a finger over the black pebble there. Indeed, the movement of the dwarf's lips, or at least, what was visible beneath his thick beard, didn't seem to correlate with the words she heard.

Vanya patted the weapon at her side. "It is perfect."

"Perfect for now. One day soon, you will earn your true weapon." Aralas cleared his throat. "Have you finished what I commissioned?"

"Yes," Master Blackhammer said. He went to the back of the building, then returned with a scabbarded sword. "Here it is, my lord."

Mai's gaze swept from tip to hilt. It had to be longer than her leg. Gauging from the size compared to the other blades the local warriors used, it must've been the one she sang to on her first day in town.

"*Tamskelti*, the Ice Reaver." Master Blackhammer pulled it from its scabbard with several tugs and proffered it in two hands. Then he winked at her. "Enchanted with the help of Miss Mai."

"It resonates with the universe." Makeda stared with wide eyes. She lifted a crystal hanging from her neck, which gave off a faint blue glow.

Head bobbling, Vanya blew out a breath. "Is this the weapon you promised me?"

"No, you will earn that blade yourself. This one…" Receiving it with a dip of his chin, Aralas hefted the blade. He backed into the street, and the people who had gathered round made way. With two hands, he swept the weapon in wide circles. The *swoosh* sent ripples through the pulse of the world, singing a song reminiscent of the dwarven marching tune from that first day. He then turned to the weaponsmith and nodded. "It has perfect balance."

"I can feel its vibrations," Vanya said.

"Yes." Master Blackhammer grinned. "It is a weapon fit for a king."

Aralas tossed the blade, sending it hilt over tip through the air. It arced right into the dwarf's outstretched scabbard.

The elf angel never ceased to be amazing. Mai closed her gaping mouth. "Will you wield it against the Tivari?"

With a grin, he shook his head. "No. This is the mission I am entrusting to you. You three, along with several guards, will deliver *Tamskelti* to the leader of the rebellion in the North so that he might use it against the orcs."

Mai searched his eyes. Maybe this was the mission which would prepare her to save her family.

He beckoned to Ku, who must've been there for quite a while. "Ku will guide you to the meeting point. While you are there, their king's consort, Regina, will teach the three of you how to bend someone to your will."

"A charm spell?" Makeda's expression brightened.

"Or a Fairy's Song." Aralas lifted his chin toward Mai, before shifting to Vanya. "Or a *bahaduur* Command. Call it what you will, the effect is the same, even if the way you evoke it varies, based on whether you are singing a Dragon Song or casting Shallow Magic."

Mai's head spun. Apparently, different forms of magic shared similar roots. And she would soon be learning something useful.

His eyes locked on hers. "Just remember, you can use an instrument, but don't use your own voice. Avarax is always listening."

Chapter 19:
Hunting Dog's Teeth

L eaves crunched under Mai's feet as their ragtag party made their way through the mountains, toward the meeting to deliver the sword to the Northerners. Up sharp paths, down twisting trails, Ku had led them and several warriors along the western ridge of Cathayi lands for a week already. According to him, Tivari priests usually stayed in the fertile lowlands, making the wooded mountains safe for travel. Still, ponchos of mottled green and brown helped conceal them from the valley below, where the maturing rice plants cast the fields in yellow-brown.

Now, from their high vantage point, the several villages seemed like bumpy spots in the swaying sea of rice stalks, looking like the dozens upon dozens they'd already passed. One of these could've been mistaken for her own village, with mud-and-stick walls and thatched roofs.

JC Kang

A lump formed in Mai's throat. The week they'd spent in the mountains was a week not learning the magic to save her friends and family. They were undoubtedly harvesting the rice, and preparing bales to sacrifice to the Tivari Gods. They only had another month or so before the flaming chariots descended on the pyramids. Then, when there was no need for field hands, Mother, Father, and Ling would become expendable.

Makeda placed a hand on her shoulder. "Homesick?" The dark-skinned sorceress, an Aksumi in her own language, had proven warmer than the Ayuri, Vanya.

Mai nodded. "If I hadn't met Aralas, I would now be in a village just like this, breaking my back over the harvest."

"So would I." Makeda's eyes roved over the valley. "This doesn't look too different from my homeland."

Mai looked over her shoulder to Ku and his comrades, who'd all been rice farmers before they'd been freed. "Do your people grow rice, too?"

"Some, but compared to the type you grow, it is longer and tougher. We grow mostly wheat." She took Mai's hands and studied them. "It's been so long since I've worked the land, I forgot what a callous felt like."

Mai's face flushed. Maybe her hands would never be smooth like Yanyan's. "Where are you learning your magic?"

"Not far from your Cathayi town, on the other side of the elf kingdom."

212

"Is that near your homeland?"

She shook her head. "Aksumiland is far, far away. However, there are no sanctuaries from the Tivari there..."

Mai tapped her pebble. It might translate whatever language Makeda or Vanya spoke, but didn't make her own language any easier. Whatever sanctuary meant...

"...so they brought several Aksumi sorceresses to live in Ankira."

"Ankira?"

"Where Vanya's people live—at least, the free ones—at the edge of the elf kingdom's protective cloak."

Wen had mentioned the spell which hid Cathay from the Tivari...and from recent experience, the Last Dragon, as well. "How does it work?" Mai asked.

Makeda pointed to the Iridescent Moon, now waning to mid-crescent, barely visible between the trees. "Did you know, the Iridescent Moon did not appear until after the Tivari conquered the world?"

It made sense, given that the Iridescent Moon never came up in the ancient Cathayi songs that spoke of brighter days. Mai shook her head.

Makeda's expression brightened. If someone spoke with the same enthusiasm, describing how rice stalks grew could sound interesting. "It is the manifestation of Riyalas, the elf God of Magic. The elves were close to extinction when he appeared and strengthened their magic. With that, they were able to create the cloak."

"What does it do?"

Makeda waved her hand in a long arc above her head. "It blocks all sound, and if you're on the outside, you can't see it. If you try to enter, save for at specific points, you'll just find yourself somewhere else."

Like the time she got lost in the forest. Mai nodded. "Are we still protected here?"

"No! We're out in the open." Lip curling, Makeda pulled at her poncho. "So ugly, and hot."

Mai stifled a giggle. Considering the Aksumi's usual clothes looked like little more than undergarments, it was no wonder she was complaining.

Makeda held a hand out, palm down, and waved it in a circle. "See? The resonance of the universe feels different than inside the Cloak of Riyalas."

Feels? Mai closed her eyes and listened. Now that Makeda had pointed it out...the pulse of the world, while still audible, sounded less concentrated than in Cathay.

A sharp whistle trilled from somewhere in the distance.

"Shhh!" Ku, at point, dropped to the ground. He motioned everyone down. Around him, the warriors all crouched low. Vanya pressed herself against a willowy tree and place a hand on her sword hilt.

Mai joined Makeda, huddling close to the ground. She looked around. *What is it?* she mouthed.

Brows furrowed, Makeda just stared at her.

Of course: the magic pebble interpreted their voices, but didn't change their words. Mai looked to Ku.

"It was a madaeri," he whispered as he bolted to his feet. "We've been spotted."

"There's no cover." One of the warriors ran a hand over the tree. Their open, wispy trunks were too narrow to hide behind.

Mai closed her eyes and listened. Everyone's heartbeats pattered. Breaths came out shallow and ragged. There were no sounds of movement, or any sign of the beasts, at least not nearby.

Ku pointed down in the valley. "It will take time for the Tivari to send out Templars. We need to keep moving, and try to evade or kill the madaeri."

Was it even possible? A madaeri that didn't want to be found usually stayed that way. Mai had never even seen one.

The trill echoed again, from somewhere to the right.

"Come on." Ku beckoned them forward. "Keep moving, deeper into the woods. Keep your eyes and ears out for the monsters."

Not easy, considering Mai didn't know what they looked like. Neither did Ku. She looked to Vanya and Makeda. "Have you seen one before?"

Both shook their heads.

"I hear they have huge fangs," Makeda said.

Vanya shrugged. "My *naga* is sharper."

The group doubled their pace, making plenty of noise as twigs and dried leaves crunched and crackled beneath their feet. There was no use in trying to be quiet, since madaeri supposedly had such good hearing. No matter how many times they zigged and zagged over the next phase, its shrill call followed them. Sometimes from behind. Sometimes from the right or left, and once, even ahead of them. Even with the narrow trees providing little cover, it stayed out of sight.

Mai felt so useless.

In the distance, the sky whined. Peeking through the treetops, she tracked the sound to its source. A flickering object drifted high above, a white line in its wake. It looked too small to be a Tivari god's chariot. She pointed. "What is it?"

Ku followed her gesture and squinted. "Tivari demon horse, probably delivering Templars. Come on."

Mai shuddered. While a Tivari god might vaporize a human, the demon horses carried Templars that would make deaths slow.

They continued deeper into the woods for another phase, the madaeri still screaming every time they changed direction.

Tall, dashing, and valiant, Vanya looked at the ground behind them. "The Templars must have found our trail by now. I say we fortify this position and fight."

Ku shook his head. "Even if we can defeat them, what happens when they don't report back?"

Closing her eyes, Mai listened. Indeed, heavy Tivari boots snapped twigs and crunched dry leaves. Though distant, they were closing fast. Around them the forest sounds fell silent.

"There's another way," Makeda said. "I can cast a cloaking spell."

Mai raised an eyebrow. "Like the one that hides the elf kingdom?"

"Yes." Makeda gave a forceful nod.

Exchanging glances with the other warriors, Ku gave an equally convincing nod. "Do it."

Makeda pointed to a tree, apart from the others, with several thin trunks flaring out. Its canopy formed an umbrella just a little higher than their heads. "Stand under there."

As Mai joined the others beneath the branches, Makeda reached into her poncho and pulled out a pouch. With her eyes closed, she circled the tree, sprinkling a red powder in circles, squares, and triangles. The pace at which she worked followed a rhythm.

Watching the sorceress work, Mai found the pulse of the world in her ears. Makeda's movements followed the beat. Too slowly.

The bootsteps grew closer.

Mai's heart picked up a notch. If Makeda didn't finish in time, they'd have to fight. Rather, the others would, and Mai would be utterly useless. Maybe she could stir courage with a song. Her clammy hands trembled as she groped for the flute in her gown.

"They are nearby," a Tivari said, his voice carrying from several hundred feet away.

"Straight ahead," said another.

Usually, the Tivari spoke their own language among each other, and when they spoke in Cathayi, it was with a throaty accent. Now, it sounded so clear. Mai tapped the pebble on her ear. Perhaps it translated *their* words, too.

At her side, Ku, Vanya, and the warriors all drew their swords. The collective rasp would surely give away their location.

The Tivari's dark shapes now flashed between the trunks.

Clasping her crystal, Makeda backed up against the tree. "Grzt zrm glkn," she uttered, over and over again. Though not translated by the magic ear bauble, the guttural syllables mingled with the pulse of the world, changing them like the ripples of a pond mixing with each other. The powder on the ground glowed red, while the crystal shed a light blue.

Seventeen Templars broke into the clearing, in grey mesh armor and with holy rods in hand. One stared at a magic mirror in his other hand. Perhaps its magic could see through Makeda's protective cloak.

"Shhhh." Ku reached for Makeda, who was still grunting out her spell.

It had a rhythm, like music.

Vanya stayed his hand. "As long as she chants, they won't see or hear us."

The Tivari leader looked up from the mirror. "They aren't here."

Mai started to blow out the breath she was holding, but then caught sight of the sweat gathering on Makeda's brow.

Not only that, her beautiful dark complexion seemed to pale, and her hands trembled. Her expression contorted like a victim of a Tivari's unholy rod.

Ku's grip tightened on his sword. "How much longer can she hold out?"

Vanya's head bobbled. "I don't know."

The crystal in the sorceress' hands flickered like a candle in a breeze.

"Oh, no," Vanya said, tightening her grip around her weapon.

All the warriors assumed fighting stances.

In this, Mai had nothing to offer. She was useless, just like back home in the village.

No.

She had the ability to hear the pulse of the world. She closed her eyes and listened. As awful as the sorceress' words sounded, they formed a harmony with the pulse of the world, the ripples of each building on the other. Maybe... Gripping the ground with her toes, bending her knees, and straightening her spine, Mai withdrew her flute and played notes at the same frequency as Makeda's spell.

The sorceress' expression relaxed. Her posture straightened.

Mai's own vitality guttered. The energy in her arms and legs seemed to drain like water from a hole in a bucket. Her trembling fingers almost lost hold of the flute. Still, she maintained the tune.

The Tivari fanned out as they marched through the clearing. They came closer, yet their eyes never stayed on the tree for more than a split second. Then, one stepped toward the markings that Makeda had left in the ground.

Through the haze in her eyes, Mai stared at the upraised foot as it came down toward the rune...

...and somehow veered at the last second and missed. The Tivari continued on his way, apparently unaware of the magic.

Maintaining her music to the cadence of Makeda's chanting, Mai shook the sweat from her forehead.

From up in their tree, the shrill cry rang out again.

Mai turned and looked.

A dark shape shifted in the leafy canopy.

"There!" Ku pointed. "Madaeri!"

She squinted.

Among the flashes of greens and browns, two blue eyes peered back. It shrieked again.

Makeda's shoulders slumped more. Her voice cracked as she chanted. Two of the warriors shook the trunks, but the snarling madaeri clung fast.

"Keep playing!" Ku said.

Her own energy flagging as she played longer, Mai scanned the backs of the Tivari. They were halfway to the other side of the clearing, when one turned back, holy rod raised.

Its gaze raked back and forth.

Mai's tune almost faltered.

Then, it turned and rejoined his comrades, unaware of the squawking Madaeri. Soon, they disappeared into the woods.

Ku turned from where he was watching them and blew out a long sigh. Wielding *Tamskelti* in two hands, he hacked through the branches. The metal sliced through the wood like a scythe through rice stalks. A mass of branches and leaves dropped to the ground. In the middle, landing lightly on its feet was a bipedal figure, only half the height of a man. Its face was caked with mud, and dirt and leaves obscured whatever clothes it was wearing. Twigs protruded from its dark, curly hair.

Mai could only stare. Her music broke for a second.

Vanya swung her sword at it so fast, the movement blurred, yet it dodged toward the edge of the circle. She cut off its escape route, chopping again. The two zigged and zagged, their motions blending together so much, it was hard to tell where the woman ended and the shrubs and mud began.

"Keep playing," Makeda said. Then, she snarled out more guttural sounds and pointed a finger. Wisps of thread coned out. The webbing entangled the madaeri along with Vanya's leg and sword arm, despite her jump to the side. The more it struggled, the more it stuck to Vanya's leg. They both tumbled to the ground. Its call came out as muffled grunts.

"The spider web again?" Vanya threw up her free arm.

"Keep playing." Makeda trudged to the tangled mess of madaeri and woman. She placed a hand on the back of the madaeri's neck and barked a single syllable. Blue light flashed, and something fizzled and popped.

Then Makeda's eyes rolled up into her head. She collapsed into the mass of strings.

Fog thickened in Mai's head. Her arms grew heavy and her legs wobbled. Her tune faltered. Hands on her knees, gasping for air, she turned to look in the direction the Templars had gone. The sound of their boots in the twigs was now far in the distance.

Catching her breath, she peered through the webbing at the struggling madaeri.

Its gaze met hers. It froze. Up close, it was easier to see through the filth and make out its boyish features. It looked not like some dreadful furry beast, but more like a human child, save for its slightly tapered ears.

Vanya, at the bottom of the pile, motioned to Ku. "Give me your knife."

The madaeri's ears twitched, and it looked in the direction of the Tivari. If it shrieked again, they'd come back. With Makeda unconscious and Vanya stuck…

Chapter 20:
Stand-Off

Mai's ears filled with the rustling and grunting of the madaeri, stuck to Vanya on the forest floor, struggling with the webs. Makeda remained unconscious on top of them, while Ku and the warriors gathered around.

Exhausted from using music to maintain Makeda's magic cloak, Mai listened again for the sound of Tivari boots. They were far away now, but certainly within earshot. Thankfully, the madaeri had stopped screaming in favor of trying to free itself.

Drawing his knife, Ku strode forward. "I'm going to put the beast out of its misery."

Youthful eyes widening at Ku's blade, it redoubled its tussle with the sticky strands. It was almost as if it understood.

It was kind of cute, just like a puppy or a child, and Ku was going to kill it. Mai's gut twisted.

"Please," it said, lip jutting out into a boyish pout. "Don't kill me."

Knotted a second ago, Mai's stomach just about leaped into her throat. Not only did it speak... "Do you understand what we are saying?"

It cocked its head. "What?"

Of course, the translation bauble. It let her, Ku, Makeda, and Vanya understand each other; but without one, the madaeri had no way of understanding. She motioned Ku over. "Give me the magic ear thing."

He crossed his arms. "Why me?"

"I can understand what it is saying. It doesn't understand us."

Ku flipped the knife in his hands and took a menacing step forward.

"It can speak!" She pointed at it. "It begged us not to kill it."

"One more step," it said, gaze locking on the knife, "and I'm going to yell loud enough for every master within a mile to hear me."

Freezing, Ku raised an eyebrow. "I don't think we can trust—"

"You don't have to trust it, but if we can communicate with it, we can make it clear that if it screams, it's dead. Then, maybe it can tell us more about the area."

"Fine." Eyeing the madaeri and sighing, he removed the bauble from his ear and handed it to her. He tugged and pulled the still-unconscious Makeda free of the webs.

Mai stuck it to the madaeri's ear. "Can you understand me now?"

Its eyes widened as it tried to reach its ear through the web. When its arm barely budged, it spit threads from its mouth. "Whoa. Yeah."

Vanya poked it. "Where did you have your hands on me?"

It blinked innocently. "It's not my fault your friend glued me to you."

Mai peered through the mess. The madaeri's other arm looked to be wrapped around Vanya's thigh.

"We need to make it to North Ridge soon. Are you making any progress communicating?" Ku pointed his blade at it. "If not, we need to kill it."

"*Him*," it said. "I'm not an *it*. And if you get any closer with that knife, I'm going to scream like your girlfriend does when we go at it."

"Stop." Mai waved Ku down. "He's going to yell."

Ku harrumphed. "So it's a *he* now?"

"You want to check my pants, axe hole?" The madaeri glared.

Mai choked, holding back a laugh. "Axe hole?"

The madaeri rolled its eyes and snorted. "No. *Axe* hole."

Vanya stopped struggling to free her leg and snorted down a chuckle. "The little madaeri has quite the foul mouth."

Mai tapped the bauble on her ear. Right, Aralas had altered them so she wouldn't hear curses.

"Fork Face. Sheet head. Go to hill." The madaeri flushed an interesting shade of red. "Dame it, please tell me I am cursing your boyfriend, and not sounding like an idiot."

Boyfriend? Mai cocked her head, and looked sidelong at Ku.

Ku's forehead wrinkled up. "What's it—"

"*He*, beech axe," the madaeri spat.

"—saying?"

Mai shook her head. "Nothing helpful."

"If it's not going to help, we have to kill it." Ku took a step forward, knife flashing in his hand.

The madaeri scuttled back the best he could, given the circumstances, though it might've just gotten him more stuck to Vanya. "I'm going to yell, fork head."

"Stop," Mai said, glaring at Ku. "If you kill him, he'll just be deadweight stuck to Vanya until Makeda's magic wears off."

The madaeri nodded. "Girl's got a point."

She held up a reassuring hand. "We won't hurt you if you don't yell."

"Deal," it said.

Mai scratched her head. "There has to be some way to get past this impasse. How do the Tivari control the madaeri?"

"Same way as us?" Vanya pulled at her leg. "Fear of the gods? Unholy rods?"

Ku chuckled. "Or maybe the way we tame dogs. Withholding foods, and a good scratch behind the ears?"

The madaeri gnashed his teeth. "Just try it, sheet head."

"Makeda might be able to use some kind of magic on it." Vanya reached over and shook the sorceress. "Wake up."

Makeda didn't stir, and only the rise and fall of her chest indicated she was even still alive.

"Too much sorcery tires her. Toss me your knife." Vanya pointed at Ku's blade.

Forehead furrowed, he took a few seconds before he threw it. When she swept it out of the air, she resumed her struggle with the strands. The more she sawed, the more entangled her leg became.

For now, they were stuck. With a sigh, Mai withdrew a piece of fire-toasted flatbread and took a bite.

The madaeri's eyes locked on it.

Mai stopped mid-chew. She moved the bread left, then right. The madaeri's eyes tracked it the whole time. She ripped off a piece and offered it.

Neck straining against the webbing, the madaeri reached with his mouth. When he couldn't quite reach, his tongue shot out and plucked it from her fingers.

Mai jerked her hand back, and shook it out like the time Cleric Pyuz's whip had scored a lash across it.

The madaeri's eyes rolled up into his head as he licked his lips. "Oh, sweet ticks of Lydath—ticks, dame it, *ticks*— that was good." His gaze fixed on the remnants in her hand. "The gods might dame my immortal soul, but give me more of whatever that was, and I'll tell you fork faces what you want to know."

Mai exchanged glances with Vanya before turning to Ku. "He says he will help if we give him food."

"Work for food?" Ku raised an eyebrow. "I still don't trust *it*."

"We don't have much of a choice. It will scream."

Ku snorted. "We do. Wait for it to fall asleep, and I'll kill it."

"I'm right here." The madaeri rolled his eyes. "And I understand. Do you want to wager on who can stay awake longer?"

Mai extended the rest of her bread. The madaeri's head lunged forward, only to get snapped back by the webs. He leaned again and took the entire hunk in two chomps. Mai pulled her hand back before he bit into her fingers, too.

"All right," he said, words muffled by his chewing. "What do you want to know?"

Mai turned to Ku. "Ku, tell him where we are headed."

"That's an awful idea." Ku glared at the madaeri. "Tell me, beast, how many more of you are there out here?"

Crumbs dribbled from the madaeri's lips, all of which his tongue shot out and caught. "Three of us."

Ku looked to Mai. When she held up three fingers, he curled his lip. "What are you doing in the mountains?"

"Tracking survivors."

Mai's stomach twisted. "Survivors of what?"

"A village harbored pale-faced escapees from the North." The madaeri's eyes welled up. "The masters tortured and murdered everyone they could find."

Vanya and Mai exchanged glances. These pale-faced escapees from the North might be the ones they were supposed to meet.

"What is it saying?" Ku shook her shoulder.

"The Tivari are hunting people from the North. They slaughtered an entire village." She turned to the madaeri.

Tears rolled down his cheeks.

"Dragon tears," Ku said. "Don't let it fool you. It's just as guilty."

The madaeri snuffled. "We don't have a choice. At least they kill *you*. If *we* turn against them and are caught, they torture us and never let *us* die."

"Do you have a name?" Mai asked.

He nodded. "Dashuralascilorimarilish."

"Dash-a-what?" Vanya's eyebrows clashed together.

It was less a name and more the sound Mai's stomach made when she was hungry.

"Dash is fine." He sighed.

Makeda let out a yawn. Rubbing her eyes, she sat up.

"Hurry up and do something about this." Vanya gestured at Dash, affixed to her leg. "One of his hands is going to get cut off."

"It's *not* my fault." A grin tugged at Dash's lips. "You were trying to chop me up. I didn't expect to get stuck to you, either."

Makeda clambered to her feet. Her voice sounded hoarse when she spoke. "I'm too tired to use any sorcery. I need to rest longer."

Vanya poked Dash. "I need to remove him from my leg, and we need to keep moving, before the Tivari come back."

"And they always find us." Dash's eyes roved right and left. "The rest of you should hurry on, because we two are as good as caught."

"No." Makeda shook her head. "It's a trick Aralas taught me. A jolt of energy over the holy commitment scar hides us from Lydath's Eye."

"Really?" Dash's eyes went round like rice bowls.

Mai rubbed the scar on the back of her neck. Of course. Aralas had touched her there twice: first before he'd taken her to the dragon bones, and again before they went to Cathay. Though if Lydath's Eye couldn't see her, perhaps Cleric Pyuz had known all along that she'd gone missing. Despite that, he'd executed Ying. As a warning, perhaps?

Dash turned to Mai. "Hey, if Lydath's Eye can't see me, I'll help you. All I need is more of that food."

Mai looked from him to her friends. "No matter what, we can't just stay here. How long until you can remove the web?"

Makeda shook her head. "A few hours."

Mai peered through the branches at the Iridescent Moon, now waning to half. It would be dark soon.

"Help me to my feet." Vanya extended her arm to Ku.

Ku took her hand and pulled her up, madaeri and all. "I really hate not understanding. When do I get my magic pebble back?"

"Once we find another way to communicate with Dash ."

"Is that its name?"

"*His* name." Dash glared, and he shook his fist the best he could, given his arm being pinned to his body. Now that they were standing, it was clear his other hand was stuck much too high up on Vanya's thigh. "Look, I have a way to throw the Tivari off. If I do it, will you give me more food?"

Ku's face scrunched up. "What is it—"

"*He*," Dash supplied.

"—saying?"

"That he can trick the Tivari," Mai said. "All he asks for is food."

Ku frowned. "Fine."

Dash grinned. "You wouldn't mind payment upfront?"

233

"If it will shut you up." Vanya reached around and put bread in his mouth.

This time, he didn't bother to chew. The bread went down in a single gulp. "Any water?"

Mai took the waterskin from Ku's pack and offered it.

Ku cringed. "I don't want its lips—"

Dash's mouth wrapped around the opening.

Ku sighed.

After several chugs, Dash licked his lips. "All right, I'm going to tell my companions to send a signal from down in the valley."

"Wait." Mai held up a hand. "Won't that give away our location?"

He grinned. Then he lifted his head and opened and closed his mouth several times. Though air gushed out, no sound did. Head cocked, his ears twitched. He then looked up, smug. "Daisimorialia agreed to do it, but she wants some of the food, and her scar zapped, too. Oh, wait." His ears twitched again. "Rushalipotakomit wants in, as well."

Mai turned to Ku. "He sent a message. His two companions agreed to help, if we help them."

Ku shook his head. "I still don't trust him."

"See?" Dash said. "*Him* wasn't too hard, was it? Now, you have no choice. If you don't agree to their terms, they'll tell the masters where to find us."

Chapter 21:
Templars

The chatter of one madaeri had been annoying; the bickering of three over food made Mai felt as if a hive of bees was buzzing in her head. Since the morning, after Makeda had dispersed the magic web, Dash had taken them higher into the mountains, deeper into the woods. After several hours, they'd met up with Rush, an older madaeri, whose white curls still had a few streaks of black.

An hour of hiking later, they'd met up with Daisy. With her short height and innocent expression, she might've been mistaken for a human child. Her hair color was hard to discern—yellow tangled with brown, which could've been dirt, given how filthy her face was. She had the unique talent of being able to eat, walk, and argue at the same time.

Ku leaned in and whispered. "They are holding us hostage."

"I heard that." Dash looked over his shoulder.

Ku harrumphed. "For all we know, they are taking our food, and leading us into a trap."

Bread crumbs dribbled out of Dash's mouth, only to be swept up by his tongue. "We'll find out when you run out of this roasted garlic on buttered baked bread."

Thank the Heavens Ku didn't understand them. Mai studied the three.

Ears twitching, the wizened old madaeri, Rush, stopped in his tracks. He held a wrinkled hand up.

The two other's ears perked up, and their eyes raked back and forth. They disappeared into the surroundings.

All the warriors sank into stances, hands on their sword hilt.

Mai's heart leaped into her throat. She'd kept her ears out for the whine of Demon Horses or the boot of Templars crunching in leaves, but hadn't heard anything. She froze, closed her eyes, and focused solely on listening. There was no sound other than the chirps and squawks of forest critters. Then again, the madaeri had keener hearing, and sharper eyes.

"What is it?" Vanya whispered.

The madaeri emerged from their hiding places.

Rush lowered his hand and turned to Dash. "Garlic bread. That's what we'll call it."

Daisy's head bobbed enthusiastically. "Much easier to say than roasted garlic on buttered baked bread. You can say it in one breath, too."

Hands on his hips, Dash growled. "I found it first."

Mai blew out a sigh.

"What is it?" Ku's fingers twitched on his hilt.

Mai shook her head. It wouldn't do to tell him. "It was apparently nothing."

"They are debating food." Makeda chuckled.

Ku glared at Mai. "Your fault. You should have just let me kill him."

Dash looked at him. "We've already sent the Templars on the wrong path, and helped you avoid some traps they set. Roasted garlic on—"

"Garlic bread," Daisy offered.

"—buttered baked bread is all it's costing you." Dash harrumphed. "You should be more grateful, Turtle's Egg."

Ku's eyes widened. "You can speak our language?"

Had he just spoken Cathayi? Mai touched the magic pebble on her ear.

"Of course, stupid." Rush laughed. "How else are we supposed to keep an eye on you? There's at least one of us in every village."

Mai shook her head. "I've never seen...or heard...one of you in my village."

"What makes you think you could?" Daisy shrugged. "We could be right beside you, and you'd never know."

"Like this." Dash pulled a piece of bread from Mai's bag. He'd just been next to Vanya.

"Since you don't need it, give me back my magic bauble." Ku reached for Dash's ear.

Dash ducked the swipe. He leaned his head to Makeda and Vanya. "I need to understand them."

Ku growled. "So do I."

"Please?" Mai reached into her food bag to get more bread, only to find it empty. The madaeri had taken not only her bread, but also the berries and nuts as well.

Ku sighed. "Come on, we need to reach the meeting point, and these pests have delayed us enough."

"This way is faster." Dash pointed to the right.

Shaking his head, Ku said, "You don't even know where we are going."

"North Ridge."

Ku's brows furrowed. "How—?"

"You said so, before you knew I could understand your language. When you threatened to kill me. That wasn't very nice."

Ku threw his hands up. "In any case, that is the wrong way. We're going this way."

Daisy tugged on Mai's arm, leaving dirt marks. "Don't listen to him. Dash knows what he's talking about."

Mai looked from Dash to Daisy to Rush. Rush's wrinkled face betrayed no emotion. Who knew what the madaeri were planning? Now that there was no more roasted garlic on—garlic bread, they could be setting a trap. "I'm sorry, but Ku is our leader."

Ku gave an emphatic nod. "Come on."

"Your funeral." Dash snorted.

"You've eaten all our bread, so run along." Ku swooshed them away with a hand.

"I'd follow you," Dash said. "Just so I could watch you eat your words. However, I don't want to end up as entertainment for the masters."

Mai exchanged glances with Vanya and Makeda. What if the madaeri were really trying to help?

"Let's go." Ku gestured them on.

Dash peeled off the pebble and tossed it at Ku. "You're going to need this."

Ku swiped it out of the air. He stuck it to his ear and stomped off to the north. The other warriors followed without question. With a last look at the madaeri, Mai hurried after him.

***

After several phases of the Iridescent Moon, they'd descended toward a vale between two mountains.

"This is the pass which will take us to North Ridge." Ku pointed to the collection of huts at the foot of the mountains, which looked no different from Sweetfield village. Nearly two ninety-nines people worked the surrounding rice fields.

Something sounded wrong. And looked wrong. Mai held up a hand. "Wait. There's no village priest."

Ku squinted. "You're right. This is good. Maybe we can get some food to replace what those varmints ate."

"No, what if it's a trap?" Mai scanned the fields again. Still no sign of a priest or his armored horse. "Dash said this was a bad idea."

"You're too trusting. He just wanted our food, and now we need more because of it." Ku waved back in the direction they'd come. "This village's priest is probably waiting for those pests to lead us into their trap somewhere. Come on."

It made sense, but Mai's stomach twisted all the same. As they weaved along a trail down the mountainside, the unsettled sensation got worse. It was too quiet. No bird songs, no squirrel chatter.

Crack. A blue bolt crackled through air. Everyone jumped.

Crack. Crack. Another blue bolt forked and stabbed into two of the warriors. Without a shout or scream, they crumbled to the ground, bodies smoking. A pungent smell filled the air.

Bile rose in Mai's throat. Poor Ying had been reduced to ashes, but these men…their bodies would rot, their flesh torn away by scavengers.

"Templars! Fall back, fall back." Ku stumbled as he turned around, but climbed back to his feet.

Makeda grabbed Mai's hand and pulled her along.

A bolt sizzled from a different angle, right through where she'd just been standing. It splintered a nearby tree.

Frozen, Mai stared at the trunk. That could've been her.

Another hand joined Makeda's in tugging hers.

Shaking off the dread fascination, Mai looked down.

It was little Daisy. "Hurry. There are eight masters. You can outrun them with those long legs."

Right. Escape. She raced off after the madaeri. Scattered to either side of her, the remaining four warriors and Ku ducked and weaved through the trees. Blue light flashed, and the air fizzled with sparks. Tree trunks snapped. One of the men stumbled and fell.

She turned her head to see who it was.

A hand shot out and jerked Ku behind a tree. A ray of energy surged right through the spot he had been running.

"Come on!" Makeda gave her another yank.

Mai looked forward and resumed her mad dash. After several minutes, the sound of crackling wood and sizzling air faded in the distance. She bent over, panting for air. Makeda's chest heaved as she crouched. Daisy didn't seem tired at all.

Presently, two of the men joined them.

Mai peered through the trees. "Where are Vanya and Ku?"

The two looked at each other, then looked back.

"I don't know!" Makeda said.

"I'll go find them." Daisy pointed deeper into the woods. "When you catch your breath, go that way. Rush is waiting."

Mai straightened and took long, quick steps. Ku was supposed to have taken them on a safe path. Now that they had run into Tivari, how useless she was! She couldn't wield a sword or even do much with magic, except putting out a candle. If this mission was so critical to the rebellion, why had they entrusted it to her, of all people?

No, she had her flute, and she could enhance Makeda's magic. She found the sorceress in the corner of her eye.

The sorceress kept pace, but often glanced back. "I hope Vanya is all right."

With the two surviving soldiers, they kept walking. The trees around them all looked the same, and with the Iridescent Moon blocked by the tree canopies, it was hard to tell whether they were just walking in circles.

Their footsteps crunched in the underbrush, their rhythm mingling with the pulse of the world. In the distance, more frequent, heavier footsteps came closer. Mai looked back. Dark shapes flitted through the trees.

Hopefully it was Vanya and Ku. Just in case, Mai grabbed Makeda to stop her. "Get ready."

The warriors turned and drew their swords. Grunting a syllable, Makeda held her hand out. A purple flame danced in her palm.

Two Tivari burst out from behind a tree trunk, their fangs bared. One's heart pounded slow and resolute.

Fighting for breath, Mai drew her flute. She'd never get a steady sound, not the way her lungs were burning, but she had to try. She blew out a discordant note. Her energy guttered, and it was all she could do to remain standing.

Both Templars pointed their unholy rods at her.

Makeda flung a ball of flames at them, engulfing one, but missing the other as it ducked behind a tree. The first didn't have time to scream as it was reduced to cinders.

From the other side of the tree, the survivor pointed the unholy rod at them. "Surrender, and your punishment will be—" Air swooshed, followed by a thud. The Tivari's head flew off and rolled a few times on the ground. Its body crumpled.

Vanya stepped out, sword slick with a black fluid. "I'm glad I found you."

"Where's Ku?" Energy trickling back, Mai craned to look past Vanya.

As if in answer, Ku tumbled out from between two trees. "Where is Dash?"

"Here." The young madaeri stepped out from behind a shrub.

Ku bowed his head. "I owe you an apology."

"A lesser man would say he told you so." Dash shrugged. "I told you so."

Ku snorted. "I deserved that."

"You can kiss and make up later." Rush, too, seemed to melt out of the foliage. "There are still at least five more behind us—"

"Three." With a shake of Vanya's sword, the black liquid splashed off.

"—and they will be calling for more masters in neighboring areas to join in the hunt."

"What about the three men we lost?" The image of their smoking bodies and memory of the sour stench sent Mai's stomach knotting again.

Ku shook his head. "They were specifically chosen because they were born in Cathay. They never went through the Tivari dedication ceremony. The Tivari won't be able to learn anything from their bodies."

"They saw Makeda and Vanya," Mai said, "and they were hunting the people from the North. They will suspect something with so many tribes involved."

"We can't do anything about it." Dash pointed back. "Even if we could kill them all, they've probably already sent messages to other masters."

"Where's Daisy?" Mai looked beyond Vanya and Ku, but there was no sign of the madaeri girl.

Vanya looked back. "She showed me the way to find you."

"She'll be fine," Rush said. "Come on."

Chapter 22:

Repercussions

Mai heard streams rustling over rocks as the party made their way through the woods. As Rush had said, Daisy had rejoined them, unscathed. Which meant the three had resumed their arguing.

"It's this way," Dash pointed down a trail.

"No, it's in that direction." Rush gestured almost the opposite way. "I'm older, so I know."

Daisy snorted. "You're also nearly deaf and blind."

Rush's thick eyebrows clashed together. "Not like I'd ever trust a girl with directions."

"And he's still got better senses than the humans." Dash shot a thumb back at the rest of them.

If they were worried about giving away their position to the Tivari Templars, their loud bickering didn't suggest it. Still, before long they'd reached a ridge without any sign of the enemy.

Down below, a river, sparkling in the setting sun, snaked through the trees into another valley.

"It's beautiful," Makeda said, brushing her thick hair out of her eyes.

Vanya sidled up beside the sorceress, scanned the scenery, and yawned.

"This is it. We are close to North Ridge village." Ku's shoulders slumped.

"What's wrong?" Mai asked.

"Had I listened to Dash, we wouldn't have walked into the Tivari trap. The others wouldn't have died."

Mouth opening and closing, Dash patted him on the back.

Ku sighed. "There's one more village we'll pass. We can reach it within a phase."

Dash waved them on. "We better hurry. Once night falls, the masters can see our body heat."

"We can see them, too," Rush said.

"Yes, but the humans *can't*." Daisy poked the older madaeri in the ribs. "They're even more blind and deaf than you."

They trailed Dash as he followed a stream through the woods and down the mountain. The trees looked different here, and they gave off a fresh, minty smell. By dark, they came to flat ground. The trees opened up into a field with rows upon rows of plants that grew almost as tall as the men. Long tubes jutted off their sides.

Straining her eyes in the twilight, Mai ran her fingers through the silky strands which poured from their tapered tips. "What is this?"

"Corn." Ku reached over and snapped a cylinder off. He pulled back the leaves and silken threads and bit into it, then passed it to her.

Mai received it in two hands and sunk her teeth in. An explosion of sweetness, like she'd never tasted before, erupted in her mouth.

The madaeri needed no prompting. They were chewing through the corn, leaves and all.

"By all the gods." Dash wiped juice from his mouth. "This is even better than the roasted garlic on buttered—"

"Garlic Bread," Daisy and Rush mumbled through their chewing.

"—baked bread."

A breeze rustled through the corn stalks, sending them swaying to the pulse of the world. Maybe… Mai pointed to the ground. "Can we bed down between the rows? Will that keep the Tivari from seeing us?"

"Maybe deeper in," Dash said. "And Rush will keep watch."

"I'm too old. I need rest."

"And I need my beauty sleep." Daisy ran a hand over her filthy cheeks.

***

While the whisper of the wind through the corn had lulled Mai to sleep, approaching footsteps jolted her awake. The sky had brightened to a dark blue and sent the stars to sleep. The White Moon hung low on the horizon.

One of the madaeri should've been standing watch. She sat up and looked down the row. Makeda still lay in her bedroll, her chest rising and falling in sleep.

Mai closed her eyes and listened. To the right and left, the others also slept. At least, their light breaths, set to the pulse of the world, suggested as much.

The footsteps carried through the earth, their weight suggesting someone large. They drew closer. Mai crawled over to Makeda and shook her. "Wake up."

Makeda just rolled over. Ever since scorching the madaeri faith scars the day before, she'd been exhausted.

Mai listened. Judging by their breath, Ku was in the row to the right, Vanya to the left. Mai pushed through the stalks to the Ayuri's sleeping form. She prodded her. "Wake up!"

Unlike Makeda, Vanya was instantly on her feet, hand on her sword hilt. "What is it?"

"Shhh. Someone's coming." Mai pointed to the source of the sound, several rows over.

Vanya drew her weapon.

"Wait." Mai held up a hand. The footsteps, while heavy, didn't sound like Tivari boots. "I'll go wake Ku."

She picked her way through the corn and found the warrior in another row. None of the madaeri were around. She shook him.

His eyes fluttered open.

Mai put a finger to her lips, then pointed in the direction of the newcomer.

Nodding, he eased himself to his feet and slid his sword from his sheath.

Back where she'd left Vanya, a grunt, followed by a thump, shook the air. Ku gestured for her to follow, and she trailed him through the corn rows.

Vanya's knee was digging into a man's chest. Her sword was pressed to his throat, and his eyes were wide; either in fear or because they were naturally that way. He kept his hands open and above his head.

Mai edged over. On closer inspection, with his dark hair and eyes, the man almost looked Cathayi.

251

His eyes met hers. "Please, don't hurt me."

"Who are you?" Vanya whispered.

His gaze shifted to the *bahaduur*, and his brow furrowed. "I don't understand."

Mai tapped her magic bauble. Maybe he wasn't speaking Cathayi. She looked over her shoulder to Ku.

"He's speaking the local language. I know a little of it." Ku pushed past her and knelt by the man. "We let you up. You scream, we kill."

Apparently, the magic pebble translated quite directly, as long as there weren't curse words.

Vanya eased up off of the man, but kept her sword pointed at him.

Eyes never leaving the weapon, he climbed to his feet.

"Where Ina?" Ku gestured to the village with an open hand.

The man hung his head, but pointed toward the village. "Dead. The priest and Templars executed her."

Ku covered his mouth. "Oh, no. Why?"

"The Tivari found out she harbored the Northerners." He pointed again toward the village. "Their bodies are hanging over there."

Bile rose in Mai's throat.

Ku looked toward them. "Ina was one of the shamans Aralas taught. If they caught the Northerners, then our mission has failed." He turned back to the man. "Tivari say Ina witch?"

"Yes." The man nodded. "But Ina was just a kind girl. They tortured her for days. They made us watch. She never said anything." A tear trickled down his cheeks.

A tear trickled down Mai's cheeks, too. How horrible a fate this Ina had suffered.

Blowing out a sigh, Ku looked to the rest of them. "There is still hope for the rebellion, as long as the Tivari didn't know what poor Ina could do. I need to know if she started to organize any of the villagers." He turned back to the man. "Ina show witch?"

The man looked from Mai to Vanya, and nodded. "She could talk to animals."

Mai sucked in a breath. Music could interact with the pulse of the world, but there was no way it could be used to converse with animals. Could it?

Ku turned back. "The shamans use the animals to communicate from village to village. If we go continue to North Ridge, we might see if she had any last messages."

"What about him?" Vanya gestured to the man.

Mai stayed Vanya's sword arm. "The Tivari will know we were here if they find his body."

Nodding, Ku placed a hand on his chest. "You promise. No tell Tivari we come."

Chewing on the inside of his cheek, the man stared at Vanya's sword, still pointed at him. "The priests told us if we see any other strange people, that we must report it, or the gods will punish us in this life and the next."

"Then you better make sure the priest doesn't find out." Vanya prodded him with the flat of the blade. "Or I can send you to meet the gods now."

The man's heart beat wildly in Mai's ears. Even if he didn't understand Vanya's words, her weapon spoke clearly enough.

"I promise," he said, placing a hand over his chest. "I won't tell."

"Hey," Dash said from behind them. "Where's Makeda?"

Everyone turned.

Dash stood there, his arm draped over an unfamiliar madaeri boy with curly blond hair.

If the villager's eyes could get any wider, they might be as large as his mouth.

"This is Flack." Dash clapped the boy on his back. "He wants his loyalty scar jolted, too."

Ku harrumphed. "Humans stay slaves, but we are freeing the madaeri."

"Hey." Dash poked him. "Win us over, and you'll have a spy in every village you pass through."

Ku turned to Mai. "Go wake Makeda."

Mai picked her way through the corn stalks, back to where Makeda was rolling over. If she was moving, perhaps she was close to waking. She shook the sorceress.

Makeda's eyes fluttered open. She jumped up, hand open. Then her eyes settled on Mai, and her expression softened. "Is it time to go?"

Mai nodded. "We are leaving soon. First, a madaeri wants you to dispel the magic of his loyalty scar."

With a snort, Makeda hefted her bag. "I should be saving my energy for more urgent matters."

Claiming her own pack, Mai guided her back to the others. The villager had already left.

Flack's eyes locked on Makeda. He scurried over and lowered his head, exposing the back of his neck.

Makeda looked to Ku, who nodded. With a sigh, she placed her hand over his neck and uttered a few harsh syllables.

The pulse of the world shook for a split second. Blue sparks crackled on Flack's scar.

"Ow!" He jerked back.

Dash clapped him on the back. "If the masters suspect we passed through here, holler."

Flack nodded. "Of course. I won't say anything about you. Now come on, before the others wake to harvest the corn."

He led them through the corn, cutting in between breaks in the rows. Then he raised a hand and beckoned them down. He jabbed a finger.

Mai sank to her knees. Low beneath the corn's leaves, she peered in the direction Flack indicated.

They were at the far edge of a village of domed buildings made of branches and mud. A Tivari priest was emerging from his two-level, square metal house. In front of it, several bloody messes of bone, muscle, and sinew in the shape of humans were strung up to poles. Three of the remains stood nearly twice as tall as the other four.

Turning away, she covered her mouth to fight down the rebellion in her stomach.

Ku rubbed her back. "Shhh, don't throw up."

She swallowed several times before the Tivari's footsteps faded deeper into the village.

Mai pointed in the direction of the hanging bodies, but didn't look. "Some of them are huge."

"Giants," Ku said. "The Tivari use them in the North for cutting paths through mountains and hauling rock."

Mai shuddered at their sheer size.

"Three survivors," Ku said, finger counting the bodies. He turned to Flack. "What happen?"

When the new madaeri spoke, his accentless Cathayi must've been translated by magic. "Fair-headed Northerners were fleeing Tivari priests. They tried to hide in the village, and Ina tried to help them. However, some were so big, even bigger than the rest of you. They couldn't hide. Some of the Northerners sacrificed themselves so the others could get away."

"Did Tivari pursue survivors?" Ku asked.

Flack shook his head. "No. It was so strange. A pretty woman with the Northerners waved her hands, and the Templars ignored the rest."

Ku turned to the rest of them. "That must be the one who is supposed to teach you. They survived. We must continue with our mission."

Chapter 23:

Potential

A horn blared, breaking the pulse of the world in Mai's ears. With the sun setting, she crouched with the others at the edge of the fields. The ruddy-skinned men and women—Kanin people, according to Ku—collected baskets full of corn and squash, and headed through the planting rows toward the collection of round huts with domed roofs.

Mai turned to Ku. "Are you sure this is North Ridge village?"

"I've been here a few times." A grin twitched on Ku's face, and he gestured toward a mountaintop whose tip pointed right to the Iridescent Moon. "The elf lands lie on the other side."

Mai's stomach twisted. "Why didn't we just pass through there? We wouldn't have lost the warriors."

Ku shook his head. "Aralas said it was impassable from this side."

Aralas... His lips had been on hers, just a week ago. Mai's heart buzzed. By now, he must've returned to Yanyan's embrace.

"The Northerners are in the village," Dash said.

Mai's soul just about jumped out of her skin. She whirled around to face the three madaeri, who'd gone ahead to scout. Apparently, from the crumbs on their clothes and chins, they'd scouted out the best food.

"It's safe." Corn juice dribbled from Dash's mouth as he chewed.

Ku growled. "What did you see?"

Dash swallowed and took another bite from the ear of corn. "The Tivari priest has been following the Northern girl around."

"How do you know?" Vanya asked.

Dash waved into the corn rows. Another madaeri shouldered his way between the others. With curly brown hair and bright eyes, he shared Daisy's and Dash's same youthful look...and the same penchant for food, if the food stains around his mouth were any indication.

"This is Scrit." Dash looked over to Makeda. "He wants his scar zapped, too."

Scrit's wide eyes looked like those of the village dogs begging.

Meeting Makeda's gaze, Ku imitated the expression. "These madaeri have proven helpful and loyal."

"So are the village dogs." Snorting, Makeda placed her hand over Scrit's scar and uttered a foul word. The syllable shifted the pulse of the world in Mai's ear. Blue light flashed, and sparks showered like rock on flint.

"Ow!" Scrit rubbed the back of his neck.

Ku turned to new madaeri. "When did the Northerners arrive?"

"Four days ago." Scrit held up four fingers.

"Were the villagers scared?"

Scrit shrugged. "At first. Then the Northerner woman waved her hands at the priest, and made him friendly. He follows her like he's in love."

Mai's belly fluttered. If she could learn to do this with music, as Aralas had suggested, she could save her family from Cleric Pyuz. How tragic that the knowledge would come at the cost of the warriors who died at the Templars' hands.

"Come on." Ku rose and started heading into the fields. "Let's meet them."

Mai clambered to her feet and hurried after him. Whatever she learned wouldn't bring the dead warriors back, but perhaps it could prevent others from dying.

Many of the ears had been plucked from the cornstalks, and many rows had already been cleared. Harvest season would be over soon. Some of the straggling villagers turned and looked at them with wide eyes before scurrying back home.

The buildings looked like the ones from back at the other village they'd passed: domed houses made of wood and mud—lodges, according to Flak from the other village— arranged in a circular pattern. From inside the village, chatter rose.

A wizened man with grey hair and painted marks on his face emerged from between two of the lodges. His breeches were made of some kind of animal skin, and a necklace of shimmering river stones hung around his neck. Bird feathers adorned his head. Wise eyes spoke of many winters, but glared at them with anything but friendliness.

Several men flanked him, all carrying stone-headed farming tools. Altogether, their hearts beat rapidly, out of harmony with each other.

As they came closer, the headman's eyes locked on Ku.

Ku's heart now raced, too.

Mai looked from him back to the leader. If this was the Northerner they were supposed to deliver *Tamskelti* to, his angry look suggested he might use the sword to chop Ku's

JC Kang

head off. However, up close, he looked more like the other Kanin people, none of whom had light-colored hair.

"You!" When the headman was close enough, he jabbed Ku in the chest. "I told you, you are not welcome back here."

Ku held his hands up. "I promise. I not lay with daughter."

"You disappeared with her every day." He beckoned.

The other men pointed their tools at Ku.

Mai glared at him. Could it be? Did Ku dally around as much as Aralas?

Vanya drew her sword. Grasping her crystal in one hand, Makeda held out her other palm, fingers curling and uncurling.

Mai's palms sweated. If someone didn't talk sense, they'd never meet the Northerners, and she'd never learn to bend the Tivari to their will. All hope for her family would be lost. Closing her eyes, she listened for the pulse of the world and the scattered heartbeats of the angry people. It would be possible to diffuse the anger with the right sound. She started to hum.

No, that risked drawing Avarax's attention. She withdrew the wooden flute from her poncho's inner pocket and played.

Her spirit soared on the notes, which harmonized all the heartbeats around her, like ripples on a pond merging and mingling with others.

262

Sounds shifted. She opened her eyes. The men had lowered their tools. The headman's angry expression had melted.

She'd done it! Excitement pulsed in Mai's veins. She –

The ground shook and rumbled. Heart leaping into her throat, she turned to face the sound, which emanated from inside the village.

The top of the lodges barely reached a bare chest so hairy, it might've belonged to an animal. The giant's hair, which was a duller yellow than corn, hung to its shoulders. It was impossible to tell where his beard ended, given its similar color to the yellow curls on his chest. Each step it took rattled the earth. A fur kilt covered his legs.

"You've arrived!" called a female voice in the giant's shadow.

Mai looked down to the woman, who, like the fair-headed man beside her, stood only as tall as the giant's waist, but nearly a head above the Tivari priest who tottered behind her. Like the behemoth looming above, she had hair the color of faded corn, and her skin was even paler than the dwarves in Cathay. Her face was so...three-dimensional, with a nose that began at her eyebrows and ended in a round point above full lips. Both she and the man wore fur clothing. When she motioned for the giant to halt, and continued forward, her eyes met Mai's.

Such beautiful eyes! They were round like Vanya's and Makeda's, but the color was a blue darker than Doctor Wu's. She held the skirts of her heavy brown dress, crossed her legs, and dipped into something that resembled a bow. "Well met. I am Regina. This is my husband, Vydas, King of the Nothori."

He stepped forward and clasped Regina's hand. Placing his other hand over his belly, he bowed.

Mai studied him. Kings had ruled provinces of Cathay in the name of the emperor in ancient times, yet it was their corruption and wickedness which had led to the empire's downfall. Or at least, that was what the Tivari claimed. This man, with his regal bearing, looked as if he could lift a kingdom onto his broad shoulders. His piercing blue eyes appraised them.

"Aralas," Vydas said at last, with a hint of disdain, "said you bear a sword which will unite our tribes when we attack the den of Tivari queens."

Queens? Mai had never heard of any Tivari royalty. Their supreme leader was the High Priest. She looked sidelong at Ku, who stood dumbstruck, staring at the giant. She elbowed him. "The sword."

Ku's eyes met hers, a look of recognition forming on his face. "Oh." Straightening, he offered the sword in two hands.

Vydas bowed as he received it. The blade sang as he pulled it free of its sheath, filling Mai's ears with the dwarves' hum—*her* hum—as well. His eyes marveled at the blue tinge, and he swung it in broad arcs. "It is a thing of beauty."

Regina placed two fingers on her brow and bowed her head. "It comes at great cost."

Behind them, the giant moaned.

Mai bowed her head. No doubt Regina referred to the dead in the last village, and it had cost Ku his friends, as well. "I'm sorry for the death of your people."

Regina gestured toward the giant. "Knut's men sacrificed themselves so that we could escape. Their deaths are especially tragic, since there are too few giants left in the world."

Mai's gaze shifted to the Tivari, who still gazed at Regina with adoring eyes. "We were told you did something to the priest."

Smiling, Regina placed a finger to her temple. "The gift of my people is empathic."

"What does that mean?" Makeda's eyes rounded like river pebbles.

"We can communicate with only our minds, plant suggestions and emotions, or even," she gestured the priest forward, "make someone obey you like a pet."

The Tivari waddled to her side. Up close, his eyes seemed glazed over, and his ridiculous grin exposed his fangs. Cleric Pyuz from Mai's village never looked so...friendly.

And even so, the villagers all stared at him with fear and hatred. If he was anything like Cleric Pyuz, he'd taken pleasure in abusing them.

Regina patted him on the head. "This is Cleric Zrt."

Mai's gaze strayed to the priest's side, where the unholy rod dangled from his belt; then to his neck, where his magic mirror hung. He was so much under Regina's control, they hadn't disarmed him. Mai sucked in a sharp breath. If she could control Cleric Pyuz like a Regina did this Zrt, her family—no, her entire village—would be safe.

"Aralas insisted I come on this quest so as to teach you some of what I know." Aralas' name came off of Regina's lips with a husky rasp, sounding nothing like her husband's disdain.

No doubt, the way the elf angel popped in and out of places, he'd left a string of lovers all over the world. Mai's neck tingled where his lips had pressed against them, even as her stomach knotted. Beside her, Vanya and Makeda both shuffled on their feet.

Regina gave a sidelong glance at Vydas before meeting their collective stares. "Come. There is much to learn."

Chapter 24:

Charms and Commands

The sound of all the women's heartbeats seemed even louder in Mai's ears within the confines of the lodge. Vanya's eyes were closed, while Makeda could not help but gaze at Regina. The headmaster's daughter, Nada—who had flashed adoring eyes at Ku—joined them as they sat cross-legged around the stone-lined fire pit. Late afternoon sun cast muted light in through the hole in the roof.

Mai turned to Regina. "You have the priest so much under control, you let him keep his unholy rod."

"Not by choice." The mentalist shook her head. "A charm will convince a target that you are their best friend, but it won't change their nature. I asked for his rod, but he refused."

Vanya fiddled with her sword hilt. "Couldn't you have Commanded it?"

Brushing her yellow hair out of her face, Regina nodded. "Yes, but Commands work only in that instant. It would also break the charm."

"Still, it is amazing." Makeda clasped Regina's hand. "What else can you do? Can you speak in our minds, like Aralas?"

"Yes, but I don't think you would understand me." The Empath—since that's what Regina called her kind—pressed on the bauble affixed to her ear. "This translates language, but not thought."

Mai nodded. "I felt that Aralas could hear my thoughts."

"He can, I'm sure," Regina said. "I can see images in your mind, and also project my mental images into yours. That's how I communicated with the headmaster when we arrived in this village."

Nada's eyes brightened. "That's how the shamans can communicate with animals, as well."

"Watch." Regina locked her gaze on each of them in turn and waved her hands in a pattern, coming last to Mai.

The pulse of the world quickened to Regina's finger movements, and stuttered in Mai's ears. An image of Aralas flickered in her mind, though there seemed to be something different about him. His eyes evoked a mirthfulness similar to when he was around Mai, and his golden hair was pinned up and out of his face. His shirt matched Vydas' in style, though the fabric looked to be deep blue.

He looked less...dashing? Usually, heat stirred in Mai whenever she thought about him; but now, nothing.

Apparently, that wasn't the case with the others. Makeda sucked in a breath.

Vanya fanned herself. "Is it safe to assume we have all been with Aralas?"

Been with was vague enough, and however it was translating for the others, one thing was clear. Cheeks flushed, and fingers fiddled with hair. All, save for Nada.

And Mai. What had passed between her and Aralas was for the two of them to know.

Makeda cleared her throat. "Are we able to do this, too? Project images?"

"I don't know," Regina said with a shrug. "Aralas hinted that the various spheres of magic are very similar, but that our different peoples have different ways of evoking it. He specifically told me to teach the art of Charming and Commanding."

Edging closer to the fire pit, Makeda's face looked like a puppy's about to receive a treat. "Please, teach."

"I can only explain how I do it, but I don't know how your magic works."

Butt sore on the hard ground, Mai repositioned herself. What if such magic couldn't be evoked through a Dragon Song? Her family and friends would surely die at Cleric Pyuz's hands. No, Aralas must've known it was possible, since he sent her here. Not only that, Yanyan had used it on her.

"First, we'll start with a Command, since it is easier than charming. Everyone's heart has its own unique rhythm. I sense it, and the rhythm of the earth, and make a connection."

How the Empath sensed it, she didn't say, but Mai nodded. *Listen. Connect.* Those had been some of Aralas and Yanyan's earliest lessons. And having been commanded by Yanyan, perhaps she could make a comparison. "Command me."

Regina raised one of her yellowish eyebrows. "Are you sure?"

"Why not?" Perhaps this would be the easiest way to learn the magic to save her family.

"Your giving me permission will make it all the easier." The edge of Regina's lip quirked. She locked gazes. Her fingers drew a mesmerizing pattern in the air, which mingled with the pulse of the world like ripples on a pond.

Mai's heart stirred. In her ears, Regina's heartbeat merged with the pulse of the world, and tangled up with her own. A wave flooded over her, just like when Yanyan had used a Dragon Song command. All sense or propriety fled.

Words spilled out of her mouth, unbidden. "Aralas kissed me, and I wanted more than that, but Ku barged in."

Around her, the women all stared.

"Ku?" Nada's eyes narrowed.

Mai covered her mouth. Heavens, had she just said that? Heat flushed her face.

"Is that all that happened?" Vanya smirked at Regina. "I think she is lying."

Makeda shook her head. "No, I felt the change in the resonance of the universe."

Regina took a breath and wiped sweat from her brow. Straightening, she gazed at Mai. "It was harder than making you stand or flee, but I gave you the mental Command to tell us if you'd been with Aralas."

"I felt compelled to speak, though I don't know why." Mai lowered her hand. "Do it on Vanya."

Vanya scrambled to her feet and backed away.

Regina laughed. "Don't fear. It was a complicated Command I gave Mai, so it tired me out. I won't be able to ask something as complex, and certainly not on a resisting *bahaduur*, until I've rested. The shorter the Command, the easier it will be to execute. And of course, they need to be able to understand you."

Brow furrowed, Makeda rose. "I think I felt how it works."

"Me, too." Vanya nodded.

Mai closed her eyes and thought back to the sound of Regina's heartbeat, and how her finger and hand motions had changed the pulse of the world. Perhaps a hum could accomplish the same thing, though that would possibly draw Avarax's attention.

"Go and practice," Regina said. "If and when can project your Commands reliably, I'll demonstrate a Charm."

***

After several days of practice in the Kanin village, along with observing Nada ordering animals around, Mai had learned to impose her will in single trilling notes on her flute. Ku must've been tired from all the sitting, standing, yawning, and other orders she'd practiced on him, and all the mistakes wore her out. It would certainly have been easier if she could actually sing, but the fear of Avarax kept her voice bottled up.

The local Tivari priest had borne the brunt of Vanya's verbal Commands, and Makeda's sorcery. Yet he still followed Regina like a docile pet, oblivious to the villagers' hatred of him. How amazing that was. Hopefully, they would all learn to charm soon.

Despite his obedience, the Kanin villagers still worked at the corn harvest. Today, Mai was helping Nada in a field just outside the village, using stone to grind the kernels. Other villagers took the flour to bake into a kind of sweet bread that was surprisingly filling.

Even away from the ovens, the heat was unbearable compared to back home. Wiping sweat from her brow, she turned to Nada. "Do the Tivari not eat the corn from the ear?"

The girl nodded. She could understand some Cathayi, apparently from her time with Ku. "They do, if the bishops visit. However, we are farther away from the pyramid than any other village. The bread keeps longer than the corn."

Mai cocked her head. "I've made the pilgrimage to the pyramid a few times during the sacrifices to the Tivari gods. I've never seen any of your people." Let alone anyone who looked like Vanya or Makeda.

Nada shrugged. "I've never been to the pyramid. A Tivari caravan of metal horses, ogres, and Templars passes through and collects our sacrifice."

Which was probably why the village was hard at work. Even if an Empath could charm one Tivari, an entire caravan was a different story. Mai looked back to the village.

Just like one of the village elders at home recounting epic battles by manipulating shadow shapes with his hands, Vanya and Makeda were fighting for control of the Tivari priest.

Sitting on a large rock nearby, in the shadow of the surviving giant, Regina clapped her hands. "I think you are ready." She beckoned Mai over.

Mai bobbed her head at Nada, set the millstone down, and trotted to join the others.

Regina greeted her with a nod. "Everyone has succeeded with the command. You are ready to charm."

Mai's pulse picked up a beat. At long last, this would be the skill that could save her family and village.

"Now, do whatever it is you do, and pay attention as I release him from my control. I will sense his heart and bend him to my will again."

Closing her eyes, Mai listened. At first it was difficult to hear anything more than the giant's pounding heart, but after a few minutes, the priest's pulse became distinct. As before, his heart beat in time with Regina's. She opened her eyes again.

Regina was making shapes with her fingers. The pulse of the world shifted. The Tivari's heartbeat slowed to a typical steadfast plod.

Mai opened her eyes.

The priest's eyes, glazed over since they'd arrived, cleared to a deadly glint. His silly smile twisted into a snarl. He drew his unholy rod with one hand and patted his waist with the other.

Regina's fingers danced in intricate patterns. The pulse of the world flitted.

The Tivari's heartbeat remained the same, failing to harmonize with hers.

Regina's eyes widened. Her fingers switched to a different pattern, changing the pulse of the world around them.

The priest levelled his weapon at her. A bolt of blue energy sizzled out.

The giant stepped between them. The blast struck him, and he let out a roar before falling toward the priest. The earth shook as his enormous body crashed into the dirt.

Had he crushed the Tivari?

No, the priest's heartbeat still thumped louder as he appeared from around the giant's body. He pointed his wand at Regina again.

Listening to his pulse, Mai set the flute to her lips and played a command, her energy guttering as she willed the him to drop the weapon.

The unholy rod slipped from the priest's grasp. The magic mirror he'd taken hold of dangled around his neck. He bent over to retrieve the rod.

Vanya swept her sword out, hacking the Tivari's hand off in a spray of black blood.

Mai stared in dread fascination, even as the Tivari retrieved his rod with the other hand. Snarling, he jumped back out of the sword's reach and pointed at Vanya. Unholy blue light sprayed from the end.

Vanya spun out of the way, but it took her even further out of reach. Around them, the village burst into commotion.

The Tivari aimed at Regina again. A green light flashed, striking the Empath. She crumpled to the ground. He turned and ran toward his house, leaving a trail of his blood.

With a foul grunt, Makeda sent sticky threads wriggling after him.

Without looking back, the Tivari sent another ray into the webs. The strands disintegrated.

"Get him!" Makeda screamed, hunched over her knees. "Don't let him reach his house."

Back near the millstone, Nada was chanting something in her language.

Vanya broke into pursuit.

Birds dove in and swirled around the Tivari. As if slogging through a driving wind, he swatted and batted at them.

There was nothing Mai could do against a priest, so she rushed to Regina's side. Her body convulsed in erratic spasms. Was she dying? Mai focused on the Empath's heart. It still beat, though fitfully.

Vaguely aware of Makeda snarling out more sorcery, Mai stood and took a deep breath to settle her own frantic heart. Calm settled through her jittery limbs. Bending her knees and curling her toes into the earth, she listened for the pulse of the world. Flute in hand, she borrowed the pulse and projected her own calm at Regina.

The Empath's heart slowed only a little, but at least it regained a fixed rhythm.

All energy seeping from her arms and legs, Mai looked toward the Tivari.

Though blood oozed from scratches over his face, he'd cleared the swarming birds. Now, with Vanya on his heels, he was working closer to his house, while the giant, Knut, lumbered toward him. *Tamskelti* in hand, Vydas ran a few steps behind.

Two more bursts of green light sprayed from the unholy rod. The first stopped the giant in his tracks, while the second felled him. His enormous, flaying limbs shook the ground.

The Tivari was right in front of his house. He put the rod between his teeth and reached for the door with his remaining hand.

Over all the cacophony and the fog in her tired mind, Mai picked out his heartbeat. She played one more song on the flute, willing him to halt.

If the priest was still reaching for the door, it was hard to tell through the darkness filling the edges of her vision. Vanya and Vydas both raised their weapons.

Vitality gushed from Mai's body like water spilled from a bucket. Her knees buckled. All went black.

Chapter 25:
Escape

The sound of frantic murmuring roused Mai from sleep. What had happened? The last thing she remembered was the priest about to enter his home. Every muscle felt like gelatin when she tried to sit up.

She blinked her eyes, but everything remained dim and blurry. Bringing her elbows up under her, she propped herself up.

"Mai's awake," one shape that sounded suspiciously like Vanya said.

Another blob knelt beside her. The smell of man-sweat and garlic identified it as Ku. "Are you all right? Wenhui would never forgive me if something happened to you."

"I think so." Mai blinked several times. The inside of the lodge came into focus, though it remained only dimly lit by the late afternoon sun through the fire hole. The shaman girl, Nada, was tending to Makeda and Regina, who lay asleep on fur bedding, while Vydas crowded behind her. Vanya sat cross-legged by the fire pit, sharpening her sword.

"How long have I been asleep?" Mai asked.

Vanya didn't look up from her sharpening. "Two phases."

"Is the giant all right?" Mai asked.

Never looking up from Regina, Vydas shook his head.

Mai's heart sank. She pointed her chin at Regina and Makeda. "What about them? Are they all right?"

Vydas tore his gaze from his mate and met Mai's gaze. He bowed his head. "Thanks to you, Regina survived."

Nobody ever complimented her. Mai's cheeks heated.

Vanya peered at both sides of her blade. "Makeda just needs rest. She expended too much of her energy trying to stop the priest."

"Did she succeed?" Mai's stomach twisted like a rag.

Ku shook his head, a grin forming on his face.

"What's so funny?" Mai glared at him. The priest holing up in his house was no laughing matter.

"*You* stopped him," Vanya said. "With your last Dragon Song. Otherwise, he would have made it into his house. He froze long enough for Vydas to test *Tamskelti's* mettle."

If the dwarf-forged sword could slice through flesh and bone like Vanya had cut off the priest's hand... Mai shuddered. "And?"

"His head is no longer connected to his body," Vydas said.

Ku's smile melted. "It's not all good, though. The giant is gravely injured."

"Not only that," Vanya said, "but when a priest dies, the Tivari send Templars to investigate."

Mai pushed herself up to sitting. This was all such a bad idea from the start. Why had they met here in the first place, where they'd put so many people in danger? "The village. They'll slaughter everyone."

"The headman is furious." Ku bit down on his lower lip, both irritated and remorseful at the same time. "He wants us gone as soon as we can move."

As well he should. Mai's chest squeezed. What had Aralas been thinking, sending giants who couldn't hide?

Vanya stopped her sharpening and looked up. "He thinks he can convince the Templars that they had nothing to do with the priest's death, that it was the giant and his friends."

Mai's stomach twisted. "It won't matter to the Tivari."

"Nada is trying to convince him to abandon the village," Ku said.

"The madaeri, Flick." Mai looked around. "Where are they?"

Vanya rolled her eyes. "Doing madaeri things."

Mai snorted. "Flick can feed the Tivari lies about what happened."

"Only if the village feeds him first." Ku's smaller eyes didn't have the safe effect as Vanya's when he rolled them.

"I don't think madaeri will risk their own hides," Vanya said.

Beside Regina's prone form, something buzzed and flashed. Everyone's heads jerked toward the source.

"The priest's magic mirror." Vydas pointed at the glassy-black oval. "We retrieved it."

"It's the second time it's buzzed," Ku said, poking at it as if it might bite.

Mai clambered up onto her knees and crawled over to join the others, gathered around the mirror. In the past, Cleric Pyuz had talked to his mirror, and it seemed to answer all of his questions. "If anyone knows how it works, it would be Makeda."

"I don't." Makeda, on the other side of Regina, rolled over onto her side and pushed herself up on her elbow. "It wouldn't be a good idea, either. Aralas said that Tivari spirits are trapped inside, and communicate with each other through the ethers. If we awaken the spirit of that mirror, it can tell others what it sees."

JC Kang

Mai shuddered. All this time, Cleric Pyuz had been communicating with spirits—which were definitely evil, if they served the Tivari priests.

Outside in the distance, something whined. Mai looked to the door. "Do you hear that?"

The others' foreheads scrunched, but then they exchanged glances and shook their heads.

The sound.... It was like...the demon skiff they'd encountered a few days before.

"Hurry," Dash said. "Templars have landed outside of the village."

Where had he come from? Mai's heart just about jumped out of her body.

Ku leaped up. Vanya sheathed her sword and helped Makeda to her feet. Nada leaned over Regina, shaking her, while Vydas stroked her forehead.

Dash jabbed his finger repeatedly at the lodge door. "Rush counted six of them."

"Come on, we need to escape." Ku pulled Mai up.

"What about the villagers?" Mai looked to Nada, whose hands trembled.

"If they find us here," Ku said, "the village is doomed."

Vydas cradled Regina's head and frowned. "She is still unconscious."

282

Outside, villagers screamed and yelled, the noise mingling with the skiff's whine. The ground rumbled.

Mai looked to Makeda. "Can you use your cloaking magic?"

Makeda shook her head. "Only if you can support me, like before, and even then probably not for long."

Closing her eyes, Mai considered her energy. Her arms and legs felt like wilting rice stalks, and a cloud muddled her mind. She sighed. "I don't know how much I can do."

Dash's ears twitched. He drew a circle in the air. "Daisy says they are coming in from six different sides, herding the villagers in. I think I know an escape path."

Mai pointed to Regina. "What about her?"

"She's not going anywhere." Vydas gazed at his mate, lip trembling. His tone sounded so resigned.

Vanya patted her sword hilt. "We can all fight."

No," Ku said. "If the Templars report back that all our different peoples were here, they will figure out that we are organizing a worldwide rebellion."

Setting his lover's head down, Vydas stood and straightened his furs. "The Tivari have known about my people's revolt for a while. I will create a diversion for you to escape."

Makeda's eyes widened. "You must wield *Tamskelti* to slay the queens."

"She is my sun, and nothing will keep that from setting." Vydas looked down at Regina. "Deivos calls her to his embrace. If he wills it, I will be at her side."

Mai blinked away tears. From what she'd gathered talking to these fair-skinned people, Deivos was their name for the sun god. Vydas had already resigned himself to death.

"We need to go," Ku said to the rest of them, voice frantic. "Aralas will have a backup plan to attack the queens' lair if Vydas falls. He never relies on just one option."

"Deivos smiles upon those who use their brains," Dash said, beckoning Vydas. "Come on."

Mai looked from Vydas to the others. Would the madaeri's appeal convince the Northern king? No matter what, avoiding discovery was the only way to save the village. Not only that, if she died here, her family would share the same fate. She stood and followed Dash out.

The sun cast long shadows. The high-pitched screams shifted above the village. Mai looked up. Flames crackled as they licked the oval underside of the skiff and scorched the tortured souls who bore it. It was tiny compared to one of their gods' chariots, supposedly driven by one of their immortal demon servants. The dreaded driver was obscured by the skiff's sides as it banked along the north end of the village.

Looking around the corner, Dash waved his hand back, motioning for them to keep close to the lodge. He darted across the space between buildings, then beckoned for them to follow.

Near the west edge of the village, one of the Templars yelled, "Gather in the center."

The villagers wailed and screamed.

A sense of foreboding crawled up Mai's spine. It was just like an inspection back home. Just like when Cleric Pyuz had executed Ying. This time, they knew one of their own had died, and there would be reprisals.

Dash gave her a stern jerk of his head. Swallowing her fear, she hurried to the next lodge. Up above, the skiff sounded as if it was banking along the east edge of the village. It wouldn't be long before the demon would see them.

They ran to the next three lodges, Vydas taking long strides even while he carried Regina on his back. Someone had convinced him to flee!

Behind him, Makeda was barely able to keep up, even with Vanya and Ku supporting her. The ground shook more. Up above, the silvery tip of the skiff came into view.

Heart lurching, Mai's body froze. Her breath hitched in her throat. She was as good as caught.

Then Dash pulled her into a lodge. Feeble light peeked in through the smoke hole.

What about the others? Surely the skiff would've spotted them.

Its whine intensified. All those souls, facing an eternity of pain. Tears formed on Mai's face as she covered her ears. The roof trembled, raining dust and dirt on them.

Then, the screams diminished and passed. Her lungs took in a labored breath.

"Where is Cleric Mrak's body?" a new Templar's voice came from the center.

"His Holiness is near his house," said the headman. "After the invaders killed him, they refused to let us honor his passing."

Dash pulled Mai back outside.

"Now," Dash said, waving his hands in broad circles at the nearby edge of the fields. "Run into the corn. Keep low as you work toward the mountains."

Mai looked back to see Ku, Vanya, and Makeda emerging from the closest lodge. Ku's hands trembled, while Makeda panted. Only Vanya looked unaffected by their brush with death. But where were Vydas and Regina? Mai turned and ran.

At the next lodge, she looked around the corner, which provided a clear view of the village center.

The people had gathered there, lined up, with men in the back, women kneeling in the middle, and children in the front. Just like inspections back home. Her stomach twisted.

Dressed in tightly-meshed armor, a Templar marched across her line of sight, its back to her, unholy rod pointing at various people. "Who is responsible?"

Bile rose in Mai's throat. He'd take his time, killing the weak and old first.

As Mai tracked the Templar, her gaze fell on Regina's form, lying back against a hut. Was she dead? Where was Vydas? He'd been not far behind them.

Her body shifted, and she let out a moan. She was alive!

"Speak now," the Templar said, "or Tivar will chain your souls to his chariot! Who is responsible?"

"I am," Vydas' voice shouted.

Yells, screams, and cries all erupted at once.

Vydas strode into view, a dozen paces from the Templar, *Tamskelti* in hand. It sang with dwarf magic as it left his hilt.

Tears gathered in Mai's eyes. He'd given up trying to escape, and was sacrificing himself for them.

The Templar pointed his unholy rod, but Vydas closed the distance fast. The shimmering blue blade chopped through the rod and hit the Templar, shearing armor, flesh, and bone. It fell to its knees, then crumpled into the dirt.

Blue rays sprayed out from the center of the village. One struck Vydas.

Mai took a step toward them.

JC Kang

"No!" Ku tugged at her. "There's nothing you can do."

Mai could only watch in dread fascination.

Tamskelti glowed a brighter blue, and though Vydas staggered back, he did not fall. The Templars unleashed more energy bolts, forcing him back.

In seconds, he reached Regina's prone form, and the Templars moved in.

He knelt down and kissed her. Using his sword as a crutch, he pushed himself up.

Then he drove his sword into her throat.

Mai covered her silent scream. Ku yanked her, and her feet moved of their own accord. Heavens, Vydas had killed his own mate. The few seconds it took to reach the cornfields dragged into what felt like an eternity. Chest heaving as much from grief as fatigue, she squatted and looked.

Back in the village, dozens of conflicting sounds mingled and clashed. She closed her eyes to sort them all out. *Tamskelti* hummed as Vydas swung it. The giant stomped. A Tivari groaned. Unholy rods discharged lightning with crackles. A swarm of birds flapped in circles. And of course, the skiff whined.

Tears trickled down Mai's cheeks. People were dying.

A hand tugged on her shoulder.

She opened her eyes.

Ku's lips drooped in a frown. *We need to go*, he mouthed, expression anguished.

Mai took one last look at the village. The fizzling and screaming of Tivari unholy rods came to a stop. It was over.

Wiping her tears, she crouched low and followed Ku and the others through the cornfields. This misadventure had ended in almost complete failure. Sure, she'd learned a Command, and the basics of a Charm, but she'd never had a chance to try the latter. Heavens knew if she understood it enough to use on Cleric Pyuz. Other than that, they'd delivered the sword, but now its wielder and his Empath lover were dead.

Mai sucked in a sharp breath. If the Tivari recognized the weapon for what it was, then they'd know the handful of rebels in the North weren't alone. Maybe they'd even guess the elves were helping. This rebellion never stood a chance. It was time to go home, to the village, and protect her family and friends from whatever happened.

Chapter 26:
Confrontation

The joyful bird songs did little to cheer Mai up as she trudged with Ku, Makeda, Vanya, and Dash through Cathay's wooded mountains in the early evening. After escaping the village, they'd regrouped with a sole madaeri, who bore a mix of sad and welcome news:

Vydas had escaped, and Daisy was helping him return home. He'd not wanted to live, carrying the weight of Regina's death by his own hands.

"It was either that, or allow her to be captured." Dash had shaken his head.

Old Rush had also remained in the area, volunteering to help organize the madaeri. Flick had corroborated the villagers' story, that Northerners had been responsible for the cleric's death. Much to Ku's visible relief, the shaman girl, Nada, had been able to mingle back in with the rest of the villagers without the Tivari suspecting her.

Now, most of the way home, memories of the disaster still haunted Mai. No doubt, more Tivari would keep a close eye on the village, and if any of the survivors had seen *Tamskelti*, they would tighten their control over all villages in the world.

She looked up into the heavens, where the Blue, White, and Iridescent Moons floated closer to each other than the night before. If what Aralas had told her that first night among the dragon bones was true, magic peaked during the conjunction; and it only happened every three hundred years.

Was it days away? Weeks? If the rebellion failed now, mankind would endure another dozen generations of slavery.

To her right, Vanya strode along, lost in her thoughts, yet still sidestepping every tree and branch in her way with nonchalant grace. A few steps behind, Makeda seemed to find joy in every last plant she passed. If they felt hurried, it sure didn't show.

Mai let out a long sigh. How many days had already passed since they left the protected town? Twelve? The harvest would conclude soon. Her family's time was running out.

She looked to Ku. "How much further?"

He threw his hands up. "Ask Dash. This is *his* shortcut."

"Stop complaining." Dash harrumphed. "I've cut two days off your journey, if your destination is where you say."

Ku sidestepped a bush. "Why would I lie?"

"Because you've tried to keep everything secret."

Mai looked from one to the other. Their jibes at one another felt less like distrust, and more like the bickering of old friends.

Vanya hurried to catch up. "You really didn't like madaeri, did you?"

Ku poked at Dash, who sidestepped the jab without even looking. "They're not all bad, especially when they don't fear the Tivari. Still, I have nightmares from when Wenhui and I fled our village. The madaeri hounded us relentlessly with their haunting cries, and there was no way we could hide from the Templars."

Dash's jovial expression slipped. "We can't help it. A human wouldn't survive the things the masters do to us for disobedience."

Ku tried to pat him on the head, but missed. "Like I said, not all madaeri are bad. One of your kind was with Yanyan when she rescued us."

That name again. Though maybe when they got back, the diva would help with the new Dragon Songs that could hopefully control Cleric Pyuz.

Dash might not have cared who Yanyan was, but his eyes widened. "What other madaeri?"

"The one who freed our pursuers and convinced them to join our side." Ku held his hand out at belly height, demonstrating his savior's height, which was about the same as all the other madaeri they'd met. "He went by the name Fleet."

"The Traveler," Dash said, his tone one of awe. "So it's true."

Ku ducked under a tree limb. "He sometimes appears with Aralas."

Dash nodded. "Nobody knows where he's from, and they say that he's old, even by our standards, and he escaped the Tivari ages ago."

Makeda raised an eyebrow. "Your standards? Just how old are you?"

Forehead wrinkling, Dash counted on his fingers. "Four."

"Four years old?" Ku glared at him. "That's not old at all."

Dash glared back, sidestepping a stump without looking. "Four *hundred*."

Mai's brows furrowed. She'd just learned what a *hundred* was in the village. "Did you see the last time the three moons met in the heavens?"

Dash's finger and thumb formed a circle. "Yes. It was very pretty, like an eye of the gods."

Vanya nodded. "Aralas called it the Godseye Conjunction."

Mai frowned. The elf angel had never told her the name.

Makeda's voice sounded wistful. "Lunasti, God of the Sea, salutes Magius, God of Magic, in Ayara's Embrace. Aralas says we will feel the resonance of the universe more strongly than ever."

"Can't you humans just appreciate something beautiful?" Dash yawned. Then, his eyes took on a sharp focus. His ears twitched. He held up a hand.

Everyone froze.

Mai closed her eyes and listened. Her hearing might not be as good as a madaeri's, but there was no mistaking the whine of a demon skiff. It couldn't be far away. She opened her mouth to warn the others.

"Demon skiff," Dash said.

Ku's mouth tightened into a frown. "I thought they weren't pursuing us."

"Maybe they are searching for Vydas." Vanya's hand went to her sword.

"Either way, we need to hide," Dash said.

"Or fight." Vanya patted her sword.

The *bahaduur* never strayed from conflict. Mai's jaw tightened. She turned to Makeda. She hadn't used sorcery for a few days, so she should've had plenty of energy. "Can you use your cloak?"

"Yes, but I don't have much of the powder component, so it would tire me even more. I don't know how long I could keep it up, even with your help."

Ku gritted his teeth. "And we don't know how persistent the demon or Templars might be."

"I know a place." Breaking into a run, Dash beckoned them along a path.

Mai rushed to keep up with him. With no clear trails, she nearly tripped over fallen limbs several times as she zigged and zagged. Branches scraped her and snagged her poncho. Up ahead, the sound of falling water grew louder.

"Templars!" Ku yelled. "Six of them."

Always six, it seemed. She looked over her shoulder.

Makeda and Vanya were close on her heels. Ku hung a little farther back, the browns and greens of his poncho flashing in the gaps between branches and leaves.

The waterfall roared now. She turned back to the front, only to skid to a stop before nearly knocking Dash over the edge of the cascade. Vanya came to a smooth stop behind her, and caught Makeda by the wrist.

Mai looked down. White foam rippled across a dark green pool below, which was perhaps more than the height of four, maybe even five men. She turned to Dash. "There's no escape!"

"Jump," Dash said.

"Jump?" Mai stared at him, incredulous. Even if they survived, there was no hiding from the Templars.

Dash pointed straight down. "There's a place behind the waterfall."

Maybe—

Makeda slipped past and leaped.

Mai could only watch as Makeda pressed her arms to her side as she plummeted. She entered the water feet-first, and sent a splash spouting back up.

"Amateur." With three steps, Vanya jumped head-first. Hands together, she entered upside-down, slipping through the water with barely a splash.

Makeda had since surfaced, and was scrambling to the rocks.

Mai shuddered. *They* might be able to do it, but this was too much. Too high. She looked back.

Ku was still well behind, now limping through the woods. The dark shapes of Templars shifted among the trees. At least the twists and bends didn't give them a direct shot with their unholy rods.

"Hurry!" Dash turned and ran *toward* them. Ducking and twisting with effortless dexterity, he reached Ku. Though too short to support a grown man, he placed Ku's hand on his shoulder.

Behind them, the Tivari were gaining ground. Their grey mesh armor and turquoise skin were clear now.

"Jump!" Ku waved at her. He cleared the woods, a dozen feet away, and staggered a few steps.

One of the Templars emerged from the tree line. He leveled the unholy rod at Ku. A blue ray flashed.

Dash stepped between them. He shrieked. Stumbling, he wrapped his arms around the Tivari's leg.

With limping steps, Ku careened into her.

The Templar yelped as Dash bit him.

With Ku's weight bearing down on her, her foot slipped backward over the edge. With a last glance, she caught a glimpse of the madaeri.

The Tivari was punching him in the head, sending red blood spraying, while another tried to pry him loose.

No! Not Dash.

Then she was falling. It must've only taken a second, but it seemed to drag on forever. The water rushed up. It slammed into her, knocking the breath from her lungs. Her head spun.

Next thing she knew, Ku and Vanya were dragging her from the water.

Makeda yelled some gibberish, her voice barely carrying over the roaring falls.

Mai blinked several times. She was at the side of the pool. Vanya slipped an arm under her, and half-dragged, half-guided her toward where Makeda waved frantically from under the cascade.

Mai risked a glance to the top of the falls, where a Templar appeared.

Then they were under the falls.

Had the Tivari seen them?

Chapter 27:
Last Chance

The pocket behind the waterfall was barely wide enough for the four of them to move about. The water's roar might not have completely muffled Vanya or Makeda's hushed whispers in Mai's keen ears, but their words still made no sense. Shivering from the wet clothes which clung to her, she felt for the magic bauble which translated their words.

Gone. It must've been dislodged by the plunge into the water. She looked to Ku, who was nodding in response to whatever the others were saying. When he pointed, she followed his finger.

Through the waterfall, the blurry forms of three Templars stalked along the opposite bank of the pool, coming closer. One dragged another shape behind it—Dash. He wasn't moving.

Mai's stomach wrenched into a tight knot. Tears clouded her vision.

Makeda poked her. The frantic sounds spilling out of her mouth made no sense.

Shaking her head, Mai turned her head and pointed to where the magic bauble had once been. "I don't understand."

"Her powders and herbs are wet," Ku said, his knuckles white around his sword hilt. "In order for her to conjure her magic cloak, she needs your music."

"What about Dash?"

Ku squared his shoulders. "I owe him my life. There are six of them, and Vanya hurt herself in the fall."

Mai looked to Vanya, who nodded. Her words, too, came out as gibberish.

"She can still fight," Ku translated, "but not as fast."

There had to be some way to help Dash, though what could they do that wouldn't reveal their hiding place?

The distorted shapes of the first three Templars drew closer. The other three now crept along the far end of the pool, one limping.

"Come out," one said in heavily accented Cathayi. "We know you are behind there."

"They know we're here." Ku gripped his sword and charged out.

No sooner had he stepped out from behind the waterfall than a blue light struck him. He collapsed.

Hobbling, Vanya started to follow, but Mai blocked her way.

"They'll just pick us off, one by one," she said. "Help me get Ku back."

Keeping low, they both reached for Ku's ankles. Several lines of multicolored light zipped close by, forcing them to duck back before they could get ahold of him.

Peering at Ku's chest to look for the telltale signs of breathing, Mai listened for Ku's heart.

It still beat.

Feebly.

"He's alive."

More lights of blue, green, and red flashed, reflecting in the curtain of water.

Mai joined Makeda as they dropped to the ground. Vanya shifted on her good leg. Energy crackled along the falls, but didn't make it through. In one spot, a hole opened up, only to be filled by the tumbling water.

The Tivari let out a dozen different unmistakable curses.

Blowing out a sigh, Mai clambered to her feet. No matter what, it was only a temporary reprieve. The Tivari need only walk further around the pool to get a clear view of them.

"Come out." The Templar leader yanked Dash's limp form up. He set the unholy rod to the madaeri's neck.

Dash screamed as his body convulsed.

Mai started forward, only to be stayed by Makeda's hand. Her words, while pretty, had a cadence, a structure, even if they made no sense.

"I don't understand!" Mai said.

Makeda made a hooking and casting motion.

Bait. Dash was bait.

Eyebrows drawn together, Vanya hobbled forward and spoke more foreign words.

Mai clenched and unclenched her hands. Even if she didn't understand Vanya, the *bahaduur*'s expression said it all. She intended to fight.

"Wait," Mai said. "They will use their unholy rods as soon as you step out."

Then again, the Templars were on the move again. Once they had line of sight, there was no room in here even for Vanya to dodge their unholy magic. Mai's fists squeezed tight. There had to be some way out of this trap. If only she could think over the torrent of falling water.

Water which splashed in a rhythm.

The rhythm of the world's pulse.

Just like at the waterfall back home. *In order to project sound farther,* Yanyan had said*, you must hear and borrow the sounds around you.* Makeda's shield had altered the pulse of the world, but there was a better way. One which she'd heard, but never had a chance to practice. She patted her pocket. The flute was gone. Humming risked drawing the attention of Avarax.

Still, Dash needed her. They all needed her.

Closing her eyes, she listened in the spaces between the waterfall's rhythmic splashes. The Tivari's hearts beat in unison as they worked their way around the pool, just like at the dragon bones. Resolute. Intent.

Regina had failed to dominate the heart of just one Tivari. Mai bit her bottom lip. How could she, who'd never even practiced a charm, accomplish what an experienced Empath could not?

Mai looked at the others. With all her weight on her left foot, Vanya looked relaxed compared to Makeda's fidgeting.

Mai closed her eyes again and settled her racing pulse with a deep breath. Listening for both the Tivari's heartbeats and the rhythm of the waterfall, she hummed at a cadence like the one Regina had used to reset her charm. The notes rose and fell, billowing out from her like the ripples on the pond.

In her ears, the pulse of the world shifted, along with the Tivari heartbeats. Along the edge of the pool, their steps faltered.

Vanya's stance relaxed, and she smiled as she spoke reassuring words.

One of the Templars' heartbeat picked back up. The others followed. They resumed their march. The first now stood in her clear line of sight. He raised his unholy rod.

Mai's heart stuttered. The hum choked in her throat. Energy seeped from her arms and legs.

Makeda pushed past and grunted a noise similar to snuffling pig. Flames darted from her fingertips and slammed into the lead's face. He tumbled into the pool with a splash. The two others jumped out of the line of fire. The sorceress hunched over, panting.

Maybe there was hope. Mai took deep breaths.

Straightening, gasping for breath, Makeda stepped out and shouted out more sounds.

The Tivari in back barked a command. The first jumped to a spot with a line of sight on them, its rod pointed in their direction. A blue ray streaked into the space between the water and the overhang, striking Makeda. Her knees wobbled, and then she collapsed, moaning. Vanya shouldered past. Her blade arced in the path of a second bolt. The sword glowed brighter blue, and her body tensed in spasms for a second. Then she pushed through the pain and closed the distance to the Templars.

Mai sighed in relief. Surely they'd be all right.

One fell, black blood spurting from the gash her sword left across its neck. The next lifted its rod into the path of her attack. The boom rang in Mai's ears, and the flash of blue light blinded her. When she blinked away the afterimage, the Templar and Vanya both lay sprawling on the bank.

It was just Mai now. Her stomach twisted. She'd failed once already, and now it was up to her to rescue the others. If they were still even alive. Why hadn't it worked the first time?

The three remaining Tivari now advanced toward the opening, no hesitation in their strides.

Maybe in her panic, she hadn't borrowed the sound of the waterfall enough to project. What had Yanyan said?

It is not the strength of the pluck that matters, but the intensity of your emotion. Once you have seized the song's emotion and made it your own, root yourself to the ground, align your spine, and let your heart impel your sound.

Her emotion...had been fear. Her root to the ground, forgotten in her panic.

The Templars now crowded toward the crevice, their unholy rods at the ready.

Taking a deep breath to settle her heart, Mai mustered all her remaining energy. She curled her toes into the ground, straightened her spine, and squared her shoulders. Then, she hummed. Note after note, she followed the rhythm of the waterfall and the pulse of the world.

The Tivari's march slowed, but didn't stop.

What had Regina done when she tried to charm the priest? The pulse of the world had shifted in her attempt to bring their hearts in harmony with hers. Then again, she'd failed, just like Mai had the first time. Even now, the Templars' steps regained their confidence. They raised their weapons; they must see her as a real threat.

Let your heart impel your sound. Mai broke off her hum and sang a song of companionship, like she'd sung around the dinner fires back home. Back then, she could hold the entire village entranced; so much so that even Ying's dour husband, Qiu, smiled.

Who knew if these Tivari even understood her words, but surely they could feel her intention. Still, her energy had just about drained. Coughing out the last few words, she sank to her knees and panted. She looked up.

Eyes glazing over, the Templars lowered their unholy rods. Their cruel smirks melted into ridiculous smiles. Heavens, had she succeeded?

The leader scurried over and offered a hand. "I am Vrk. Are you all right, my friend?"

Heavens, it had worked. Mai stared at his smooth turquoise fingers. A Tivari had never extended a kind gesture before, and it was hard to believe he wouldn't just pull her into a stab of his ceremonial knife. She tentatively took his rough hand. "Thank you."

"You are all wet." He pulled her up and reached into a belt pouch. It looked much too small for the mesh cloth he drew from it and offered.

Accepting a Tivari's help to stand was one thing, but their towel was another. With a long look at the cloth, she shook her head. "No, thank you. I am fine. But what about my friends? Can you check on them?"

Vrk's lower lip jutted out between his fangs. Was that a pout? It guided her back out and barked out a few words to the remaining two. They leaned over and checked on Ku, Makeda, and Vanya.

He then turned to her. "We just stunned them. They should be all right."

"Why stun?"

"Because the uh, High Priests want to capture you."

A shiver ran down Mai's spine. No doubt bad things would happen to captives, but... "Why?"

"To know why there have been so many incidents over the last several months."

"Well, tell them that we escaped."

Vrk jaw squared. "We will be punished."

Not that it mattered to her, but Regina had said a charm had limitations. They probably wouldn't remain so friendly if asked to endanger themselves. She looked back to her companions, now pushing themselves up and looking suspiciously at the Tivari. Up ahead, Vanya moaned and propped herself on an elbow.

"Are you all right?" Mai peeled Ku's magic bauble from his ear and affixed it to her own.

"I think so. I jumped back and only took part of the blast." She looked dolefully at her *naga*, now mangled. "It absorbed some of the energy."

"I'm surprised," Vrk said, walking past to his fallen comrade. He knelt down and picked up the unholy rod, also twisted and bent. "I didn't think there was anything your weapons could do against ours."

"Oh, no." Vanya pointed.

Following her finger, Mai's gaze fell on Dash, lying at the side of the pool.

The rise and fall of the madaeri's chest was so slight. She rushed to his side and knelt.

One hand was bent at a strange angle, and one eye was swollen shut, but the other opened a slit. His voice came out weakly. "Mai. I'm glad you're all right. How is Ku?"

She found Ku in the corner of her vision. He was now wobbling on his feet.

"He's fine, just a little groggy. Don't worry about him. We need to get you to a healer."

Dash's face contorted. "It hurts too much to shake my head, but I'm a goner."

308

Mai's stomach knotted. The madaeri had proven to be invaluable. And loyal.

Stumbling over, Ku fell to his knee at Dash's side. "You can't die. I owe you my life."

"As long...as you know." Dash took a few labored breaths. "Come closer."

Mai and Ku leaned in close.

He whispered, "The Tivari carry a mushroom powder...they snort it for recreation. It makes them happy. Will put them to sleep...and give them good dreams. Offer to sniff it together..."

Ku shook his head. "I don't want to take a nap with them."

"No...it doesn't affect humans. It will give you a chance...to get away." Then, the light faded from his eyes and his body went limp.

Tears flooded Mai's vision. First the warriors, then Regina and the giant. Now Dash.

Ku threw himself on top of Dash's body. "I'm so sorry. I'm so sorry."

Grief sapped the last of Mai's energy. The Tivari had killed Dash. She blinked away the tears and looked to Vrk. "You did this!"

Vrk shrugged. "When they go bad, we have to put them down. They're too dangerous, otherwise. He's lucky it ended fast."

Heat burned in her head. The turtles' eggs would pay for their cruelty. Squaring her shoulders, Mai lifted her chin to the Vrk's magic mirror. "What have you reported back to your High Priests?"

"That we're in pursuit of rebels."

"Did you say it included Aksumi and Ayuri people?"

He shook his head. "We just found out now."

"Be a good friend and say everyone looks like me and him." She tilted her head toward Ku. "Tell them that you are still in pursuit."

Ku raised an eyebrow. "What are you planning to do?"

"Send them in the wrong direction."

Chapter 28:
Accusations

T he pulse of the world thrummed louder in Mai's ears as they approached the entrance to Cathay. It had been two days since the Templars had used a pungent herbal poultice to heal Vanya's knee. Afterwards, Mai had followed Dash's suggestion with the mushroom powder. It'd stung the inside of her nose and given her a mild headache, but as the madaeri had said, it knocked the Templars out.

Ku and Vanya ended them, with her using one of their own knives. Then, after taking the remaining mushroom powder, Mai and her companions had fled, unfortunately with no time to bury Dash. It wasn't long before Ku recognized the surrounding area and led them home. Maybe it was luck, especially since their best fighter was without her weapon, but they made it back without any more sightings of Tivari or demon skiffs.

Now, just like the first time she'd come to Cathay, Kang was busy painting on the cliff face, adding more details to the coiling silver dragon and the silver-haired woman. She bobbed her head in greeting, but made an effort not to look at his work.

She passed through the elf cloak and looked on the tiny Kingdom of Cathay again. Unlike the first time, the town of elegant sloping roofs didn't hold the same sense of wonder. Too much had happened since then.

Still, the familiar warrior shouts and the hammering at the dwarves' anvil were comforting. She closed her eyes and listened for two particular sounds within the countless sounds that sang in concert with the pulse of the world.

There. Whether Aralas and Yanyan hid in her house, or behind their waterfall, or Heavens knew where, their unique heartbeats intermingled with one another, building upon each other.

Hot rage rose to Mai's head. Neither had bothered to come to help when they'd faced the Templars. It wasn't as if they were that far away, not that distances even mattered to the elf angel. Maybe Dash would've survived.

She hurried down the path into the basin, leaving behind Ku, Vanya, and Makeda. When she got to the bottom, she took a deep breath to settle her anger, and then closed her eyes to find Aralas—just like the first time she'd come, months ago. She zigged and zagged among the buildings, using only her ears to guide her. People would shout greetings, but beyond an acknowledging nod, Mai kept up with her search. Even with her eyes closed, she knew exactly where she was.

The dwarven forge. The dining hall. Doctor Wu's house. Although acupuncture would do her body and spirit good now, there were more pressing matters; it didn't sound like the doctor was even there, anyway.

Mai continued through the town, every place now familiar based on their sounds. The training grounds. Wenhui's house. Oh, how she wanted to tell Wenhui about their mishaps and small victories, but that would have to wait. As she continued deeper into town, Aralas and Yanyan's rapid heartbeats grew louder and easier to pick out.

At last, Mai opened her eyes at the palace gates. The guards bowed and let her pass. Inside the palace grounds, dozens of officials and warriors bustled about. A gust of wind sent bells chiming, carrying Aralas and Yanyan's sounds. They were in the Hall of Harmony.

Where he'd kissed Mai, after their drum duet. In her mind, this was supposed to be her special place, with that special memory. Yet he was here, with the Dragon Charmer.

Gritting her teeth, Mai ignored the eyes that fell on her and marched to the entrance. That Turtle's Egg and his whore might each have more magic than her in their little fingers, but that wouldn't stop her from...from.... She pushed open the doors.

Between the drums, Yanyan was straddling Aralas, bending over him with their tongues locked in a duel. Her gown pooled in her elbows, leave her upper body bare. His left hand cupped her right breast, while the other was under her skirts, probably on her butt. Whether he was clothed or not, it was impossible to tell from the way her skirts covered the both of them. An urgent moan hung in her throat.

Mai's heart squeezed tighter than the vice at the dwarven forge. Jealousy mingled with anger. Heavens, why did she have to like the rakish elf angel so much? "Turtle's Egg!" she screamed.

While Aralas' hands continued whatever they were doing, Yanyan reclaimed her tongue from between his lips and turned to look over her shoulder with a smirk. "My apprentice has returned."

Some apprentice. Mai lowered her hand from where she'd wrapped a tangle of hair around her finger. "Maybe if you actually taught me, we wouldn't have lost so many people."

Aralas' hands stopped. He sat up, sending Yanyan sliding down to the floor with a delighted squeal that grated in Mai's ears. With her skirts dropping, it was clear he was wearing the usual hooded cape over his tight grey clothes. Even if he did have magical man parts that came out like a duck's, they couldn't possibly be rutting with his clothes on. He tightened the cloak over himself.

He shook out his tousled golden hair, which all cascaded into a perfect frame around his face. Had he lost weight? His chin seemed shaper, the jawline more defined.

"What happened?" he asked, gaze sharpening. Again, his voice pitched slightly higher, as it always did when he was with Yanyan.

Mai jabbed a finger at him. "If you cared, you would already know, wouldn't you?"

"Despite what you might believe, my magic has limitations. We lost contact when you reinforced Makeda's magic cloak. Very impressive, by the way." He looked sidelong at Yanyan, whose lips pursed.

We again? "Where were you?" Mai snarled.

While Yanyan resumed kissing his neck, he fiddled with their intermingled hair. "Oh, all over the place. This rebellion is a coordinated effort. I trust you delivered *Tamskelti* to the Nothori King?"

Mai nodded. "Yes, but Regina and his giants died in an ambush."

"Most unfortunate. She was the most talented Empath we've trained. Thankfully, there are a few others who will soldier on in her place."

Soldier on? Fire raged in Mai's head.

"How can you be so uncaring?" Mai said when she'd recovered from her shock. From the image Regina had shared, she'd been another in a long trail of lovers. Yet he didn't seem the least bit concerned.

Aralas leaned away from Yanyan and met Mai's gaze. "I *do* care. However, this is the fact of war. People we care for will die."

People that Mai cared for still might. As angry as she'd been, she'd almost forgotten her other reason for coming here. "Send me back to my village now. I know how to charm the priest."

A grin formed on Aralas' lips. "I had planned for you to accompany Yanyan as she continues charming priests all along the east, and winning the hearts of their villages." He lifted the diva's chin.

Mai gritted her teeth. "Continue? Why didn't you send me with her at first, so I could learn the magic from a real Dragon Singer, instead of trying to piece it together from an Empath?"

The elf angel yawned. "It made you use that petulant brain of yours, and you succeeded in figuring out the basics. Being forced to use magic under pressure made you better. Stronger."

And nearly killed her. Mai's fists clenched.

Aralas' narrowed eyes shifted to her hands. "Working with Yanyan will give you more practice before you confront Cleric Pyuz on your own."

"*Now*. I've charmed three Templars already."

Lifting his gaze to meet hers, he nuzzled into Yanyan's neck, eliciting her annoying giggle. "Yanyan charmed at least a hundred before I let her try by herself."

A hundred was a number she hadn't even known before coming to Cathay, not much less than the total number of villagers who might face Cleric Pyuz's judgment at the end of harvest. "I am ready."

"What if you fail?" He raised his eyebrow. "What if you're captured or killed?"

"Then you will have others to *soldier on*." Mai turned and glared at Yanyan, who only smiled her poisonous smile.

"Very well." Aralas untangled himself from Yanyan and picked himself up, careful to keep himself covered with his cloak. "You will practice the drums with Yanyan while I confer with my spy in your village. He'll give me a time and location for you to meet him, and he'll get you safely into your village."

"Spy? How long have you had a—"

Aralas spoke a word and disappeared with a pop of air.

Yanyan stood and smoothed out her skirts. She pointed her chin at the drums. "Shall we begin?"

Anger burning in her chest, Mai glared at the diva.

Yanyan shrank back for a split second before straightening and laughing. "My, my. If the Tivari clerics had your eyes, they wouldn't need their unholy rods."

"Just get on with it." Shocked by the petulance in her own voice, Mai swept up a pair of sticks and took her position in front of the center drum. Her heart pounded in her ears, angry and turbulent like waterfalls fed by spring melt.

Yanyan's, on the other hand, remained firm and resolute. With a dismissive smirk, she took her place across from Mai.

Mai's first strike of the drum sent a tangible shudder through the room. Yanyan gawked. The drum dance duet, long ignored during her journey, came to her without conscious thought. Turning, she faced the lower drum and rapped out a pattern. Unlike the earlier times, where her spirit soared with the notes, her anger now coursed through the beats.

On she drummed, Yanyan mirroring her. The logic of the dance and rhythm had brought order and discipline to her heart in the past; now, it became calculating and scheming, like a master tactician plotting out a ruthless ambush. The sounds took control of Mai's body, pushing and pulling her through the three drums like a puppeteer.

Soon, Yanyan struggled to keep pace. Her conceited expression melted. Her brow furrowed, and her lips tightened into a thin line. Unlike their first duel on the pipa, which Mai could never hope to win, this battle among the drums turned to her favor. As her drumming waxed, Yanyan's waned.

The duet continued, the music propelling Mai through the routine. When the song reached crescendo, a bead of sweat trickled down the diva's forehead, and she blinked it out of an eye. Still, she managed to keep up as they prepared to end the song on one last beat. In their planned performance before the emperor, it was meant to stir the assembled soldiers into a confident fervor.

Listen. Connect. In Mai's ears, Yanyan's heart stuttered.

Let your heart impel your sound. Mai channeled all her anger and resentment into that last strike, timing it to Yanyan's heartbeat. The sound reverberated from the drum, shaking the hall.

The diva collapsed to the floor with a gasp.

Mai stared at her. She'd done it. She'd overcome the Dragon Charmer, who sprawled before her with wide eyes. Her usually perfectly coiffed hair had fallen free from its hairpins, giving her a disheveled look.

"Fool! This is a Dragon Song duet! Our music is supposed to build on each other's. You turned it into a duel." Yanyan hissed the words through her panting, but then hung her shoulders. Her hair flopped into her face. "But you knew that."

Had she? Mai wetted her lips and listened. Despite the rebuke in Yanyan's tone, there was something else. Uncertainty? Self-doubt?

Those were the emotions Mai had experienced throughout her life. She now saw the diva in a new light.

She was just a human. Proud, for sure, but that was armor to hide her own insecurities. The two of them were too much alike.

In that moment, Mai saw where her own petty desires for acceptance would lead her. The anger which had invigorated her now drained from her limbs, and her wobbling knees gave way.

She tumbled down beside the diva. Forcing her eyes open, she met Yanyan's gaze, and an understanding passed between them.

Chapter 29:

Homecoming

The sound of rustling waters greeted Mai as she and Aralas reappeared by her favorite river pool. The pool glowed light blue in the night sky. Her heart stirred at the nostalgia. For as long as she could remember, she'd come to the river daily to collect fresh water for the workers and steal a few minutes to watch the ripples. It had been months since she'd visited, and only now did it make sense: the light from the Blue and White Moons danced in its ripples, following the rhythm set by the pulse of the world.

Aralas' heart beat in time with it, so resolute and steady compared to earlier in the day. Chuckling, he blew the hair out of his face. When he spoke, it was again in that slightly deeper pitch than when he was with Yanyan. "You could always hear the pulse of the world, but it is only now that you realize that is what fascinated you about this pond."

How did he know? "It couldn't have been chance that I met you." Mai searched his eyes.

They were so beautiful, especially in the blue light. His mischievous smile, too, cooled the entire afternoon of rage she'd felt while practicing with Yanyan. It was so hard to stay angry, especially when the diva wasn't sucking on his face.

When he looked at her, his gaze seemed less sharp, more kind. How quickly he could change! "No. I've known about you for some time." He tucked her hair behind her ear.

"Because you would need someone to soldier on if Yanyan died?"

Brow furrowing, he cocked his head. It was as if he'd forgotten he'd spoken the words.

Snorting, she said, "How did you know about me?"

"Me." A male voice behind her nearly scared her soul out of her body.

She whirled around, her old dress so scratchy compared to the silk gown she'd worn in Cathay.

Just a few feet from her stood a madaeri with curly brown hair and dark brown eyes. Unlike any of the others she'd met, this one was clean. He bore a striking resemblance to Dash.

Her heart squeezed so tightly, she found it hard to draw a breath.

He extended a small hand. "My name is Fleet."

Fleet. Her eyes widened as she stared at his fingers. This was the so-called Traveler that the madaeri all spoke of in hushed whispers. She turned to Aralas. "Has he always been in my village?"

"I'm down here," Fleet grumbled. "And no. I travel all over the world. It's only been in the last two months that Aran—I mean, Aralas here—insisted that I keep an eye on your parents."

Mai stared at the elf angel. Apparently, he cared more than he let on. "Why didn't you tell me?"

He shrugged. "We needed to give you an incentive to learn fast. And it's not as if Fleet could save them if Cleric Pyuz decided to kill them."

"You underestimate me," Fleet muttered.

Aralas snorted. "Anyway, Fleet will sneak you back home. I trust he's bribed the village madaeri to keep from reporting your return to Cleric Pyuz."

Somehow, Fleet was now standing by Aralas, pulling something out from elf angel's cloak. "Nothing that the promise of a little snack can't accomplish."

Aralas swatted Fleet's hands away. "Good. Now, I suggest you hide at home for a while and practice listening to Cleric Pyuz's heartbeat. Maybe even try to chip away at his resolve with your magic while you remain hidden. When you're ready, try to bring him under your control."

She patted the new flute she'd borrowed from the Hall of Harmony. "What if I fail?"

"Best not to think of the consequences," he said.

"No, I need to know."

"I imagine he will make you watch as he exterminates your entire village. Then, he'll take you to the High Priest."

Mai sucked in a sharp breath.

"Remember, use your flute. If you sing or hum, Avarax will hear it. If he appears now, the rebellion is doomed."

Heart squeezing, Mai gave a tentative nod. Still, the only way she knew how to charm a priest was with a song of comradery.

"Are you sure you are ready?"

Was she? She nodded.

"Once you succeed, tell him not to harass the villagers, and to keep reporting back to his superiors that everything is normal. Then, I'll take you back to Cathay so you can train for your own mission."

"Mission?" She raised an eyebrow.

"To charm Avarax."

Fleet whistled.

Memories of the enormous dragon circling over Cathay sent shudders through Mai's body.

Aralas set his hands on her shoulders. "The rebellion relies on you. Everything you have gone through was meant to prepare you for a confrontation with him. If the Last Dragon allies with the Tivari instead of us, all hope is lost. If we can turn him against the Tivari, however…"

"I need more training."

"You're the one who insisted on coming here."

Her shoulders slumped. In her rush to save her family, she risked not only herself, but all of Cathay. Who knew if she'd even survive a confrontation with Cleric Pyuz?

"I don't want to lose you. If you are in danger, squeeze this." He pressed a black cylindrical stone into her palm. It was smooth, and much lighter than it appeared. "It will let me know."

"If you cared so much, why didn't you give it to me on the mission to deliver *Tamskelti*? It could have saved so many people."

He chewed on his lower lip. "There is only one. Yanyan had it."

Always Yanyan first. Mai's shoulders stiffened. Probably the only reason he cared now was that she was the one whose voice Avarax responded to.

"May the Heavens smile on you. I am going to check on Makeda and Vanya. I will give them your regards. Now, I will leave you in Fleet's small but capable hands." The elf spoke a word and disappeared with a pop of air.

"My hands aren't that small, are they?" Fleet turned his hands over and back.

"*You* are small." Had she just said that? She needed Fleet's help. But maybe it was his resemblance to Dash.

Grumbling, Fleet beckoned her. "Come on."

With the moons as their guide, they crept along the irrigation ditches, the frog trills and insect chirps their only company. Whereas she might've been afraid of roving ghosts in the past, she'd travelled enough at night to know they were only a Tivari story to keep mankind controlled.

The harvest was almost over, leaving most of the fields covered in dry, shredded rice stalks. She rubbed her hands together, the callouses a memory of many past harvests. Not far in the distance, the dozens of hovels that made up her village shone in the moonlight.

Her eyes locked in on her own house. Heart soaring, she broke into a run.

Fleet's hand, surprisingly strong for his small size, seized her wrist. "Down, girl. You're like my grandma whenever she saw sweet biscuits."

"It's faster this way." She tugged back.

"Cleric Pyuz knows your habits. He has eyes on your favorite routes."

Mai looked from the village to him. "But Aralas said—"

"Aralas says a lot, but they can teleport themselves out of a mess with a single word."

"It's as if Cleric Pyuz knew I'd come back."

Fleet nodded. "Now you're thinking. He also knew you'd leave."

Mai gawked. "How?"

"He knew you'd started learning magic. He rightly guessed that if he killed Ying, it would send you running to your teacher."

Mai's stomach twisted. Ying's blood, and that of her unborn child, was on her hands.

"They sent out Templars to track you, but they had no idea you'd teleported." Grinning, he tapped the back of his neck, revealing his own loyalty scar. "Even now, they don't know about the elf angels, or how they've sown the seeds of rebellion across the world. They—"

Mai held up a hand. The rest of his story could wait. "So I can't go into the village. How am I going to see my parents?"

"I didn't say you couldn't, you just can't take your usual path."

Mai nodded, then trailed behind the madaeri as he took a long path around to the other end of the village.

At the edge of the fields, he crouched low. "All right, wait here."

Mai squirmed. She was so close. "Where are you going?"

When he spoke, his voice sounded suspiciously like hers. "I'm going to draw your family out with a *Ghost Echo*. Remember to keep your reunion as quiet as possible."

Would they brave venturing out of the village at night? Mai tracked the madaeri for a few feet before he seemed to melt into the background.

She was now alone, with only her thoughts as company. She'd waited for this moment for months, never knowing if her parents still lived. Cleric Pyuz had used them as bait this whole time; and like the worms the village boys used to lure fish, they might not survive even now.

Was the risk to her family and friends worth it? As brutal as Tivari rule was, if she'd just gone about with her life, they could've lived out many more years.

A ghost's low moan pealed through the night sky. Mai's soul just about jumped out of her body.

No, not a ghost. All along it'd been madaeri, forced by the Tivari to trick mankind into submission. Her eyes followed her ears, to where dark shapes moved inside the village.

Three of them, near her hut, ventured out now and approached. Her heart pattered. It could only be—

Father's bent-over, shirtless form hobbled along, supported by Mother and Little Sister Ling in their bulky dresses. He hadn't been so slow just a few months ago. Mai's stomach clenched. It was all she could do not to run up to them.

The three paused every so often, their heads raking back and forth, no doubt alert for ghosts. Fleet was nowhere to be seen. Every nerve wound tightly, Mai sprung up and ran to them.

They froze in place. In the dim moonlight, their expressions twisted into shock...and horror.

Mai stopped.

Mother held up her hands. Had she always smelled so...ripe? "Mai? Is it really you?"

"Yes!" Mai took another step—

Her family faltered back.

"What's wrong? It's really me." She reached out with spread arms.

Father turned to Mother. "It really sounds like her."

"Of course it's me."

Little Sister Ling took a tentative step forward. "Ghosts don't speak so clearly, though."

Mai cocked her head. Ghosts didn't speak at all, did they? If there even were such things. "I'm not a ghost. It's me. And please, quiet down."

"We just heard your voice," Mother said, "calling us here."

Mai's jaw tightened. Maybe Fleet had embellished the ghostliness of her voice. "I swear by the Heavens, I'm alive."

Mother extended a hand. "Is it really—?"

In two steps, Mai crossed the distance between them. She took Mother's hand and put it on her chest.

"Your hands! They are so warm. And your heart…it beats!" Mother's eyes widened. "By Lydath's grace, you're alive."

It'd been so long since anyone had invoked the Tivari gods, Mai almost cringed.

With a sharp breath, Little Sister Ling pushed past and threw her arms around Mai. Tears in her eyes, Mother wrapped her in a hug so tight, it nearly squeezed the air out of her.

Now without anyone's support, Father hobbled over and joined in the embrace. He patted her head. "After you fled, Cleric Pyuz questioned everyone. Poor Li, he—"

Li! Mai's heart would've leaped into her throat had everyone not been squeezing it so tight. She pushed back out of everyone's embrace. "What happened to Li?"

Mother sighed. "He was the last person to see you. Cleric Pyuz had him tied to the post in the village center for three days, without food. He was whipped several times a day."

Tears threatened to spill. All her fault. Mai took deep breaths to settle her heart. "What about now?"

Ling's tight shoulders relaxed. "Cleric Pyuz gave him a chance. He could only redeem his soul by harvesting twice his quota, to make up for your loss. Father, too." She tilted her head toward him.

Guilt bore down on Mai's chest. Her escape had been so selfish, and everyone had been punished because of it.

"Where did you go?" Father asked. "Cleric Pyuz proclaimed that Tivar smote you."

"He lied." An obvious answer, but one which slipped through Mai's tightened lips.

Mother gave a hesitant nod.

"The Tivari have lied to us for generations. Tivar is a god of evil. He didn't create us."

The three looked at her, mouths gaping wide.

"Hush," Father said, voice rising. "You'll be punished in the afterlife for such blasphemy!"

Mai pointed to her cheek. "I was healed by the grace of the true gods. And please, not so loud."

"Witchcraft!" Mother screamed, shaking her head in slow arcs.

People stirred in the village. Mai looked up. Several shadowed figures peeked out from their huts.

Father beckoned. "Come on, we will go to Cleric Pyuz and beg for forgiveness."

Mai held up a hand. "No. Listen to me. The stories of Cathay are true. I've seen it with my own eyes."

"If what you say is true," Father was nearly shouting, "then you must've been corrupted by their decadence. Cleric Pyuz must cleanse your soul, or you will pull Tivar's chariot in the afterlife."

Like the ones she'd seen on her mission to North Ridge. Mai shuddered. Whatever lies they may have been told for generations, at least the chariots had been true. Still, she held up a hand. "No. Our people were not meant to be slaves of the Tivari. See? I am alive, and I am here to show you Cleric Pyuz's unholy rod is nothing compared to the magic of the True Gods."

The doors to Cleric Pyuz's house slid open, lighting up his stout silhouette, and the unholy rod he held in his hand. Her boast was about to be tested.

Chapter 30:
Taming Lesser Dragons

Mai's heartbeat pounded in her ears as Cleric Pyuz marched toward them, several of the villagers in tow. She hadn't had a chance to listen to the rhythm of his heart, nor try to weaken him while she remained hidden. It was too soon to confront him. Hands trembling, she pulled the flute from her dress.

Running ahead of Cleric Pyuz was another familiar form, not much more than a shadow in the darkness. With its height and broad shoulders, though, it could only be Li.

If Mai's heart raced before, it sprinted now. With the harvest nearly over, the Tivari didn't need anyone for another season. Li and her family might all die here and now if she failed. As he drew closer, the moons lit his prominent nose.

He was a good-looking man, but not nearly as handsome as she remembered. Objectively speaking, he was plain compared to even Ku. And compared to Aralas… Mai's heart squeezed at the thought of the elf angel in Yanyan's arms.

"Oh, by Lydath's Grace." Li stepped forward with outstretched arms. "Mai! I thought you were dead."

Had he always smelled so…sour? Mai's nose crinkled of its own accord as she took a step back. Still, his smile was as sweet as she remembered. The tightness in her shoulders started to ease, and she strode forward into his embrace. She buried the side of her head into his firm chest. He seemed more bony, less muscular than before.

Still, the hug provided a sense of nostalgia, even if it didn't send the same tingles up and down her spine. What had Aralas said the day she left the village? That after everything was said and done, she might not even feel the same for Li anymore? She'd scoffed at the idea then, but now his prophecy had come true. Still, no matter what, he'd always be her first love.

Cleric Pyuz's heavy boot steps drew closer.

She lifted her chin from Li's chest and looked over his shoulder.

With one hand resting on the hilt of his ceremonial knife and the other gripping his unholy rod, the priest strode with purpose. His heartbeat was slow and intent; steadfast, like every Tivari she'd ever listened to. Maybe even without preparation, she could charm him. She tried to push away from Li, to reach her flute, but he held her firmly.

Cleric Pyuz arrived. "So, our little witch has returned." His forehead scrunched as he lifted his hand from the knife's hilt and glanced at his magic mirror. He leveled his unholy rod at them. "Step aside, Li."

Li released her, but turned around, interposing himself between the two of them, and stretched out his arms. "Cleric, Mai has returned. Of course she would. She is obedient."

If only he knew. With the extra space, she tried to slide her hand into the fold of her dress to retrieve the flute.

Li took a step backward, pressing against her.

"I will not warn you again, Li," Cleric Pyuz snarled. "I will invoke Tivar's wrath and reduce you to ashes."

Li's voice cracked. "No, please don't kill her. She just came back to me."

Shaking his head, Cleric Pyuz grinned. "Oh, I'll kill *you*, if I have to. I don't plan to kill *her*. The High Priest wants her alive. Seize her, Li, and we can save her soul."

Li's heart beat like Cathay's flag in a storm. One hand pushing between his shoulder blades, Mai stepped back and pulled out her flute.

Cleric Pyuz grunted something. Green light flashed from the unholy rod. It struck Li, lifting him off his feet and sending him back. He careened into her. The flute slipped from her grasp as she tumbled to the ground. She reached for it, but Li's weight pinned her down, also pressing Aralas' magic tube between them so she couldn't reach it.

Around them, people screamed. Somewhere nearby, Father limped toward her.

Li didn't move, but his heart still beat. Fitfully. The green light must've been the same fell magic the Templars had used on Regina. She'd saved Regina then, but it'd left her exhausted. She stretched again for the flute.

Cleric Pyuz's boot came down, just missing her hand, but crushing the wood instrument.

Mai yanked her hand back. All was lost. Aralas had been right, it was too early to confront the priest.

Now, Cleric Pyuz loomed over her, unholy rod pointing at her. His smirk exposed his tusks.

Closing her eyes, Mai took as deep a breath as possible with Li's weight crushing her. Her pulse rattled back to normal. It no longer echoed through her, and now Cleric Pyuz's own heartbeat filled her ears. Steadfast.

She bent her knees so her soles and spine were flat on the ground. Finding the pulse of the world, she spoke a command to his heart. "Drop it."

The priest's hand opened. Everyone gasped. The unholy rod dropped right on top of her. Even with her flagging energy, she clawed the earth, snatched it up and pointed it at him. It felt cool and smooth in her hand. Still, even if she could remember the sounds the Tivari used to invoke the rod's unholy magic, her mouth couldn't possibly imitate them, and in all likelihood, the Tivari gods wouldn't listen to a human.

Given his gawk, Cleric Pyuz probably thought she could use it. He took a step back, hands in the air.

Straining her neck to keep him in her sights, and the rod trained on him, Mai squirmed enough to get out from under Li. His heart still beat, erratically, and maybe, just maybe, she'd have enough energy to save him.

But what if she passed out? She'd be at Cleric Pyuz's mercy. Glaring at the priest, she rose up on to one knee.

"Mai," Mother screamed. "Don't be foolish."

Li's body started convulsing, just like Regina's had. His mouth gulped for air, like a carp taken from the Cathayi palace's pool. Li's mother screamed.

"Seize him." Mai pointed at the priest. "Otherwise, I can't save Li."

"Your witchcraft won't work." One side of Cleric Pyuz's lips quirked up. "But I can save him, with the grace of Tivar."

"Please!" Li's mother dropped to her knees by him.

"I need the holy rod." Cleric Pyuz extended his hand. His lips arced into a full grin now, with nothing but cruelty in them.

"Give him the holy rod!" Skinny Fang said.

The other villagers joined in. "Give it to him!"

With several deep breaths, Mai let the pulse of the world reinvigorate her. Just a little more… She held up a hand. "Have you ever seen Cleric Pyuz heal anyone? He can't! His gods are evil. They can only harm!"

Murmurs erupted among what must be over half the villagers. Despite the seeming disharmony, the underlying beat of their chatter followed the pulse of the world.

Mai rose and looked to her family. Their heads shook. What were they thinking? After a lifetime of dedication to Tivar, they had no reason to believe her. If she gave them the unholy rod, they might return it to the priest.

She'd just have to bluff more. Locking her toes into the ground, she straightened her spine and squared her shoulders. The pulse of the world coursed through her. Listening for Li's ragged heartbeat, she took a deep breath to settle her nerves. She rose her voice in song.

She wasn't sure what words spilled off of her lips, only that the melody was soothing. Her spirit soared as it could only when singing, and she projected her calm into Li.

Around her, everyone fell silent, eyes wide. Li's body relaxed, and his gasps settled into regular breaths. Mai's energy flickered. The unholy rod felt so heavy in her hand.

With a snarl, Cleric Pyuz reached for his ceremonial knife—then patted at his side. It wasn't there. He looked down, then left, then right. He took a step forward and tripped over his feet. He stumbled, and fell with a thud just a few feet away.

Panting, Mai looked toward him. He squirmed to free himself from the dry rice stalks entangling his ankles. How lucky!

Or maybe not luck. His ceremonial knife was missing, too, and she'd seen it as he approached. But how? Nobody had dared come closer to him. Now they all watched, gaping, as he crawled up to gain his feet.

Mai closed her eyes and breathed. Her energy still wavered. The song of charm on the Templars had almost knocked her out, and then, she'd borrowed the waterfall's rhythm.

Li's mother gasped.

"Li!" Skinny Fang, who hung back with the others, pointed.

There was a rhythm to their shouts. Mai turned.

Li eased himself up onto his elbows. "Mai?"

Silence. Everyone stared and gaped, no one more than Cleric Pyuz himself.

"He's alive!"

"Li's okay!

"Mai did it!"

"You did it," Li shouted.

Their excited cries followed the pulse of the world, filling Mai with more energy. Maybe...

Eyes turned to Cleric Pyuz.

"Witchcraft!" He drew his whip with one hand, and with the other reached to his neck, where his magic mirror hung.

Mai patted her skirts for Aralas' tube, but then stayed her hand. He hadn't said how long it would take him to respond, or even how he'd respond. If he sucked her through the ethers to safety, Cleric Pyuz would call Templars to wipe out the entire village. His hand was on the mirror.

Listening for his heartbeat, and the rhythm of chattering villagers, she straightened her spine and dug her toes into the soft earth. Borrowing the evening sounds and the chattering of the villagers, she raised her voice in song. With her heart impelling her sound, she chose the same song of friendship she'd used on the Templars.

Her vision faded at the edges. Her voice started to crack. If this didn't work...

Cleric Pyuz's head cocked to the side, and his frown relaxed. Still, he was lifting his mirror.

Mai kept singing, switching to the song of camaraderie that she'd used on the Templars.

Her energy guttered, and the black of night filled her vision.

***

The sound of Cleric Pyuz's heavy breathing roused Mai from sleep. She bolted up from where she was lying on the ground. Bright rays of sun stabbed her eyes. She blinked to clear the gunk, and when her vision cleared, she looked around.

Cleric Pyuz was crouching with his back to her, facing out toward a circle of weary villagers, including her parents and Little Sister Ling. His unholy rod…

…was still in her hand.

"Mai!" Mother shouted.

Cleric Pyuz turned around. "Mai, you've finally woken! I was so worried when you passed out."

Her head felt like an anvil. She blinked a few more times. "What happened?"

"You sang the most beautiful song." He waved his hand toward the villagers. "I was afraid this rabble was going to burn you for witchcraft."

"Of course we weren't." Father limped a step forward. "We told you, we just wanted to help her!"

Cleric Pyuz shrugged. "I couldn't take that chance, and you wouldn't let go." He pointed to the unholy rod.

It was so strange to see Cleric Pyuz so…friendly. Mai rose to her feet and surveyed the people who remained: Mother, Father, Ling, Li, Skinny Fang, the headman, and a few others. All looked so tired. She looked to the Iridescent Moon, now waning past half. She must've been asleep for hours.

"Have you stayed here all night?" she asked Father.

"Of course," Cleric Pyuz answered. "I couldn't risk them harming you."

Mai snorted. "Of course. It's all right, though. My family wouldn't hurt me."

"Of course!" Li said. "You saved my life."

Mai beckoned the headman. "We need to talk."

"What about?" Cleric Pyuz asked. His eyes were big and round, like the village dogs when waiting treats.

"I…" Mai took a deep breath and flashed her friendliest smile. "Cleric, you must be so tired. Don't worry about the villagers, they won't hurt me. You mustn't hurt any of them either. Never again. Give me your mirror and go back to rest."

"Mirror? Oh…" His hand shot up to his neck. "I really want to, but the High Priest will punish me."

Mai chewed on her lip. In the end, Regina had died because her charm had failed while the North Ridge priest still had his unholy rod and mirror. It was a risk, but at least she had his unholy rod. "Very well. I am concerned about you, though. Go back and rest."

The Tivari pout was just unsettling this time as it had been when the charmed Templar had done it. Still, Cleric Pyuz turned around and stomped back to his house in the village.

The others watched him go.

Father's eyes rounded. "How did you do that?"

"And you made Cleric Pyuz drop his holy rod," Little Sister Ling said.

Li grinned. "And healed me."

Never before had so many people praised her at one time. Heat flared in her cheeks. "A Dragon Song. Our people are capable of so much, and the Tivari have kept it from us."

Mother shuffled over and embraced her. "I'm so proud."

"There are many people like me, in Cathay."

Father sucked in a sharp breath. "Cathay was destroyed."

Mai shook her head. "Not completely. A small part of it is hidden by elf magic—"

"Elves?" Lines formed on Li's forehead.

Clearly, this wasn't an easy story to tell, and they probably wouldn't even believe her. "Yes, they went into hiding and have waited until now to reveal themselves. The elf angel, Aralas—"

"Angel?" Mother tasted the word.

Mai sighed. If they kept interrupting her, she'd never finish telling the story. "Yes, the elf angel took me to Cathay and taught me how to use Dragon Songs. I need to go back and continue training, so that I can charm Avarax—"

The headman's eyes rounded. "The Dragon?"

Who'd probably heard her sing. All the more reason she needed to leave soon. "Yes, so that we can overthrow the Tivari. Everything they've told us for generations is a lie. I—"

"This is all hard to believe," Little Sister Ling said.

Mai threw her hands up. Now even Little Sister was interrupting. Even if the villagers now admired her, they probably couldn't get past the fact that she was just plain Mai. How could she possibly change minds that had been decided for thousands of years?

"It's true," a voice said from beside her.

Mai's soul just about jumped out of her body. Given everyone else's shocked expressions, they were just as surprised. She looked to her side.

Nothing was there. She looked to the other side.

Fleet stood there, twirling Cleric Pyuz's ceremonial knife around his finger. "You're welcome, by the way, for taking this and tying up his ankles."

Mai could only gawk. How had he even done it? "Why didn't you take his magic mirror?"

"Mirror? Oh." Fleet stood on his tiptoes, stretched his arm out and wiggled his fingers. "Can't reach it. At least, not without being seen."

The headman waved a finger. "Is that… Is that...an elf?"

Fleet's face scrunched up. "Ewww, no. You won't see me dancing naked in the moonlight."

A picture of Aralas dancing naked flitted through Mai's imagination. Heat rising to her cheeks, she shook the image out of heard. "He's madaeri."

"Madaeri?" Almost everyone said in unison.

The headman shook his head. "He has no fangs!"

Fleet bared his teeth. "Not last time I checked."

"Or fur!" Father said.

"Close enough?" Fleet lifted a hairy foot and wiggled his toes.

Li pointed to the foot. "And he's walking on two feet!"

Fleet shrugged. "If you want me to crawl, you'll have to give me some pretty good food."

"Everything we thought about madaeri was wrong," Mai said. Though maybe not everything: they could stay out of sight, and their howl could make one's blood run cold.

"In any case," Fleet said. "What Mai says is true. All the enslaved peoples of the world—humans, dwarves, and my kind—will rise up against the orcs during the Godseye Conjunction. Your village must be prepared."

Chapter 31:
Stranger

S cythes swished through rice stalks as Mai walked among the villagers harvesting the last fields. The water bucket dug into the crook of her elbow. To think, the village might actually be able to keep the rice, instead of sacrificing it to the Tivari gods. All the playing children would never again worry about dying from starvation.

After explaining the rebellion and the elf angel to more of the village, she'd squeezed Aralas' magic tube. When she hadn't been swept through the ethers back to Cathay, she decided to make herself useful and go back to her old work. The sounds were all so nostalgic, save for the new addition of Cleric Pyuz actually working. Now, he grunted as he hefted bales of rice, grinning at her every time he passed.

The attention never failed to send a shudder up her spine. The Tivari who'd left so many scars on her back and murdered Ying now followed her like the giggling village girls followed Li. Still, as long as he didn't harm any of the villagers, she could leave at any time.

A commotion erupted near the edge of the fields.

Mai rose to her tiptoes and swayed back and forth, trying to get a better view over the taller men. Finding no success, she zigged and zagged her way through the workers toward the front, where an arc had formed around...

...a naked man.

A handsome one, at that. The bronze skin tone, dark hair, and rounded features looked so much like Vanya. An Ayuri! How had one of their kind made it all the way here?

She stopped behind the first row of onlookers. On more careful examination, though he had rounder eyes, instead of Vanya's brown irises, his were a bright blue, almost like Regina's and Vydas'.

The headman jabbed a finger at him. "Put on some clothes!"

The newcomer's eyes roved over the crowd. His bare body shivered. The poor man was either scared or cold, or perhaps both.

"I said, put on your clothes!" The headman cocked his head. "Who are you, anyway?"

Someone had to explain, before the Ayuri man died of fright.

Then again, he didn't seem that frightened. He reached over and ran a finger through the headman's eyebrow. Such strange behavior! Perhaps this was their form of communicating, and Vanya had simply learned local customs.

The headman covered his eyebrow. "What? You've never seen eyebrows?"

The Ayuri's eyes roved back and forth over everyone. Then he wiped his own eyebrow. Maybe he was simple-minded. It was such a rarity to see in an adult, since the Tivari usually adopted those children during their first pilgrimage to the pyramid.

A knot formed in Mai's stomach. Perhaps those children weren't actually adopted, but... She shook the thought out of her head, and cleared her throat. "The poor thing."

The newcomer craned his neck until his eyes met hers. He brought his hands up and squeezed his chest muscles. He was a simpleton, without a doubt.

She flashed her warmest smile. "This man must have travelled from down south. Look how dark he is. And his eyes are so round."

Murmurs broke out. The men all nodded.

The Ayuri looked up and down his arms, as if he was just seeing them for the first time, then swept his gaze over them all. His eyes spoke of cunning, too much for him to be a simpleton.

The headman took off his poncho and offered it.

The newcomer snatched it, then squirmed and wriggled as he pushed his arm up through the neck hole, and his head through the sleeves.

A giggle escaped her, unbidden. She slipped through the last row of people and tried to adjust the clothes. Her hand brushed over his neck as she tried to fit his arm in the right place.

His man-part sprung to attention. Disgusting!

Then it twitched. His eyes met hers, and he grinned.

Heat rushing to her cheeks, she averted her gaze. "Uh, just wrap the shawl around your waist."

He reached out for her breasts. When he spoke, it was in perfect Cathayi, like how Aralas' magic bauble translated. "I don't have these."

The heat fled from her head. Neither Li nor Aralas had tried to touch her there. Screaming, she slapped his hand. "Pervert!"

The chatter fell silent, and the others rushed forward.

"You can't do that to a woman," the headman yelled.

The Ayuri grinned and pointed at her. "Let's breed."

Heavens, the nerve! Mai's eyes widened. If her face could scrunch up anymore, she'd look as old as the headman.

The man opened his eyes wide while wrinkling up his own face.

She cocked her head. Was he imitating her expression?

He, too, tilted his head.

The Turtle's Egg! She glared at him. "Are you mocking me?"

"Mocking?" He sighed. "Of course not. I just want to mate."

The intensity of his gaze was as unsettling as his words. Her face burned as she took several steps back. Thankfully, the villagers pushed forward, interposing themselves between her and this strange man.

The man waved his hand in an arc from left to right. A ripple swept from his fingertips, crashing through the pulse of the world. Her protectors parted like leaves before a gust of wind.

An Empath? Mai's jaw slackened. The newcomer couldn't possibly be a Northerner—his skin color was much too dark. Perhaps it was sorcery? No, he was too light to be Aksumi, and he had those blue eyes which sparkled in the sun.

With a grin, he took a step forward.

Mai's chest squeezed. Her feet froze in place, even as her mind screamed to flee.

"You! Back to work!" Cleric Pyuz snapped his wrist, sending his whip out.

It lashed across the newcomer's back.

Never in her life was Mai more grateful for Cleric Pyuz. Surely a Tivari priest would scare the visitor. Mai studied his expression.

His eyes rolled up, and his. His shoulders tightened. It looked less like a reaction to pain, and more like little Dash when he first tasted garlic bread. Then the man's expression relaxed. Hand on the side of his neck, he spun to face the priest.

The whip cracked again.

The man caught it.

How was that even possible? Mai's gasp joined everyone else's.

Then, cheers broke out.

Oh, Heavens, no, the hostility they felt toward the priest might break the charm.

Even now, his heartbeat shifted. Cleric Pyuz looked from him to the others and back. His mouth locked into a tight frown. He gave the whip a sharp tug.

The Ayuri didn't budge. Not only that, he started pulling back, a smirk forming on his lips.

Digging his feet into the dirt, the priest drew his unholy rod.

The villagers backed away. "The holy rod," several said in unison.

351

Mai's blood ran cold. She'd hidden his unholy rod in her home, but perhaps he had another back at his house? She should've kept closer watch on him. Now, something had to be done before Cleric Pyuz hurt or killed this newcomer.

"Zzzzzt!" the Ayuri hissed through his lips.

Something buzzed like an angry swarm of bees in the man's chest. Like when Makeda invoked sorcery, the pulse of the world jolted. The whip went taut of its own accord as sparks sped from the man to the priest.

Cleric Pyuz's body went rigid. Then, he collapsed into a smoking pile. The stench of burning flesh filled the air.

Mai's heart leaped into her throat. She turned and ran back to the village, squeezing Aralas' magic tube over and over again. With the priest dead, the Templars would attack the village. And who knew what this visitor was, or what he wanted. She looked over her shoulder as the people gathered around the Ayuri with excited chatter.

The buzz was subsiding in the Ayuri's chest. Still, it sounded familiar, like... Vanya, when she fought? No, the *bahaduur* seemed to be energized by the pulse of the world. This man seemed to create his own pulse.

Hands holding up her skirts, one of the village women was hurrying from the village to the fields.

Mai tried to grab her sleeve, but missed. "Mother.... Where is my mother?"

The woman pointed back.

"Don't go out there, it's dangerous!" Mai reached for the woman again.

The woman batted her hands away. "I need to deliver a message to the headman."

Mai looked back out to the fields, then resumed her run. Where was Aralas? Too busy sleeping with Yanyan again, as likely as not. She reached the edge of the village, ran among the huts to the center…and skidded to a halt.

A group of the women, who should've been cooking, all laughed and giggled.

In their midst, Aralas was grinning ear-to-ear. It looked like he was flirting with Mother. Mai's stomach twisted.

His hair fell into his face as he looked up, forcing him to puff it away. "Oh, Mai, there you are. I was just telling your mother—"

"I squeezed your cursed tube so many times, my hand hurts! Why didn't you come for me?"

He settled a kind gaze on her. "I knew you'd come here."

She pointed back to the fields. "Back there, there's a man. He—"

The elf angel pulled her to the side, brushed her hair behind her ear, and whispered, "…is Avarax."

"Avarax?" Mai gawked. How could Aralas be so nonchalant about it? "Are you sure?"

"Yes."

Fear crept up Mai's spine. That's why the buzzing in the visitor's chest had sounded so familiar. It was the same as when he'd flown over Cathay. "Why didn't you tell me he could take the shape of a man?"

"Did you not see Kang's murals in Cathay? One shows the Guardian Dragon taking human form."

"How was I supposed to know that's what it meant?" Mai threw her hands up. It'd been a silver dragon coiling around a woman. "Why is Avarax here?"

"He must've heard your voice and come. I told you to use your flute."

Mai shuddered. She'd brought the dragon here. "Why didn't you come get me earlier?"

"I'm here now."

She waved back to the field again. "Why not out there?"

Aralas nodded. "I can't risk him seeing me. Not yet."

How could the elf be so unconcerned? "Can't you stop him?"

"Maybe on the night of the Godseye Conjunction, at a place where the pulse of the world wells up, I could. Maybe." Aralas shrugged. "*You*, however, can. Any time, any place, with the right training."

It was just as Doctor Wu had said months ago, when Avarax flew over Cathay. Mai's voice called to Avarax's Dragonstone. It was too heavy a burden to bear. Who knew if it was even possible? She chewed on the inside of her lip. Still… "My village is in danger!"

"It's you he wants. If you're not here, the village is as insignificant to him as the ants beneath your feet are you to. We sent a girl to tell the headman to invite Avarax to dinner."

"Dinner?" If Mai's jaw could hang any lower, she'd have to pick her chin off the ground.

"He's learning about his new body. Dinner will stall him." Aralas wiped his hands against each other, making a clapping sound. "Are you ready to go?"

If this was the only way to save her family… Mai looked to Mother. "Mother, I must continue my training."

"When will we see you again?"

Aralas gazed into the heavens, then met Mother's eyes. "One week. Keep the stranger here, and he will protect your village."

Mother reached out with both arms.

Before Mai could hug her, Aralas' arm wrapped around her.

He spoke a word. Colors swirled. The village disappeared.

Chapter 32:

Look Who's Coming to Dinner

The roar of wind assaulted Mai's ears as she and Aralas materialized on a path in a gorge. Some thirty feet below, a stream bubbled over rocks, the sound echoing off the sheer, white cliff walls. The scene might've been beautiful if her head didn't hurt so much.

Mai's legs wobbled.

"Focus," Aralas said.

Closing her eyes, Mai took a deep breath. Though it was loud, there was an order to the sounds. As with everything else, the pulse of the world formed the underlying beat.

She opened her eyes. "Where are we?"

"Hualian Gorge."

Mai drew a sharp breath. The old legends spoke of the scenic ravine, where even whispers would carry for as far as the eye could see. Wenhui and Ku hailed from the area. Mai, Li, and Ying had always daydreamed about singing here. Then again, with the wind and water, how would any sound, except for a projected Dragon Song, carry through the ravine?

Aralas pointed downstream. "This stream flows into Teardrop Lake."

Where Guanyin's tear fell to earth, and the Cathayi people sprung forth. At least, that was what Aralas had said that first night, so many months ago. "Why did you bring me here?"

He tucked her hair behind her ear. "To practice listening."

Now? With the Last Dragon doing knew who what in her village? "I've been doing that ever since we met."

"You can always get better." He took her hand and gave her a tug. "Come on."

Taking a deep breath, Mai closed her eyes and listened as she walked. With the wind and rapids, it proved harder to hear the echo of her footsteps. On more than one occasion her toes came perilously close to the edge of the path, and it was only Aralas' pull which kept her from tumbling over.

A new sound hid among the others, riding on the pulse of the world. Steadfast, it would've also been strong had the other sounds not masked it.

Mai opened her eyes and searched for the source.

It came from a dozen feet above, right in the face of the cliff.

Aralas grinned. "You heard it."

"What is it?" Mai stared at the rocks.

"Listen."

She closed her eyes again. The muted pulse sounded like Makeda's cloak, only much more powerful. Like the cloak of elf magic over Cathay. She opened her eyes and turned to Aralas. "It's magic. Similar to the kind that hides Cathay from the Tivari Gods' flaming chariots."

"Very good." He blew the hair out of his face.

Something within called to her. "Can you disperse it?"

"Yanyan asked me the same question when I first brought her here."

Her again. Mai frowned. "And?"

"I told her, if she can hear it, she can dispel it herself."

The Turtle's Egg enjoyed speaking in riddles. "How?"

With an open hand, he arced his hands up and down. "The ripples of magic have a certain frequency and strength. If you sing between the beats with the same frequency and intensity, you can disperse it."

Mai closed her eyes and listened. The strength of the pulse was beyond what she'd ever created with her music. It was impossible. She started to shake her head.

Wind gusted through the ravine again, blowing hair into her face and joining the roar of waters below. That was it. Like at the waterfall, she could borrow the sounds to increase the intensity of her song.

Waiting for the next gust, she listened to the pattern of the cloaking magic. It rose and fell like the ripples across a pond. The water tumbling over the rocks sang its own song. She started a hum, joining it.

The wind roared again. Curling her toes into the ground, Mai raised her voice. She tied the wind's sound, and that of the water, to her song. The magic cloak's pulse wavered, but held fast.

Maybe she'd attract Avarax again. Still, note after note, she bent all the other sounds to fit into the magic cloak's waves, like matching Yin to Yang, like...male to female.

Heavens, had she just thought that? Memories of Aralas' lips on her neck in the Hall of Harmony fluttered through her mind.

Maintaining her song, she looked sidelong at the elf angel, whose beautiful golden hair whipped with the wind. His heart beat intensely, like the magic cloak. Smile forming, he nodded. "Yes, borrow all sounds around you, even mine."

The wind eased, but the beat of his heart took over in her music, matching hers. His eyes gazed into hers, adoring, just as he looked at Yanyan. If only he'd join her in song!

Even though he didn't, her chest swelled. Energy surged through her. The magic cloak's pulse flickered, and then faded altogether.

Above them, the white rocks wavered, then disappeared. A cave mouth yawned open in the cliff face, nearly three times as big around as she was tall.

Still singing, she afforded it a glance, but then returned to Aralas. Their hearts beat with one another. If she stopped singing, maybe their hearts would stop, or at the very least, go their separate ways. With a decisive step, she seized the distance between them. She slid her hand into his cloak, across the cool smoothness of his clothes, and wrapped him into an embrace.

Pulling his elbows in, he pressed his palms into her shoulders. She pulled him toward her, to claim that last space between him, but he pushed back.

Maybe it had all been a trick, the way he'd gazed at her just a few seconds ago. Her song stuttered to a stop.

No sooner did she stop than his lips met hers. She would've yelped, but his tongue pushed forward, urgent. Was this really happening? She parted her lips, and his tongue darted in, tracing a path around hers. Her breaths came out heavy. Heat flared inside her. Tingles shot up and down her spine and all through her hands and feet, more intense than the energy it had taken to disperse the magic cloak. A moan rumbled in her throat.

His tongue withdrew, like a turtle head returning to the safety of its shell. He pulled back, panting. She tried to reclaim his mouth, but he leaned his head back beyond her reach.

He set a finger on her lips. "I'm sorry. I had…I had to release the echo of your Dragon Song."

An excuse? The heat inside fizzled, like water thrown on a fire. She swatted his hand away. "You Turtle's Egg."

Head hanging, he pushed her back. "I'm sorry, but there's no time. We need to get into the cave and reestablish the cloak before Avarax comes looking for you."

Mai let out a long breath and looked up to the cave. "How do we get up there?"

His chuckle sounded nervous, like a bride on her wedding night. He slipped an arm under hers.

As hateful as he was, her body melted against his. He spoke a word, and they rose off the ground. Her heart jumped into her throat. Higher and higher they floated, until they reached the cave. He took a step from mid-air to the opening, and then pulled her in.

With a single word and a swipe of his hand, the pulse of the world shifted. The magic cloak's sound returned. The outside world appeared as a haze. How simple it was for him to do it, compared to all the effort it had taken her. Perhaps he could've dispersed it just as easily.

She turned to him. "Could you disperse the magic cloak over Cathay?" If so, maybe he could re-establish it.

Aralas laughed. "It was created by thousands of elves, using several different forms of magic over the span of days."

Thousands was a number beyond her fathoming; it was only recently that *hundreds* made sense. "Were they the ones who created the cloak over the cave?"

He shook his head. "No, this magic isn't as old as the one over Cathay, Ankira, and the elf realm."

"Wenhui said that cloak is losing its power."

"Yes. It's held for several millennia, but it's been shrinking in recent years."

Mai shuddered. If the Tivari gods' flaming chariots flew over Cathay after the cloak failed, they'd surely find it. "This is mankind's last chance, isn't it?"

"Everyone's last chance. If we fail to defeat the Tivari now, it will have consequences that reach farther than you can imagine."

She could imagine her family suffering at the tips of unholy rods, and that was enough.

He pointed deeper into the cave. "And the reason why is in here."

"Where does this go?" Mai peered through the darkness. A dim, blue light glowed.

"You will see. Follow your ears."

Mai closed her eyes and listened as she walked. The energy of the world pulsed loudly here, perhaps even more than at the dragon bones.

No, there were two beats. One riding on top of the other, both powerful. She opened her eyes. "What is it?"

Aralas motioned forward. "Why don't you go see?"

She studied him.

His expression revealed nothing.

With a sigh, she followed the tunnel as it descended deeper. The floors and walls were smooth, with patches of glowing blue rock. The spots grew larger and brighter the further she went.

"What is this?" she asked.

"What does it look like?" He gestured to a particularly bright spot as they walked past, high above in the ceiling.

It was such a luminous color, like... "The pool where I met you."

He nodded. "And?"

Where else... "Avarax's eyes."

"Very good. Anywhere else?"

"Vydas' sword, *Tamskelti*."

If Aralas was really just playing with her heart, his kind eyes didn't suggest it. They showed none of his usual mischievousness, only adoration. "It comes from a mineral called *istrium*. It makes magic stronger, and there is a lot of it in this world. The orcs force the dwarves to mine it, to use in their chariots."

It all made sense. No wonder Tivari magic was so powerful. She nearly tripped over a rock. "There doesn't look like much here."

"There's more, the deeper you go." He waved his arm in an arc. "This vein runs under Teardrop Lake, all the way to the pyramid."

"Why did the Tivari abandon this mine?"

Aralas dragged his hand over the walls as he walked. "No dwarf pickaxe dug this hole."

If not the dwarves… "Then who did?"

"The one who put the magic cloak over the entrance. Do you hear it?"

The little hairs on the back of Mai's neck stood on end. The sound that rode on the pulse of the world, though nearly inaudible, was becoming more and more distinct.

The passage opened up into a cavern large enough to hold an entire village. Mai gasped.

Istrium covered the walls, illuminating a floor sparkling with gemstones and shiny disks. It was hard to tell in the blue lighting, but the disks looked to be the same gold that gilded the chariots of the Tivari gods. The pulse of the world seemed to echo and intensify among them. Swords, knives, axes, metal armor, and more lay among the rest of the clutter. Her gaze fell on a pole about her height, with a short sword blade attached to one end.

"What is this place?" She turned to Aralas.

He wasn't there. Head darting right and left, she searched.

The elf angel was nowhere to be found.

Light footsteps echoed from a tunnel on the other side of the cavern. Aralas must've magicked himself to the other side. Another test, no doubt.

Then a gust of wind whipped through the cavern. The pointy stone fingers hanging from the ceiling vibrated, singing with the pulse of the world.

An enormous chain of silvery white scales, like countless mirrors, burst in from the opposite tunnels. The blast of wind knocked Mai to her butt. She shielded her eyes, and just barely made out the head of a dragon.

Chapter 33:
To Charm a Dragon

Heart thrumming in her ears, Mai scuttled back from the dragon as it drew nearer. Her stomach twisted into a knot, threatening to rebel. Its head alone was easily four or five times larger than her. It came close enough that its silvery whiskers brushed across her cheek, soft as feathers, before veering off.

Mai froze. None of her limbs would obey her command, and she nearly wetted herself.

It raced past with a gush of wind, each huge scale reflecting Mai's dumbstruck expression as its body waved up and down. Without wings, it swam through the air like a carp through water, as if dancing to the pulse of the world. It was beautiful. If what Aralas had said before was true, about the only dragon left in the world beside Avarax, this must be the Guardian Dragon.

JC Kang

Mai's head spun. Her bodily functions lurched and jerked between fear and wonder. Deep breaths only partially settled her racing pulse.

It circled one more time, then hovered right in front of her. Luminous eyes, like the patches of istrium on the wall, bore into her. Unlike Avarax's scheming expression, this one's looked noble and dignified. "Wei Mai, you are trespassing. Why should I not eat you?"

Like the tolling of the palace bells, the voice rang. Its energy rolled over her. All the deep breathing in the world couldn't keep her throat from squeezing, choking out her words. Her mouth just opened and closed. Heavens, it even knew her name, down to the arbitrary surname chosen by the census official.

"Speak!"

The pulse of the world shifted. Just like when Regina commanded her to speak, the words spilled out of her mouth. "Aralas brought me here."

"I'll be sure to thank that rascal for the snack if he dares show himself."

Mai's breaths rasped. Apparently, the Guardian Dragon wasn't the benevolent creature everyone in Cathay thought. She took a step back. This was it. The end. With her death, nothing could control Avarax. The rebellion would fail. Cleric Pyuz would... Cleric Pyuz was dead, killed by Avarax's magic. Which meant that Templars would investigate her village...

No, she couldn't die. Not now. She had to find Aralas, wherever he'd run off to, and somehow convince him to protect the village. Closing her eyes to shut out the image of the dragon's head, she took a deep breath. Her heart slowed only a beat.

Heavens, the dragon's energy throbbed, strong and deliberate. That's what she'd heard from all the way out in the valley, riding on the pulse of the world. Like the magic cloaking the cave entrance, it was so powerful. And yet, she'd dispersed the cloak.

Aralas wasn't here to loan his energy, nor were the sounds of water and wind. But there were the teeth hanging from the cavern ceiling, vibrating. Indeed, they seemed to mute the pulse coming from the dragon—from its dragonstone, if what Doctor Wu had said was right.

The pulse of istrium carried in the coins, all available for her to draw on. Yanyan had charmed the Guardian Dragon years ago. Maybe Mai could, as well.

Eyes still closed, she held the image of playing hide-and-seek in the rice fields with Ying, Li, and Fang. She raised her voice in the song of friendship, joining her music with all the sounds in the cave. Note after note sought to connect her heart to the dragon's.

All the pretty words about comradery and companionship rose and fell from her lips, yet they seemed like a pebble thrown in river rapids, barely making a ripple in the sound of the dragon. It was impossible to match the intensity of the dragonstone, not with the sounds available in the cavern. Not only that, her voice didn't connect like it had to the Templars.

It laughed. "I applaud your effort. I will make your death painless."

Energy wavering, Mai was almost screaming her song. If only she had an instrument, like Yanyan's pipa, or the drums in the Hall of Harmony, maybe she could connect to the dragonstone. The pipa had supposedly been made from one of the Guardian Dragon's scales, while the drums had come from its shed skin.

That was it! Lowering her voice, Mai listened and sorted out all the sounds in the cavern. Most, like the small metal disks, echoed with the pulse of the world. Others had their own frequency. But there....

She opened her eyes. Several bowl-like objects, swirling with colors like the Iridescent Moon, vibrated with her song, halfway bridging her voice and the Guardian Dragon's dragonstone. And there! Among the swords and knives, a long pole with a small sword on the end resonated exactly to it.

Gasping out a last note, Mai ran for the weapon, nearly slipping on one of the metal disks.

"Foolish mortal. You cannot escape me." A talon swiped, just barely missing.

Let it believe she was trying to escape. Mai zig-zagged through the treasures, like she had run among the trees when fleeing the Templars. She dived under the dragon's tail and reached for the weapon. Her hands closed around the long handle, which was wrapped in black cord. She rolled over and pointed the tip at the dragon.

Its laugh shook the cave. "Foolish, but spunky."

The blade, which didn't look metal, vibrated with the Dragonstone. Mai sang her song of friendship to the weapon, letting her voice mingle with its pulse.

The dragon froze, its beautiful eyes locked on the blade.

Then it laughed. "You're smarter than the last one, but your voice isn't matched to my energy. No medium you sing through can change that."

Of course. Yanyan's voice was matched to the Guardian Dragon, while her own was… "Avarax."

Were those its eyebrows clashing together? "What did you say?"

"Avarax. My voice resonates with his dragonstone."

It snorted. "That is a bold claim."

"Doctor Wu said so." Mai's stomach flipped and twisted. Not like the Guardian Dragon would know who Doc—

"The Daoist priestess?"

"Yes." Whether it was true or not, it was buying her time. Not to mention, she was actually holding a conversation with a dragon.

JC Kang

"A wise woman."

From the other end of cavern, Aralas laughed.

Mai turned to see him lower the hood of his cape. The Turtle's Egg! He'd been here the whole time, watching, not caring if she got eaten.

"You see, Celastya," he said, "Mai can help solve your Avarax problem, as well. Will you help me teach her?"

Teach? Mai looked from elf to dragon. What had started as chance to charm Li, and evolved into a means of protecting her family and village, had now thrust her into conflicts between elves and Tivari, and Celastya and Avarax.

The dragon's whiskers quivered. "What do you expect me to do?"

"You know the song of Avarax's dragonstone better than anyone else. Sing its song, so that Mai might hear it and learn a song of charm specifically for him."

Mai's heart, racing from fear just a few moments ago, started to calm. She stared at him.

He shrugged. "There's no better way to learn a Dragon Song than from a dragon."

"Charm Avarax?" The dragon belched sparks. "You are delusional, elf angel. No human can channel enough power to charm a dragon."

Mai cleared her throat. "Yanyan charmed you, didn't she?"

372

The dragon's eyes, glowing a brighter blue, locked on Aralas, who strolled to her side now. His head made two slight shakes.

It blew out a few a puff of air from the side of its mouth, which sent its whiskers aflutter. "Yes. Sure."

Mai's face scrunched up. There was more to this story, if Aralas' blank expression and the dragon's reaction were any indication. Even now, the two of them just stared at each other, expressions twitching. Or at least, if a dragon could have expressions, that's what it would look like. Was he speaking in its head like he'd done with Mai? Would that even work on a dragon? Or maybe it was speaking in *his* head.

"Her voice," Aralas said at last. "Because it already harmonizes with his dragonstone, it will be easier for her."

"Very well." Doubt still hung in the Guardian Dragon's voice. "How much time do you have?"

Aralas held up a finger.

"A century?"

Aralas shook his head.

"A decade?"

Aralas shook his head again.

"A year?"

"A week," Mai said.

If a reptile could roll its eyes, that was undoubtedly what the Guardian Dragon was doing. "Impossible. This is a human we are talking about."

Were humans really so weak and insignificant? Mai channeled confidence she didn't have. "I can do it."

The dragon snorted. "Not by yourself, you can't. There might be another way."

"How?" Mai asked.

"If you can fashion a musical instrument from one of those." The dragon pointed a claw.

Mai followed the talon. It pointed to the bowl-like objects, whose colors swirled like a soap bubble. Aralas nodded in slow bobs.

"What are they?" Mai asked. They had resonated with her song earlier, and mingled with the sound of the dragon's dragonstone, even if the effort hadn't worked.

"Eggshells." The dragon's voice cracked.

"Yours?"

"And Avarax's."

"But, but…" Avarax had wings, whereas the Guardian Dragon had none. He'd been blood red, and she was silver-white. His head was triangular with sharp horns, while hers was more rectangular, with antlers. Heat flared in Mai's cheeks. "You look so…different."

Sadness hung in the dragon's laugh. "No more different than you and say...an elf."

Heat in her face, Mai found Aralas in the corner of her eye.

His expression could only be described as bored.

The dragon's chuckle sounded more genuine this time. "Maybe not *that* elf."

Though all logic screamed that Aralas was wrong for her, her heart pounded all the same. Why not him? Because he was not just an elf, but an angel as well?

"Pay attention." Its neck craned back to the egg shards.

Mai shook impossible ideas out of her head. She walked over to the shells.

"Your voice already matches with Avarax, but your power is not strong enough to affect him. The eggshells have a piece of him, though they would work even better if you used the eggshell he hatched from."

"Where can we find that?"

Both the dragon and Aralas burst out laughing. Heat burned in Mai's face.

When the elf angel choked back his laugh, he cleared his throat. "Avarax was ancient even when the elves ruled over this world. Nobody would even know where he was hatched. It would be just as easy to use one of his scales or whiskers."

"And how do you plan on getting something like that?" The dragon snorted. "Unless you have any better ideas, fashion an instrument from this shell. It will loan you a little of my dragonstone's song. Even then, you must choose a location where the energy of the world wells, on the night when Guanyin's Eye is fully open."

The dragon bones, perhaps. Or perhaps the pyramid. Getting all the conditions perfect seemed impossible.

Chapter 34:
Ulterior Motives

Outside the dragon's lair the winds had died down, leaving only the rustling of the stream in the gorge. Mai looked up. Shadows from the setting sun made the entrance to the lair even harder to pick out from the surrounding rock; or perhaps that was just the magic cloak hiding it.

She closed her eyes and listened. Just as before, the cave's cloak hummed in her ears, along with a hint of the Guardian Dragon's unique pulsing. In her hands, an eggshell the size of her face echoed the sound.

She opened her eyes and turned to Aralas. The setting sun set his golden hair ablaze with red highlights. He was so beautiful. It kept her from shoving him off the ledge. "You risked my life. Again."

"It was another test to prove your worth." He shrugged. "To see how well you could think and act when faced with dragonfear. Avarax will be even scarier."

Just the memory of being face-to-face with the Guardian Dragon sent a shudder through her. If Avarax was even more frightening… "Would you have saved me?"

He searched her eyes. "Of course."

There was so much he wasn't saying. He and the dragon had communicated mentally, the way he'd spoken in her head, or the way Regina had planted an image. "What does the Guardian Dragon have to gain from helping us?"

"She lives in constant fear of Avarax."

Mai shuddered. The fear both evoked had made her lose control of her body. "So he is stronger than her?"

"Yes. He's kept her weak by mating. Her dragonstone is weakened when she lays eggs, which he eats."

Before now, she would've never imagined dragons laid eggs, like chickens. To think that Avarax forced himself on Celastya. Mai shuddered again. In human form, he'd tried to grab her breasts and demanded to mate. She pointed up at the cave. "So the cloak hides her from Avarax?"

Aralas shook his head. "It would, except he knows where her lair is."

"Why does she stay there, then?"

"This location, so close to a large istrium source, gives her power, which is magnified by the resonance of her hoard. It also hides her from the orcs. If they knew she existed, they'd hunt her down, just like they did the dragons who helped them conquer the world millennia ago."

The dragon had been so huge, and its power so vast. Even an army of Templars with unholy rods didn't seem like a match for her. "I can't believe they could even harm her."

"It might take several of their gods on flaming chariots, but eventually, they would prevail." He searched her eyes again. "That said, she is a good and just being. A servant of the gods, like me."

Mai snorted. The dragon hadn't seemed good; Aralas even less so.

He grinned. "If you can charm Avarax, and we banish the orc gods, then surely she will help mankind against the orcs."

"How is it even possible to banish the orc gods?"

Aralas lifted the eggshell shard from her hands. "Raze the Temple of Tivar. Tear down the Golden Bowl at the Shrine of Lydath. Strip Frawdok's Purse of its silver threads. Destroy the Lair of the Orc Queens."

Mai's gawked. Cleric Pyuz had told stories of all the famous holy sites, though maybe no human had ever laid eyes on them. Tivar's grand temple lay high in the mountains in a faraway land, accessible only by magic. The Shrine of Lydath supposedly had a gigantic bowl, gilded in gold and platinum, which faced the heavens to catch the holy tears of Lydath.

She shook her head. The High Priest, archbishops, and Templar Master dwelled in these places. "Those sites are protected by Tivari angels and countless Templars."

"There are over a hundred humans for every orc in this world. As long as they don't suspect the elves' involvement, the worldwide rebellion will draw them away from our targets."

On the one hand, the plan made sense; but something didn't sound right. If the Tivari came to put down the rebellion... If the rest of the villages in the world were like hers... Father, hobbling from Cleric Pyuz's abuse. Li and Skinny Fang, armed only with hoes and shovels. Mother and Ling, with no weapons at all. A pit formed in her stomach. "Countless humans will be slaughtered."

"Before the Templars reach their targets, we should have begun our assault on these sites. They'll rush back, but not before we are done."

Should. "You are too willing to risk human lives."

If his glare could get any sharper, it would cut even more easily than the sword they'd delivered to the Nothori king. It looked nothing like his typical indifference. "I will challenge the High Priest to single combat, to draw him away from the Temple, so that others have a chance."

She returned his stare. "You can teleport away at any time. You don't care about us at all. We are just your tools to defeat the Tivari."

His lips pursed. "I am going to show you something. I'll be back soon." On a word of Shallow Magic, he disappeared into the ethers with a hollow pop.

Mai threw up her hands. The Turtle's Egg was now abandoning her, near the lair to a dragon which might change its mind and eat her anyway. Like every other human not named Yanyan, she was expendable.

With nothing better to do, she continued along the ridge, listening to the sound of waters and the occasional roar of a wind gust through the gorge. The scenery was beautiful really, and she might've appreciated the view more had Aralas not left her in such a sour mood.

Before long, the ravine widened, as did the stream below, and opened up into a lake with shimmering blue waters. Well off in the distance, the pyramid rose along the shore, its gemstone sparkling at its tip. The flickering matched the pulse of the world.

Her stomach rumbled at a very different rate. She looked back to the Iridescent Moon, now waxing to half. The sun glowed red at the horizon. After sheer terror had smothered her appetite, it was coming back now.

The air popped in front of her.

She turned.

A figure clad in grey hooded robes approached. The embroidery at the robe's hems and sleeves marked it as…a Tivari acolyte. Like the ones who'd prepared her for the initiation rites at the pyramid so many years ago.

Her heart lurched. She took several steps back and listened for its heart, ready to sing a song of charm. How had an acolyte found her?

It lowered the hood, revealing Aralas. Like before, pursed lips and a tight jaw replaced his usually nonchalant expression.

She blew out a breath. "Don't scare me like that. What are you doing in their robes?"

He extended his hands, offering grey cloth, embroidered like his robes. "Put this on."

"Why?"

"Because where we are going, you will want to look like one of them." He thrust a hand into his robe. His form shortened and broadened. His beautiful features thickened to blunt ugliness, and his skin tone darkened to turquoise. Tusks emerged from his lower jaw. He looked just like an acolyte. He withdrew his hand and opened his palm, revealing a glass ball similar to the one Makeda had used to shine light.

She cocked her head.

"Take it," he said.

"What is it?"

"It creates an illusion, like the one I am using." He waved his hand over himself. "You will look just like any other orc."

To think that once, she had believed the Tivari to be beautiful. Or at least, she'd convinced herself they were. Did she really want to look like one? Her hand closed around the glass.

Nothing seemed to change with her, but Aralas shifted back to his original form.

He chanted a few melodious words and drew a circle in the air between them. In that space, a mirrored surface, like the ones Makeda created, reflected her new appearance. She looked just like Aralas' Tivari illusion, with the blunt features, tusks, and turquoise complexion.

He studied her. "As long as that touches your bare skin, you will look like one of them."

"What about you?" she asked.

Snuffing out the mirror, he withdrew another marble, and his appearance changed back to that of a Tivari. "Put on the robes."

The robes wouldn't fit over her dress. If Aralas watched her, especially looking like a Tivari... Or maybe not, since she couldn't keep ahold of the bauble while changing. She ran her finger in a circle. "Turn around."

With a snort, he spun and faced the other direction.

She waited a few seconds. When it looked like he would stay facing the lake, which would provide a prettier view for him than her skinny body, she set the bauble down, shimmied out of the roughspun dress, and shrugged on the robe. She poked her head through the hood.

He was looking over his shoulder, eyes fixed on her.

Her heart jumped into her throat for what must've been the tenth time today. Harassed by Avarax in human form, threatened by the Guardian Dragon. Neither felt as traumatizing as having the elf angel watching her change. Heat flared in her cheeks.

"Sorry," he said, tone actually apologetic. "Human bodies look so…sturdy, and round, compared to ours."

Was that what he thought of Yanyan, as well? Sturdy? Mai couldn't bring herself to make eye contact. She knelt down and picked up the glass ball.

He cleared his throat. "Where I am taking us, you mustn't speak. It will give us away."

"Where are we going?"

"The pyramid." He pointed across the lake, to where the gemstone sparkled atop the massive structure.

"Whatever for?" Her stomach churned. Before the initiation rites, acolytes had bathed her and dressed her in smooth white robes. It had been a joy then, but now knowing the Tivari were evil changed all that.

"To prove that I care about humans."

Chapter 35:

The Wrath of Koralas

The chants of human children singing praises to Tivar carried through the cool evening air, roiling Mai's stomach. Long ago, she'd been one of them, so overjoyed to be accepted as a follower of the Tivari gods. She looked through the grove of trees to the pyramid. As always, the gemstone at its top sparkled and pulsed in the night sky.

Aralas had teleported at least four times this day, so he clearly had a lot more power than he admitted. He left her side and walked to a tree several feet away, placing his hand on its trunk. Even with his Tivari illusion face, he looked up at it almost the same way he looked at Yanyan. Her jaw tightened. She started to speak.

He held up a finger. Though his lips didn't move, his voice spoke in her mind. *Shhh. We are dressed like orcs, but you don't speak their language.*

Of course. She placed her hand over her mouth.

His preoccupation with the tree was like the village dogs in the woods. Unlike the wispy trees surrounding it, this one had a single trunk, and would've been too big for her and Aralas to clasp hands if they stood on either side of it. Not even the elf trees on Cathay's border grew so large.

When she approached, an unsettled feeling, like a madaeri howl before she knew what they were, sent the hairs on the back of her neck prickling. She swallowed hard.

There are several more like it in the grove, his voice spoke in her head. *Spread out so that their leaves are hidden among the canopies of the slickbarks.*

She looked around. Indeed, there appeared to be a single row of this tree—

Trees of Light.

—running through the middle of the grove. What was so special about it?

Put your hand on it and listen.

Closing her eyes, she placed her palm on the gnarled bark. It throbbed beneath her hand, sending energy surging into her...no, past her. The beat followed the... She opened her eyes.

Aralas nodded. *You don't hear the pulse of the world here, do you?*

She shook her head. It had been so strong in the ravine, and even in the grove up until...

Take a few steps back.

She backed away. The pulse of the world filled her ears again. How could it be?

The tree's resin draws istrium energy through it, up into the leaves. He pointed up. *Look.*

She squinted. Countless dots of dim blue light shone between the slickbarks' thick canopies. She sucked in a sharp breath.

He nodded. *I planted these closer together so they wouldn't grow so tall, but in the elf realms the trees are easily a dozen times thicker and taller.*

Whatever for? Mai's forehead scrunched of its own accord.

The original plan to defeat the orcs was a ritual spell, invoking the wrath of the gods. When complete, the istrium energy in the air would pulse so fast, it would kill every living thing on this planet, save for the plants.

Mai staggered back a few steps. What kind of god could be so cruel?

He shook his head. *If you could fathom how far istrium allows orcs to spread their evil, you would understand.*

No. It didn't make sense, under any circumstance. The elves lived hidden away, and most humans would rather live as slaves than die.

Yes. You see, when the gods sent me here, my job was to plant Trees of Light in the elf realms. The elves would gather beneath the canopies and be safe when the Wrath of Koralas was unleashed.

Of course the elves would be protected. If he'd brought her here to prove he cared about humans, it wasn't working. She squeezed her fists tight.

Eyes widening, he shook his head. *The gods thought you were mindless slaves. It was only when I was searching for hidden elf villages to plant Trees of Light in that I first met one of you. I realized humans were sentient, self-aware. And beautiful.* He reached toward her face with an open palm.

She took a step back and pointed to the trees. "You said you planted these trees recently. The ritual spell is still being cast, isn't it?"

His eyes darted toward the pyramid and back to her. He put his finger on his lip. *Shhh. Yes. It is timed to be completed the morning after the harvest moon.*

Of course, during the arrival of the Golden Flock. The seven stars which shone above the pyramid each year represented the Tivari gods receiving their sacrifice.

That's why I planted these trees here. He gestured toward the Tree of Light behind them. *Humans will gather around all the pyramids worldwide to make sacrifices to the* orc gods. *Before the spell is cast, other elf angels will bring them to the safety of the trees. It will save as many of you as possible.*

Still, hundreds upon hundreds...no, *countless* humans would die, including her parents, who weren't scheduled for the pilgrimage this year.

His Tivari illusion eyes looked sad. *It is a last resort. If we can raze the Temple of Tivar before then, we will stop the spell.*

Mai counted on her fingers. The rebellion was to start when magic was the strongest, on the night of the Godseye Conjunction... She gasped.

Yes. The same night as the Harvest Moon this year.

"There's not enough time!"

He set his finger on her lips. *Any later, and humans will start returning to their villages. Even more will die.*

Why couldn't it wait?

The cloak over the elf realms will fail soon, among other reasons.

The heartless Turtle's Egg! These plans just proved he didn't care about humans.

If not for my protests to the gods, all of you, all the dwarves, all the madaeri, everyone but elves would've died. His glare looked even more ferocious with the Tivari face.

389

She snorted. If the Wrath of Koralas never happened, humans would still go on living, at least.

Lips pursed, he withdrew a four-inch wooden flute and handed it to her. *If you need to use magic, use this. We don't want Avarax swooping in.*

She tucked it into the robe, and he put a hand on her shoulders and uttered a word of magic.

The grove swirled in colors, and was soon replaced by darkness. The pulse of the world was so strong here, stronger than anywhere she'd heard. Where were they?

Inside the pyramid, Aralas' voice spoke in her head.

Her steps wavered. She'd only been inside once in her life, as a child. Right before the initiation ceremony, when the acolytes had bathed and robed her. A complex mix of nostalgia and nervousness now mingled with dread.

She'd heard the pulse of the world during the rites, though it was only now that she knew what it was.

Make sure the bauble is secure against your skin.

Mai patted her hip, where her undergarments kept the glass secure against her.

Tivari grunts echoed off stone, somewhere nearby.

She blinked several times. Something pinched her ear.

The Tivari's guttural language shifted. Aralas must've attached a translating bauble again.

"The next batch is almost done with washing," one said, its voice still echoing.

"There are at least two that need to be culled. A boy and a girl."

Culled?

You don't want to know what that means.

She did. Even if it was horrible, she had to know.

Very well. First, you will watch. Aralas' hand closed around hers, and he pulled her along.

Since it was so dark, she closed her eyes and listened. The sound of their light footsteps echoed, suggesting that they were in an enclosed hall, certainly much smaller than the Hall of Harmony in Cathay. The stone was cool beneath her feet.

Aralas' hand fell away.

A Tivari called from up ahead. "You two, we need hands at the bathing."

"Yes, sir," Aralas said, apparently in the Tivari language, given the fluency of the magic bauble's translation. He thumped his chest.

Come along.

Up ahead, bright light outlined a rectangular opening into a larger room. Lines of brighter light rippled on the walls, to the rhythm of sloshing water.

She blinked again to allow her vision to adjust to the light.

The bathing room was just as she remembered it: about the same size as the Hall of Harmony in Cathay, with undecorated smooth stone walls. Several pools occupied the center, where several young girls stood naked in knee-high water. With eyes closed, they clasped their palms together. Barefooted Tivari acolytes in grey robes sponged them in the bathing ritual...

No, they were examining the children.

As a child, she remembered them as they ran a thumb between her eyebrows, marking her with a turquoise dye. Most of the children now bore that smudge.

One girl, however, with one of her arms hanging limply at her side, had been marked in red. She looked so angelic. Her attending acolyte gestured to another. "This one has a defect. Take it to culling."

Aralas stepped up and thumped his fist on his chest. When he spoke, his words came out forced. "Yes, sir."

Mai's stomach churned. Her childhood friend, Fei, had disappeared right after bathing, just like this little girl would. Cleric Pyuz had told Fei's parents that she'd been chosen for a position of honor. Maybe that's what culling meant.

No. Aralas' voice trembled in that one syllable, sounding like a little boy, or even a little girl.

She looked up at him.

A tear glistened in his Tivari eye.

"W—" —hat would happen to her? What had really happened to Fei? Bile rose in Mai's throat. She blinked several times.

The rest of the girls had lined up by the door.

"Not you." A High Acolyte gestured to Aralas. "Take this group to the robing."

Aralas thumped his chest, the sound almost masking his hard swallow. With a last look at the girl marked with red, he gestured to the children. When he spoke, it was in Cathayi. "Come, young ones." Then he gestured to her. "You take up the rear." Though he'd spoken in Tivari, and the bauble translated it, his voice still cracked.

Mai looked at the girl marked in red, standing at a different passageway with another acolyte, then back to Aralas. They couldn't just let her...

We must obey the command. Sadness hung in his mental voice. *After we deliver these children to the robing room, we will come back and save her.*

They marched through lit passageways, the children still pressing their palms together. If they were like her at the same age, they'd be rehearsing the songs of devotion in their head for the ceremony, with words that a child's mind wouldn't even really understand.

The next room might've been exactly the same as the bathing room in size and plain appearance, save for the pools.

Simplicity, they were taught, was a virtue for all humans to embrace.

Several acolytes stood at the head of the room. Just as when Mai was a child, these girls went to the front and bowed. The acolytes helped them into the robes. How proud and scared she'd been herself. How foolish she'd been. How they all had been, and still were.

"Last batch of the day," one of them muttered to another's knowing nod.

Mai's stomach knotted. To the Tivari, these adorable children weren't even a group of people, but rather a batch, like something to be cooked. It had gone on like this for countless generations.

Aralas pounded a fist to his chest to the last group of acolytes and guided the girls toward the last chamber. The voices of chanting children grew louder.

Every step felt heavy as she walked. It was about this time as child when she'd noticed that Fei was missing. Now, these girls marched, unaware of the next step in the so-called culling.

As they entered the room, the girls mingled with boys who came in from a hallway on the opposite side. Boy-girl, boy-girl, the choreography of creating several lines had been practiced in their home villages for weeks before their arrival at the pyramid. When all had entered and stood in neat rows, the archbishop at the front of the chamber raised a hand.

The children all bowed their heads.

Just as she remembered, the archbishop was handsome for a Tivari. Of course, everyone said Tivari were good-looking, but perhaps no one would ever say aloud how ugly most of them were. All but the bishops, archbishop, and High Priest.

"Children," he said in Cathay's language. "Welcome. You will prove your knowledge of Tivar's Canon."

Mai closed her eyes and thought back. She'd once been a five-year-old, back home, practicing the lines. She opened her eyes again.

"Tivar created the Tivari in his image."

"...and humans to serve," all the children droned.

The archbishop nodded. "Hard work in life..."

"Will be rewarded in the afterlife with Tivar's Rest."

"Laziness in life means—"

"Eternal labor in the afterlife," they all finished.

"The wicked..."

"...will pull Tivar's chariot for eternity."

Mai shuddered. No matter what Aralas said, the Tivari gods' chariots were proof of their divine power. All those souls, screaming under the flames... Her ears buzzed at the memory of the flaming chariot drifting above Cathay's valley, drowning out the rest of the recitation.

She took a deep breath. It looked like the recitation was over.

The children all bowed low and spoke as one. "I swear obedience to Tivar and his children on earth from now until I am granted Tivar's Rest."

She'd made that oath years ago. No longer. She'd do everything in her power to make sure no more human children would have to swear this oath again.

The archbishop motioned to a set of double doors. "Now, you face your last test. You will go back outside and be blessed by the bishops, and receive a benediction from the High Priest himself. Acolytes, lead your line."

The doors swung open from the outside. Mai walked beside Aralas. The group of children behind them raised their hoods, as the ritual demanded, and followed a few steps behind. The cool evening air greeted them.

The acolytes at the head of the lines should've turned and veered back to the pyramid's central landing, but instead they kept going straight toward the grove surrounding the pyramid. Up ahead, bishops stood ready to receive each child. When she'd undergone the ritual herself, it had been at the base of the pyramid.

She turned to Aralas. *This isn't right*, she mouthed.

The lines in his brow suggested he knew. He looked over his shoulder toward the pyramid.

She followed his gaze. The pyramid landing, where the high priest usually stood, was empty.

Oh, Koralas' Ass. For the first time, Aralas voice carried a tone of panic.

Chapter 36:

Initiation

T he joyous chants of misguided children behind Mai joined in with the crowds of hooded kids marching toward the platform. Despite the hundreds of singing voices, it was hard to hear above the furious throbbing of her heart in her ears. It nearly drowned out the pulse of the world. If Aralas was worried, they must be in trouble. His eyes were locked forward.

She followed his gaze.

The platform rose just outside the tree line. Though hard to make out from the wispy trunks and leaves, the figure atop it wore white robes with embroidered with symbols of Tivar's Scythe. With such robes, it could only be the High Priest.

Just a step behind him stood a similarly dressed Tivari, hands behind his back. Never in any of her previous two pilgrimages had she ever seen someone occupy the same station as the High Priest. Then again, the High Priest had never given the blessing from the grove. Whoever it was must've been important.

Yes, very important. Aralas' mental voice cracked. *That is Gen…no, their King. He's not supposed to be here.*

A king? Like the man who ruled over Cathay? The Tivari didn't have royalty, only priests of different importance.

It's all a part of their lie. There was an urgency in his voice like never before. *If the king is here, they must suspect there is something more to the scattered uprisings they've put down. Of course, all the work we've done must've drawn their attention.*

Though their line of singing children was far from the center of the platform, it became easier to pick the King out from the trees as they got closer. She studied him when they came to a stop in front of a bishop. If the archbishops and bishops were handsome, no words could describe how beautiful the King was. He might've rivaled Aralas himself.

As she and Aralas turned to face each other, with enough space for a child to pass between them, he snorted. *I'd worry less about his looks, and more about his military genius. If anyone can figure out our plans, it is him.*

Mai's stomach clenched. If they went through with the rebellion, so many humans would die, and possibly for nothing.

This explains the change in ritual. He can't get close to the pyramid.

How strange, that a holy figure couldn't even come close to one of the Tivari's holiest sites.

It's not easy to explain. It's...a curse. Remember, he's not a real priest. The bastard has slain several of my comrades over the years. Aralas was fiddling with something under the acolyte robes. The furrowed brows of his Tivari illusion face didn't even seem possible for the average Tivari.

Hopefully the hood would hide his expression, but the fidgeting would certainly be a giveaway. For someone who seemed so stubborn about maintaining appearances, he was doing a bad job. At least the sound of chanting children would keep anyone from hearing his shuffling.

She gave him a nudge with her elbow.

No, I can't risk you. I need to... He resumed the appropriate pose, palms pressed together. Even so, his heart, barely audible over the pulse of the world and the changing children, pattered.

Couldn't risk her? Wasn't she just a tool? Wouldn't he find someone else to soldier on?

Chest rising and falling, he locked gazes with her. It might've moved her heart had he not looked like a Tivari.

Then, the magic bead slid at her hip. She caught the hard bump and kept it pressed to her skin. Heavens, sweat had made her skin so slick.

The bishop in front of them raised a thick eyebrow. Instead of a magic mirror, a red amulet, representing the Red Sun of Tivar, hung from his neck.

Adjusting the hem of her undergarments so the bauble stayed snug, she straightened.

"Tivar's grace is upon you," the High Priest called.

Mai's gaze jerked up as the children's singing quieted to a low hum.

The High Priest held his arms stretched out as he rambled on about Tivar's grace.

Beside him, the King's eyes swept over all the children. He twirled an unholy rod around his finger, apparently caring little about upholding the deception of the ritual's sanctity.

Still, all the humming children focused on the bishop in front of them, while the acolytes kept watch over the children. The only one watching the King was Aralas.

The elf angel's fists were squeezed tight, his illusory Tivari jaw locked.

"Now," the High Priest said, "step forward and receive your mark."

Mai stepped to the side to allow the children to pass. Aralas, however, didn't budge. Eyes darting to the platform, where the King's head started turning toward them, she cleared her throat.

Aralas' glare at the King fluttered, then settled on her. He stepped aside.

The King's eyebrows drew together, though certainly not as dramatically as Aralas' had just a few moments before. Had he seen the breach in ceremony?

Mai's stomach twisted.

The King's gaze shifted back to the pyramid, from which more lines of children emerged.

She would've blown out a breath had the bishop in front of her not already been staring. The first in line, a boy, stepped past her. With the words to his song changing to an oath to Tivar, he knelt before the bishop, lowered his hood, and bowed his head. The back of his neck was smooth, unmarred by the dedication scar.

The bishop smiled, revealing his fangs. He started to set the red amulet on the boy's neck.

The orcs test the children to see if they will be a threat in the future. Aralas' voice sounded tight in her head. *Don't worry, none of these children have the spark of magic. They are safe.*

If Mai's stomach had twisted at first, now it was in knots. How did he even know? When she'd gone through the ritual before, the boy in front of her had died. Would he have become a threat if he'd lived? Why hadn't the magic killed her, or Wenhui, or Makeda, or anyone else who could use magic?

Their gods are looking for only one type of spark, when in fact there are several.

"I'm so tired of doing this to these vermin all day." The bishop pressed the amulet onto the boy's skin.

"At least it's only during harvest time," a bishop said from the line beside them as he placed his amulet on a girl's neck.

It took all her discipline to keep her jaw from dropping. What she'd assumed were prayers in the Tivari language, the magic translator revealed to be just idle banter.

All of the amulets at the head of the few dozen lines hummed.

Both children, and the one on the other side, ground their teeth, no doubt wincing against the pinch they'd been warned about. The bishop pulled the amulet back, revealing a rectangular scrape on the back of their necks.

Aralas lifted his chin. *As long as the magic remains in the scar, the orcs will always know where you are.*

Mai's own scar itched, or maybe it was just her imagination. It had to be, since Aralas had zapped it before he'd taken her to Cathay.

"Welcome to Tivar's flock," the bishop said in Cathayi. "You will serve the Tivari until you receive Tivar's Rest."

Mai blew out a breath. The first children had made it. They filed off to the side, then back around toward the pyramid. More children came and received their marks. She found the King in the corner of her eye.

His gaze seemed distant, unfixed. It didn't seem like the look of a military genius.

Looks can be deceiving. If he recognizes me, the rebellion has no way of succeeding. He fiddled with something in his robe again. *Our only chance, if he knows elf angels are involved, will be for me to kill him. My magic won't affect him. If you can't escape in the confusion, I want you to prepare yourself...for death.*

Mai's heart leaped into her throat. If Aralas' magic couldn't affect the King—

I will fight him hand-to-hand. If I'm losing, I will disintegrate myself with a holy rod.

Her eyes settled on his hand in his robe. Had he kept an unholy rod there this whole time?

Holy. My rod works through the divine will of Koralas. Anger tinged his voice. Even now, his heart beat loudly enough for her keen ears to pick out.

Mai's, too. Sweat drenched her, threatening to send the bauble sliding from her hip again. She took a deep breath to settle her nerves.

Aralas, too, needed to calm down, lest he draw too much attention. Both his hands crossed into the opposite sleeves, and whatever he was doing with his holy rod was making too much of a clicking noise. *It's hopeless.*

The elf angel had never panicked, not when they'd hidden from the Tivari at the dragon bones, not when they'd faced the Guardian Dragon. There must've been something about the King.

He killed one of my sisters.

No wonder. Who knew angels even had siblings, or perhaps all angels were brothers and sisters. Still, if Aralas did something stupid right now, the rebellion would fail. Though maybe if it never got started, humans would continue living, though as slaves.

Or maybe the Tivari would slaughter everyone and start fresh.

Mai closed her eyes and listened. The pulse of the world was so loud here. The children's hum, too, as they continued with the ritual. Their sound didn't follow the rhythm of the world, but at least she could use it to mask her own hum. Would Avarax hear it? The last time, it'd taken him half a day to appear.

She curled her toes into the ground, thankful that acolytes didn't wear any kind of shoes. She straightened her spine and bent her knees. The pulse of the world, so strong here, surged through her. Focusing on Aralas' heart, she joined her hum with the children's. Her own beat was different, but hopefully, their louder sounds would hide hers. She projected the energy of the Dragon Song into him.

His rapid breaths calmed. His heart slowed.

JC Kang

Hopefully he wouldn't do anything stupid. Mai slowed the rhythm of her hum. Surprisingly, she wasn't tired at all.

His fidgeting eased. His fists loosened.

Thank you.

Mai blew out a breath and looked.

The last of the children were finishing the ritual. Up to now, it didn't look as if any of them had been murdered in the name of a false religion.

As I told you, none of these children has the spark of magic, at least not the kind that the orc gods are looking for.

How did he even know, beforehand?

Angels of Koralas watch these ceremonies. We make sure the children with the spark aren't discovered by the orcs. Which reminds me, we need to find the girl they separated earlier before she is culled.

406

Chapter 37:
Unenviable Choices

Mai's footfalls padded on the stone floors as she hurried after Aralas. They'd just finished delivering the children in their line back to their families, and now rushed through the bowels of the pyramid to rescue the little girl with the limp arm. In the dark halls, she had to rely on hearing the echo in order to keep pace without tripping on uneven stones or running into walls.

The air grew cooler, and goosebumps erupted over Mai's arms and shoulders. The stone felt colder on her feet. "Where are we going?" she whispered.

Shhh, just speak in your mind. We are headed to the holding pens, where they keep the handicapped children before...culling. Aralas' mental voice shuddered.

She still didn't understand what culling was, and now he was talking about *handicapped*.

People who aren't fit enough to work in the fields. They are culled.

The Tivari always said these special children would attend to the bishops, and if they performed their duties well, their injuries would be healed by the Grace of Tivar.

It's a lie told to make these poor children's parents feel better. Come.

Mai's stomach twisted. Poor Fei, from her childhood, had never returned healed.

Voices carried from a lit chamber ahead.

"C-cleric, I'm so c-cold. When c-can I see my m-mommy?" Fear hung in a girl's chattering voice as she sniffled.

"Be quiet and stand still. You must pass this test if the High Priest is to accept you into his service. The gods will punish you if you make too much noise."

"I j-just want to go home."

"Shut up."

A sense of dread squeezed Mai's chest. Just a few more steps and they'd be in the room.

Aralas held a hand up.

She pushed past him.

Her stomach twisted into knots.

Several children stood in niches in the wall, not much wider or taller than them. Save for the shivering girl, none moved. In fact, their eyes were all closed, and their complexions were pale.

Too pale.

The girl's palm pushed forward, but the air in front of her looked solid.

Facing the child, an acolyte leaned back on a chair with fluffy black cushions, his bare feet propped up against the chamber's smooth walls. His fingers were interlaced behind his head.

Mai cleared her throat. "Why is this one being culled?"

Shhh!

The acolyte turned. His eyes roved up and down over her. "I don't recognize you. And why are you speaking in their tongue? And your voice…" His words came out, translated through the magic bauble.

Turtle's Egg! Of course they'd speak their own language among each other, and in her urgency to help the girl, she'd forgotten.

"P-please," the girl said. "I'm so cold."

Mai stared at the acolyte. "I just came from Ayuri lands. The archbishop there told me to practice only the Cathayi language."

"Archbishop? And you already speak the language better than anyone else." The acolyte's narrowed eyes fixed on her while he edged forward in his chair and reached for his magic mirror.

Mai listened for his heartbeat. She withdrew the flute and played the song of charm. Here, where the pulse of the world was so strong, it was too easy.

The suspicious glare melted, replaced by a broad, stupid smile. He lowered his hand from the mirror. "What an interesting instrument."

She held it up for him to see. "A souvenir from down south."

"Well," he said, showing no interest in the flute, "I'm Drtz. Welcome to this miserable corner of the world. I'll let you know which of the halflings digs up the best mushrooms."

Back in the shadows of the corridor, Aralas shuffled on his feet. *Not bad*, his voice said in her mind. He sauntered in and clapped her on the back. "Fmrz, there you are." He turned to the acolyte. "She's lucky to be here instead of stuck in some backwater village."

The acolyte laughed. "You'll see one soon enough. You're here to join in on the eradication of Sweetfield village, right? It's as backwater as it gets."

Her village. Her family. Mai's heart just about leapt into her throat.

Aralas turned to her, then back to Drtz. He gave a tentative nod. "We heard something about it in Ayuri lands."

The acolyte's laugh came to a sudden stop. He spat. "The humans first killed my friend Pyuz, then somehow wiped out three units of shock troops."

Three units? Mai would count on her fingers if it wouldn't give away her disguise, but with each unit having six Tivari, it had to be close to twenty. There was no way the entire village could have overwhelmed a single priest, so it must've been Avarax who'd done that.

Drtz made a fist. "The general plans on leading an entire battalion of our most seasoned shock troops to torture and kill every last man, woman, and child."

Shock troops, battalions, the words didn't make sense to Mai. Still, it was clear her village was in danger. "When will that be?"

Drtz shrugged. "I've heard the scouts will be back in a few days. Maybe a week. I hope I can join in."

"Us, too." Aralas gestured at the shivering girl. "But for now, we have orders to relieve you here."

Drtz looked from him to Mai, and raised an eyebrow.

She nodded. "Yes."

He stood. "Very well. I'll introduce you to that halfling, if I can find him. Sneaky little beasts." He tapped his magic mirror.

411

No sooner did Drtz march out of the room than Aralas was at the girl's niche. Head shaking, eyes wide with fear, the girl pressed against the back.

Aralas turned to Mai. "Keep an eye out to see if your friend returns."

Friend, indeed. Mai snorted.

He adjusted his robes. The turquoise skin color of his illusion changed back to its usual tone. He lowered his hood, revealing his gold hair, in his face as always.

The girl's eyes widened, and she rushed forward, only to hit up against the solid air. "You! Y-you're th-the angel who b-broke my arm."

"Yes," Aralas said, blowing the hair out of his face.

Mai's eyes darted from the corridor to him. How could he do such a horrible thing? "When did this happen?"

"Weeks ago." Aralas spoke a guttural word of Shallow Magic and waved his hand in front of the girl.

She tumbled out.

He caught her in an embrace. "There. You're all right now." He spoke another word, and the pulse of the world shifted.

She looked up at him. Her voice came out more smoothly. "Wait, you're not her. You're a boy."

That was debatable. Mai harrumphed.

412

The girl looked at her, eyes wide and fearful.

Of course, the Tivari image. Mai pulled the illusion marble away from her skin and folded cloth around it.

Aralas laughed. "Boy, girl. It doesn't matter. You are safe now. Here, I will heal your arm." He sang a few notes, similar to the song he'd used to heal Mai's cut.

The girl's eye widened as she moved her arm in wide circles. "It works again!"

He nodded. "Yes. I'm so sorry I had to paralyze it. But like I told you before, it was to save you."

Mai's head spun. It was as he said. He needed to keep the talented children from facing Tivar's red amulet. Hope rose in her chest. "Did you save my friend Fei, too?"

Aralas' head turned in slow shakes. "It could be that she had a real disability, like these children." He pointed to the other niches.

Her eyes raked back and forth over all the poor children. "Are they dead?"

"No. Orc magic keeps them frozen, but alive."

She counted five girls, three boys, all unmoving. She reached out to touch them, but her palm hit an invisible barrier. It buzzed with Tivari magic. Her stomach sank. "What will the Tivari do with them?"

He put his hands over the girl's ears. Tears welled in his eyes. "The…babies…of the orc elite will eat them."

Mai's stomach went from sinking to churning. As horrifying as it was, it made sense. Except, as gross as it was… "Why don't they just use people who have already died?"

"They need live people. And not just any people, but children no older than six or seven."

Mai blinked away the tears. "Why?"

Aralas cleared his throat. "I suspect…it's the same reasons evil sorcerers sacrifice children to make their elixirs of long life."

Mai shuddered. There were stories of that from Old Cathay. She jabbed a finger at the niches. "We need to save them."

He shook his head. "There's nothing we can do. If we thaw them, they will die."

"Can't you use your magic to heal them?"

He snuffled. "No. I've tried many times. It only makes them suffer."

There had to be something they could do.

"Not for these children, no. There's nothing we can do. But for all future children. Now let's go, before Drtz comes back."

Mai looked over the poor boys and girls, all unmoving and too pale. She closed her eyes and listened. Their heartbeats were so slow, so weak, almost imperceptible. If

414

they couldn't be saved, perhaps they could be spared a gruesome death. "Then kill them."

Aralas' beautiful eyes widened. He put his hands over the girl's ears again. "I...I can't just kill children."

"It's better than being eaten alive."

"They won't feel a thing."

There had to be a way to convince him, using a reason he would understand. "It will mean less food for the Tivari babies."

He shook his head, so immediately he probably hadn't even considered her logic. "If the orcs discover dead children, they will suspect something. Now come."

Mai gulped hard. She'd dispersed the dragon's cloak over the lair; maybe... "What if the Tivari magic failed...ran out like the magic cloak over Cathay?"

He blew out a long sigh. "It could work. However, their blood will not be on my hands. If you truly believe it is the right thing, I will not stop you. But make it quick."

"If I disperse the magic, will the children suffer?"

"Not if you sing them into the next world."

Mai shuffled on her feet as she memorized each of the children's faces. Their parents and older brothers and sisters would be in the encampment, thinking about a child they believed to be serving the Tivari bishops. She closed her eyes and listened.

The Tivari magic buzzed like a wasp. Maybe—

"No," Aralas said. "Sing to *them*. Their hearts. Like a mother mourning her dead child."

Mai nodded. If she did this, she would be a murderer. But still, it was for the children's sakes. "I will do it."

"I shall take this girl to Cathay. I'll be back." On a word of magic, he and the child disappeared with a pop.

Leaving her alone to do a dark deed. Taking a deep breath, she curled her toes into the stone. The pulse of the world coursed through her. She straightened her posture, allowing its echo to course into her spine. Holding the image in her head of poor Ying with a baby in her belly, murdered by Cleric Pyuz, she lifted the flute to her lips and played.

Sad. Grief-stricken. She projected the sound into them, and slowed each note. The sound of their hearts slowed. And finally stilled.

The children looked no different than before, but her ears didn't lie. Their hearts beat no more.

Mai blew out a quick breath. Slumping to the ground, she drew her knees to her chest. Tears ran unchecked down her cheeks. It didn't matter if the Tivari heard the crying. Let them come. Let them kill her now.

A warm presence settled down beside her. An arm draped over her shoulders.

She didn't need to look up to see it was Aralas. His heartbeat was so distinct, even though now it pulsed as slowly and sadly as hers. She leaned into him.

"I know." He patted her. It was so gentle, so soothing.

She sniffled. "How do you do it? How do you make these choices?"

"I've been fighting this war for longer than you can imagine. I've had to make many hard choices. It doesn't get any easier. A little bit of me dies each time I have to choose one person over another."

Maybe she'd misjudged him all this time. Maybe he wasn't a monster. Or maybe she'd become one herself.

He gestured toward the children. The children she'd murdered. "I wish it didn't have to be so, but innocents will die."

Maybe her own family, too. Perhaps she'd have to make the decision to kill them herself. She cleared the stickiness out of her throat. "Would you have risked all those children at the dedication ceremony if you had a chance to kill the King?"

He reached into his robes. When he withdrew his hand, he opened it, revealing a clear crystal with a sharp point. Silvery impurities were veined in regular patterns through it. "I did have a chance. This could kill the King. I really wanted to. However, your song of calm helped me think clearly. Killing him would have given away the elf angels' presence in the world, and the orcs gods would've summoned demons to suppress the rebellion. It wasn't worth risking all those children."

Had he really cared that much? She searched his eyes.

They were so sad, so beautiful. The arm around her pulled her close. "It wasn't worth risking you."

As cruel as he could be to her at times, it was times like these that broke down her resolve to spite him. Heart fluttering, she leaned her head toward him. Their lips met, tasting of salty tears. She wouldn't let him go, not this time.

Footsteps echoed in from the corridor.

Again?

He broke the kiss and spoke a word. Colors swirled and flashed.

When she blinked, she found herself in a cavern lit by dim blue patches. The pulse of the world hummed in the teeth hanging from the ceiling.

The Guardian Dragon's lair.

"We don't have much time to save your village," Aralas said. "Keep practicing here, where the cloak will hide your voice from Avarax. I'll be back in a few days."

A few days. Maybe her village might not have a few days. Maybe she couldn't improve enough in such a short amount of time to charm so many Tivari. "Where are you going?"

Aralas held out the eggshell the dragon had given them. "I'm going to fashion a musical instrument from this. Its magic will help you project dragonfear into the orc army. It will certainly attract Avarax's attention."

Mai swallowed hard. Still, perhaps there was opportunity in this disaster. "Can you have Fleet send a message to his friends? To tell the Tivari that many masters of magic will gather at the village?"

He searched her eyes. "Why would you want them to think this?"

"To draw as many of them as possible. If Avarax comes, I will turn him against the Tivari."

If only she were as confident as her voice...

Chapter 38:

Beginning of the End

The song of Celastya's dragonstone, resonating in the stalactites and stalagmites, became Mai's constant companion in the three days she spent practicing her music in the lair.

At least, it must've been three days, based on when she got sleepy and hungry. Without the sun or the Iridescent Moon, it was impossible to tell. Really, it felt like three tortuous weeks, each second not knowing when the Tivari would attack the village.

Celastya—on the rare occasions she appeared to bring food—had been kind enough, teaching Mai about how istrium increased a dragonstone's energy, and how gold amplified istrium radiation. More importantly, she proved to be friendly companionship to help keep her mind off the village.

Now, the Guardian Dragon was gone, off on another journey into the world, apparently unafraid of discovery by the Tivari. Perhaps she could use invisibility, like Aralas, or could walk in human form like Avarax.

It didn't matter to Mai. She was left alone with dark thoughts. Who knew if her idea of drawing the Tivari to her village would even work? Or even if the Tivari did come, what if her plan failed?

Just when she thought she'd go crazy, the cave burst into bright white light.

Mai squinted and shaded her eyes with a hand. Head raking back and forth, she found the source.

Aralas stood there, one hand suspiciously held behind his back, the other outstretched. Light coming from a clear, fist-sized gemstone in his palm illuminated his beautiful features.

At last!

"I have news from my spies," he said, blowing the hair out of his face. "Your suggestion worked. The Orc King believes your village is the center of the rebellion. He has assembled his best soldiers and will lead the attack himself, from astride a flaming chariot."

Memories of a Tivari god's chariot rumbling across the horizon sent a shudder down her spine.

He flashed a wry, knowing smirk. "Several of his own sons—bishops and archbishops—will participate. Their goal is to capture everyone in the village and question them. I hope you know what you are doing."

Mai's stomach knotted. "Me too."

"This will help." With his other hand, he held out a pipa.

It was the most beautiful instrument Mai had ever seen; even more beautiful than Yanyan's. Made from dragon eggshell, the resonator shimmered with swirls of color. The sound plate glittered with gold, while the strings caught sunlight like a spider web at dawn.

Mouth agape, she took it in two hands.

And nearly dropped it.

It had a pulse of its own, somewhere between Avarax's and Celastya's dragonstones, but also harmonized with the beat of Mai's own heart. As if it belonged to her.

Aralas grinned. "A strand of your hair is twisted into each of the strings."

When had he taken her hair? She could only gawk.

"I have one more gift for you, one which I was hesitant to entrust to you. It was hard to pry it away from Yanyan, as well."

She swallowed hard. The pipa was gift enough.

He took her hand and pressed the shining gemstone into her hand. "You will need this, too."

"What is it?"

"A starburst. The ancient elves, during their war against the orcs, discovered twelve of them in the Glittering Caves. They helped magnify their magic, and turned the tide of the conflict. The elves might have won, had they not lost their magic during the Year of the Second Sun."

One of twelve. Mai studied the clear gemstone, which had dozens of facets. Wenhui had mentioned it, and Kang had depicted it in his painting of Aralas. "I don't think—"

"You will need all the magic you can draw on. It will help replenish you. Please try not to lose it."

She bowed her head. "I will protect it with my life."

"That's what I'm worried about."

She pleaded with her eyes. "Then help me fight the Tivari, in case Avarax doesn't come."

"He will. As for me, we've moved our timeline up because of your plan. While you draw away the orcs' best troops, I will lead the attack on Frawdok's Purse, with Vanya and her *bahaadur*. Makeda will storm the Golden Bowl of Lydath. Vydas will raid the Lair of the Orc Queens, while Master Blackhammer and his dwarf kindred will raze the Temple of Tivar. It is all up to you."

The weight of responsibility bore down on Mai's shoulders. If she failed…

"If you fail, you die. Very slowly, in all likelihood. Your family and friends will be slaughtered. However, because of the risk you are taking—the choice you made in the pyramid—far fewer humans will be put in harm's way."

423

Bile rose into Mai's throat. She'd unwittingly chosen to risk the people she cared for the most over countless strangers.

No, not unwittingly. Just like when she'd sang those poor children into death, she'd chosen her village. After all, the Tivari were going to attack there anyway.

Nodding, Aralas rubbed her back. "Are you ready to go?"

"No."

"Me either." He reached out, touched her shoulder, and uttered a word of magic.

***

With the distant whine of demon skiffs in her ears, Mai ran through the fields toward the village. Cradled in one arm, the pipa strings' powerful pulse, embodying the might of two dragons, calmed her nerves. Still, sweat gathered on her brow.

It had to be from the heat of the midday sun, and not the fact that a Tivari army would arrive soon, most likely followed by Avarax.

"Go back to your homes," she yelled to the villagers who were finishing the harvest. "The Tivari are coming."

Some stared, while other gave hesitant nods.

She pointed in the direction of the approaching craft. Hopefully they believed her, but perhaps it didn't really matter. If she failed, everyone would die anyway. She reached her hut, where her parents were weaving baskets with dried rice stalks.

Mother looked up. "Mai, you are home! Oh, what a beautiful instrument!"

Mai wrapped her in a hug, then pulled back. "What happened to the Ayuri stranger? Is he still here?"

"He was amazing!" Father held up all his fingers, closed them, and then flashed eight fingers. "Templars came, the day you left. They were going to kill us all, but the stranger…"

Little Sister Ling clapped her hands. "He shot lightning from his fingers and killed them all."

Mother grabbed Mai's arm. "He wants to marry you!"

Mai shuddered, then shook the image of Avarax flying over Cathay out of her head. "Where is he now?"

"He left," Father said. "He said he'd return when you did."

Left! She looked in the direction of the demon skiffs. Though they still hadn't appeared on the horizon, the wail of tortured souls propelling them grew louder. And with it, another sound…

A flaming chariot of their gods, sending tremors through the ground.

Mai's throat tightened. How long would it take Avarax to respond to her music? Maybe he wouldn't get back before the slaughter began.

Bending her knees and straightening her spine, she cradled the pipa and strummed out a song of greeting. The throbbing of the starburst in her robes filled her with vitality. The music would draw the villagers in, so they wouldn't be caught out in the open.

Hopefully, Avarax would hear it and come as well.

The skiffs grew larger, and behind them, a flaming chariot. It settled to the ground in the near distance, while the skiffs rumbled overhead, shaking the ground.

There were so many, more than Mai had ever seen at once. She took deep breaths to calm her heart, to keep her fingers from fumbling on the strings. Ahead of them, the villagers scrambled back.

Where was Avarax?

The skiffs all hovered above the fields surrounding the village. She looked down the paths that spread out from the square, to see Templars jumping out. They formed up in ranks with bishops at the head. The precision of their rhythmic march would have been beautiful if they weren't there to torture and kill everyone.

They closed in on the village like a slipknot drawing around a chicken's neck. The villagers screamed and yelled as they stampeded in chaos.

Only deep breaths kept Mai from joining them. The marching boots now shook the ground.

She lowered the pipa. Even if the starburst had kept her energy from guttering, it would still be better to stay fresh. Surely Avarax had heard her by now. She waved toward the hut. "Hide inside!"

Mother grabbed her arm. "You too. We won't lose you again."

A voice boomed from the chariot. "Everyone line up in the village square!"

Was it the voice of Tivar himself? Or any of the other fell gods?

Around her, whimpering men, women, and children fell to their knees and pressed their foreheads to the ground.

Templars marched down the paths, their unholy rods leveled.

Mai clutched the pipa. Its resolute pulse gave her courage. She scanned the skies.

No sign of Avarax.

She closed her eyes and listened.

The telltale hum of his dragonstone was nowhere within earshot.

The Templars reached the square. Instead of grey robes, the bishops wore the same supple armor as the priests and Templars.

The archbishop, recognizable from the pyramid, strode forward and met her gaze. "Mai."

Heavens, she was the only one standing. And he knew her name. Now where was the King? She had to stall them long enough for Avarax to come. If he came at all. She squared her shoulders. "Archbishop, to what do we owe the pleasure of your visit?"

He held his magic mirror in his palm, facing up. He waved his hand over it and uttered words in the foul language of the Tivari.

A lifelike image of her, charming the three Templars at the waterfall with her song, flashed above the mirror.

The villagers all gasped.

Another appeared, of her crying and talking in the pyramid. She'd been with Aralas at the time, but he wasn't in the scene now.

The archbishop waved his hand again, and the images blinked out. "You are guilty of practicing and teaching witchcraft. If you explain how you learned the dark arts, and reveal your students, your death will be quick and your parents will be spared."

Mai shook her head. "It is just me. I taught myself, and no one else."

The archbishop broke into laughter. "The gods know you are lying. If you do not answer now, I will invoke Tivar's wrath on your father. The divine magic will burn him from the inside out. It will take him an agonizing week to die, but die he will, and then his soul will spend all eternity pulling Tivar's chariot." He fiddled with his unholy rod and pointed it at Father.

The Turtle's Egg! Anger surged through her. Mai dug her toes into the ground, straightened her spine, and strummed the pipa. Just like when Yanyan had sent her reeling back in the duel of music, the chord tore out from the strings.

The archbishop staggered back and fell. His eyes fluttered, and white foam, flecked with black, gathered around his tusks.

The Templars all pointed their unholy rods at the villagers. At her.

And Avarax was nowhere to be found.

Chapter 39:
Last Stand

The pipa pulsed with the rhythm of both Avarax's and Celastya's dragonstones, filling Mai with courage, even with all the Tivari surrounding her. A single chord had knocked the archbishop unconscious. Perhaps she didn't need to charm Avarax to defeat them.

Still, he was only one Tivari. Meanwhile, one bishop knelt by the archbishop, and the Templars spread out in a line, their unholy rods trained on her and the villagers.

Borrowing the pulse of the world and the energy of the starburst, Mai plucked out the song Yanyan had played to repel her, which had felt like a spider stalking across a web. Propelled by the power of two dragons, the notes crept out of the pipa, clawing and skittering. She rose her voice in song, choosing words of death and destruction.

The villagers behind her whimpered and wailed; but around them, the Templars paused and lowered their weapons. Their cruel grins contorted into fearful eyes.

Mai improvised a few more notes, letting the magic of the pipa's eggshell pour into her music. It came out as the keen of a tortured ghost. Her voice carried on its waves, crashing like a waterfall into a pool.

The Templars and bishops staggered back several steps. Their ranks broke. They turned and fled.

In the distance, even the god's chariot rose and spun mid-air. The flames scorched the souls bearing it with an intensity unlike anything she'd seen before. The chariot roared back in the direction it came, faster than she could imagine, leaving a trail of smoke.

Heavens, had she just repelled a *god*? Pride filled her chest as she continued playing. The Templars had cleared the village, and looked to be stampeding in a crazed frenzy.

She'd routed them with only a song, but without Avarax coming for her to charm and turn on them, they'd eventually regroup.

Not today, though. With the pulsing starburst replenishing her energy, she continued singing. The waves of her voice rippled out...

...and met another presence. One which pulsated with immense power.

It trudged through her song, like a farmer through flooded rice fields, coming closer and closer.

431

Mai looked up the path from which the sound emanated.

The Ayuri human—no, *Avarax*—slogged his way through her music. No longer naked, he wore shiny gold armor. With a nonchalant wave of his hand, he brushed aside any Tivari who fled too close to him.

Her eyes widened as they met his. Now was her chance to charm him. To use him. Listening to the vibration of his dragonstone, she changed her song to bring him under her influence. She plucked out each note, and sang each word to bend his dragonstone to her will. Once she turned him, she would command him to destroy the Tivari.

His steps picked up stride. The promise in his wicked grin had nothing to do with attacking the Tivari.

She screamed out the next few syllables, but then her fingers froze over the pipa strings. Her mouth opened and closed, but no sounds came out. She staggered back several steps.

"It's okay." Behind her, Father rose and ventured to her side. "He's the one who destroyed the Tivari patrol."

Of course he was; and now, he'd heard her song and come.

And here she was, fingers unable to move, unable to even attempt a charm. Had he done that with his magic? And now, with no music to scare the Tivari, their boots had slowed into a sense of order. They were regrouping. All was lost.

Mai turned to Father, eyes never leaving Avarax. "The Tivari came back today to investigate. Revealing my power just now may have taken away the element of surprise. Without that, the rebellion doesn't stand a chance."

Avarax's shoulders squared and his neck leaned back. Maybe it would look intimidating, if he had wings and a long neck. "I will protect you."

For his own purposes, no doubt. She shook her head. "This isn't about my safety, it's about the future of humanity. You wouldn't understand." Even if he looked it, how could Avarax even comprehend the suffering of mankind?

"The Tivari!" someone shouted.

"They are regrouping," said another, voice trembling.

The villagers' collective scream sent cold crawling up Mai's spine. But even that sensation wasn't as terrifying as the Tivari boots marching in unison, coming closer and closer.

Mai's fingers remembered how to move again. Her sweaty hands tightened around the pipa. She tasted the words of power in the song of charm, and found them flavorless. She had no magic to influence Avarax. Not only that, the Tivari… "I stopped the song too soon. It won't work as well the next time!"

Avarax held out a hand. "Come with me. I will save you."

"I can't let my friends and family die." Though maybe if she couldn't charm the Last Dragon, she could negotiate

433

with him. "You can save all of us. Show them your true form."

He cocked his head. "If I do this, will you come with me?"

To mate, if he still had the same ideas as the first time they'd met. Mai fiddled with a loose lock of hair. No. He'd taken Celastya against her will. There was no telling what he'd do to a human.

Then she looked past him, to where the Tivari were closing in. Around them, the villagers scattered. There was no other way. She took a deep breath to calm her nerves and bowed low. "Yes. Please."

"Tzrf," he uttered. The single syllable resonated with his dragonstone, different from Celastya's, different from the eggshell. The pulse of the world jolted. She experimented with the frets of the instrument until his sound vibrated in the strings of the pipa. There it was, the means of influencing him. Digging her toes into the ground, she looked up from the instrument...and gasped.

Avarax's human form shifted. The gold armor popped open as he grew. Brown skin transformed into red scales. His size swelled as arms bent into forelegs and wings sprouted. Hands and fingers curled into talons, while his tail sprouted, thickened, and elongated.

Every fiber of her being screamed to flee, even as her feet rooted to the ground. Not just her, either: villagers and Tivari alike gawked and screamed.

It was just like when he flew over Cathay so many months ago, only this time, he was so close. So huge. His dragonstone seemed to inflate him with each pulse, so that now his belly could've covered three or four of her villages. His shadow cast the world into twilight.

With a deep breath, her body calmed just enough for her to move her fingers again. She curled her toes into the dirt, bent her knees, and straightened her spine. Holding the chord which resonated with his dragonstone, she strummed.

The sound came out, eerie but beautiful. It echoed in his dragonstone. Now, she just needed to change the song of charm to match the new tune. She opened her mouth—

He sucked in a breath. His dragonstone crackled. Then, he roared.

Her ears felt like they'd been lit on fire. The ground rattled, throwing her off-balance and breaking her connection to the ground.

Flames erupted from his mouth and billowed into the Tivari. Bishops, Templars, all burned. None of their unholy magic could protect them. Not a single one screamed or yelled. Their bodies just turned to charred blobs. The skiffs caught inside the flames crackled and fell to the earth.

At the edges of the fire, Avarax's front feet crushed the surviving Tivari as he took a couple of steps. He cleared the village and turned around.

Sun flared in Mai's eyes. The song! Here was her chance. She brought her fingers to the strings.

He reached over with his enormous foreclaw and plucked the pipa out of her hands. It must've taken the same precision and control as a human picking an ant off of rough ground. With a flick of his talon, he sent it flying away.

"No! That was a gift from Aralas." She jerked her head to track it. There it was, at the far end of the village, lying on one of the paths. She ran toward it.

Rought, hot claws scooped her off her feet and knocked the breath out of her.

Chapter 40:
Verbal Jousting

Mai might have enjoyed flying if she weren't enveloped in a dragon's foreclaw. With trembling arms, she hugged her shaking knees to her chest. Sweat gathered on her brow as she panted in the oppressively hot air.

Careful to avoid the razor tips, each as large as her torso and sharp as a Tivari knife, she nudged her face out between iron-scaled fingers. The cold wind roared in her ears and whipped through her hair.

She squinted as freezing air pricked at her eyes. Far below, the hills, rivers, and forests drifted by. Maybe it would be her last sight. As a human, Avarax had wanted to mate; now, as a dragon, maybe he'd just eat her.

To think, it had been her idea to lure him to fight the Tivari.

She retreated into the confines of his claws. It must've been the rush of wind in her eyes that coaxed the tears out. Not the fear of being torn limb from limb and devoured.

If she was just a snack, he would've eaten her by now. Not like she, all skin and bones from a life of hard labor, could even begin to sate the appetite of such an immense creature.

Mai suppressed a wry laugh. Only she would think of such a silly notion. She closed her eyes and listened.

The dragonstone pulsated from deep within his body, just as Doctor Wu and Aralas had trained her to hear. Rapid as a dragonfly's wings, violent as a summer thunderstorm, it was the key to vanquishing him. She'd been so close when she'd found the right chord on the pipa.

Now, it was gone. Lying on a path in her village, perhaps shattered by the force of his flick.

She still had the starburst, though. Maybe—

Her stomach lurched into her throat. Blood rushed from her head. Her ears clogged, sounds muffled. With a hard swallow, her hearing cleared. Braving the wind and cold, she peeked out again.

They were now descending in lazy circles toward a lone mountain. The rocky crag jutted up from vast plains, the likes of which she had never seen before. Villages dotted the expanses. If what Celastya had said about Avarax's lair was true, these villages were home to humans who looked like Vanya.

All of humanity was relying on her to charm Avarax, to turn him on their enslavers. He'd already killed so many of their bishops and Templars. Had the King escaped? It sounded like he rode in the god's flaming chariot, which had retreated from the dragon's onslaught.

A poof of air, like the whipping of gigantic sheets, roared in her ears. Her heart sank into her stomach at the sudden slowing.

Despite his enormity, the dragon landed lightly near the top of the peak, close to a gaping hole in the rock. He crawled inside, plunging her into darkness.

Mai's heart jittered as she listened. With each of the dragon's quaking steps, the floor jingled and clinked. From somewhere deep within the mountain, the rapid vibration of istrium hummed.

The dragon opened his foreclaw. She tumbled out and fell to her side on the cool, shifting ground. Heart racing faster, she patted around for a solid surface.

He uttered one guttural word, his breath reeking of burnt flesh. The cavern flared into brightness.

Mounds of gold, silver, and jewels sparkled. So much treasure, creating a priceless landscape across the enormous cavern. She gasped. It had to be several times larger than Celastya's hoard, enough to gild a dozen of the Tivari gods' enormous flaming chariots.

If he, like Celastya, benefited from gold and silver magnifying istrium, maybe she could turn it against him with her voice.

The dragon loomed above. Red like cinnabar, he marred the cave's glittering beauty. He bared his fangs, each as long as she was tall. His glowing blue eyes bored into her.

Mai scuttled back several feet. Her chest constricted, forcing short breaths.

His laugh shook the cave, sending her sprawling again.

A word of magic shifted the pulse of the world. There it was again, the song of his dragonstone. Her only chance to connect to his life force and control him.

The dragon's hideous form shimmered and shrunk. His wings disappeared into his body, and his limbs shortened and thinned. Now standing bipedal at twice her height, he looked almost human, save for the scarlet scales and horned reptilian head.

And the spade-tipped tail, which whipped out and entangled her ankle.

With a single tug, the dragon-thing dragged her closer. His hand seized both her wrists. The vice grip chafed as he yanked her arms above her head and jerked her to her feet. He pressed his scaly face to hers.

The stench of burning death filled Mai's nose. Her heart pounded in her ears, drowning out any coherent thought. There was no escape, unless she regained her wits. Using the breathing techniques Aralas had taught her, she closed her eyes and inhaled a slow draught of air.

Her heart slowed, and coolness washed over her.

The torrential vibrations from his dragonstone rang in her ears, as strong and rapid as when he was still a dragon.

"You will entertain me," he said with a malevolent grin.

Entertain him? Every muscle threatened to tense. Her voice trembled as she spoke. "Let me sing for you."

The dragonman's hand withdrew. He cocked his head. "Sing?"

She nodded. "A song like you've never heard before."

He loosened his grip on her wrists. Pins and needles flared in her arms as Mai lowered them. She grabbed the savaged neckline of her dress and pulled the severed flaps together. Such a perfect cut; not a single frayed thread. Those claws could do the same to her flesh.

"Well?" His glowing blue eyes entangled her reflection, magnifying and distorting her trembling lips.

An icy tendril crawled up her spine. There was no way to draw a breath, let alone sing. He'd toy with her, like the village cats did with mice. After he grew bored, maybe he'd torture her before eating her. Tears blurred her vision.

No.

Aralas had taught *her*.

The fate of humanity depended on *her*.

Not Yanyan.

Mai blinked away the tears. Sinking to her knees, she pressed her forehead to the ground, just as she would to Cleric Pyuz. "Glorious Avarax, you honor me by hearing my song."

"Rise." His voice echoed into her, the vibrations of his dragonstone bending the rhythm of her heartbeat.

Compelled, she rose to her feet like a puppet pulled by its master. The effect of a command, just as Regina had taught *her,* to use on *him.*

The dragonstone buzzed like an angry swarm of bees. Just as Doctor Wu had explained.

Borrowing the energy in the cavern, amplified by the starburst, she sang the song of camaraderie. She enunciated dozens of notes in rapid succession, tying her voice to his dragonstone. With each verse, she slowed her cadence just a little, lulling river torrents into a meandering stream, to bend him to her will.

On quivering legs, his eyelids drooped. His breath lightened. Aralas had been right. Of course it would work. Soon, very soon, they would—

"What is this?" Avarax's eyes flared open, then narrowed. His dragonstone's pulsations quickened.

No! She couldn't let the power slip away. When she failed, it would doom the rebellion.

She raised her voice.

The dragonstone vibrated faster. The dragon's forked tongue darted over jagged teeth. He raised his claws, reaching back, ready to swipe at her.

The charm had failed. Nothing could save her now.

Except her own wits.

Listen, Yanyan had said.

Still singing, Mai closed her eyes. Each note she sang reverberated into Avarax's dragonstone. Making the vibrations stronger. The opposite of when he'd compelled her to stand.

There was no way she could charm him, but maybe there was another way. Mai abandoned the song, subtly transitioning to a lullaby her mother taught her. Sweet. Heartfelt. Lulling.

He lowered his claw, and his head cocked.

His dragonstone responded. Avarax's eyes sagged again, his upright frame slouching over. Note by note, she unwound the dragonstone's vibrations and bound them up with her own. Slower and slower, weaker and weaker.

His eyes fluttered again.

Her eyes, too.

His power was so strong, his dragonstone echoed back into her heart.

His legs buckled.

Her knees, too.

Shoulders slumping, he crashed to the floor, sending coins and jewels jingling.

Mai too collapsed. Her vision darkened at the edges, the dragonman her last sight.

Chapter 41:
Revelations

A chorus of angels coaxed Mai out of peaceful sleep. Her head was cradled on something soft—a pillow, or perhaps even a cloud. It was cool, like an early autumn afternoon.

Her eyes fluttered open, revealing a blurry mass of gold. She blinked a few times.

A cute chin and delicate jawline, framed by gold hair, came into focus above her.

Heavens, she was lying in someone's lap, and that someone was humming the most beautiful song. Combined with the softness, the crisp air, and the blue sky above, it was so soothing, so peaceful.

Aralas looked down. Breaking off the song, he blew the hair out of his face and flashed a smile.

"Am I dead? Have you taken me to the heavens?"

He laughed. "No. You are so connected to Avarax that when you sang him into a magically-induced slumber, you fell asleep yourself. Like him, you would've stayed asleep forever had I not woken you."

So she was alive. Mai tried to sit up, but her spine complained.

"Easy, now." He eased her back down, and cradled her head in his arm.

It felt so comfortable, so *right*. Still… "Where are we now?"

"We are back in Cathay."

Cathay? She listened. The sound of the magic cloak no longer buzzed in her ears. "I don't hear the cloak."

"The magic faded."

So soon? "How long have I been asleep?"

"A week. I've been singing to you his whole time, trying to break the effect of your Dragon Song."

A week! So much could have happened in that time. "What about the Tivari?"

"Thanks to you drawing away their best troops, we were able to accomplish our objectives. The Temple of Tivar, the

Shrine of Lydath, Frawdok's Purse, the Lair of the Queens...all damaged or destroyed. Their gods can no longer descend to the earth. Even now, humans around the world are rallying to fight the remaining village priests."

She smiled. "A great victory."

"Not without losses." He sighed.

Mai's stomach knotted. "My family?"

"They are fine. Avarax killed every orc that threatened your village."

If not them, then... "Makeda, Vanya, Vydas, Nada..."

"All survived. They are leading their people."

"Fleet?"

"It would take more than a war to kill him. He's like a cockroach."

"Wenhui and Ku?"

"You will see them soon. And your family. Tonight, the emperor will address you all. As we originally planned, you will perform on the drums to rally the warriors for the last offensive against the orc holdouts."

She sighed. "With Yanyan."

His head shook in slow arcs. "Her Dragon Song summoned a storm which sent an orc god's chariot from the sky. It was amazing, but she was already depleted from other feats. Without the starburst to replenish her at the time, she has permanently lost her voice and her magic."

Mai gasped. It was all because he'd given *her* the starburst, to face Avarax. How awful it would be, to be so talented and adored, but to lose it all. "I'm so sorry." Was she?

"The warriors admired her," he said, showing no more concern for his lover than he would a rank-and-file soldier. "They felt that as long as she sang at their head, they couldn't lose."

Now, without their figurehead... "Can they still win the war?"

"Perhaps. Morale is a powerful thing, and they might have lost it."

Mai swallowed hard. "Then I will become her voice. Let her lead, and I will sing from the shadows."

His expression brightened. "Would you do that? Become the voice of Yanyan?"

Mai's belly twisted. Like Yanyan, all she'd ever wanted was to be appreciated. With this arrangement, the diva would still get all the praise, and cast a long shadow from which Mai might never emerge.

"There is a benefit to this." Aralas' heart beat strong and steady, a rhythm so distinct, it sang to hers. Leaning over, he pressed his lips to hers.

They were so soft. Mai closed her eyes and savored in their warmth.

Then, he pulled back. "There's also a complication. I'll explain it to you tonight, at the drum dance."

***

The chill evening air sent goosebumps up Mai's arm as she stood by the three drums on the palace parapet, sticks in hand. Dressed in Yanyan's vibrant robes, hair held up with pins in an elaborate style, and with one of Aralas' illusion baubles pressed against her skin, the countless warriors and citizens below would never guess her true identity.

Her chest squeezed. Future generations would speak of Yanyan's amazing feats, perhaps even giving her credit for singing Avarax to sleep. Yanyan herself would probably always eat bitterness, knowing that it wasn't her who deserved all the credit.

A gong rang from the entrance to the palace.

Mai let out a long sigh and looked.

Dressed in ornate yellow robes, the emperor emerged. He took his time as he worked toward the front of the parapet with several guards, including Ku, at his side.

That was her cue to start the drum duet, but where was her partner?

The pulse of the world shifted, guiding her to strike the drum in front of her without conscious intention.

At the same time, another beat joined from the far drum.

Mai's heart nearly leaped into her throat. There was another drummer, obscured by the middle drum, rapping out a beat in perfect synchronicity with her. As she started a spin to the center drum, she caught a flash of red robes on the opposite side, just like hers.

Yanyan, maybe? No, Aralas said she'd lost her magic, and Yanyan's dress—the one Mai wore now—was one-of-a-kind.

She continued her dance through the drums, letting the beat guide her, but still trying to steal a glance at her partner, who circled step-for-step on the opposite side of the center drum. When she rotated right, her partner spun left. When she rounded the center, her partner mirrored her on the other side.

On one switch in position, she caught sight of a pointed ear. Aralas? No, it was certainly a woman's gown, and not the shiny grey fabric he always wore. She closed her eyes and listened.

The breathing pattern, the rhythm of his heart...they pulsed at a rapid beat, like the times he'd dallied with Yanyan.

It was him! How funny it would be to see him wearing a gown! And she would see him, at the end of the performance, when they would finish in a formation facing each other.

They continued the dance through the drums, their hearts beating as one. Unlike the first time in the Hall of Harmony, though, it didn't feel like her Yin joining with his Yang to form a perfect whole, but rather female energies building on each other. Still, they moved in perfect harmony, and like the time she'd caught him and Yanyan in the Hall of Harmony, the energy in the sounds grew and projected out into the audience.

In the sky, a new pulse joined in. The silver scales of the Guardian Dragon flashed in undulating circles around the conjoining moons. Below, in the courtyard, the people gasped and pointed. They joined in with chants. Mai's heart soared.

The emperor had nearly reached the platform.

One final pass around the center drum. Soon, she would see Aralas dressed like a girl. Giddy, Mai pounded out the last beats.

On the last turn, she pirouetted into a cross-legged squat, one stick high and the other low, facing...

An elf maid.

In a cross-legged squat, she held a mirror pose. She looked so similar to Aralas, though she wore her golden hair in a style identical to Mai's. Her eyes were Aralas' same shade of violet, though even more stunning, with long lashes and eyeshadow. Glossy red brought out her lips, though no makeup could hide the sadness in her expression. The low cut of the gown revealed the shallow cleft of small breasts.

Still, the rhythm of her heartbeat was his. Or at least, his when he was with Yanyan.

How could it be?

You've discovered our secret. A voice like Aralas', but in the slightly higher pitch from when he was with Yanyan, spoke in her head..

Whatever the emperor was saying now, Mai's pulse drowned it out. Her gaze locked on the elf maiden. Was it just an illusion bauble, like they'd used at the pyramid?

No, not it's not an illusion. Aralas does not truly exist. Just like future generations will forget you and speak only of the legend of Yanyan, they will never know me. Aralas is not one individual, but several elf angels assuming a single identity.

Of course. The image Regina had projected into her mind had been slim and feminine. Which meant…

Yes. Regina knew my sister, Siena, who trained and organized with the fair-skinned people of the North.

More than one… Of course. Aralas had used *we* when referring to himself, and Fleet had used *they* when speaking of the elf angel's ability to teleport. At the time, she'd thought it strange, but shrugged it off as a slip of the tongue. If this one had a twin sister named Siena…

My name is Kierra, also a woman.

Which would explain the lack of man parts. Maybe male elf angels weren't like ducks.

No. Kierra snorted. A sad smile quirked on her serene expression.

But why? Why must they remain faceless? All Mai ever wanted was to be *seen*.

Because we are all flawed as individuals. Infallible legends have the power to inspire.

The gong sounded again, signaling their dismissal. Kierra and Mai spun back up, again rotating in perfect harmony.

Mai cast her eyes down, unable to meet Kierra's gaze. She'd kissed another woman. Done more than that. The Tivari priests had taught that that was wrong, but they'd used religious dogma to control humanity. It hadn't *felt* wrong.

No, Kierra's voice said. Her expression looked sad, wistful. *It's not wrong. We love who we love. This is what worship of the True Gods will teach you.*

But...

And we didn't kiss.

If not Kierra...this Siena? But no, in Regina's mind, Siena had looked different.

Down below, the people cheered to the pulse of the world. Up above, the Guardian Dragon circled again. It met Mai's gaze, winked, and then disappeared.

The gong sounded a third time, and its echo wrapped around another form at the far end of the platform, hidden in the shadows of the battlements. Mai turned to look, but nothing was there.

At least, nothing she could see.

But a heart beat there, its rhythm steadfast and familiar. Across from her, Kierra's pulse skittered.

"What's going on?" Mai demanded, looking first to Kierra then to the corner. She marched over.

When the figure lowered its hood, golden hair fell into its face. A puff of breath blew it to the sides, revealing kind violet eyes and sharp features.

"Siena?" Mai asked.

With a bitter chuckle, Kierra shook her head. "That's Aran, our triplet."

Triplet? Mai staggered back a step, mind reeling. It was a word she'd never heard before, yet one whose meaning could be guessed from the context of the term for *twins*.

"How... how is that even possible?" she asked.

"There's always a chance," Kierra said, "but we were conceived by three people."

Mai's head spun. "Three? Was there more than one male?"

Laughing, Aran shook his head. "Our species sometimes has a rare gender, neither male nor female, or perhaps both. Their energy is tied to a Life Tree, and children conceived with their help are special."

A third gender? Tied to a tree? It was all too confusing. Mai looked from Aran and Kierra. The two looked similar, though now that Kierra was wearing makeup and a dress, she was clearly a woman.

Mai had been interacting with two different siblings. Aran's hair always fell into his face, while Kierra's tresses were always perfect. He was constantly blowing it out of his face, while she fiddled with hers.

"Which one of you did I kiss?"

Kierra's gaze shot to Aran. "You kissed her?"

Aran's grin could only be described as sheepish. When he spoke, his pitch was barely perceptibly lower than Kierra's. "I thought it was you? You're the one who's left a trail of human lovers. Yanyan, Vanya, Makeda, Wenhui, Kang…"

Kiera placed a hand on her chest.

"Which one of you was it?" Mai demanded, heat rising to her ears.

In two steps, eyes shifting from her eyes to her mouth, Aran covered the distance between them. Though it must've taken only a second, every moment stretched into an agonizing eternity. Need built inside her.

Brushing her hair behind her ear—he'd done that often, whereas Kierra was always lifting Yanyan's chin—he leaned in.

It was just a gentle peck, one which promised more, if only she'd take the invitation.

Eyes closed, she claimed his lips with unbridled urgency.

*For the extended, explicit scene, either join the ***Legends of Tivara Facebook group****, or pick it up from Bookfunnel. The story continues below.*

Epilogue

Mai was dying.

Orange glowed on the inside of her eyelids as the afternoon sun warmed her face. Propped up on her bed, she coughed.

"Master Yanyan, have a sip of tea," a young woman's voice said.

Yanyan? Hadn't she been slain in the final attack on the Tivari? Mai's eyes fluttered open, and she looked around the room to locate the Dragon Charmer.

A dozen women and two men dressed in white robes surrounded her bed. One girl was offering Mai a porcelain cup filled with steaming liquid.

Right. She was Yanyan now. Had been, for the last fifty years—and these were her Dragon Singer students. Over the years, the elvish illusions had come closer and closer to Mai's actual appearance; she hadn't used a bauble for nearly two decades.

Her arm, despite being not much more than skin and bone, was too heavy to lift and take the teacup. She nodded to the girl—Yina—who bowed and brought the tea to her lips. The liquid was hot and soothing in her dry throat.

"What was I saying?" she asked.

A middle-aged woman cleared her throat. "You were recounting the story of how you and Aralas rescued me from the Tivari initiation rite."

That's right. It was Lu, the little girl they'd saved that night, on the eve of what was now called the War of Ancient Gods, so long ago. Mai smiled at her. "Yes, Aralas and I had been within a few feet of the Orc King himself."

Several of the students whispered among themselves, and though Mai's hearing had deteriorated over recent years, her ears were still sharp enough to decipher whispers.

"Yes, killing the Orc King would have prevented the nuisance he's become. Still, there was no guarantee that Aralas would've succeeded, and the attack would've given the Tivari forewarning of the revolution."

At least, that's what Aran had said at the time.

"So how did you stop him?" asked a young man, eyes rapt with attention.

Mai chuckled. "How do you use any Dragon Song?"

"Listen!" they all answered in unison.

A laugh came from the door. "I'm glad you finally learned that lesson in your dotage."

Mai turned to see a silver-haired woman with blue eyes standing at the threshold.

"Doctor Wu!" Mai said. It'd been fifty-five years since she'd last seen the woman, who didn't appear to have aged a day. "Why have you come?"

"All you youngsters, let your master rest. Lessons can wait." The doctor shooed the students away.

They all turned to Mai, expressions curious and questioning. With a nod, she dismissed them. Something deep and primal told her this would be the last time she saw them. Tears gathered in her eyes as she watched them file out.

"Why have you come?" Mai asked, even though she knew why.

"It is time. Can you hear my heartbeat?"

Mai closed her eyes and listened. The doctor's heartbeat buzzed, buzzed like… Mai's eyes shot open.

Doctor Wu winked. "You know who I am, then."

"How did I never guess before?" Mai asked.

"How, indeed?" The doctor's hands closed around Mai's.

They were soft and warm and comforting. If this was to be her last hour, it was nearly perfect. It'd been a charmed life, blessed by devoted friends, gifted students, and the occasional lover. The Kingdom of Cathay had flourished, and the emperor had showered her with rewards. It turned out that becoming Yanyan hadn't been so bad, after all.

If only Aran were here now. With roving bands of Tivari still causing trouble in the years after the war, he'd popped in and out of her life, each time merging their hearts in song, then merging their bodies in lovemaking. During a close conjunction of the three moons twenty-two years ago, he'd disappeared forever. It would've been nice to see him one last time.

Another hand closed around hers.

She turned, but nobody was there. Closing her eyes, she listened.

There.

A heartbeat. Steadfast and resolute.

Her own heart soared. "Aran."

His form shimmered into being as he lowered his hood. He blew the hair out of his face. Like Doctor Wu, he hadn't aged in the last thirty decades.

She struggled to lean forward in the bed, to no avail.

"I came as soon as I could," he said, his fingers interlacing with hers. "I'm sorry to have been gone so long. War waged in the heavens as the orc gods embarked on a last effort to hold on to their power. Siena, Kiera, and all the other elf angels were summoned by our gods to fight."

"How are your siblings doing?" Mai asked, even as her flagging energy made the words difficult to speak.

"Siena remained in the Heavens. Kiera continues to watch over the pyramids with me, here on Tivara."

Kiera had tormented her so much in the early days, Mai was happy not to have seen that triplet. She buried those memories, and instead savored the joy of seeing Aran again.

He brushed her hair behind her ear and kissed her forehead. Then, he spoke a word.

A pipa—her pipa, made from the Guardian Dragon's eggshells—appeared in his hands. Sitting by her on the bed, he strummed, each note filling the space between her heartbeats. Then, he raised his voice in song.

The joyous chorus stirred fond memories of her seventy years walking the earth. Her parents, holding her tight. Laughing and singing with Ying. The wonder of visiting Cathay for the first time. The thrill of evoking magic the first time. The awe of beholding the Guardian Dragon. And the ecstasy of becoming one with Aran. The pride when her first students made their first breakthroughs.

His song quieted, its beat growing slower, coaxing Mai's eyes to close for one last time.

JC Kang

Acknowledgements

First, I would like to thank my wife and family for the patience they have afforded me as I pursued my childhood dream of fiction writing.

A shout-out goes out to my old Dungeons and Dragons crew: Jon, Chris, Chris, Paul, Conrad, and Julian, for helping to shape the first iteration of Tivara twenty-five years ago. Huge thanks to Brent, who contributed so much backstory to the new literary version.

A huge thanks to my sister Laura for her spectacular job with the maps.

Thanks to writers over at critiquecircle.com who motivated and helped me along the way.

These writers on Critique Circle were particularly helpful in the revision of this story: as always, first and foremost, Jason Nelson; and then the others who stuck through the entire mess: Ana Johns, Leanne Yong, Ligia de Wit, Tracy Leonard Nakatani, and Catesquire.

Special Thanks

My continued writing is supported by many generous pledges from Patreon. I would like to especially acknowledge Elena Daymon and Samantha Mikals. I'm humbled by your support; as well as Dianeme Weidner, Spring Yang, Nicholas Klotz, Scott Engel, Mary Luu, Dexter Bradley, and Lindsay Shurtliff.

About the Author

JC Kang's unhealthy obsession with Fantasy and Sci-Fi began at an early age when his brother introduced him to the *Chronicles of Narnia*, the *Hobbit*, *Star Trek* and *Star Wars*. As an adult, he combines his geek roots with his professional experiences as a Chinese Medicine doctor, martial arts instructor, and technical writer to pen multicultural epic fantasy stories.

Made in the USA
Middletown, DE
23 October 2021